Whispers in the Dark

Haarlock's Destiny

Book 3

J. Tyler Pennington

Yellow Sign Publishing

Published in Dayton, OH, USA.

Generative AI was not used in this novel's production.

Cover Art by Claire Scarth

Word Count: 99,493

Print ISBN: 978-1-7351166-7-9

eBook ISBN: 978-1-7351166-8-6

Library of Congress Control Number: 2026908713

1st Edition – 2026

Special Thanks

Claire S.
Scott M.
Avery M.
James A.
Victor B.

DRAMATIS PERSONAE

Huerto de Vid Azul

Amal Thmyia
Lord,

Janice
Maid

Jan
Bailiff

Aripine
Mayordomo

Rafael Malisco
Solicitor

Ostia

Lizza
Server

Camilla Albertine
Marquise, Consular General

Jean-Baptiste Bachelete
Bodyguard

Quinn
Sky Druid

Ladrón
Raccoon

Aldo
Steward

Unnamed Boy
Door Guard

Diego
Thief

Mr. Renquest
Butler

Haarlock
Lord, Shadowdancer

Marcon de la Garza
Couturier, Lemurian Spymaster

Unnamed Man
Pedestrian

Gabriel
Footman

Zachary
Grifter

Samantha
Enchanter

Acorn
Cat Burgler

Manuel
Sentinel

Roboute
Illusionist

Unnamed Man
Door Guard

Alejandro
Thief

Mateo Cabrera
Courier

Unnamed Woman
Server

Dominic
Work at Travel Companion

Glen
Messer

Continued

DRAMATIS PERSONAE

Ostia

Gerard Parnell
Blank Face, Thieves' Guild Guildmaster

Chester McCafferey
Manager

Dominic
Assistant

Unnamed Man
Bartender

Lilou
Assistant

Unnamed Elf
Seneschal

Justine
Blade Thief

Callista Sooztorn
Clerk

Unnamed Men
Ostian Guards

Raoned Shein
Paladin, King of Lemuria

Balthazar
Captain of the Hygeia

Micca Barecna
Lord, Ostian Guard Captain

Zeline Aetos
Seer

Haverstrand
Portreeve

Frederick
Tailor

Unnamed Elf
Noble

Marcus Eplin
Ostian Guard Lieutenant

Patricia Lee
Clerk

Unnamed Orc
First Responder

Elaria
Clerk

Claville

Simon
Thieves' Guild Guildmaster

Sjena
God of Shadows

Unnamed Human
Owner of Treasure Hunter's Dream

Pierre
Door Guard

Kilec
Phantom Blade

Continued

DRAMATIS PERSONAE

The Fallen Kingdom

Sofia de Costa
Attendant

Antonio Rivera Salamanca
Scribe

Aran
King

Bianca Molina
Courtier

Esmerelda
Noble

Belmora County

Basterlit Cratery
Anointed Shadowsmith, Emissary

Drigen Elmaris
Count

Mr. Chandler
Butler

Unnamed Elf
Footman

Burning Sands
Sathe
Ostia
Turbenton
Azure Inlet
Claville
Lorth
Kingdom of Lemuria
Portsmouth
Zilgas
Namedian Commonwealth
Arras
Bay of Azol
Trintos
Silver Tip Mountains
Lamorales
Trellisberg
Grecklewood Castle
Goswell Gulf
Nippon
Empire of Sanyo

1

Haarlock didn't like the cold. His hands and feet hated it. It didn't seem to matter how many layers he wore, they always hurt in the winter.

And winter was on its way.

Ostia, the capital city of the Kingdom of Lemuria, lay at the base of a massive mountain range. And now, in mid-November, the wind off those mountains was *cold*. Though the cloudless sky allowed the sun to beat down unabated, the occasional gust cut deep.

Too bad Haarlock was in disguise. He'd rather be wearing his wool-lined adventuring cloak. Now, though, he sat outside a small bistro wearing appropriate noble attire. Sure, his tunic and breeches had layers, and his face a bushy beard, but his head? Nothing but medium-length hair. The only thing keeping Haarlock sane was hot chocolate. Lots of it.

A server walked over to Haarlock's table. She wore a heavy green dress and a fur hat. A few strands of blonde hair hung down her temples. Haarlock wished he had remembered to bring his hat.

"That's your third one, m'lord. Will it be a fourth today?"

"No, Lizza, I think this will be my last."

The young woman smiled. "Of course. Same as last time, your bill comes to an even 80 copper."

"Same as last time, keep the change." Haarlock laid a single silver coin on the table.

"Most generous, m'lord." Lizza dipped her head and took the coin.

Haarlock watched Lizza walk off and couldn't help but give a small smile. The server was friendly, funny, and attractive. It almost made him want to make this place a regular stop and maybe ask her to dinner.

I wonder if it's appropriate for a noble to ask out a commoner?

He assumed not due to the power imbalance. He was a lord, and that title gave him ownership of a hamlet, Farncombe, and command over its nearly 70 residents. Plus, *The Blue Pearl* lay on the southeastern side of Ostia. That was almost a two-hour walk from the guildhall and more than a five-hour carriage ride from his estate.

Probably best not to risk it.

While Haarlock's mind wandered, he received a psychic message from Ladrón, his raccoon familiar.

*"*Maybe. Found.*"*

"Where?"

*"*Approaching. South.*"*

That was from Haarlock's rear. He didn't dare turn around to look.

"How close?"

*"*Soon.*"*

Ladrón watched from the top of the four-story, mixed-use building across the street. It provided an excellent view of the entire block.

"What color is his outfit?"

*"*Color?*"*

Haarlock chided himself. Raccoons don't see in color.

"What's he wearing?"

*"*Hat. Fancy.*"*

Just like Ladrón said, a fancy hat-wearing elf walked past Haarlock. His outfit was a blue tunic, black pants, and a red beret with a pheasant feather in it. Fancy indeed. But was this Mateo Cabrera? His race and headwear fit the bill, though Haarlock didn't dare stare long enough to see if he matched the elf's hand-drawn picture.

The elf entered *The Blue Pearl* through the front entrance. Haarlock couldn't see inside since the shutters were closed, so he sipped his drink and tried to people-watch. If the elf didn't come out in two minutes, he probably went out the back. Haarlock brought up the quest notification to review his task.

Investigate Mateo Cabrera

Guild Quest

The Crown thinks Mateo might work for Blue Jira.

Bring him in so they can ask.

Time Limit: 3 months

Rewards: 2,000XP

Time drug on as Haarlock waited. The bistro was a popular place for warm drinks, thus busy this time of day, so it would make sense if it took longer to get an order.

Haarlock let out a breath he didn't know he was holding as the fancy hat-wearing elf reappeared, steaming drink in hand.

"Follow on the rooftops best you can. Let me know if he turns a corner."

Ladrón sent a confirmation ping. Haarlock waited a minute before downing the last bit of his drink, then dropped a few silver next to the cup and left.

The elf went another three blocks west before turning north. Haarlock kept back a block to hide himself in the busy post-lunch commute. Another block north, then one west, and the elf stopped. Ladrón messaged their target browsed at a street vendor.

Haarlock's instructions were to investigate anyone or anything Mateo interacted with. He just needed to confirm that this was his target first.

Though Haarlock didn't win the yearly Academy tournament, he proved his worth and accepted a position in the adventuring guild Shattersong. A small guild, they worked hand in hand with the crown on various sensitive matters, one of which was the looming invasion by Lemuria's southern neighbor, Sanyo.

It's suspected Mateo Cabrera works with an information broker called Blue Jira. Who Blue Jira is, no one knows, but it's believed they're the primary method by which Sanyo's rogues, called shinobi, communicate. The goal was to find and capture Mateo, then use him to get to Blue Jira.

It took Haarlock a few minutes to catch up to his target. Though now he moved across the street and under a long colonnade, walking down a hundred feet before entering a business.

Haarlock followed the elf inside, and a wave of tobacco slammed into him. The interior was nearly a hundred feet long, and cigars, cigarettes, and loose-leaf tobacco filled every available space. A dozen other men browsed the shelves and bins. The target had his back turned to the door as he looked over a countertop of loose-leaf tobacco.

"Watch the entrance. Tell me which way he goes when he leaves."

Cigars weren't Haarlock's favorite, but he liked them more than cigarettes. Then again, Haarlock only ever smoked modern-day cigarettes. Were the ones in *The Game* better? He assumed so because of the lack of chemical additives.

Since Haarlock had no experience buying cigars, he watched what the guy next to him did. Mimicking the man, he picked up a cigar and smelled it. The rich scents of wood, leather, and tobacco filled his nostrils. Haarlock checked the price: one silver.

A quick look in a wall mirror confirmed Haarlock's target still browsed in the same area. He didn't know the capabilities of Couriers, but he suspected it involved dead-dropping messages.

How am I going to check every cigar he touches?

Haarlock turned around to browse the bins behind him. He still needed to confirm the elf's identity. Haarlock also needed to monitor exactly what he touched. So far, the elf seemed content to look at what Haarlock assumed was the high-priced shelf. A sign on the wall read *10 silver each.*

The elf turned around, put his hands behind his back, and bent over to look at whatever was in the bin. Blonde hair hung down, preventing identification. The elf nodded a few times, then moved towards the door.

Haarlock waited a moment before going to where the elf browsed. He hoped to find a dead drop, and if not, it was a good way to let his target get some distance.

Canny Observer worked overtime as he examined the multitude of boxes on the shelf. After a minute, Haarlock's curiosity got the better of him, so he looked over his shoulder at the door and saw the elf standing there. The picture matched exactly. It was Mateo Cabrera.

Unfortunately, Mateo's eyes met Haarlock's, and the elf smirked before he dipped outside. Haarlock bolted to the door while telling Ladrón to follow their target. When Haarlock made it outside, Mateo was gone.

"Which way did he go?"

*"*Gone. Lost. Sad.*"*

Haarlock exhaled hard through his nose. Now his cover was blown and his target would be on alert. His first lead was thin at best, and now he had no others.

"Whelp, guess we'll head back to the guildhall."

*"*Hungry. Food?*"*

"Sure." Haarlock couldn't help but laugh at Ladrón. The raccoon never let failure stop him from eating. *"What are you thinking?"*

*"*Soup.*"*

A bowl of hot soup on a wintry day sounded perfect. Hopefully, it would warm his frigid mood, too.

2

The walk back to Shattersong's guildhall took two hours but felt like five.

Ladrón was in a mood and wanted to stop and smell every food stall. Haarlock wasn't sure how he could be hungry after two large bowls of hearty soup...actually, he did. Whatever becoming a magical familiar entailed, it gave the raccoon an almost bottomless stomach.

Luckily, skewers of roasted meat kept Ladrón content. As did Haarlock's shoulder.

I think I'm getting scoliosis.

When they finally reached the alley behind Shattersong's public entrance, Haarlock went to a recessed door made of dark wood and metal bands. He could feel a minute tingle of magic as he unlocked the door. Down 20 steps and through a door on the left, Haarlock entered the guildhall proper.

A wave of heat poured across Haarlock. Ladrón hopped off his shoulder and ran to the fireplace at the far end of the room. Haarlock followed, pulling up one of the nearby chairs and sitting as close to the fire as he dared. It took a few sniffs before Ladrón felt comfortable enough to lie on the lion-skin rug. One of the other guild members, Samantha the Enchanter, had a fox familiar named Jaakuna. The two animals did *not* like each other, and Ladrón wouldn't sit anywhere near where the fox had been in the last few hours.

It only took a few minutes for the warmth of the fire to cause Haarlock to drift off. Before sleep overtook him, a pair of voices brought him back.

"...if that's the only option."

"I'm going to say you're right."

Haarlock turned around in his seat to see Jean-Baptiste Bachelet the Bodyguard and Zachary the Grifter coming up from the training floor. Both men wore their usual attire, though with thicker garments. Jean-Baptiste's chainmail shirt partially hid beneath an unadorned white tunic. His long brown hair draped over his left shoulder, and a small, black-sheathed dagger hung from his belt. Zachary, dressed to kill in a hard-edged, solid black one-piece, had his mutton chops waxed flat against his face.

Were the men dressed alike, the only two things that would tell them apart were their accents and hair. Jean-Baptiste spoke with a moderate French accent and kept his face clean-shaved and hair long. Zachary's voice, on the other hand, was rich, with a slight British accent. The Grifter's hair reminded Haarlock of Roboute's: a coiffed pompadour of singular poise. Zachary's mutton chops give the man's otherwise formal appearance a rough edge.

"Welcome back, Haarlock." Zachary smiled. "Did you have luck with your mission this time?"

"No." Haarlock stood and slumped his shoulders in defeat. "I found Mateo, but he made me and bolted."

Jean-Baptiste's eyebrows shot up. "Comme c'est malheureux. This presents a challenge."

Haarlock grumbled in agreement. "That's an understatement."

"Tell us what happened." Zachary motioned for everyone to sit in front of the fireplace.

"Since I wasn't sure when he'd return from vacation, I've been waiting at Mateo's favorite bistro for the last week. Intel showed he visits there, like clockwork, everyday around 1pm. Today, finally, Mateo came in for a drink, so I followed him a few blocks until he went into a tobacco shop. Not sure what I did, but Mateo made me. Ladrón lost him in the crowd, and here we are."

"Couriers are a slippery bunch." Zachary rubbed his chin in thought. "They have Class Abilities that allow them to detect if they're being followed."

Haarlock touched the Talent obscuring ring on his left index finger. He assumed Mateo used a Class Ability or a Feat. "How'd he vanish so easily?"

"You have the Talent *Nondescript*, yes?" Jean-Baptiste shrugged. "There's no doubt Mateo possesses a similar, though far more powerful, version of that."

Nondescript passively provided the user a, well, nondescript appearance, be it through gait, speech pattern, or body language. It wasn't a powerful effect, but it would hinder any efforts to track the user.

"Wonderful." Haarlock sighed. "What do we do now that he knows someone's onto him?"

"That is a question for our imperious leader." The Bodyguard looked at the wall clock. "I believe she'll be here for dinner."

***

Shattersong's members came and went regularly. The guild's Steward, Aldo, kept a running tab of everyone's schedule and ensured a meal would be ready when appropriate. Tonight was such a night.

Marquise Camilla Albertine, the guild's unofficial leader, along with Jean-Baptiste, Zachary, and Haarlock, all sat at a table near the fireplace. Ladrón lazed in front of the fire.

"I didn't think this quest would be more trouble than it's worth." Camilla stirred her bowl of chicken noodle soup. Her long, curly, multicolored hair lay in a messy ponytail, creating a stark contrast to her black dress. "Do we have Mateo's current place of residence?"

"We do, but he'll already be gone." Zachary dipped a hunk of bread into his bowl. "We should have taken him at his home the day he returned."

"True." Camilla thought to herself for a moment, then addressed Haarlock. "We shouldn't leave a stone unturned. Take Zachary and Acorn with you and see what you can find. Maybe we'll get lucky."

"Understood." Haarlock nodded to Zachary. "You know where Acorn went?"

"She's teaching a class on lock picking at the..." Zachary stopped suddenly, then looked at the non-rogues suspiciously. "Actually, we'll discuss it on our way there."

"We know you're a rogue, Zachary. And that the Thieves' Guild exists." Jean-Baptiste sighed. "It's not a big secret."

"To you, perhaps. But we rogues must keep the faith."

***

Haarlock, Ladrón, and Zachary made their way through the city, heading towards one of the Thieves' Guild's sub-guildhalls. The approaching sunset brought a nasty chill to the air, and both men kept their wool-lined, hooded cloaks closed tightly in front. Ladrón's fur kept him warm enough that he didn't want to wear anything other than his armored harness.

With so many rogues operating in Ostia, there needed to be a way to stem the tide of quests coming into the Thieves' Guild. The solution was to set up locations specialized in different rogue aspects: thieving, spying, assassination, and sabotage. Acorn, as a Cat Burglar, frequently found herself at the thief branch.

Tonight the gnome taught a class on lock picking. As a master of the Skill, she felt it her duty to teach the guild's new rogues on the finer aspects of the subject. And to show off.

Much like the main guildhall, the thief branch was located underground. This entrance, though, was through a warehouse a block from the lake's northern coast. The two rogues wound through the buildings, eventually stopping down the street from a two-story brick structure. Large letters spelled out the word *Exports* on one side of the building.

"This is it." Zachary looked at Haarlock. "You've never been here, yes?"

"Correct."

"It'll be strange if we arrive at the same time. Wait five minutes, then go inside. There will be a back room. Knock twice on the door, and then a guard will ask you a question. Whatever they ask, the answer this week is *marmalade toast.*"

Haarlock pursed his lips in annoyance. "Really?"

"This branch's leader likes simple responses." Zachary took a step forward, then stopped. "What is it again?"

"Marmalade toast."

"Good."

The Grifter walked down the road, stopping by a large, rounded column. He looked around for a moment before entering the building. Haarlock waited the requisite time, then followed.

When he entered the structure, Haarlock found small groups of men going about their business, moving, filling, or unloading boxes of varying sizes. Most were human, with a few orcs as well. None bothered to look at Haarlock as he walked past them towards the back room.

Shaped like a corner office, the room's only entrance was a single, windowless wooden door. Made of dark wood, it didn't have a handle on the outside. Haarlock rapped twice and took a step back. A soft voice came from inside.

"Hey, I wondered when you'd get back. What did you get?"

I hope Zachary isn't messing with me.

"Marmalade toast."

The door creaked open to reveal a young boy no older than 12. He looked up at Haarlock, then at Ladrón, smiled, and moved out of the way. Haarlock entered the room and found a spiral staircase in the floor. *Canny Observer* let him hear the ever so faint sound of voices coming from the dark recess.

As he went down the stairs, the noise grew to shouting. A light at the end of the long tunnel was the source. Both Haarlock and Ladrón covered their ears as they approached.

Four people sat around a square table inside the large room: his guildmate Acorn, an obese human man, and two male elves. Each worked furiously at a lock while those around them cheered. Haarlock watched as someone went around taking money and handing out bet slips. Zachary stood off to the side, drinking an ale, and waved Haarlock over.

"What's the challenge?" Haarlock had to yell to be heard.

"First person to open a Masterwork lock with basic picks."

"Who's winning?"

"Hard to say. Acorn is good, but those elves are no slouches."

Haarlock watched for a moment. "Who's the big guy?"

"Correllen, the leader of this branch. He's decent with a lock, but he's no Acorn."

The challenge went on for another five minutes before the elf on the right cheered as he slammed down his lock. The elf on the left cheered, too. Acorn cursed as she threw hers on the floor, while Correllen sighed as he put his down gently on the table. Cheers and groans sounded out, and those who cheered went to collect their winnings.

Zachary sighed as he hung his head. "Acorn is going to complain. A lot."

The gnome hopped down from her chair. A grimace went across her nut-colored face, and she stormed towards the bar, ignoring both of her guildmates as she climbed onto a bar stool.

"Bartender. I need whiskey."

The bartender, a skinny man with a bald head, poured the shot and slid it to Acorn. She downed it and slammed the glass on the bar top. Zachary and Haarlock exchanged glances.

"Keep staring, you two." Acorn grumbled to herself.

"There's no need to fret." Zachary gave a soft smile to the back of the gnome's head. "It's only money."

"Money I no longer have." Acorn ordered another shot and drank it just as fast as the last one. She looked over her shoulder and put on a fake, toothy smile. "What brings you boys here?"

Zachary sat next to Acorn. "Are you sober?"

Acorn tapped the side of her glass. The bartender poured another, and she downed it.

"I am now." The gnome left a handful of coins on the table and then turned around in her seat. She sighed before she jumped down. "Oh, great, they're coming to gloat."

Haarlock turned to see the two elves approaching. They sported the standard black hooded cloaks but wore exposed chainmail shirts over their tunics. With a full view of their face Haarlock saw their identical features. Twins.

The one on the left spoke in flawless, perfectly accented Elvish.

"It is a pleasure to meet you, Lord Haarlock. And you, Ladrón. I am Diego, and this is my brother, Alejandro."

Alejandro spoke next. "We hoped to meet you one day. It is rare that a human speaks our language well enough to impress an elf from the homeland."

Haarlock replied in kind. "I am at a loss as to whom you speak."

"Count Perez." Diego put a hand on his brother's shoulder. "He is a cousin. We had dinner with him a few weeks after Gabriella's quinceañera. It saddened us to miss it."

Guess those dialect lessons in college paid off.

"It was important I spoke as authentically as a native in my last line of work."

"Ah, yes." Alejandro smiled. "You were a mercenary in the previous world. It is a tale you must tell us some day."

"My brother is right. We are very interested in hearing it. But it will have to be another time." Diego switched to Common. "We have winnings to collect and supplies to buy."

The brothers looked at Acorn in unison. The gnome's light brown skin blushed red with anger, then she removed a pouch from her belt and slung it at Diego. He caught it with a huff.

"Thank you, Acorn." Diego nodded to his brother, and they both left.

"Yeah, we'll see how welcome you are..." Acorn mumbled under breath as she stared daggers at the backs of the elves.

Zachary raised an eyebrow. "You're not one to be a sore loser."

"I'd be less sore if they didn't cheat."

"How do you know they were cheating?"

"Because *I* was cheating!" Several other people looked Acorn's way. She frowned, then looked at the ground. "If I cheated and they beat me, it was because they cheated, too."

*"*Acorn. Sad. Me. Sad.*"*

"Ladrón is sad because you're sad."

Acorn perked up and looked at the raccoon with sorrow in her eyes.

"Oh. My. Gods. I am so sorry, Ladrón." Acorn took a piece of candy out of her pocket. "I hate that I made you sad."

The gnome presented the candy as an offering of peace. Ladrón climbed down Haarlock, sniffed the shiny red orb in her hand, then put it in his mouth and crunched it.

*"*Thanks. Tasty.*"*

Acorn looked up at Haarlock, and he winked. The gnome smiled and gave the raccoon chin scratches.

"I love this little guy."

"He ain't so little, trust me." Haarlock rolled his shoulder. The one Ladrón regularly sat on. "He's pushing twenty pounds. At least."

"You should put him on a diet." Zachary huffed with a smile.

"Try telling a raccoon that can speak psychically in your head that he can't have as many snacks as he wants."

"Can't you block it?"

"I can, but I get a little buzz every time he talks to me. Last time I did the buzz didn't stop for several hours."

"Sounds like you shouldn't have given him an intelligence enhancing necklace."

Haarlock looked down at the golden bangle tied around Ladrón's neck. It roughly doubled the raccoon's intelligence, and once the animal became a magical familiar and Haarlock took Improved Animal Bond, Ladrón's intelligence nearly tripled, coming to 17. Haarlock's intelligence sat at 30, but this didn't make Ladrón half as smart as Haarlock. It made him three times as smart as a raccoon.

"Hindsight is twenty-twenty."

Both men shared a smirk.

"Losing money made *my* hindsight pretty damn clear."

"How much?" Zachary looked down at Acorn with pursed lips.

"Six platinum."

Haarlock let out a low whistle. "Should have cheated better."

Acorn shot a look of pure venom at Haarlock, then shrugged. "I would stay mad at you, but you have a Ladrón."

A soft chitter of contentment issued from the animal. It wasn't hard for either man to see Acorn's heart melt with joy.

"Well, small stuff, we have a job for you." Zachary crossed his arms and smiled when the gnome looked up at him. "Interested?"

"Anything is better than being here."

3

Three figures moved through the shadows toward a six-story tenement building.

They stopped a few alleys down, then one figure moved into the moonlight and approached a pair of people smoking outside. Several coins went to the smokers, both for their information and to leave. The figure talking to them signed in *Thieves' Cant* to their two companions in the alleyway *not home*.

The smallest figure, no larger than a child, climbed effortlessly up the building's side to the fourth floor. She paused at the window, opened it, then darted inside. Several seconds went by before she stuck her head out and signed *all clear*. The other two figures went inside the building's front door.

As Haarlock and Zachary approached flat 13D, its door opened to reveal Acorn sinisterly backlit by the moons in the large window.

"He left in a hurry."

The state of the living room confirmed the gnome's assessment. Several glass containers lay broken in the middle of the floor, along with a handful of small trinkets and paper, and one sock. Two empty bookshelves and a dresser with its drawers on the floor in front of it were the only furniture left.

"Grab everything." Haarlock pulled out a pouch and handed it to the raccoon on his shoulder.

Ladrón jumped to the ground and went to work.

Though Zachary and Acorn's sub-specializations were geared toward thieving, they were still mid-level rogues. That meant *Canny Observer*. Zachary pulled a light orb out of his pocket and activated it, filling the room with soft light. He handed one to each of his companions. Even with *Darkvision*, Haarlock wouldn't risk missing something by not using the orb. Haarlock took it and headed to the kitchen.

It looked much like one in the previous world: cabinets above countertops and cupboards beneath. The sink, a large bowl set into the counter, lacked running water, but it had a drain. Several large buckets sat in a space where a trash can might go.

Many years ago, Haarlock took part in an escape room. One clue, a key, lay flat against the bottom of a high-up cabinet. The only reason Haarlock found it was because he ran his hand across the surface. Just like he was doing now. What few containers remained held only stale rice and some kind of dried foliage.

If there was something hidden in the kitchen, it was beyond Haarlock's ability to find.

His area searched, Haarlock went back to the living room where Zachary worked. The Grifter used his orb to see inside the empty dresser.

"No luck in the kitchen."

Zachary's head was stuck partly inside the dresser. "Pretty much the same for me. The only thing I'm finding is cobwebs. Hopefully Acorn has...what's this?"

Once he found the right angle, the Grifter put his other arm inside, then brought out a small piece of paper. Zachary held the light orb close to it and squinted.

"This is some kind of cigar label, I think." He stood and moved closer to the window for additional light. "Acorn, come here, please. We found something."

The gnome appeared in the bedroom doorway with Ladrón beside her.

"Whatcha got?"

"A cigar label, I think."

Acorn took Zachary's place at the window and examined the piece of paper with an appraising gaze, then smelled it.

"Rich leather and wood. You're right, this is from a cigar. An expensive one."

"Do you recognize the label?" Zachary crossed his arms while he held his breath.

Even Haarlock felt the tension in the room. This was a clue, a small one, and it could make or break their search for Mateo.

"Can't make out the brand mark, but this partial symbol here means it's imported." Acorn thought to herself for a moment. "I'd hazard to say no more than three or four places in the city carry something like this."

"Expensive means scarce." Haarlock sighed. "This might be from a small, single-run batch, or a product line. There could be hundreds of those brands."

Acorn nodded her head. "And they might not sell to the public. Could be sold from a backroom stash, or through a private club."

"That presents a problem." Zachary shrugged. "But problems are to be solved. And we have a clue to point us in the right direction."

Haarlock smirked. "I think I know someone who can help us with that."

"Who?" Acorn cocked her head to the side.

"Roboute."

***

The next day Haarlock made his way east to Roboute's mansion. The Illusionist's home, his *large* home, sat nestled in an affluent neighborhood surrounded by canals. Three covered archway bridges allowed entrance to the area, each guarded by a no-nonsense, well-dressed orc. Across the bridge and a quarter mile down a curving street, Haarlock arrived.

Four stories, 26 bedrooms, and more than a dozen staff, the mansion took up the space of four other buildings in the neighborhood, with triple the square footage. The estate grounds were relatively small, though a respectable scattering of shrubs and small trees dotted the area.

Three raps on the large, dark wood door and Mr. Renquest answered.

"Good evening, Lord Haarlock and Ladrón." The aged human man bent at the waist respectfully. His black-tailed jacket and white dress shirt looked as impeccable as ever. As did his gray mutton chops. "May I ask the reason for your call?"

"And a good evening to you, sir." Haarlock patted Ladrón as the raccoon gave a bow of his own. "I would like to ask Roboute for help with a quest. If he's available, of course."

"Lord Roboute is always available to you, m'lord."

Renquest moved over and gestured inside. Once Haarlock entered the foyer, the Butler asked him to wait, then disappeared into the house. A few moments later, the refined British accent of Roboute called out.

"Haarlock, my dear protégé, come in, come in!"

Haarlock went into the hallway to see Roboute walking towards him. The Illusionist's pompadour stood proudly on his head, as did the goatee on his face. His outfit, though, looked like a terrible combination of comfort, style, and color.

"What on earth are you wearing?"

Roboute stopped, looked down at himself, then back up with a sheepish smile. He walked up to Haarlock and shook his hand, then gave Ladrón a pat on the head.

"Forgive me. I'm attempting to invent a new style. There's a big to-do party next month, and I want to be the belle of the ball, so to speak."

Haarlock's eyebrow raised. "I'm going to go out on a limb and say you're a little too old for that."

*"*Agree.*"*

"Fair point." Roboute looked down at himself, then frowned and snapped his fingers. The outfit changed to a simple suit of dark browns. "The joys of being an Illusionist. I'm never without appropriate attire. Come."

Roboute led Haarlock to the study where a pair of Footmen laid out steaming cups of tea and plates of biscuits. Haarlock sat in an overstuffed chair and took a biscuit while Ladrón hopped off his shoulder and onto the nearby table. The animal shoved several of the baked disks into his mouth.

"Flaky, buttery, and with just a hint of orange. These are superb."

Ladrón nodded in agreement as he ate another three.

"Indeed." Roboute took a bite of his own. "I'd be a larger man if I didn't have a modicum of self-control."

"You'll have to share the recipe with me. These would go well at the bodega."

The Illusionist smiled and looked towards the room's entrance. "Renquest?"

"Yes, my lord?" The Butler appeared without a sound.

"Please bring Lord Haarlock a copy of the biscuit recipe."

"Right away."

Roboute gave one of his shark-like smiles. "Anything else I can do for you this evening?"

Haarlock pursed his lips. It was both annoying and absolutely unsurprising that Roboute knew more than he should about what was going on.

"What makes you think I came here for anything but your riveting conversation?"

"Our relationship is more transactional than friendly. So, tell me, how may I assist you in finding Mateo Cabrera?"

Haarlock sighed. "Camilla told you I was coming?"

"Not at all."

"Then how did..."

Haarlock stopped when Roboute gave another of his toothy smiles.

"Secrets are best kept by those who have them." The Illusionist chuckled to himself. "You were saying?"

"Mateo caught me following him and cleared his flat. No doubt he's gone on the lam, which means he'll be next to impossible to find again."

Roboute rubbed his goateed chin. "This presents a problem."

"I'm hoping the fact that you're a Level 53 mage will lessen that problem."

"Yes, I'm sure it will. Leave your pet and walk with me."

The Illusionist stood and made his way out of the study. Haarlock followed as Ladrón moved towards the remaining biscuits.

Down the hallway and a set of stairs, then into a storage room. Roboute wove his hands in front of him in a spiral pattern, and the far wall shimmered in response. The taste of magic filled the room as the wall turned from wood paneling into brick. A tunnel appeared, receding into darkness. *Darkvision* allowed Haarlock to see a room further ahead.

When Roboute walked into the open space, he snapped his fingers, filling it with soft light from an unseen source. Shelves filled with books, jars, and boxes lined much of the walls. A ritual circle was inlaid into the floor and ceiling, and magical diagrams and sigils covered the walls where the shelving didn't.

"Welcome to my private study."

Haarlock's mouth couldn't have been more open. He blinked a few times and closed it.

"Damn, Roboute. This is something."

"Indeed. I spent the better part of four decades building this place."

It didn't take long for Haarlock to find himself running a finger across the spines of books. All were old, with titles in languages he couldn't read. The ones he could ranged from magical treatises to literary works.

"This book. It's *The Iliad.*" Haarlock gently pulled the volume from its spot and opened it. "How is this here?"

"If you read the foreword, the author says it's his fading recollection of the story and is far from complete."

"How valuable is it?" Haarlock closed the book and put it back. "Actually, don't tell me. I don't want to know."

Roboute smirked. "Let's see about your problem, shall we?"

"Finding a needle in a haystack." Haarlock walked to the center of the room to stand with Roboute. "Which I'm told is quite difficult."

"Luckily, it's not *that* difficult. Ostia is home to many people, yes, but a small percentage of them are elves. And roughly half of those are male."

"How many does that leave us?"

"About ten thousand. We can eliminate children and the elderly, which brings us to under seven thousand."

"And you just happen to know those demographics?" Haarlock gave Roboute an eyebrow raise.

"You know things when you've been around as long as I have." Roboute winked. "Now, the trick will be finding one elf among those seven thousand. I can't find his exact location, but I can identify where he's been. That should allow you to narrow down your search."

Roboute waved his hand, and a table with a city map appeared. He went to a shelf and removed two pouches from a box, then sat them on the table and opened them. Colored crystals filled one, and sand the other.

"Take a red and blue crystal from the pouch and hold them in either hand."

Haarlock complied. Roboute took a green crystal in his right hand, then held out his left hand, palm facing Haarlock. The Illusionist spoke under his breath for a few seconds, and when he opened his right hand again, the crystal was gone.

"Think of Mateo while looking at the map." Roboute took a handful of sand from the other pouch and sprinkled it on the map.

As the grains landed on the parchment, they swirled around the city, forming piles in 14 places.

"These are Mateo's most visited places in the last six months. Do you recognize any of them?"

Haarlock looked at his now empty hands. He felt the magic flow across and through him as Roboute spoke, concentrating on the crystals he once held. It must have been a high level spell for it to have consumed so many components.

"This one, here, is where I first found Mateo. Here is his apartment. These other ones I don't know."

The sand piles lay on the eastern side of the city, from the coliseum all the way to the city walls to the south and east.

Roboute looked at the map as he tapped a finger to his lips. "Unfortunately, I have no way to determine which place is his most visited, nor the timeframe of those visits."

"Can you track the location of an object, too?"

"Of course."

"I was hoping you'd say that." Haarlock produced the cigar wrapper piece. "Found this at his apartment."

"You believe this will help find him?" Roboute took the wrapper and looked it over.

"When I followed Mateo the first time, he went into a tobacco shop. After finding that wrapper, my thought is he went there because it's familiar to him. Habits are subtle like that."

"Clever, Haarlock. Very clever."

"I like to think so."

Both men shared a laugh. Roboute went back to the shelving and retrieved a small wooden bowl and a vial of liquid. He put the wrapper and liquid in the bowl, then produced a match. The contents went up in a flash of green and blue light. A breeze blew across the map, removing the sand from all but three places.

Roboute pointed at a sand pile. "Makes sense Mateo's apartment would remain."

"What about the others?"

"This, I believe, is an import warehouse. The final location must be the place it was sold."

Haarlock crossed his arms and nodded to himself a few times. "This is what I needed, Roboute. Thank you."

"Of course. Your quest is important."

"Right. Mateo might lead us to Blue Jira." Haarlock frowned and looked at Roboute. "How did he even come on the radar?"

"Radar?" Roboute raised a questioning eyebrow.

"Right. Um, it's a device that can track things in the air."

"Like birds?"

Haarlock sighed. "Never mind. Anyway, how did you find out about Mateo's involvement with Blue Jira?"

"Pure happenstance, as it turns out. As you so cleverly discovered on your own, Mateo enjoys tobacco. Including snuff. For reasons beyond me, the Crown has seen fit to heavily tax snuff, which in turn creates a black market for it. Especially the more illicit blends. Mateo just so happened to be purchasing a tin of untaxed snuff when the city guard raided the shop. They confiscated Mateo's tin, levied him a fine, and that was it until a few months later."

"And no one bothered to tell me he liked tobacco? That would have been a useful piece of information to have."

The blank, annoyed look Haarlock gave the Illusionist was returned with a shrug.

"Anyway, I take it something was in the snuff tin?"

"Exactly. Some months later, a Clerk, during a routine archival consolidation, examined the evidence from that raid and uncovered a coded letter hidden in the tin. That letter made its way to Marcon, and lo-and-behold..."

"Our mysterious coded text. Talk about luck."

Six other instances of the coded text, all in a cipher none could crack, linked the shinobi activity together. Without finding who created it, or what ability they used to encode the text, it would remain gibberish.

"At this point, we will take any we can get."

Haarlock crossed his arms as he looked at the map. "With months having passed without incident, Mateo has no reason to believe he's being targeted. Except he caught me following him."

"I wouldn't worry about that. Mateo is a top-notch Courier, and to be a top-notch Courier is to be followed. And sometimes robbed. It's unlikely he works solely for Blue Jira, if he works for him at all. Mateo may have been a third-party contractor and is a dead end."

"Wonderful." Haarlock stared at the map again. "Do you really think capturing Blue Jira will help root out the shinobi?"

Roboute looked at Haarlock with a grave expression. "The shinobi plaguing us are too well organized and informed. Someone must be directing them. Someone high in the government. If we can find Blue Jira, we can find the mole."

"It's hard to believe, after all that's been done to find them, the mole is still out there."

"Hence why we need Blue Jira." Roboute sighed. "If Sanyo invades before we've gotten our house in order, the war will be lost before it even starts."

"Once again: wonderful." Haarlock huffed. "Sounds like I need to get my raccoon and come up with a plan."

"I'll walk you out."

It was no surprise when Haarlock found Ladrón still in the study, passed out on a plate of half-eaten biscuits. Crumbs covered most of the animal, doubly so on his face. Loud snoring filled the room.

Haarlock crossed his arms. "Mr. Renquest?"

The Butler appeared from a hidden door in the corner.

"How many biscuits did you give Ladrón?"

"As many as he wanted, m'lord."

4

Haarlock sat across from the smoke shop *Luxe Leaf*. To either side of him sat Camilla Albertine and Quinn the Sky Druid. All wore the hoods of their cloaks up to hide their identities. And Camilla's colorful hair. One other member of Shattersong joined them: Manuel the orc Sentinel.

The orc spent little time at the guildhall, instead putting his skills and size to work guarding important people visiting Ostia. Coming in at 6'7", with a broken tusk and a gnarly scar from his right ear to his collarbone, his mere presence made a statement. That and the three-foot-long cleaver hanging from his belt. Manuel showed it to Haarlock when they first met. It weighed at least 50 pounds.

Manuel stood a few dozen feet in the alley next to *Luxe Leaf*. He waited for either the store to close, or the raccoon sitting on his shoulder to give him the signal. Ladrón liked Manuel's height. It allowed him a better ability to look for food and/or things to steal.

This was the middle of their sixth day.

It was anyone's guess if and when Mateo would show. Their clue was a thin one. Mateo could very well have a month's supply of cigars, or he may have found a new brand to smoke. But they agreed to follow the lead for another four days.

Their target would, almost assuredly, be in disguise. But Shattersong had ways around that. Quinn possessed an ability that allowed her to see active spells, like those used to change one's appearance. She can use that ability while seeing through the eyes of her familiar, a hawk named Volar. Camilla's Consular General class allows her to recognize a face no matter how different it looked since she last saw it. It worked through magical effects and with pictures, too.

With both women on the lookout, it didn't matter if Mateo used magical or mundane means of altering his appearance. They'd find him.

It took them several days to figure out what to do with Mateo once they did.

The Courier class offered several abilities, many of which keep any knowledge secret. It didn't matter how much they tortured him; Mateo literally couldn't give them the information they wanted. That left following him.

Following someone was hard to begin with. Most people aren't actively looking for a tail, but they aren't oblivious to one, either. The subconscious mind is a powerful tool, and if you're not careful, the target will notice you, eventually. Things become far more difficult when the target knows they're being followed. Doubly so when *The Game* provides people with abilities.

They know Mateo is Level 27, which means he possesses the Class Ability *Sense Follower*. If anyone within 200 feet has the intention of following him, he would be alerted. Mateo wouldn't know *who* it was, though, and that's why he ducked into the tobacco shop the first time Haarlock followed him. It forced Haarlock into a small space so he could be easily identified.

Triggering this ability was part of their plan.

"Female orc coming from the east wearing a blue cloak and a gray fur hat."

Quinn's eyes were glossed over as she looked through Volar's eyes. The hawk soared high above the city, far outside the range of Mateo's abilities.

Two minutes later, the target came into view. Camilla watched the woman for a few seconds before shaking her head. It was the third person with an active spell to pass by that day.

Another hour. Quinn absently played with the charm woven into her dark brown hair while Camilla read a book. Back in the previous world, Haarlock sat for long periods of time surveilling a target. He didn't like it then, and he didn't like it now. But he knew of a few mind games to play to keep the boredom from getting too painful.

Suddenly Quinn straightened in her chair.

"What?" Haarlock tensed, his dagger in his hand.

"Someone with an active spell went into *Luxe.*"

Camilla's eyes shot up from her book and toward the store's door. "Why didn't you see them sooner?"

"Volar was at the wrong angle. They came out of the alley across the street and went right in. I almost didn't see them."

Haarlock sent a mental nudge to Ladrón. The raccoon would give the signal for Manuel to get ready and then hide.

Quinn watched the windows of the store, following the people inside. "I see a faint trace of their magic. Camilla, it's the person in the black jacket."

"I see them. Their back is to me."

"They've moved towards the door. I think they're checking out."

Three pairs of eyes watched the front of *Luxe.* It took an agonizing minute before the black jacket came into view. Camilla flashed the *Thieves' Cant* sign for *Confirmed.*

Lucky for them, their target went in the right direction.

Haarlock met eyes with the orc hiding in the alley right next door and nodded. With the grace of a boulder, Manuel walked into the street and turned directly into Mateo.

The elf, disguised as a human, flew backwards and landed flat on his rear. The small paper package he held fell to the side and burst open, spilling out a dozen cigars. Camilla, Quinn, and Haarlock all focused on Mateo and their intention to follow him.

Their efforts had the desired effect. Mateo's confusion turned to concern in an instant. He went stiff, and even from this distance Haarlock could see his eyes moving rapidly as he darted his head from side to side.

It took Mateo a few seconds to regain his composure and look up at the orc towering above him. The elf scooted back a few feet, but he didn't get far before he was grabbed. Haarlock didn't need to hear them to know what Manuel was saying.

"Sorry, I didn't see you there. Let me help you up."

Manuel dragged the elf to his feet, then Mateo said something to make the orc laugh.

"No, no. It was my fault. Oh, look at you. So dirty."

The elf received a *vigorous* dusting off.

"See, all better." Manuel picked up the dropped cigars, wrapped the package up neatly, and handed it back. He laid a coin on top. "My recompense. Au revoir."

The orc walked off down the street while the confused Mateo looked around again. He frowned, then left both his package and the coin Manuel gave him on the ground before walking away.

***

Manuel's hearty laugh filled the Shattersong guildhall. Everyone else, save Acorn, was present and laughing along: Haarlock, Camilla, Samantha, Quinn, Zachary, and Jean-Baptiste. Ladrón, and Samantha's fox familiar Jaakuna stayed in their respective master's rooms. They did *not* like each other.

"And the look on his face? Étonnant!"

Haarlock was in awe of the Sentinel's personality. The vast majority of the time Manuel acted as stoic as a rock, with barely a word or expression. But when he found something hilarious? His laugh sounded like a dozen men.

The orc gestured to Haarlock. "Good idea using his own abilities against him."

"Thank you. I wasn't sure it'd work, but I'm glad it did."

"Oui. I would have handled him a little rougher if not."

"I'm glad you didn't." Camilla gave Manuel a stern look. "Attention does not benefit our quest."

Manuel bowed his head. "Of course."

"And how is our target, Samantha?" Camilla looked past Manuel to the gray-haired woman in the corner.

The Enchanter leaned against the wall with her arms crossed and head tilted down, causing her pixie cut hair to shadow her face. Normally, the late 50s woman talked a mile a minute, moving her hands as much as her mouth. Now she focused on a tracking spell. The one on the pebble Manuel slipped into Mateo's pocket.

"He's visited a dozen different places in the last hour alone. Busy boy."

"Don't forget to identify those locations on a map. We'll send that information to the kingdom Spymaster and let him do the tedious legwork." Camilla smirked. "We'll be the ones to bring the target in."

"Speaking of." Jean-Baptiste cleared his throat. "We'll need to hit him hard and fast so he can't destroy any intel."

SSE. Sensitive site exploitation. Back in his special forces days, Haarlock went on many raids. Each time they took every piece of evidence, from laptop to legal pad, that they could find. It wasn't his job to analyze the intel, but he knew its value. Just like with Mateo, even the smallest clue could lead you to the next target.

"Good point as always, Jean-Baptiste." Zachary nodded to the Bodyguard. "Mateo cleared out with haste last time, which means anything important would have been quickly accessible. Which also means it's just as easy to destroy with a simple fire spell."

"You think he knows magic?" Haarlock raised an eyebrow.

"Perhaps. It's more likely he has a container that will immolate anything in it with the press of a sigil. One he will have on his person." Zachary shrugged.

"Quinn can counterspell any active magic in the room." Camilla gestured to the druid. "How fast can you cast those?"

"It will take me only a moment to cast, but I have to identify the magic before I can. That can take several seconds."

"I have something." Haarlock pulled out a braided leather necklace with a shimmering yellow gem hanging from it. "Suppresses fourth-level spells and lower in a twenty-foot radius."

<u>Nullstone Necklace</u>

Rare

Abilities - Magic Nullifying Field

"That's a find." Jean-Baptiste nodded in appreciation.

"And a double-edged sword." Quinn eyed the stone. "I'll be useless once that's activated."

Camilla tapped a finger to her lips. "It would be better to have Haarlock sneak in and disable all magic in one go."

"All this cloak and dagger stuff is boring me."

Everyone looked over at the brooding orc.

"Yes, Manuel." Zachary rolled his eyes. "We all know you like to break stuff."

Manuel squinted at the Grifter. "Just because I'm big and an orc doesn't mean that's *all* I want to do. I have hobbies."

"Like what?" Haarlock genuinely didn't know.

The orc looked at Haarlock for a second, squinted, then smiled. "I like to paint. In fact, I painted that one right there."

Haarlock looked over his shoulder to where Manuel pointed. On the wall between two bookcases hung an oil painting of Ostia's castle. The shining white fortress stood proudly on the mountain, with its banners flying in the wind. Even from this distance Haarlock could see the detail in the stone walls.

"Impressive."

"Merci!" Manuel put a hand on his chest and dipped his head. "Do you have any talents outside of adventuring?"

"Me?" Haarlock frowned. "Now that I think about it, not really. Just stayed busy with work."

Jean-Baptiste. "Adrenaline is my hobby, so I understand where you're coming from, Haarlock."

"Talk of hobbies is fine and all, but we have a job to do." Camilla looked between the men. They nodded their attention. "I think it would be best to have Haarlock enter Mateo's residence and activate his anti-magic necklace, then have Mateo and Jean-Baptiste do the apprehending. Haarlock can provide backup muscle if needed. Thoughts or concerns?"

Samantha, still focusing, kept her eyes closed and head down as she spoke. "Quinn and Volar can be lookouts, and I'll be magical backup for the boys."

"Sounds good to me." Though she shouldn't see it, Quinn gave the older woman a nod.

"What about Acorn and me?" Zachary raised an eyebrow at Camilla. "And you?"

Camilla gave the Grifter a considering look as she thought for a moment. "We don't have the durability of our fighters, nor the damage output of our mages. The three of us will be in the surrounding area in case Mateo escapes the others."

"Speaking of, where is Acorn?" Haarlock looked around the room.

"Running down a few leads on Mateo's whereabouts." Camilla shrugged. "It's almost assured she'll get nowhere, but we can't leave any stone unturned."

"What leads?" Haarlock raised an eyebrow.

"Acorn is visiting every high-end cigar dealership in the city. Hopefully, the bag of money she has will get someone to talk."

Zachary chuckled. "Spending money? I know she's loving that."

Jean-Baptiste shared a series of enthusiastic nods with the Grifter.

"Alright, we have a plan." Haarlock thought to himself. "How long before we go after Mateo?"

Camilla gestured to Samantha. "When we know where Mateo beds down."

"We're going after him tonight?" Quinn raised her eyebrows in surprise. "After this morning, he'll be on edge."

"True." Camilla gave the Sky Druid a smirk. "And while he might expect it, he won't be expecting us."

5

Haarlock slinked through the shadows, a raccoon following close behind. He looked up to see Volar in the sky, backlit by the bright moons.

Each member approached on their own. They didn't know what kind of surveillance Mateo might have, but an eight-person group at night drew attention from even the most casual observer.

It took until midnight before Shattersong was confident Mateo would stay put. The Courier found himself in an apartment building two blocks south of the coliseum. There were too many exits and too many blind spots. Underground tunnels littered the entire area, and nearly every building connected to its neighbor in some manner. If Mateo escaped, it was likely they'd never find him again.

The building lay down an alley and across a plaza. Haarlock slowed to a walk and put Ladrón on his shoulder. When he made it to the apartment's opposite corner, Haarlock leaned against a wall and waited.

A few minutes later, Jean-Baptiste and Manuel strolled down the thoroughfare in front of the apartment. They chatted about a random topic, laughing from time to time. A three-person group came from the opposite direction, nodding respectfully as they passed. The pair stopped in front of the building, and once the other group moved further away, Manuel lit a pipe.

Haarlock cast *Shadowstep* and appeared in the alley across the street, then looked for a chalk marking near the ground. Part of the mage's scouting efforts included finding where in the building Mateo stayed.

Fourth floor? Good thing I took Agile *as a Talent.*

As Haarlock heard others walking down the street, he would dip into a shadow, allowing *Wrapped in Shadow* to obscure his presence. His cloak, enhanced with Stealth, didn't hurt, either. So long as he didn't move, it would take a dedicated observer to find him.

Ladrón stayed below to signal the fighters when Haarlock got into position.

With the Feat *Magic Novice,* Haarlock could sense magical energies. Samantha provided a replica of the spell used to track Mateo, giving him something to recognize. All Haarlock needed to do now was find which room had the right magical scent, as it were. Lucky for him, or not, each room faced the outside.

Haarlock climbed around almost the entire building before he felt the correct magic.

Thick curtains blocked all light from the room, but the living room curtains were slightly ajar. *Canny Observer* and *Darkvision* revealed the room's interior. A corner bookshelf, two sitting chairs, and a small table covered in papers filled the room. An open kitchen lay on one side, and doors to two rooms on the other.

A mental command to Ladrón sent the animal poking his head into the street and waving his hands.

Manuel laughed again, then the sound of a door opening and closing filled the quiet street. Ladrón scampered up the wall, nimbly hopping from downpipe to windowsill. What took Haarlock almost three minutes, Ladrón accomplished in 20 seconds.

The inside hallway cast light under Mateo's door, and it didn't take long for two figures to stop in front, casting shadows as they did so. Haarlock *Shadowstepped* into the room and moved between the bookshelf and the wall, then activated the magic nullifying necklace. Its area of effect would cover the entire room with ease.

Less than a minute later, Manuel kicked in the door.

Splinters of wood flew across the room as the orc burst inside, cleaver at the ready. Jean-Baptiste followed, manacles in hand.

One of the room's doors opened and an orc just as big as Manuel rushed out. He slammed into the Sentinel, knocking his weapon from his hand and hitting him to the floor. Jean-Baptiste reached for his sword and received a backhand for his trouble. The Bodyguard hit the wall with an *umph*.

Manuel got to his feet in an instant and tackled the other orc back into the room he had come from. It took a little longer for Jean-Baptiste to recover, but once he did, he joined his friend.

Haarlock left his hiding place, and as he went towards the other room, Samantha appeared in the doorway. The Enchanter motioned with her hand, and when nothing happened, she looked down at it with confusion. Realization dawned on her, and she looked up at Haarlock.

"The necklace." She pointed to Haarlock's hand. "Get rid of it!"

With a 20-foot range, the only place for it to go was out the window. Haarlock grabbed a heavy book from the shelf and threw it as hard as he could toward the glass. Ladrón, watching things unfold with his face plastered against said glass, screamed as he dived out of the way.

The book went through the window and out into the alley, followed shortly by the nullifying necklace. Samantha's hand flickered with magic a few seconds later. She cackled maniacally and joined her two compatriots in the other room.

Haarlock knew his guildmates could take the other orc, even if the violent sounds coming from the room suggested otherwise. He needed to get Mateo and prevent him from destroying evidence. Haarlock kicked the other room's door open and found it empty.

In a panic, Haarlock rushed to the blinds. They were closed tight, as were the windows behind them. He went to the bed and laid a hand on it and felt warmth. Whoever lay here hadn't been gone for long. Haarlock flipped the mattress off the frame, but nothing was underneath.

Where did you go?

There had to be something. Anything. Haarlock tuned out the sounds of fighting from the next room. *Canny Observer* and *Magic Novice* went into overdrive, seeking any hint of where Mateo had gone.

Samantha's magic filled the air, but something else hid there. Behind.

Haarlock turned and looked around the room. Something odd about the corner caught his attention. The way the shadows from the window lay on the wall was wrong, as if there should have been an object there, but wasn't. He blinked, and a standing mirror appeared.

An illusion spell, a simple one, diverting one's attention away from the object so it remained unnoticed.

Clever.

Faint sigils lined the mirror frame, and Haarlock recognized the energy they gave off. He felt it before in *The Dolphin*. The warden possessed a statue bust enchanted with *Teleport*.

Where it went was anyone's guess, but Haarlock knew what waited on the other side: Mateo.

Fortune favors the bold.

Haarlock took a deep breath and placed his hand on the mirror. The world flashed black as a whip-crack of sound filled his ears. When his eyes finally adjusted to the new, dull white glow of magical light, he found himself touching a near-identical mirror to the one in the bedroom. Only this one was somewhere else entirely. Where, Haarlock didn't know. The cool, damp air and the old, cracked brick walls made him think of a cellar. None of that mattered because Mateo stood in front of him, holding a round object in an outstretched hand.

"Take another step and I drop this."

Haarlock slowly put his arms out to his sides, palms facing out.

"Your team is good. Real good." Stress oozed from Mateo's words. "I didn't think you'd find me again so quickly."

The elf laughed nervously. Haarlock eyed whatever was in his hand.

"I assume that's some kind of bomb?"

"Big enough the overpressure will kill us both."

"That's not what I'm here for, Mateo."

"Oh, I know what you're here for." Mateo clenched his jaw and stared daggers at Haarlock. "You've ruined everything. *Everything*!"

Not that it would help, but Haarlock cast *Magic Armor* on himself.

"Let's talk this out. We only want to ask you questions."

Mateo huffed. "It doesn't matter now. I'm dead."

"We can protect you."

"Please." Mateo put his arm down. His face went from anger to despair and back repeatedly. "They can get to me anywhere I am."

"Who can?"

"Don't!" Mateo pointed the bomb at Haarlock again.

Haarlock knew what was going to happen before *Alert* triggered. He could see Mateo's hopeless expression.

Tears welled in the elf's eyes as he opened his hand, and Haarlock watched in slow motion as the bomb fell towards the ground. Haarlock turned and dived towards the mirror as he tossed his guild ring to the side.

Haarlock felt the *Teleport* spell activate as white light filled his vision and burning fire licked across his body.

6

Haarlock hit a wooden floor, then screamed as searing pain wracked his body. Consciousness came and went, but eventually soothing relief poured across and through him. How much time passed, he didn't know, but when he awoke, he found himself in his room at the Shattersong guildhall, now clad in a simple set of dark linen clothes.

Before he could do much more than sit up on the bed, a *massive* ball of fur tackled him from behind, knocking him to the floor. Soon it climbed up his back and attached itself to his head.

*"*Hurt. Sad. Better. Happy.*"*

"Yeah, glad to see you, too." Haarlock laughed as he hugged Ladrón. *"Mind letting me up?"*

Ladrón climbed off Haarlock's head and did circles on the floor, chittering with joy the entire time. Haarlock stretched out the soreness across his entire body, and as he rubbed his hands over his face he felt something, or the lack thereof. He no longer had a beard.

I can't remember the last time I was clean-shaven.

Haarlock put on the slippers by the door and went out into the guildhall proper. Samantha, Jean-Baptiste, Camilla, and Quinn mingled around the fireplace at the far end. It didn't take long for them to notice Haarlock, and all stopped and stared as he approached.

"Um, hi guys."

Samantha walked up, tears in her eyes, and punched Haarlock in the chest. She wasn't strong, but her bony knuckles hurt.

"You worried us something fierce." The Enchanter stared at Haarlock for a moment before slamming into him with a hug. "The healer said it'd take a couple of days for you to wake up, but we were going to get another one if you didn't wake up after three. Glad you're okay."

"Sorry. A crazed elf tried to blow me up."

Haarlock hugged her back for a moment. Samantha moved away and pulled the magic nullifying necklace from a pocket.

"You dropped this." Samantha handed the necklace over.

Camilla walked over and shook Haarlock's hand. "Did you say Mateo tried to blow you up?"

"Oh yeah, you guys don't know about the mirror."

Haarlock explained the teleporting mirror, Mateo's desperate rantings, and the bomb.

"Once we subdued the orc, we found you half-burned to death in the other bedroom." Jean-Baptiste looked upset just talking about it. "Nothing else was fire damaged, so we had no idea what happened."

Quinn tilted her head and frowned. "The explosion must have destroyed the mirror on the other side, dispelling any magics on its companion item. Samantha, can you backtrace a teleport spell?"

"I can give you a rough idea of the direction and distance, but nothing exact after this much time has passed."

"Good thing for us I left behind my guild ring." A sheepish smile overcame Haarlock when everyone looked at him. "I didn't have time to activate the homing spell on it, but it's there." Haarlock looked at Samantha. "Can you track it?"

"You better believe it." The older woman smiled.

Camilla stood. "We can't wait on the others. Quinn, once the ring is located, you'll *Teleport* yourself and Jean-Baptiste in. Clear the space, then bring the rest of us."

"I'll need an hour to prep the spells."

"Then we leave in an hour."

***

A whip-crack heralded Haarlock, Camilla, Samantha, and Ladrón.

Mateo Cabrera, or what was left of his charred remains, lay under a canvas tarp in the middle of the room. A soot-covered room that stank of burned flesh.

Jean-Baptiste gestured towards the ground, then towards a doorway to his left. "The bomb destroyed everything in this room, but almost all of what's in there survived." He handed Haarlock his guild ring. "This will need to be polished."

The blackened ring looked undamaged, though soot filled every nook and cranny. Haarlock slipped it on a finger and gave the Bodyguard a nod. Even though he stood with only a set of basic winter clothing on, his guild and signet rings gave Haarlock some semblance of normalcy. His equipment wasn't in operational shape after the firebombing.

Quinn stood in the center of the other room, hands on hips, as she surveyed the space. Hung on the walls, stacked tables, piled on shelves, and scattered on the floor were documents. Hundreds of them. Mateo's bomb damaged much, but only destroyed those documents within a few feet of the doorway.

"By the gods." Camilla walked to one table and ran a hand across the papers.

"My sentiments exactly." Jean-Baptiste flipped through a book he found on the floor. "This looks like some kind of ledger, and in that bundle are architectural drawings."

Haarlock walked around the room as Ladrón continued to sniff through things on the floor. How this much material survived the explosion, he didn't know. It looked as though a spell prevented the fire's progress, with an obvious line of demarcation between burned and not.

A thought came to Haarlock. "How much of this do you think is a false flag?"

Everyone in the room looked at him.

"What do you mean?" Camilla frowned.

"This room didn't burn from the firebomb?" Haarlock gestured to where the fire had stopped. "And who in their right mind would keep this much information in one location?"

"We're underground in a place that can only be reached by teleportation." Quinn gave Haarlock a confused look. "Where else would they keep it?"

The mage had a point. Haarlock came from a world where you could store tens of thousands of documents on a device the size of your fingernail. Here in *The Game*, paper could only store so much data.

"Fair point." Haarlock put his hands on his hips. Mateo killing himself sat weird with him, and this only added to it. "Still. This seems...excessive."

"Be that as it may, I'll take it." Samantha grabbed a bundle of papers and arranged them neatly on the table, then stuck them under her arm. "Let's get moving. I don't enjoy being underground."

"No." Camilla shook her head at the Enchanter. "These documents are too sensitive. We can't risk removing them from a secure location like this one. I'll inform the spymaster and his people can perform the retrieval. Everyone, put things back the best you can remember, and let's get out of here."

***

Congratulations! You have completed the quest: Investigate Mateo Cabrera. *You have been awarded 2,000 experience.*

Haarlock sat in front of the fireplace in Shattersong's guildhall, reviewing his latest notification. The fire, magically enchanted to stay forever aflame, bathed him in warmth. The pot of tea helped, too.

Ladrón napped in the chair next to him, lying on his back, head hanging off the edge and tongue hanging out of his mouth.

What was next? With Mateo dead and his hideout found, it would likely revolve around what the cache of documents revealed.

With any luck, Marcon and Roboute will locate several of the Sanyo moles.

Sanyo. The invasion.

How many shinobi are there? In what positions are they hiding? What happens when they're activated?

Even a single operative could wreak untold havoc. Depending on what access they had, vital messages could go missing, supplies delayed, or troops redirected. If there were more?

Haarlock shook his head. Thoughts like that didn't help. Until a target presented itself, there was no sense in worrying. But what to do until then?

The training floor beneath him was an option. In the past weeks, with help from Acorn, Haarlock's *Lock Pick* Skill increased from *Skilled* to *Expert*. The gnome was an *excellent* teacher. Maybe Jean-Baptiste or Manuel would offer tips on sword fighting?

Going back home sounded good, too. There was never a lack of work at the bodega, even for the lord of the land. Haarlock's contract with the guild specified he would spend no more than a single month away from his estate at a time. It'd been close to that since he started the Mateo quest.

Haarlock left Ladrón and the fire to go upstairs and find Camilla.

The Clerks and Accountant already left for the evening, leaving Aldo and Camilla at the front desk. Haarlock walked into the middle of their conversation.

"...back to haunt us." Camilla frowned as she looked at the paper in her hand. "And an expensive haunting, too."

Both looked at Haarlock as he entered the room.

"We're haunted?"

Aldo stood on a small stool while Camilla kept the document low enough for him to see it. Even for a dwarf, the Steward was short.

"In a way." Aldo ran a hand across his short, bright red beard. "This building needed renovation sixty years ago. Now it's a problem that can't be ignored."

"Really?" Haarlock looked at where the walls met the ceiling and floor. "I've been in some crappy places before, and this isn't one of them by any stretch."

"It's a problem you can't see, Haarlock." Camilla handed the paper to him.

Haarlock looked at the document, a blueprint of the guildhall, and saw many areas circled in red. Notes next to each circled detailed structural instability because of soil erosion and poor foundation design.

"This looks expensive."

"It will be." Aldo grumbled.

"Any idea of the cost?" Haarlock grimaced as he looked at Camilla.

The woman sighed. "Repairs will be several thousand gold by themselves. Then we need to consider the cost of replacing the magical enchantments seeded throughout. Samantha will price that out, but I imagine it will be several times the cost of the repairs."

"You need to find the agent who sold you this place and have a conversation." Haarlock huffed.

"She died of a heart attack a few years after the sale." The dwarf shrugged. "And her firm went out of business twenty years ago."

Haarlock raised his eyebrows. "I didn't think Shattersong had been around that long."

"The guild purchased this building forty years ago, shortly after it was formed." A faraway look came across Aldo's face. "The roster has changed twice since then." He gestured to Camilla. "You've been here what, ten years now?"

"Eleven in March. Jean-Baptiste's eighth anniversary is in May."

"Time flies, doesn't it?"

"Very much so." Camilla frowned at Haarlock. "Shouldn't you know all this? We gave you an onboarding packet with a history of the guild."

"I left it in my room." Haarlock gestured over his shoulder towards the stairs. "Kinda forgot I even had it until just now."

Camilla gave Haarlock an *of course you did* look. "I suggest you take the time to review it."

"Speaking of time, I'm wondering if there's anything else for me to do. And where my equipment went."

"Yes, you've been on mission for nearly a month." Camilla handed the blueprint back to the dwarf. "Aldo plans to retrieve your equipment from repair on his morning chore run. After that, you're free to go about your business. You have lands to manage after all."

The Steward excused himself and left.

"True." Haarlock nodded to himself. "Nothing else the guild needs me for?"

"Nothing current that suits your abilities. Jean-Baptiste is guarding a visiting dignitary, Quinn and Samantha are teaching a class at the Adventurer's Guild, and Acorn is testing a bank's security."

"A bank?" Haarlock chuckled. "I know she's loving that."

Camilla smirked. "Especially since she's paid ten percent of whatever she can steal."

"What's the most she's ever made?"

"Sixty-four platinum."

Haarlock choked on air. "Holy *shit*. What'd she take?"

"A two-kilogram bar of solid orichalcum."

Created by suffusing a copper-zinc alloy with massive quantities of magic, orichalcum is one of the rarest substances to exist in *The Game*. A bar that size would take years of effort to create.

"You should ask if she needs any assistance." Camilla raised an eyebrow. "If you're concerned about such things, that would help your status in the Thieves' Guild."

That wasn't a terrible idea. Haarlock waffled internally for a moment as he weighed the choice.

"Actually, you know what? I *will* go and see."

7

Clad in his freshly repaired gear, Haarlock made his way south across a few marketplaces. A set of recessed stairs led to a sturdy wooden door, and behind it, an unnamed tavern. He didn't know the grim-looking bartender's name, but Haarlock gave the man a nod anyway before heading to the back.

The storeroom at the end of the hallway held several beer kegs. Haarlock turned the handle on one and pushed, revealing a false wall and a spiral staircase set into the floor. Down the stairs, and at the end of the stone hallway at the bottom, lay a reinforced metal door. The door's viewport opened as Haarlock approached, and a set of eyes looked out.

"We're closed." The gruff voice sounded equally annoyed and bored.

"Hi." Haarlock smiled. "I'm here to help a gnome rob a bank."

The viewport slammed shut. A moment later it slid back open again.

"Ain't no one here knows about a gnome or a robbery."

"Does anyone know about a raccoon?"

Ladrón chittered proudly from Haarlock's shoulder.

Once again, the viewport slid closed, and a few seconds later the door swung open to reveal Acorn. Her wide eyes fixed on Ladrón immediately.

"I'm robbing a bank with a raccoon?!"

Haarlock smirked. "You better believe it."

Ladrón waved his paws triumphantly.

The gnome woman excitedly clapped her hands in rapid fashion. "I'm *so* going to be the talk of the guild. Come in, come in!"

Acorn waved Haarlock inside as a newly acquired quest notification pinged him. In the middle of the guildhall's recessed area sat two figures Haarlock knew. Save Brea the Bartender, a tall, muscular woman with red hair and a look like she'd eat you alive, and the door guard; the place was empty.

Ladrón chittered as he sniffed the air, and with the grace of a ravenous animal, he leaped to the ground and scurried towards the bar. Brea was already setting out a plate of peaches.

"Where is he going?" Acorn's face turned from joy to betrayal in an instant.

"While there's no doubt you have a special place in Ladrón's heart, I know for a fact he forgot about us both the instant he smelled something sweet."

Acorn chuckled softly as she went to the table and sat down between the two others.

Justine, second-in-command of the Thieves' Guild sat to the left. Pointed, heavily bejeweled ears poked through the medium-length brown hair lying loose around her shoulders. Bright red lipstick stood out against her fair skin, and her tight clothing, a combination of linen and leather, left little to the imagination. The circular, silver pendant adorned with three sapphires dangling just above her breasts helped, though. She leaned back in her chair and nodded once to Haarlock.

Her boss, Guildmaster Gerard Parnell, sat with excellent posture between the two women. His features were *bland*, almost comically so. At a glance, he looked like a dozen different people Haarlock knew from the previous world. His clothing, a brown tunic and black trousers, held just as much character as his short brown hair.

The man spoke in an equally bland tone. "May I ask how you knew about our meeting, Lord Haarlock?"

"Camilla."

"Of course. She's always trying to help me win these so Shattersong gets some credit." Acorn shook her head. "I assume you want to help so you can get a percentage?"

"Not really." Haarlock walked over to them and took a seat. "Figured it would be a good boost to my status in the Thieves' Guild. That, and I've always wanted to rob a bank."

"So you *don't* want paid?" The gnome squinted at Haarlock in an accusatory manner.

"No, Acorn." Haarlock laughed. "Unlike you, I'm not in it for the money."

"But I am." Justine leaned forward and smiled. "We were just negotiating my cut."

"And, like I was saying, twenty-five percent is too much."

The two women stared at each other.

Gerard looked from one to the other, then to Haarlock. "Since you have no interest in payment, Lord Haarlock, perhaps you can settle the matter."

Justine leaned back, crossed her arms, then nodded once to Gerard. The gnome watched Justine for a moment before looking at Haarlock.

"Fine." Acorn scoffed.

"Is Justine doing twenty-five percent of the work?"

Gerard spoke. "Likely more." He looked at Acorn.

The tiny rogue thought to herself for a moment. She looked at Gerard, then at Haarlock, and finally at Justine.

"You better help steal a *lot* of stuff."

"Oh, don't you worry your little head about that." The lithe elf smiled deviously.

"What about you, Gerard? What role do you take?" Haarlock gave him a once-over. "I doubt anyone could find you in a crowd. Be a great getaway man."

"I am merely the organizer and sounding board. The client contracted the guild for a quest, and as guildmaster, I chose the best tool for the job." Gerard gestured to Acorn.

"Damn right I'm the best."

Haarlock raised an eyebrow. "No offense, Acorn, but you're not the highest-level rogue in the city. Wouldn't the bank want someone better suited to test their security?"

The gnome gave Haarlock a blank look.

"As I said, the best tool for the job." Gerard, in a rare moment of expression, smirked at the gnome. "Acorn is far more clever than she lets on and has absconded with more than her fair share of treasure from other well-secured vaults."

"Allegedly." Acorn held up a finger.

"And how do you fit into all of this?" Haarlock looked at Justine. "One tool not enough?"

"Our target has top-end clientele, with a security system that puts the kingdom treasury to shame. Acorn might be good, but she isn't *that* good." Justine looked at the gnome and mouthed *sorry*.

"Who are we robbing exactly?"

"*Raven Rock Holdings*." Acorn stuck her tongue out at the elf. "It isn't your average bank, and our goal isn't just to rob it. Unfortunately, as the lovely elf said, it's got excellent security."

"What's wrong? Worried you'll get caught?" Justine's expression was equal parts friendly and stabbing.

"Haven't been caught yet."

Haarlock frowned. "*Isn't just to rob it*? What else were you hired to do?"

Acorn steepled her fingers and rhythmically tapped the tips together. "We're after the manager. Robbing the place is just a pretense."

"Interesting..." Haarlock went to rub his bearded chin but stopped for a second when he felt smooth skin. "Um, what sort of plan do you have so far?"

"A poor one. These are personnel files." Gerard produced a stack of papers from somewhere under the table, then a map. "This is a two-year-old map of the first floor. Renovations were finished ten months ago, so this is assuredly out of date. We know of at least one basement level we don't have a floor plan of. The security system is as thorough as it is sensitive, with layers of detection magic, mundane locks, and guard stations. You need an appointment to get through the front door, and without some form of clout, wealth, status, or combination thereof, you don't get an appointment. Even if you get inside, guests are escorted at all times or otherwise locked in a place they can't leave."

"Good thing I've seen a lot of heist movies." Haarlock nodded several times as he stared at the map.

Acorn looked at Justine, then at Gerard. All of them looked at Haarlock.

"Oh. Right. Sorry. Movies are like a combination of a play and a book. You can watch the play anywhere you want, just like you can read a book. If that makes any sense."

"It absolutely does not." Justine leaned in and met Haarlock's eyes. "You'll have to tell me about it more sometime."

"Oh my god, woman!" Acorn looked at the elf as if she had three heads. "Keep it in your pants."

Haarlock's cheeks flushed hot as he looked at Gerard for help. The man's blank face stared back.

"Anyway." Haarlock cleared his throat. "I have an idea of how to get us all in the door, and, hopefully, make it look like we stole something."

"Already?" Acorn looked less than convinced. "We've been planning this for two weeks, and all we've come up with are explosives."

"Well, it's all about misdirection." Haarlock held out his left hand, and once everyone looked at it, he snapped his fingers. They watched for a moment before looking up at Haarlock again. "And voilà!"

Haarlock's right hand came up from under the table with a key in it. The key that opened the Shattersong guildhouse's rear door. Only this one wasn't his.

"Check your key ring, Acorn."

The gnome's hands moved with lightning speed as she reached for her belt. Metal jingled for a moment before she slowly looked up at Haarlock with daggers.

"How'd you do that?"

"Like I said, misdirection." Haarlock moved back in his chair, and a raccoon head popped up from between his legs. "And a Ladrón. You three forgot about him when he went to the bar, and our ability to communicate telepathically let me set the trap. I think something similar might work at the bank."

Acorn smiled warmly at the animal. "That was a masterful piece of thievery, Ladrón."

Ladrón chittered in appreciation.

"So, Haarlock, what does this misdirection plan of yours entail?" Gerard tilted his head ever so slightly.

"The long and short of it revolves around using me to get the others inside. Then Justine and Ladrón make a distraction while Acorn robs the place. It's rough, but I think it'll work."

The elf and the raccoon looked at one another and exchanged a curt nod.

"I'm going to assume *Raven Rock Holdings* doesn't do cold calls." Haarlock looked over to the bar at Brea. She leaned against the back counter while polishing a glass. "And I'm assuming she isn't here just to serve drinks."

Gerard looked at the woman while he spoke. "Brea is here to provide material and logistical support, yes."

"Good, because we'll need some pretty specific supplies. We also need to see what assurances *Raven Rock* gives its customers and what happens if those assurances are broken. Oh, and Acorn, do you think Camilla will let us borrow something?"

8

A well-appointed carriage stopped in front of a single-story stone building. Gargoyles sat on the roof corners, and swirling patterns adorned the structure's facade. A sculpted wooden sign that read *Raven Rock Holdings* stood proud over thick, dark wood doors. A doorman in a high-collared wool coat waited at the ready to accept any visitors.

The carriage driver dismounted, extended the stairs, and opened the door. Lord Haarlock, bedecked in a one-piece, all-black jumpsuit made of fine linen and trimmed with red lace, stepped out. Next came Acorn, similarly dressed in a blue jumpsuit, with a large leather satchel draped across her chest. The pair walked towards the entrance with purpose, and the doorman opened the doors and bowed as they entered.

Two figures, one elf and one raccoon, remained in the carriage.

"Ah, Lord Haarlock!" A voice echoed in the large, open space. "You're right on time."

Haarlock watched as a clean-shaven, middle-aged human man stood from behind an oak desk in the center of the room. He wore a muted red tunic, black slacks, and a green chaperon hat adorned with a white goose feather.

"Welcome to *Raven Rock Holdings.* I am Chester McCaffrey, branch manager and your personal assistant today."

"Thank you, Mr. McCaffrey."

"Please call me Chester. And please, please sit." He gestured to the two chairs across from his desk. "I wasn't aware there would be two of you today. May I ask your name, miss?"

"Leater Quint." Acorn smiled brightly and nodded once. "I am Lord Haarlock's attaché."

"Yes, of course."

Chester waited for his customers to sit, then took his own chair. A ledger lay open on his desk. He took a feather quill, loaded it with ink, then poised it on the right-side page.

"First, I must thank you for thinking of *Raven Rock Holdings* for your security needs. Adventurers and nobles alike have used our services for many years without complaint."

"Hence this meeting. What I have requires the most discrete accommodations."

Haarlock gestured to Acorn, and she tapped the satchel for effect.

"Absolutely, m'lord." Chest wrote something in a smooth, flowing script as he nodded enthusiastically. "We have many secure containers for items of that size."

"What kind of security?"

"Physically, our vault is beneath our feet, secure behind a three-foot-thick foundation of magically solidified and hardened stone. Anti-teleportation, scrying, and divination spells encapsulate the building, in each room, and, depending on which package you purchase, individual containers. We have thirty-second response times from the city guard, and on-site security that is more than capable of taking care of anyone attempting to abscond with our customer's valuables. And more, of course, but that's proprietary information."

Haarlock looked around the space. The lacquered wood-paneled walls gave the room an air of aristocracy, though the lack of windows made it feel somewhat smaller than it was. A smattering of flora kept the space from seeming bland, even with the absence of artwork. One thing he didn't see was the aforementioned security. Perhaps they were behind one of the three doors at the far end?

"Where might this security be?"

Chester beamed. "The doorman? He's a retired adventurer of some renown. You'll see the others once we continue the tour."

"Of course."

"Now, your item. May I ask what it is?"

Acorn looked questioningly at Haarlock, and he replied with a single nod.

"Unfortunately, you are unable to know the actual contents as they are considered diplomatic material." From the leather satchel, the gnome removed a bright yellow pouch emblazoned with ***DIPLOMATIC CONTENTS***. "I understand you may need to know what type of contents are in the pouch."

The manager's eyes widened as he wrote in his ledger. "Ah, yes, an item of the utmost discretion. I can assure you, Ms. Quint, my inquiry is only to provide the best security possible. We at *Raven Rock Holdings* do not presume the need to know why your items are to be stored with us, just their general demographics so we can ensure proper handling."

"Of course." Acorn sat the yellow pouch on top of the satchel. "The contents are non-magical and non-biological. Fire and water protection are a must, though."

"Hmm, yes." Chester wrote more in his ledger. "A tier-four, medium-sized unit will ensure your item's safety."

"What about price? I may be a noble, but I am not without my limitations." Haarlock smirked.

"The ever-looming specter of money. How many days will you be storing your item with us?"

"Six."

"Six days with a medium tier four, initial enchanting fee, first-time discount..." Chester wrote out the pricing formula as he spoke. "Four hundred and sixty-two gold."

Acorn cleared her throat at the price, and Haarlock had to stifle a laugh.

"The fee may be steep, yes, but our security is top-notch. Your property will not leave this building except in your care."

Haarlock rubbed his newly beardless chin as he considered the offer. Considered for a little *too* long.

"Perhaps that tour of our facility will help ease your mind?" Chester smiled.

"Actually, yes, that would be an excellent idea." Haarlock nodded as he looked around. "Would you happen to have something warm to drink? I was hoping once we were inside the cold would wear off, but it appears that wasn't so."

"Of course!"

Chester snapped his fingers, and a few seconds later, a Footman appeared from one of the far doors with a tea service. He set out the cups and poured boiling water from the kettle with practiced ease, and once he laid out a small dish of biscuits, he disappeared. Both Haarlock and Acorn liberally applied sugar to their cups, though the gnome went with chamomile while Haarlock took chai.

With steaming tea in hand and the diplomatic pouch returned to the satchel, Chester led the two new customers towards the three doors in the back. When he turned his back, Haarlock used *Sleight of Hand* to add a little something extra to his drink.

"Like I mentioned before, we have additional physical security beyond the door guard. Like the foundation below, the walls above are magically strengthened, three-foot-thick solid stone. Guards would arrive long before anyone could penetrate them."

Haarlock sipped his tea, fighting back his disgust at the bitter flavor.

"Now, inside the rightmost door is our security checkpoint." Chester led the pair to the door and opened it with a key. "We check each person entering the lower floors to make sure they bring no weapons or other illicit items with them. Please, after you."

Inside the room looked like any hundreds of airport security checkpoints Haarlock had been through. To the right lay two long tables with small trays, and behind them stood two well-built, blandly dressed guards. Both orcs and both bored looking.

"These are also retired adventurers, Arnold and Guy." Chester nodded to them, and they nodded back. Haarlock noticed a hand sign flashed between them. "Please remove all items from your pockets and place them in the trays. The guards will ensure nothing dangerous is present, then check your person with a simple passive wand detector."

Arnold pointed to Haarlock, then his table's tray, while Guy did the same to Acorn. They inspected each item, then person, Chester included, then waved a wand over each person's body. Haarlock could feel the slight tingle of magic as it passed. Chester told Guy about the diplomatic pouch and how it couldn't be opened but ensured a thorough inspection of the leather satchel.

Haarlock held his breath as he watched the orc pass a wand over the satchel, then turn it inside out. He knew they were searching for active enchantments, hidden compartments, or anything surreptitious. And they searched *thoroughly*, checking even the seams for tampering.

Once Guy finished his inspection, Haarlock covered his stress-laden exhale by blowing on his tea. Acorn, though, looked as though this was something she'd done a dozen times before.

The handful of items were returned and Guy opened the inner door using a ring heavy with keys. Beyond lay a short hallway, and at the end, a large spiral staircase.

"Come, come." Chester motioned as he stepped into the hallway, talking as they went down. "Next is the private room."

"Private room?" Acorn perked up. "I assumed there would be only vaults down below."

"While there is a vault, yes, clients still need to access, inspect, or otherwise interact with their items in private. Hence the rooms. There are additional refreshments there, if you like."

Haarlock cleared his throat with a raspy cough. "That would be excellent. It appears the dry air has somewhat parched me."

"Of course, m'lord. As I was saying, each room is fully protected from both magical and mundane eavesdropping, so anything discussed inside is confidential."

The wide-set stairs, easily capable of holding four people abreast, continued down several levels, opening into a wide hallway lined with wooden doors.

"And here we are." Chester brought the pair to the second door on the right and unlocked it. "Please make yourselves comfortable while I retrieve several of our secure containers for your inspection."

Chester held the door open while Haarlock and Acorn entered. Much like the top floor, dark wood paneling covered the walls, though far more furniture, all dark and overstuffed, adorned the space. A small table of refreshments lay in one corner, and a large, empty table sat in the middle. Soft light came from orbs set in the walls, blanketing the space in a calm glow.

Acorn watched the door close behind Chester, then snapped her head to look at Haarlock. "Is it working?"

"Yeah, I'd say so." Haarlock coughed again, though this time it sounded far worse. "My throat feels like sandpaper. And I'm getting lightheaded."

"Let's hope the alchemist got the dosage right." The gnome shot Haarlock a smirk. "And you didn't lie about your weight."

"Hardy har harr." Haarlock coughed again, wincing at the pain. It was all he could do to croak out a few words. "You ready?"

"Ready as I'll ever be."

The gnome took several deep breaths as Haarlock stumbled over to one couch. His heart raced and his lungs burned, and he ran through the plan to keep himself conscious for as long as possible.

Step 1: I pass out.

Step 2: Something about...a doctor. Or was it Ladrón?

Step 3: Chaos.

Haarlock wondered why he couldn't remember the finer points of his plan, but figured it was because of his oxygen-starved brain.

9

With a massive, ragged inhale, Haarlock jerked back into consciousness. Justine kneeled over him, with Chester and one of the orc guards, Guy, flanking either side of her. Worry covered the two men's faces, but Justine's showed only pure deviousness.

Haarlock looked to either side as he blinked rapidly. He was back in the lobby, lying in the center of the room with his head propped up on a small pillow.

"Oh, thank the gods." Chester exhaled and fanned his face with his chaperon hat. "You had us worried, m'lord. Worried something fierce."

Justine stood and picked up a small leather doctor's bag, tucking it under her left arm. Unlike her normal, risqué outfit, she wore a demure set of dark, heavy linens and a hooded cloak. A cloak too big for her petite frame.

"Really, Lord Haarlock, you need to be more careful about what you drink." Justine shook her head. "That chai tea nearly killed you."

"Yes, silly me." Haarlock's croaking voice was barely understandable even to him. He coughed, dislodging something in his throat and making his voice far clearer. "Apologies for causing so much worry."

The manager nodded to himself a few times as he wrung his hands, while Guy stood passively staring at Haarlock.

"It is a wonder you thought to bring your doctor along." Chester regarded Justine for a moment before looking back at Haarlock. He dropped his hands to his sides. "I hate to pry, m'lord, but are your health issues so great you need a personal physician with you at all times?"

"Unfortunately so, Mr. McCaffrey." Haarlock smiled as he extended a hand towards Guy, and he grunted as the large orc pulled him to his feet in a single, smooth motion. "Silly of me not to check what you offered."

"Yes, silly indeed."

Haarlock watched as suspicion crossed Chester's face.

Whelp, time to get the party started.

Giving Justine a wink, Haarlock turned his attention back to the manager and the orc. Both looked at him as if something was wrong, but they couldn't figure out what.

"Tell me, Mr. McCaffrey, how well does your security hold up against raccoons?"

Bursting out of Justine's oversized cloak, Ladrón screamed as he latched onto Guy's head. Chester screamed in kind as he backed away into Justine's waiting arms. The elf quickly tied the manager's hands behind his back, then forced him to the floor and bound his feet. A pair of self-tightening cords ensured the man was out of the fight.

As Guy desperately tried to peel the animal off his face, Haarlock slipped one of the cords around his feet. The large orc went down in a huff; his breath knocked from his lungs.

Ladrón bolted away as the doorman burst in to investigate the commotion. Haarlock and Justine looked at the doorman, then at one another, and split apart and ran to either side of the spacious room.

Arnold exited his security checkpoint, eyes going wide at the chaos. He looked between the doorman chasing Justine and Haarlock picking the lock on the door to the back offices. Choosing the active threat, Arnold rushed at Haarlock.

Alert allowed Haarlock to roll out of the way just as the second orc guard swiped at his head. Springing to his feet, he squared up against Arnold. The guard put his hands up in a classic boxing stance and smirked when Haarlock did the same.

I'm going to regret this.

Haarlock juked left, jabbing with his right, feeling the slab of granite that was Arnold's arm. The orc sent out a haymaker and missed Haarlock's head by *this* much, even with his dodge abilities.

Now out of his leg bindings, Guy went after Ladrón. The orc moved with surprising quickness, herding the animal into a corner as best he could. Ladrón wasn't in fight-or-flight mode: he was doing the leading.

Once they reached the corner, Ladrón's *Nimble Climber* let him scurry up the nearly smooth wall, and Guy found him with a screaming raccoon on his face for the second time. Lucky for him, that didn't last long.

True to Chester's word, a dozen city guard poured into the building 28 seconds after the commotion started. Per protocol, they rounded up everyone, employees and all, securing them with bindings until identities were confirmed.

***

Haarlock, Acorn, and Justine sat on a couch in the middle of *Raven Rock Holdings,* hands tied in front, with six city guards surrounding them. Ladrón sat in a cage in one corner, his own guard watching him closely. Chester McCaffrey looked at their possessions laid out on the floor between them.

"I must say, this is the worst robbery I've ever seen." The manager sighed as he shook his head.

Acorn looked to either side at her compatriots, then turned to Chester and gave him a toothy smile.

"What's so funny?"

"Oh, just that this wasn't the *worst* robbery." Acorn shrugged. "Because you're going to pay us."

Chester scoffed. "And why might I do that?"

"Because *Raven Rock Holdings* has never been robbed. And so long as you pay us, it never will be."

"What are you going on about, gnome?" Chest's face scrunched up in displeasure.

Acorn used her chin to gesture to the inside out leather satchel. The one covered in arcane runes, sitting next to the yellow diplomatic bag.

"You brought me, thief extraordinaire, into your vault with a magic bag. When Lord Haarlock here had a little medical emergency, you left me alone. In your vault. With said magic bag. One that let me bypass your security and bring in all kinds of nasty safe-cracking tools. And then I robbed you. A *lot*."

Chester's left eyebrow rose comically far on his head. He looked at the city guard to his right, but the man only shrugged.

"We searched you. The only things you lot have are those laid out here. And besides, no magic you could bring in here would work in the vault. Not expanded storage, dimensional pockets, or teleportation. Whatever that bag is supposed to do, it didn't."

"But how can you be sure?" Acorn gave a tight smile.

"Your so-called diplomatic pouch?" Chester absently waved his hand toward the yellow bag. "Of course we searched it. It's a fake."

It was small, almost imperceptible even to *Canny Observer*, but Haarlock noticed the man's hesitation. Acorn and Justine would have seen it, too.

"Really? Because it looks to me like the seal isn't broken. The seal ensuring legal repercussions against anyone opening it, save an official Lemurian diplomat, of course."

Haarlock could feel the excitement pouring off Acorn. It was all he could do not to smile as he looked down at the heavy piece of tape covering the opening.

Their plan was working.

The diplomatic seal was not a simple thing to come by. Neither was the bag. It took both Acorn and Haarlock over two days to convince Consular General Camilla Albertine, diplomat of Lemuria, to provide them with it. Two days of assurance the items would not be used for any nefarious purposes.

Technically, this isn't nefarious.

"You are obviously mistaken."

"Yeah, well..." Acorn shrugged. "You didn't look inside it. And since you didn't look, that tells me you think it's real. And if you think it's real, I'm going to go ahead and say there's a chance you think I actually stole something."

Chester stared at the bag for a long moment before looking up at Acorn with hate in his eyes.

"Fine, have it your way." The manager picked up the yellow bag, then held out his hand towards the guard to his right. "Your dagger, please."

The guard provided his blade, and as Chester brought it to the diplomatic seal, Haarlock cleared his throat. Chester stopped and looked up.

"You know, if that bag *is* real, it's a state crime for you to open it. I don't know the exact punishment, but it's at least prison time." Haarlock made an exaggerated grimace. "You know what? Don't take our word for it. I'd get someone who can attest to the item's authenticity. We'll be happy to wait."

"And I assume you know someone who can do that?" A smug look crossed Chester's face.

"Two people, in fact."

***

It took nearly two hours for Lord Micca Barecna, captain of the Ostian Guard, to arrive at *Raven Rock Holdings*. Marquise Camilla Albertine arrived an hour later. Neither seemed pleased to be there.

Micca looked every bit what Haarlock thought of when he heard *captain of the guard*. Somewhere in his fifties, Micca's short, balding, flame-red hair gave him a fierce look. The deep voice accentuated his appearance, as did the polished breastplate and its embossed horse under two crossed swords. Barecna's yellow tunic differentiated his rank from the white and red of the other guards in the room.

Camilla's multi-colored hair hid under the jet-black hooded cloak she wore. The woman said nothing once she identified herself, and now stood off to the side, alternatively glaring at Haarlock and Acorn.

"Lord Haarlock, once again I find you in custody." Barecna's left hand rested on the hilt of the sword at his hip while the right ran through his hair as he looked around the scene. "I'm not sure why I'm here, though. Just because we're neighbors doesn't mean you'll be treated any easier under the law."

"Of that I have no doubt, captain." Haarlock nodded. "But I hope it comforts you we haven't actually committed a crime."

Chester scoffed so loudly that it drew everyone's attention. "You surely jest."

"We jest not, Mr. McCaffrey." Acorn nodded her head towards Camilla. "Lady Albertine can confirm that the Ostian Thieves' Guild was hired to test the security of *Raven Rock Holdings*. Justine can confirm it, too, but I figure no one would believe her."

Justine shot the gnome an annoyed look, then shrugged. "You're not wrong."

"And, once the guild received the quest, I was subcontracted. Lady Albertine sent Lord Haarlock to assist me, and I enlisted Justine. Together, the three of us successfully completed the test."

"Successful? You've been caught. That's not what I'd call a success." Chester rolled his eyes.

Barecna turned to Camilla. "Can you verify any of this, Lady Albertine?"

"Unfortunately, yes." Annoyance oozed from the marquise's words. "I was contacted by the Thieves' Guild to schedule time for Acorn to be away for this particular job, and I suggested Lord Haarlock assist her. The two of them even asked for my assistance, under false pretenses though it was."

Chester jerked his head around. "You assisted them?"

"Where do you think they got the diplomatic bag and seal?"

"Captain, this is preposterous!" Chester gestured stiffly as he spoke. "You have confessions of thievery from these three and a confession of aiding and abetting from her."

Camilla squinted at the man.

"Actually, Mr. McCaffrey, if they were hired to test your security, this isn't a crime." Barecna eyed Haarlock for a moment before speaking to Camilla. "Lady Albertine, beyond your word this is a legitimate enterprise, can you provide actual proof?" The captain looked at the trio. "Can any of you?"

"I can do that, captain." Justine lifted her hands towards the guard standing next to her. "Just need my hands freed."

Barecna nodded, and the guard cut her free. With her right hand, Justine reached into the top of her tunic and pulled out a sealed envelope.

"What? How?" Chester frowned in disbelief. "You were searched!"

"I'm an elf, Mr. McCaffrey. I may look half your age, but I'm almost thirty years older. That means I have a lot of levels in rogue, and a lot more tricks than this one."

Justine winked at him and offered the letter. He snatched it from her hand and examined the seal, an image of a stylized bird, wings spread, hovering over a rock. Barecna walked over to him.

"Who does the seal belong to, Mr. McCaffrey?"

It took a long moment for Chester to reply. "It appears to be the seal of Count Richard Glasdale, the owner of this company."

"Please verify if the document corroborates their story."

Chester cracked the seal and removed the folder parchment inside. He looked between the three rogues on his couch as he unfolded the paper. Justine spoke as he read, staring directly at the manager the entire time.

"I would imagine it says something about hiring the Thieves' Guild to test your security, then paying out ten percent of the value of whatever we abscond with."

"Yes. It does." Chester visibly shook. "Why wasn't I informed about this security test?"

"Because you'd have shored up any deficiencies before we arrived and suspected every new customer. Wouldn't be a very good test of your security then, would it?"

The elf smiled, and the manager glared.

Barecna cleared his throat. "Sorry to interrupt the staring contest, but has a crime been committed here today?"

"No, it appears there hasn't." Chester smirked. "Especially considering they have *not* removed any items from the property."

"At least not yet." Acorn tilted her head.

"Whatever you may have removed from our vault, and I'm still not convinced you did, is in there." Chester pointed at the diplomatic bag. "And since you got caught before you could leave, you failed in your task." Chester turned to Camilla and jabbed his finger back at the yellow bag. "You're a diplomat, right? Open the bag."

If looks could kill, Chester would have died from Camilla's eye twitch alone. She walked up to the manager, her eyeline matching his, stopping at an uncomfortably close distance.

"You are speaking to a noble, Mr. McCaffrey." The flat tone of Camilla's words caused the manager to gulp. "I suggest you use proper decorum when doing so."

"Um, yes, of course, Lady Albertine." Chester took a step back and bowed his head for a moment. "Forgive my rudeness, but I implore you, my lady, these three stole from us. They've been caught, so their mission has failed. Open the bag, please."

The marquise looked over the man's shoulder at the trio, squinting with suspicion when Acorn looked at the diplomatic bag then back at her and winked. Haarlock noticed Micca Barecna pick up on the wink, too, squinting at Haarlock with pursed lips.

"Unfortunately, Mr. McCaffrey, I will not be doing that. Diplomatic bags are not something to be trifled with based on hearsay alone, and it's your word against theirs. Technically, it's the reputation of *Raven Rock Holdings'* impenetrable security against their word. And to be honest, I consider *Raven Rock* the more reputable party in this situation."

"But my lady!" Chester stammered as he rapidly blinked.

Acorn's mouth couldn't have been more agape, and the subtle smirk from Camilla only caused it to widen further.

Chester turned to Barecna and looked at him with pleading eyes.

"Sorry, Mr. McCaffrey. Not only do they have a letter, verified by you, no less, authorizing their presence and actions here today, there's no proof that anything was taken. Without the opening of the diplomatic bag, of course, and it doesn't appear that's happening. With no crime having been committed, and no evidence to show they've attempted to remove anything from the premises, I see no reason to hold these individuals any longer. Unless you have an inventory of your vault's contents and would allow a search of them, of course."

Barecna gave the manager a few seconds to stew before he snapped his fingers. A pair of guards removed the restraints on the remaining two rogues while another let Ladrón out of his cage. The entire guard cohort, save Barecna, marched out of *Raven Rock Holdings* without a word.

Acorn picked up the diplomatic bag and gave it a little toss. She went to leave but stopped after a few steps and spun around on her heels.

"Actually, Chester, I like you." The gnome crossed her arms and regarded the utterly defeated manager. "I'll make you a deal."

"Dare I ask what that might be?" Chester sighed heavily as his shoulders slumped.

"See, there's no doubt you're getting fired for this."

"Since I'm the one who allowed this establishment's reputation to be tarnished, I'm sure I will."

"And I don't want that." Acorn gestured to her two compatriots. "None of us do."

Chester rolled his eyes. "And what, pray tell, could you offer me?"

"I'll open the bag and give you back what's inside."

"You will?" Hope crossed the man's face, turning to suspicion in a moment. "What's the catch?"

Acorn smirked. "There's always a catch, and this time it's money. Lots of it."

"Typical."

"Don't be like that, Chester. We get paid ten percent of the content's value if I walk out the door with this bag. If it actually *is* stuffed full of jewelry, I can only imagine ten percent will be a *lot*. But I don't know how much it is. Not yet at least."

"Ah, I see." Chester huffed. "You're extorting me."

"Extortion? Hardly." Acorn waved dismissively at the man.

Something clicked in Chester's head and he perked up. He looked between the three rogues with wide eyes.

"This is a trick!" The manager jabbed a finger at Acorn. "You didn't actually steal anything!"

The look of exasperated disbelief Acorn put on caused a snort from Barecna. "Me? Trick someone?"

"This is all an elaborate ruse to get me to pay you for a job you didn't do."

"I mean, maybe." Acorn tapped a finger on her chin. "Maybe we did try to trick you by going through all the effort and expense to acquire an authentic diplomatic bag, enchant it with a dimensional space, and for Haarlock to risk his life just to get me alone, past your guards, where I could do any number of things. That seems more likely than us successfully robbing you. *Way* more likely. Or maybe the fact that we got the enchanted bag past you in the first place shows your security isn't as perfect as you think."

The manager stared hard at the gnome while Acorn acted as if she were bored. As they continued their standoff, Ladrón climbed onto Haarlock's shoulder.

*"*Success?*"*

"We're about to see."

Both Camilla and Barecna watched with interest. Haarlock wondered when they caught on to the scheme and how much of their stonewalling of Chester played into that.

"Thirty seconds, Chester, before I walk out."

The manager's low growl filled the space as he clenched his fists. Justine and Haarlock exchanged glances.

Chester reached a hand out when Acorn turned around. "Wait!"

"We have a deal?"

"Yes." The man grimaced. "How much do you want?"

"Six platinum. Each."

"Eighteen platinum? I don't have that sort of funding!" Chester looked at the two rogues standing behind him, then to Camilla and finally Barecna. "This is illegal."

"You're right, Mr. McCaffrey, extortion is illegal." Barecna looked past the manager to Haarlock and Justine and received an enthusiastic series of nods. "If you would like to press charges, I can bring everyone down to the local outpost, file an official report, and request the State Department to force the diplomatic bag to be opened at that time. Of course, then they'll have succeeded in their breach of your security. It'll be a *very* public affair, but perfectly within your legal rights to do so. Would you like to press charges, Mr. McCaffrey?"

Chester fumed as he looked at those around him. Haarlock could see the gears turning in his head, and the exact moment they stopped.

"How do you expect me to pay that sort of money? I might make two platinum in a year with my bonus."

"Oh, you're not paying us, Chester. *Raven Rock Holdings* is."

"How do you figure?"

"We know there's a petty cash fund to woo over potential clients. *Rich* clients. You can pay us out of there." Acorn put up a single finger. "Think of it this way: eighteen platinum is likely a lot less than your employer will pay us if this bag goes out the front door. Gems are valuable, and a lot can fit in a bag this size, ya know?"

"It appears you have me between a rock and a hard place." Chester sighed. "But I capitulate. You'll have your money."

Acorn gave herself a little fist pump.

"But! I want a contract written up. You're not backstabbing me anymore than you already have."

"Worry not, Chester." The gnome gestured to Justine, and as the manager turned around to look, the elf removed another letter from her shirt. "We have one prepared. Oh, and lucky for you, there's an Ostian Guard captain and a marquise here to witness it."

A look of pure, unadulterated contempt turned Chester's face into a scowl unlike any Haarlock had ever seen.

***

"You should have seen the look on his face!"

Acorn's squeaky laugh echoed throughout Shattersong's guildhall, followed closely by others. Manuel, Jean-Baptiste, Justine, Zachary, Samantha, Quinn, Haarlock, Ladrón, and Camilla joined the gnome by the fireplace, drink and food in hand and paw.

Zachary downed the rest of his wine. "I'm still in shock at your unmitigated gall." The Grifter turned to Haarlock. "This was all your idea?"

"Partly, yes." Haarlock shrugged. "I'm a fan of heists, and mostly they rely on acts of extreme chicanery. A little misdirection here, some pressure not to get fired there, and voilà! Besides, there was no way we could steal anything from there; we just needed to make it appear it were possible."

"And yet, steal we did." Acorn produced six platinum coins, her eyes widening as the fire's light danced across them. "Too bad Chester took the bait and paid us out."

With a mighty laugh, Manuel gave the comparatively tiny gnome a pat on the back. "Your greed never ceases to impress, mon amie."

"I take that as a compliment."

Quinn slowly shook her head. "Seems almost cruel to trick and extort someone like that."

"Don't worry your blonde head." Justine gave the mage a friendly elbow nudge. "*Raven Rock Holdings'* owner, Count Glasdale, guarantees the best security money can buy for his customers. A manager who can be extorted isn't one worth having."

The mage nodded in contemplation.

"Next time, let's leave my status as a Lemurian diplomat out of your planning, shall we?" Camilla fed a piece of meat to Ladrón, speaking more to the animal than anyone else. "Diplomatic bags are to be used for *official* kingdom business only."

Acorn cleared her throat. "Yeah, sorry for the misleading request."

"Oh, no, I knew you weren't giving me the complete story, Acorn." Camilla looked up with an amused expression. "I gave you the bag so I could see what shenanigans you would get into."

The gnome smirked as Samantha leaned forward and rested her elbows on her knees, then let out a long *hmm*. Everyone looked at her.

"Makes me wonder if real enchantments would have bypassed their security. Been fun to try."

"I could taste the residual magic floating in the air." Haarlock shook his head as he thought back. "I can't imagine what sort of crazy counterspells and damping enchantments are coursing through those walls."

"Fair." The Enchanter nodded before returning to her plate of food.

Haarlock turned to Jean-Baptiste. "No comments?"

"I'm wondering where you got the idea to poison yourself. Seems you took a risk assuming they'd let Justine in and not search her for a raccoon. Or you'd not die before she could get to you."

"Justine, any comments?" Haarlock shot the elf a faux-contemptuous look.

"Hey, you're the one who agreed to being poisoned."

"And you're the one who suggested poisoning me."

"It worked, didn't it?" Justine gestured to Acorn with her cup. "Besides, she's the one who convinced you."

"Don't put that one on me!" Acorn sat straight. "I wanted to use a knockout drug, not poison. Someone didn't think it'd be authentic enough."

Both women looked at Haarlock.

"Authenticity is key, right?" Haarlock shrugged.

The room erupted in laughter.

Another half hour went by as Acorn wrapped up the story. In the end, after Chester McCaffrey paid 18 platinum from petty cash, he assured the trio they would be banned for life from the premises. He would also file complaints against Camilla for improper use of a diplomatic bag, along with a general complaint for...something against Captain Micca Barecna. Since the manager rubbed the marquise the wrong way, she looked forward to spinning the situation to make him look bad. Haarlock may not have known Barecna all that well, but he suspected the captain wouldn't blink an eye at whatever complaint Chester conjured up. That's if he bothered, considering his employment at *Raven Rock Holdings* would end in the immediate future.

Shortly afterwards, the group broke apart. Haarlock headed back to his room with an unconscious, overstuffed raccoon in his arms. He laid Ladrón in his own corner bed, then kicked off his outfit, changed into pajamas, and climbed under the covers.

In all the excitement and exhaustion of the day, Haarlock had yet to check his notifications from the successful quest.

CONGRATULATIONS! YOU HAVE COMPLETED THE QUEST: TEST RAVEN ROCK HOLDINGS' SECURITY. *YOU HAVE BEEN AWARDED 4,000 experience. You have been awarded 40 Renown. You have been awarded 80 Infamy.*

You have leveled up! Would you like to apply one (1) levels to Rogue?

Your one (1) levels have been applied to your Rogue class. Your stats have been adjusted accordingly.

NAME: Haarlock
RACE: Human
AGE: 30
RENOWN/INFAMY: 670/288
STATS:

CLASS: Shadowdancer
LEVEL: 19
EXPERIENCE: 72,627
TITLE: Lord
GUILD RANK: Copper

HP - 130	STR - 25	DEX - 70	INT - 30
WIS - 25	CON - 53	CHA - 40	

SKILLS:

Master	Expert	Skilled	Proficient
Dagger	Stealth	Tracking	Sleight of Hand
	Survival	Athletics	Simple Weapons
	Unarmed Combat	Spycraft	Skinning
	Lock Pick	Bow	Vintner
		Bartering	Estate Management
			Magic Theory

CLASS ABILITIES:	FEATS:	TALENTS:
Thieves' Cant	Alert	Canny Observer
Sneak Attack	Magic Novice	Resilient
Uncanny Dodge	Pass Without Trace	Hidden Blade
Deft Hands	Wrapped in Shadow	Improved Animal Bond
Darkvision		Shadow Dance
Chink in Armor		Nondescript
Murder		Silent Kill
		Agile

SPELLS:

Cantrips	1st Level	2nd Level
Mage Hand	Umbral Step	Shadow Tendrils
Mend	Magic Armor	
Shadowstep		

Haarlock frowned at how he received more Infamy than he did Renown. Then again, he *did* sorta rob a bank and extort the manager for a sizable payout. Mr. McCaffrey would assuredly slander his name for the foreseeable future. Six platinum would do nicely to offset that problem, as did another level.

Almost Level 20. Whatever will I take when I get there?

Another question was what to do about his seemingly never-progressing *Stealth* Skill. He needed Mastery to complete the requirements for Phantom Blade, but doing enough sneaking around to get it seemed difficult. No, not difficult, just time intensive. How many quests would Haarlock have to do in order to finally advance? 10? 30? The kind of quests mattered, too. He'd probably need to spend some time slinking around the city with Acorn.

Whatever the answer, Haarlock needed to head back to his estate. He is a lord, and lords need to manage their lands. Plus, he liked the open spaces of the countryside. And the food.

10

Huerto de Vid Azul, Elvish for Blue Vine Orchard, and Haarlock's home.

The estate's three-story bodega came into view as Haarlock's carriage rounded a small copse of trees. Perched alone upon a snow-kissed hill, the three-story building's marble structure shone in the setting sun. Forty-five acres of grapevine surrounded it, and fields of wheat, barley, and corn surrounded those.

In the distance to the south, several columns of smoke identified where Farncombe lay. Haarlock was glad for Jan, the hamlet's Bailiff. Though a proud man, he ran Farncombe with a tight, efficient hand. The bell tower of the hamlet's church, helmed by Father Jessup, could just be seen peeking over a hilltop.

The carriage rolled to a stop, and Haarlock exited. Ladrón leaped to the ground and scurried around, chittering the whole time. Four hours in a carriage made anyone restless. *Especially* a raccoon. Ladrón ran to the estate's entrance, a stone archway, and climbed to the top, knocking snow off as he did so. He looked out over the fields towards the bodega.

*"*Aripine. Dubois. Friends.*"*

Haarlock chuckled. The estate's Majordomo, Aripine, always kept plenty of snacks on hand. Dubois, their resident Chef, seemingly had an understanding with Ladrón and exactly how much and what kind of food the animal wanted.

Before he walked through the archway, Haarlock looked up at the shining metal sign at its peak. A vine with large, three-pointed leaves stood in relief, matching the signet ring on his finger. Haarlock tipped his head to the sign and went through the arch and down the stone path towards the bodega. Ladrón followed, darting in and out of the rows of grapevines.

Haarlock took several deep breaths of the evening air through his nose as he walked. While he wasn't a fan of the cold, there was nothing like winter air filling one's lungs. It always energized him.

A quarter mile down the path Haarlock passed a cluster of buildings overlooked by the bodega. Though Farncombe held most of the estate's population, the bodega's workers and their families lived here. The few residents outside tipped their heads as Haarlock passed.

As he climbed the hill, Haarlock heard the unmistakable clicking of metal on tile. Large double doors opened to reveal Aripine. The elderly gnome wore her usual attire of a ruffled shirt, vest, and slacks. Fur boots replaced polished leather shoes, and a wool hat hid her long, gray hair.

"Greetings, m'lord. I wondered when you'd return." The woman's voice softened when she looked at the raccoon by Haarlock's feet. "And you, too, Master Ladrón."

Aripine's eight-legged mechanical chair bowed, and Ladrón jumped into the woman's lap, chittering happily.

"It's good to see you, too, Aripine." Haarlock suppressed a shiver. The wind was especially fierce on top of the hill. "I could use something warm to drink."

"Fantastic idea." Aripine called over her shoulder. "Janice. Fetch a tea service, please."

A voice came from inside. "Yes, ma'am."

"I have a fire going in the living room and will have one started in your room as well."

"Thank you." Haarlock walked inside and looked around. "Feels good to be back."

"It's good to have you back. Wasn't sure when you'd return. Neither did Count Elmaris." Aripine moved to Haarlock's side and held out a thick stack of envelopes. "Your correspondence has been requested. Repeatedly and with haste."

Haarlock sighed. "For?"

"He wouldn't say but stresses the importance he knows of your return."

"Fantastic." Haarlock looked at the other senders. One he recognized. "Lord Thymia again."

"He wants an in-person meeting to discuss the offer."

"This is, what, the tenth letter?"

Aripine shrugged as she petted the raccoon on her lap. "Seems your sawmill will be of more use than you thought."

Haarlock considered that. The sawmill's purpose, along with the cooperage, was for the estate to have a start-to-finish production line of wine barrels. Once they fine turned the process, they expected a 14% increase in profits the first year.

Lord Thymia's interests lie in reducing costs for his lumber business. Using the estate's sawmill would save a third of the cost of transportation, not to mention turnaround speeds.

"I'll deal with the count after Thymia."

"Of course, m'lord. Are you hungry at all?"

Ladrón perked up. "**Food. Hungry. Want.**"

"It seems we both are."

"I'll fix something then. Tea should be waiting for you by the fire."

***

Lordly duties include replying to correspondence. *Lots* of correspondence. The stack of letters Aripine gave Haarlock contained only the important ones. Sixty-three more awaited.

When he left for his quest to find Mateo, Haarlock told Aripine not to respond unless necessary. He is lord, and the lord should take time to reply to each person. That was a mistake.

Now I know why Aripine smirked at me when I said that.

Hand writing each letter gave him a lesson in humility. Aripine could write in flowing script with speed, finishing a whole page in five minutes. Haarlock struggled to get two done in an hour before his hand cramped. Eventually, he broke down and asked for help.

It took four days to reply to them all. Four. Haarlock was sure he had never done that much writing before in his life, and he hoped to never again. Luckily for him, one of the Maids kept a muscle-relaxing balm for just such an occasion.

Sporadic guests came during this time. Travel in the winter slowed, but warm food and strong spirits saw one or two customers per day. Ladrón enjoyed meeting new people, and they enjoyed tales of the raccoon's heroics.

Snow and freezing temperatures arrived on the fifth day, blanketing everything in an inch of white. Lord Amal Thymia arrived that afternoon.

Haarlock came downstairs to find Aripine talking to two men in the foyer. Heavy leathers and furs covered the tall human's lanky frame, and his partially braided hair combined to give him a druidic vibe. The other, an elf, couldn't have been more different. His long, platinum-blonde hair lay in a single braid over the left shoulder of his dark wool cloak. Expensive leather boots shined to a near-mirror finish and supple gloves went well with his black leather satchel.

"Ah, Lord Haarlock." Aripine gestured to the taller man first. "I introduce Lord Amal Thymia and his Solicitor, Rafael Malisco."

Thymia took a step forward and spoke in a deep voice. "Greetings, lord, and thank you for hosting me. Apologies for my late arrival; the weather took a turn rather suddenly."

"No problem at all." Haarlock gestured towards the fireplace. "Would you like to warm yourself by the fire? Perhaps some tea?"

"That won't be necessary. I would like to tour your facilities at once."

"Absolutely. Aripine can summon our carriage while I get my cloak."

"I would prefer to walk."

Haarlock's brow rose in surprise as he looked at Aripine. The gnome gave a subtle shrug.

"I'm not wearing appropriate attire. Please give me a few minutes to change."

"Of course."

Ladrón begged, *a lot*, to come along as Haarlock changed. The animal loved to explore, and the construction site was a perfect place to go. Haarlock knew better, though. Not only would Ladrón get soaked from all the snow on the ground, but he would also want Haarlock to carry him back. A wet, freezing cold raccoon wasn't great for first impressions. Or anything else, for that matter.

And so, with a thick cloak and wool undergarments on, Haarlock walked away from the bodega with a pouting raccoon in his mind. Luckily for him, the range of their psychic communication was only a few hundred feet.

***

"That fence next to the large oak? To the left are the blue vine grapes. We only have two acres, but we're also only one of three places in Lemuria that grow them."

Thymia replied with a single head nod, the same as he had for the other tidbits about Huerto de Vid Azul. Rafael seemed enamored by it all, even if he didn't speak. The snow slowed them some, giving Haarlock plenty of time to exposit as much as they'd listen. They arrived at the construction site after half an hour.

Like the other two, Haarlock had yet to see the site. He had yet to see the recently completed windmill, too. Haarlock mentally chastised himself for slacking on his lordly duties.

The site, an area of flattened ground, piles of materials, and partially erected frames, lay a hundred feet from the forest's edge, nestled in a small dip between the hills. When completed, the sawmill would be 58 feet long, 15 feet tall, and 30 wide. The cooperage would be a squat structure 24 feet wide and 40 feet long.

Each building required specialist equipment: saws, planers, and hoisting equipment for the sawmill, and firepots, presses, and charring machines for the cooperage. None of the equipment was particularly specialized, which saved on cost, but it required skilled tradesmen to operate. Those weren't cheap. The gnomish steam engine that would power the sawmill wasn't cheap, either.

Haarlock took the men through the site, using a copy of the blueprints to identify the buildings' footprint and where the internal equipment would rest. Thymia asked questions about transportation routes, road capacities, production schedules, and methods of storage. Much of it was beyond Haarlock's knowledge, and he assured Thymia the information would be sent to him as soon as possible.

With the hour-long tour over, Thymia walked to the middle of the cooperage site and stood with his arms crossed. He looked around for a moment before tapping the heel of his boot into the ground several times.

"Is there something wrong, Lord Thymia?" Haarlock walked to his side.

"The ground is already frozen, and you have building materials on site. I take it your work crew is equipped for the task of a winter build?"

One of the many useful things about magic: construction in the winter.

In the previous world, bad enough conditions, especially in the winter, could and would shut down a job site. With the right spells in *The Game*, one could heat the earth, melt snow, dry material, and mitigate the negative effects of any weather. It costs more, sure, but having an additional three-plus months of construction per year saves money in the long run. And those extra months would get the wine barrel stock up to par just in time for next year's harvest.

"Absolutely. Once we source the last bit of materials, they should have both structures up and be ready for production by the middle of March."

Thymia gave the site another examination. Once he found whatever it was to his liking, he nodded once to Rafael. The elf, who up to this point had stood silently off to the side, perked up and walked over to Haarlock. Rafael's face was one big smile, and his voice sounded like every other lawyer Haarlock had ever heard.

"Lord Haarlock, my liege is satisfied with your site and would like to return to the bodega and begin negotiations. Your Mayordomo and I can take care of the paperwork once the details are decided."

Haarlock blinked several times at the elf. "Um, yes. I'm glad to hear that."

"Excellent. Lord Thymia is also eager to try Chef Dubois' culinary delights. I hope it won't be too much trouble to have an early dinner?"

"Not at all."

***

Chef Dubois stood to the side as Maids sat plates of steaming food before the guests. A discerning eye ensured each item faced the correct way. Utensils and drinks were already placed and served, though one glass looked a centimeter too low. A refresher course on proper serving guidelines would need to be held.

Their guest, Lord Thymia, moved with the grace and precision of someone with a lifetime of training: perfectly sized portions, excellent posture, and not a single wasted movement. Lord Haarlock, though, tried his best.

Proper decorum precluded the appearance of Master Ladrón, but few rules applied to the animal. A small side table held a veritable feast for the gluttonous creature, and try as he might, Ladrón's idea of etiquette was only eating one pawful at a time.

Dubois didn't mind Ladrón's antics. When a new recipe needed testing, or a bad one disposed of, there was no better method than that of a raccoon. The cabinets and pantry needed to be locked, *securely*, though.

The four-course dinner went more than adequately in Dubois' eyes. His team prepared flawless dishes, and the two guests made the appropriate comments to verify this. Namely clean plates.

11

"He sure is an interesting character."

Haarlock huffed in amusement as he watched Lord Thymia's carriage disappear over a hill. The chair-bound gnome to his left frowned, then nodded slowly several times.

"Yes, m'lord, he is."

"Have you had dealings with him since you've been here?"

"If I remember correctly, Lord Thymia took over his lands in the last fifteen or so years. His mother was elevated to baroness when she took a position with the Crown, and he stepped in to run things. I've sent her cases of wine over the decades, but never him."

"Now it seems we'll be sending carts of planks."

A stiff gust of wind caused them both to shiver. The top of a hill was a terrible place to stand in winter, after all. Haarlock followed Aripine inside.

"When will you be visiting Count Elmaris?"

"He's expecting me the day after tomorrow."

Aripine went to the small writing desk by the front door and removed an envelope thick with documents. Its wax seal held the estate's sigil. "Tax reporting is due, and if you could save me a trip, I'd appreciate it."

"Not a problem." Haarlock took the envelope and weighed it in his hand, letting out a low whistle. "How many trees did it take to make this?"

"Enough." The gnome exhaled. "It contains *detailed* records of our purchases, expenditures, copies of all permits, and my handwritten report thereof."

"Do we owe any outrageous fees?"

"Is that an increase from last year? Yes. Is it more than expected? No. The windfall from the Vid Azul brandywine sales, increased production from the windmill, and more guests here at the bodega raised our taxes by about twenty percent. It'll be at least quadruple next year with the new sawmill and cooperage in operation."

"Ah yes, the more you make, the more it costs you." Haarlock shrugged. "No escaping taxes, though."

"Never."

"Speaking of brandywine, how many bottles of Vid Azul do we have left?"

"One hundred and ninety, m'lord."

"You weren't kidding when you said they'd be hard to sell."

"Two thousand gold per bottle is steep even for the well-off."

Haarlock huffed in amusement. "Apparently. I think we can afford to make a well-placed donation, wouldn't you?"

"Count Elmaris is a lover of all things expensive, especially when he doesn't have to pay for them."

***

The trip north to the Elmaris estate might be long, but damn, was it beautiful.

After a few hours, the roads turned to paving stones lined with manicured hedges. Copses of oak trees dotted the landscape, as did tranquil frozen ponds and the occasional white marble building. Snow-covered mountains in the distance lent a feeling of majesty to the scenery.

The grove of gargantuan oaks surrounding Elmaris' manor looked like something from a fairytale. As did the stream meandering through the area.

Balconies jutted from the dark stone and wood manor house's three floors, each looking out over patios and trellises.

Haarlock's carriage pulled to a stop in front of the portico, and a well-dressed elven Footman in a red jacket and black slacks opened the door. When he stepped out, the Footman gave him a once-over. The full adventuring gear Haarlock wore, along with the raccoon on his shoulder and a small wooden box in his hands, had to be an uncommon look for guests.

"Welcome back, Lord Haarlock." The elf bowed. "Do you have baggage for your stay?"

"Yes, one suitcase."

A snap of his fingers summoned another Footman. The second went to the back of the carriage, stopping when he saw the contents. Haarlock caught the look they shared.

"The case of red is my compliment to the staff." Haarlock winked.

"Once again, m'lord, you are too kind."

The subtle nod put the second Footman back to work, and the first led Haarlock to the front door. Inside the foyer stood Mr. Chandler, the estate's rotund, well-jowled, dwarven Butler. He wore his typical tailed black jacket and slacks and a white dress shirt. His respectably trimmed beard and salt-and-pepper hair completed his look.

Next to him was someone who wore anything but what could be called typical: Count Drigen Elmaris.

Everything the count wore was a different shade of blue, from vibrant sapphire to milky turquoise. Other than the color, his clothing conformed to the common style of dress shirt, long coat, and slacks, with dyed leather boots. Numerous jewelry adorned his hands and neck.

"Lord Haarlock! You look as dashing as ever." Elmaris smirked as he looked at Ladrón. "As does your companion."

Ladrón, wearing his intelligence enhancing necklace and armor, perked up. *"*Handsome.*"*

"Thank you, count. You're quite a sight yourself."

"I couldn't help myself, really. Too many outfits and not enough reasons to wear them."

Mr. Chandler cleared his throat. "Lord Haarlock and Master Ladrón. Your room is prepared, and we can see you to it immediately if you wish."

"Good evening to you, Mr. Chandler. Thank you for..."

"No need for rest. Lord Haarlock here has missed dinner and must be hungry, yes?" Elmaris' eyebrows rose in excitement.

*"*Food?*"* Ladrón stood on his hind legs, one hand on Haarlock's head. *"*Now?*"*

"Ladrón is always hungry, and yes, I could eat."

"Excellent!" Elmaris clapped his hands together. "Please follow me. I must know what's in the box."

Elmaris led Haarlock down the well-appointed hallway towards the dining room. Pictures, foliage, and artifact adorned tables lined the walls.

"Thank you for accepting my invitation." Elmaris' expression turned serious. "I know the trip is long, especially with the weather this time of year."

"No trouble at all. I'm on break from the guild, so I have nothing but time."

"Yes!" Elmaris' face lit up in an instant. "You'll have to tell me all about your adventures thus far. I'm sure you've jumped right into the deep end."

Haarlock smiled at the man's enthusiasm. "Speaking of telling tales, I'm wondering the reason for your invitation."

"I'm sure you found the whole situation to be very mysterious."

Count Elmaris didn't look his age; his Elvin heritage causing his 46 years to look closer to 26. This gave a strange quality to his mannerisms, making him seem insincere. Haarlock knew that wasn't true, and he couldn't help but smirk at Elmaris' look of pure deviousness.

"Very mysterious, yes." Haarlock gestured to his adventuring-clad self. "I assume you have a problem needing taken care of?"

"Oh, no. Nothing like that." The count gave a dismissive wave. "I'm merely the middleman."

Haarlock frowned. "For what?"

"A surprise, of course." Elmaris motioned for Haarlock to follow. "But first, something to eat."

The Footman at the end of the hall opened the dining room doors and bowed his head as they walked past. At the enormous table sat a male gnome, Basterlit Cratery.

The diminutive man left his chair and approached, a toothy smile on his face. His clothing, a wide-sleeved black shirt under a red felt vest and skin-tight black slacks, gave the gnome a vaguely Spanish swashbuckler look.

"Many greetings, Haarlock lord. Pleasure mine."

Basterlit put a hand on his waist and bowed. The dark, jeweled rings adorning his fingers shone oddly as they moved in the room's light.

"Yes, when I heard Basterlit was staying in Lemuria a couple of extra months, I, of course, offered the hospitality of my estate." The count beamed. "It's not every day one hosts a diplomat."

"Drigen." Basterlit looked at the man with a contemptuous eyebrow raise and spoke in a foreign tongue.

Whatever he said made the count chuckle.

"I must apologize, Lord Haarlock." Elmaris gestured to the gnome. "Basterlit and I are old friends. I shouldn't have misconstrued the nature of his stay."

Basterlit nodded once to the count. "Thanks many."

"As you can see, he keeps me from inflating my ego too much."

Leashing the count's ego? That's something I never thought possible.

"Introductions aside, I'm still curious as to my being here."

Haarlock saw Elmaris give Basterlit a slight nod.

"Dear lord, a gift for you." The gnome bowed again. "Much help with honor during the tournament."

"Oh, you're talking about the duel." A chill ran down Haarlock's spine as he remembered seeing the blade sticking out of his chest, and the park bench in an endless field of clover. "And you're giving me a gift?"

"Yes. A mighty gift of shadow and metal." Basterlit held up his right hand and made a tight fist.

Haarlock moved only his eyes as he looked at Elmaris, then gave an eyebrow raise. Before anyone else could speak, a Footman appeared and rang a small chime.

Elmaris patted his stomach. "I almost forgot about dinner! We'll discuss more about Basterlit's gift later, Haarlock. One can't miss a meal, after all."

As Haarlock assumed, the opening courses were entirely too much. Plate after plate of tiny food came and went: grain-fattened songbirds fried in brandy, ten-layer sweet cakes, and hearty soups of winter vegetables. The main course was a delicacy from Basterlit's homeland: a breed of large rabbit, stuffed with tart cranberry sauce and glazed in honey and rotisseried for six hours. It requires an expert chef to prepare it, for if not done correctly, the sauce turns sour, ruining the entire dish.

Sides of chunky mashed potatoes and seasoned green beans gave Haarlock the feeling of Thanksgiving.

Ladrón, in a rare episode of restraint, waited patiently as his own fleet of plates came and went. Granted, each portion went into his mouth as quickly as he could manage, but he didn't complain about the delay between them.

"Dear Drigen, the feast is too great." The gnome wiped his mouth on a white napkin, then balled it up and tossed it onto his clean plate. "Compliments for chef."

The count beamed. "He is a rare skill indeed. I hear yours is as well, Lord Haarlock."

"Dubois?" Haarlock nodded as chewed the last of his green beans. "I've never seen someone use jarred ingredients so artfully."

"When I have time from my busy schedule, I'll be sure to taste his menu."

"We'll look forward to your visit, count."

"Most excellent. I'll need to get another bottle of your brandywine while I'm there, too." Elmaris chuckled, then glanced at Haarlock's wooden box on the table by the door. He eyed it for a long moment before looking back at Haarlock. "Dare I ask?"

"I may have anticipated your needs."

Haarlock went to the box and removed the lid, then took the bottle out from inside. When he turned around, the count exhaled and fell back into his chair.

"By the gods themselves, Lord Haarlock!" Elmaris' body froze in amazement.

"Forgive my understanding, lords. What bottle is it?"

Elmaris blinked and looked at the gnome. He spoke a few sentences in the same language as before, and Basterlit nodded his understanding.

"Many years past I remember the drink. Very excellent."

Without prompting, a Footman appeared with glasses while another took the bottle from Haarlock and poured for them.

Basterlit and Elmaris each took a gentle sip and let out a satisfied *ahh* in unison.

"Quite the exquisite treat, Lord Haarlock."

"Yes. Much good." Basterlit sipped again.

"Well, count, the rest of the bottle is yours. My gift to ensure I stay on your good side."

Haarlock's wink brought a hearty laugh from Elmaris. The count took a larger, though still reserved, drink and set his glass down.

"Please, Haarlock. It would take a great breach of trust for you to get on my bad side." Elmaris looked at the remainder of the bottle on the table. "Or if you withhold this magical liquid."

The three men shared a laugh.

"No worries there, count. We have plenty left."

"Good!" The wall clock started the hourly chimes, drawing Elmaris' attention. "Ah, how the time flies. Basterlit, do you want to start tonight?"

"Yes." The gnome gave a curt nod. "Need two hours. Forge not ready."

"That's right, you're a smith." Haarlock tilted his head. "I'm excited to know what you're making for me."

"See soon. Must prepare."

Basterlit downed the last of his brandywine and excused himself, and Haarlock noticed how Elmaris watched the gnome with a sense of wonder.

"This will be something, Haarlock." The count gave him a *just you wait* kind of look. "It's rare for male gnomes to leave their cities. Rarer still to have their crafting equipment on hand."

Haarlock thought back to every time he saw a gnome, and, besides wine distributor Lazrie Pendleboot, Basterlit was the only other male he'd seen. Come to think of it, besides Katten Danderly, the rogue at the kingdom tournament, all female gnomes worked some kind of administrative job. Granted, Aripine was once an adventurer, but she, like Katten, seemed the exception, not the rule.

"What do you think he'll make?"

"Hard to say, really. Basterlit can forge just about anything, so you might get a ring or a sword."

A ring?

The only other magical ring Haarlock possessed was the Talent obscuring one. Well, the *Etiquette* enhancing ring Aripine gave him was magical, but he found little use for that. Spreading his fingers out on his legs, Haarlock wondered how many he could wear at once before they looked gaudy.

"...so really, it's quite the experience."

Haarlock looked up at the count. "Yes. I'm excited to be part of it."

"Good!" Elmaris shot to his feet. "Let's have another drink in the lounge. You can tell me all about that little windmill I paid for while we wait."

***

The pair went to the back terrace and through a sculpted hedge garden, then down a stone path towards a large barn nestled between a stream and a pair of giant oak trees. A door opened, and out stepped Basterlit Cratery, the Level 68 Anointed Shadowsmith.

He wore a leather apron over a simple outfit of pristine white linen. On Basterlit's forehead lay a black leather band with a shimmering purple crystal set in it. The nearby flickering torchlight played oddly on the jewel's surface. Even the gnome's shadow seemed to sway in the wrong direction.

The gnome put a hand on his chest and bowed his head. "Pleasure is mine for this opportunity."

"It is I who should be grateful." Haarlock bowed in return.

The count walked over to the gnome and placed a hand on his shoulder.

"Your actions to challenge the slight to Basterlit's honor, and the injury you received in turn, have weighed heavily on his mind."

"Yes. Heavy." The Shadowsmith frowned, then looked up at the count and nodded.

"Basterlit is unable to convey his thoughts adequately in the common tongue, so he has asked me to translate. Please come inside."

A gnome-sized blacksmith's forge lay in the center of the barn. Tools and containers sat on a bench to one side, buckets of liquid and straw to the other, and an anvil in front. Basterlit stopped at the anvil and placed a hand on top. He stared at the metal as a contemplative look crossed his face.

It took a long moment for the gnome to speak. Elmaris translated in real time.

"Your actions at the tournament showed me the truth of your character, Lord Haarlock. I prayed to my god, Sjena, many times in an effort to understand that truth. As if a specter, He appeared to me on the third night."

The gnome moved to the table and retrieved an ornate hammer. Inset gems, not unlike the one in his headband, flanked its sides. Geometric patterns surrounded the faceted stones, glowing faintly of their own power.

He laid a pointed metal stick on the anvil and lightly tapped his hammer next to it three times. The fourth strike landed hard on its end. Basterlit struck again and again, turning the rod over each time until the tip shone a deep red. He moved to the forge and plunged the glowing rod into the bed of coals. Flames of shadow engulfed them.

Haarlock frowned as his eyes tried to understand what he saw. Their beauty entranced him, and it took Basterlit's voice to break his gaze.

"My religion's texts speak of Sjena's appearance and the significance of its meaning. It is all too common for Him to appear perhaps once in a devotee's lifetime. For me, His appearance is the fourth such occurrence."

The gnome turned his head toward Haarlock.

"I asked Sjena what gift would suit someone such as yourself. Should it be wealth? Land? Titles? It was only for a moment that He thought, then He smiled and in my mind I saw an image of a dagger. Do you own a dagger, Lord Haarlock?"

"Yes."

"If you would allow me to see it?"

Haarlock drew his weapon and handed it to the gnome. Basterlit tested the blade's weight and balance, then tapped the dull back edge against the anvil. The noise it made caused him to frown.

"I do not know this metal."

"It comes from the previous world and is called titanium. Non-magnetic and very strong for its weight."

"Unbreakable and Never Dulling. Fascinating." The gnome nodded his head in appreciation before meeting Haarlock's eyes. "This weapon can be improved. Would you allow me to do so?"

That caught Haarlock off guard.

Should he? *Could* he? The dagger came with him from the previous world, and, like his clothing, served as a reminder of where he was from. He never thought to get rid of it, let alone allow someone to alter it. Would changing it allow the memory-altering effects of *The Game* to gain a stronger foothold?

Haarlock felt the pull between practicality and emotion working on his answer. Would Basterlit be insulted if he said *no*? Would the smith's deity, Sjena? A few long seconds passed as he considered his answer, and in the end, practicality won over emotion. He would take what was given.

"Yes."

"Thank you, lord." Basterlit placed a hand on his chest and dipped his head.

Elmaris smiled as he gestured to two chairs against the wall. "This will be a rare sight to behold, Haarlock. Few witness a Shadowsmith in action."

Basterlit dismantled the dagger, setting the handle and cross-guard on his bench and the blade on the anvil. He removed an ingot of dark, shimmering metal from a box on the bench and laid it next to the blade. Three pumps of the forge's bellows brought the shadow flames to a whispering roar.

Twenty minutes passed as Basterlit stoked the forge. When they pleased him, he sat the dagger in the fire with a set of tongs. For nearly an hour he moved it back and forth through the burning coals, watching with intensity. Once the metal was to his liking, the gnome brought it to the anvil.

The vibrant orange glow of the titanium dimmed as Basterlit laid the ingot of shimmering metal on it. Light flowed into the ingot, slowly drawing the two metals together into a single billet. As this happened, Basterlit soaked a large sheet of paper in a bucket of watery clay. He wrapped the conjoined metals in it and coated them in a thick layer of straw.

Back into the forge the billet went. Bellows worked to help heat the metals as Basterlit worked it through the coals. Another twenty minutes passed before he brought the billet back to the anvil. A single strike of his hammer shattered the clay capsule.

With slow, deliberate blows he worked the billet, sending sparks of purple with each strike. As the metals cooled, they were reheated, then folded in half and forged together once more. A dozen times this happened. Two dozen. Basterlit worked until great beads of sweat poured down his arms and face.

Each time he struck, the gems on his headband and hammer surged in brightness as magic filled the air. Slowly the metal lengthened and took form, no longer a military combat knife but a long, slender dirk. Basterlit gave the blade a final bath in shadow flames before quenching it in a bucket of oil.

Once the blade cooled, Basterlit worked a metal rasp across it. He changed to finer tools as the cutting edge was honed to razor sharpness. A maker's symbol stamped on the forte signaled the blade's completion. With the handle and cross-guard returned, Basterlit laid the dirk on the anvil and stepped back.

The gnome spoke. "For you, Haarlock. A gift."

It took a moment for Haarlock to register the words as his mind still lingered on what he had just watched. What he experienced. It was as if he had been the one being forged. Did he really feel each blow from the hammer? The heat from the shadow flames? The cool kiss of the quenching oil?

"Yes." Haarlock shook his head. "Of course."

Haarlock stood and walked to the anvil. He reached out for the blade but stopped just before he touched it.

"Problem?" Basterlit tilted his head.

"There's no problem." Haarlock smiled softly. "I'm just...unsure how I feel right now."

Elmaris spoke in a somber tone as he walked to Haarlock's side. "I inherited my father's lands when he passed. They were his one day, and mine the next. Nothing changed, yet everything changed."

"I don't understand."

"Your clothing, Haarlock. The first time we met, I could see they were altered. And now this weapon, the last reminder of your life in the previous world, is gone. Yet not gone. It has changed as you have changed. Like I changed when these lands became mine."

The count was right. He changed the instant he came to *The Game*. When he left his world for this one. Dwelling on things one can't affect is useless.

Haarlock took the weapon in his hand, surprised by its lack of weight. It wasn't heavy before, though now it felt as if a breeze would blow it from his hand. The blade itself shimmered like Basterlit's gems, and up close, looked as if it would fade from existence at any moment. The gnome's mark, an anvil crossed with twin flaming hammers, slowly faded in and out of sight. Haarlock examined the item.

Sjena's Gift

Unique Dirk

Damage (Piercing) - 75

Damage (Slashing) - 25

Abilities: Blessed, Dual Natured, Featherlight,
Never Dulling, Unbreakable

Unbreaking and *Never Dulling* were two abilities the dagger came into *The Game* with. *Featherlight* reduced the weapon's weight to nearly nothing, just like the giant sword in the Hero's Tomb dungeon. As for *Dual Natured* and *Blessed*?

Elmaris translated for the gnome once again.

"*Dual Natured* allows your blade to strike creatures who exist not wholly in our reality. Ghosts, succubi, and the like can be attacked directly now, along with people under certain spells. As for the last ability..." The gnome touched two fingers to the gem in his headband as he dipped his head. "...Sjena saw fit to guide my hand as I worked, leaving His mark upon your weapon."

"His mark?" Haarlock frowned.

"Sjena's mark is only for those who follow His teachings. As you are not of His flock, whatever benefit it may provide will be unavailable to you."

Haarlock frowned. "Why give it a mark if I can't use it?"

"He has taken an interest in you. And if you are lucky, Sjena will appear and offer His patronage."

Joining a religion? That wasn't something Haarlock ever thought of doing, even before *The Game*. He never considered himself religious, and barely even spiritual. But he'd seen the powers wielded by those who followed a god of this place. To have that ability, too, would be a boon Haarlock couldn't pass up.

"What sort of patronage?"

"Sjena's domain is that of the shadows. As you are a student of the shadows, He would likely enhance your abilities or give you a new one altogether. But Sjena is a fickle god. Knowing Him is like trying to grasp a shadow."

Basterlit gave Elmaris a nod, and the count spoke to Haarlock on his own.

"As usual, Lord Haarlock, you impress me with your serendipitous fortune." The count smirked. "You've been here less than a year and already you've acquired a Unique weapon, and the interest of a god. Most impressive."

"Thank you, count." Haarlock tipped his head, then held out his new dirk in front of him, turning it side to side. "I'm going to have to practice with this. It's far longer and lighter than I'm accustomed to."

"Yes, well, that will have to be another time, I'm afraid." The count yawned. "It's probably close to sunrise."

"Very tired." Basterlit blinked his eyes several times, then rolled his right shoulder. "Take down forge, then sleep."

"Do you need help?" Haarlock looked at the forge, but he knew nothing of blacksmithing. "I can at least carry things for you."

"No. Self must do."

"Well, old friend, you know where your room is." The count turned to Haarlock. "Yours is on the second floor. One of the servants can show you."

12

Haarlock left Elmaris' estate just after lunch, returning to the bodega in the early evening. The previous day's snow turned some of the rural roads into a muddy mess. But not those on Haarlock's land. One of the first things he did was to have them all paved in stone.

Granted, it wasn't the smoothest ride in some parts, but it made for steady travel.

I wonder how much it'd cost to pave them like Elmaris' roads?

The scent of freshly baked bread wafted through the air as the carriage pulled up. Dinner wouldn't be for two more hours, but Haarlock wasn't all that hungry. Elmaris served a lavish brunch fit for more than one king.

Ladrón, of course, didn't let that stop him. He scurried out of Haarlock's lap and out the carriage window, then over the terrace fence and into the bodega through a partially opened window.

With far more grace, Haarlock went inside to find Aripine and Bailiff Jan sitting by the fire. At first, he wondered if something was wrong, but the two calmly chatted about a random topic. The large, bald man held a well-endowed cup of wine, and as he went to take a drink, he noticed Haarlock and stood.

"Oh, good afternoon, m'lord. I didn't know you'd be back today."

"Neither did I, really." Haarlock shook the Bailiff's hand. "How are you?"

"Well." Jan gestured to Aripine. "Just come to give our Mayordomo an update on the construction progress."

"Please sit." Both men sat, and Haarlock poured himself a glass of wine from the nearby tray. "What's going on with the construction?"

"Supply problems. The contractor's mage requires certain spell components, and apparently there's a shortage of them. That means a price increase."

Haarlock hung his head. "Of course it does."

The real question is whether they increased because of normal market fluctuations or the machinations of Sanyo's shinobi. Then again, considering what Marcon said about the volume of those shinobi, *normal* might be anything but.

"What kind of increase are we looking at?"

"Depends on how soon you want things completed, m'lord. We can have them purchase everything now, but that's another five hundred gold to the cost. Waiting could see the prices go up or down. That also means a delay."

"I'm not worried about the overall cost, Jan. What I am worried about is getting ripped off." Haarlock swirled his wine as he thought. "Is the foreman reputable? What about his suppliers?"

Might be something to have Marcon and/or Roboute look in to.

Jan took a generous drink. "They're the same crew who put up the windmill. Count Elmaris doesn't hire anyone but the best, so I wouldn't worry about the workers. As for the mage and his supplies, that's beyond me. I can put feelers out to some people I know in the city and see what they're saying."

"I suggest we buy upfront." Aripine studied her own glass of red liquid. "A delay now means more delays later. I agree we should have concerns about price gouging, but I'm more worried about having to buy barrels when we could have made them ourselves. Kinda defeats the point."

"Well said, Aripine." Jan nodded once to the gnome. She returned the gesture. "This is already causing a slight delay, but it shouldn't hurt production times."

"Good." Haarlock downed his glass. "Are you staying for dinner, Jan?"

"I never turn down a meal." The Bailiff gave a low rumbling laugh as he patted his ample stomach. "If you can't tell."

"Indeed. Unless there's anything else for me, I'm going to retire for a while."

"Not at all." Aripine's chair adjusted itself to walking height. "Jan, let's get the payment authorization paperwork done."

"Yes, ma'am."

The two flights of stairs showed Haarlock just how tired he was. He didn't get much sleep after Basterlit's crafting session, and what he got wasn't very good. The nap in the carriage helped little because of the bumpy roads and the cold. A heating stone kept the chill away, but it must have been undersized, malfunctioning, or something, as it didn't exactly make it warm. Luckily, a cuddling raccoon helped with that.

And speaking of a raccoon, one was splayed out on Haarlock's bed. Ladrón continued to snore when Haarlock put him in his own bed.

Haarlock changed into a robe, then put his attire on the armor stand near the closet. Haarlock had the stand made in Farncombe before his last outing but hadn't been able to use it since then. With the stand decorated, Haarlock stood back and looked over his kit.

Overall, it still looked out of place for *The Game*. The vest, even with the extra armor obfuscating its profile, was the most obvious *not from this world* piece of equipment Haarlock had. Under his cloak, the fatigues could be mistaken for regular garb, but not the vest and the dozens of loops covering its surface.

The black fatigues, with *Stealth* and *Acrobatics* enhancements, looked and felt just like real ones, even with 15 armor built into them. How Marcon kept the material so soft, light, and pliable was anyone's guess. Then again, the elf said *I'm almost as good of a tailor as I am a spy. And I am a very good spy*. He must be an excellent spy indeed.

Luckily, the boonie hat wasn't too out of place, fashion wise. No one else wore something exactly like it, but there were similar enough styles for it to pass unnoticed at a glance. Same with his combat boots. Long since without polish, they would pass as common footwear to anyone but the most observant.

At least the greaves and bracers are actual medieval armor.

Haarlock huffed to himself before turning towards the smoldering fire. It was always kept just barely alive by the Maids, but it did little to warm the room. Luckily, a stack of firewood sat beside it. Kindling and five logs went in, and with a little stoking, the flames came to life. When Haarlock stood, he came face to face with Roboute's clock, a wooden dove perched on top of it.

The wily Illusionist gave him the magical clock shortly after they first met. With the right words, it would bring the messenger bird to life, allowing them to keep in regular communication. Haarlock sent the bird to Roboute a few days ago with an update about his explosive efforts to find Mateo, and it being here now meant a reply. So did the rolled-up paper in the bird's feet.

The trove you found proved enlightening, and that means more work for you.

Your task will take you on an extended trip far from here. When you've made the necessary arrangements, write back when you can meet me at the restaurant where you killed a dwarf.

The *Crimson Biscuit*. Haarlock faux assassinated a dwarf forger there during the Academy tournament's Assassination Game. It wasn't surprising Roboute knew about that. In fact, it annoyed Haarlock how Roboute seemed to know so much random information about him.

Into the fire the note went, and into the bed went Haarlock. Worrying about Roboute was a problem for tomorrow.

***

"Sorry to head back out again so soon, Aripine."

Haarlock stood on the terrace, wrapped in his wool-lined cloak, and looked out across the rolling hills in the morning light. White covered everything, and the orange sun turned it into a beautiful scene.

"Worry not, m'lord. We here at Huerto de Vid Azul will keep things running in your absence."

Aripine stood next to him, her chair adjusted higher so she could see over the banister. Even with the legs extended as far as they could, the woman's head only came to Haarlock's chest.

"Glad to hear it. I always feel bad about leaving."

"Why?"

"These are my lands, and I should be around to manage them."

The gnome chuckled. "You still have much to learn, m'lord. I'd be surprised if a noble spent a quarter of their days at home. Dinner parties, hunting trips, and the like take up a lot of time, after all."

"Fair." Haarlock nodded a few times. "Still, I don't like it."

"Good thing you have me, then."

Haarlock looked down at Aripine with a smirk. She smiled back.

"However long I'm gone for, try not to let the builders bankrupt us."

"A strongly written letter to the appropriate guilds has already been drafted." Aripine grumbled. "They should know better than to sneak a price increase like that. Very unprofessional."

"Well, I'll leave you to it." Haarlock sent a mental ping to Ladrón to meet him at the carriage. The animal was in the kitchen saying his own goodbyes to Chef Dubois. "I'll see ya when I see ya."

"Safe travels, m'lord."

Haarlock went through the terrace gate and to the waiting carriage out front. The driver stood with the door open and nodded respectfully as Haarlock climbed in. A few seconds later Ladrón scurried through the window, and they were off to Ostia.

13

Many taverns, tailors, smiths, and restaurants surrounded the city's towering coliseum. The volume of people coming and going in the adjoining blocks provided an excellent means of cover. You'd be hard pressed to find someone in the winding streets and alleys, let alone in the dozens and dozens of businesses crammed into every nook and cranny. And that's without hooded cloaks obscuring their faces. Haarlock, having come and gone from this area for over two months, still found it confusing.

The vagueness of Roboute's letter suggested that their meeting necessitated secrecy. One of the more popular, though less reputable, establishments perfect for this sort of thing was the *Crimson Biscuit*.

Haarlock had the carriage stop three blocks away. Even with his relatively distinctive gear and moderate notoriety from the Academy tournament a few months ago, barely anyone paid him a second glance. Only Ladrón rated a few pleased smiles from young people.

A few minutes later Haarlock found himself across the street from the *Biscuit*, absently window-browsing a boutique as he tried to get a read on anyone paying a little *too* much attention. He wasn't sure why he was being so cautious. It wasn't as if Haarlock hadn't met with a contact in public to discuss sensitive topics a dozen times before. Whatever the reason, the cold seeped in. He jogged across the road and into the tavern.

When Haarlock closed the door, the sound of music and the warmth of fire slammed into him. A stocky dwarf man in green sang and played the lute at the far end, glorifying the story of two heroes fighting against all odds. Fifty other people filled the space, and many of them watched the performer with interest.

Before Haarlock's eyes adjusted to the dim light, a server walked up to him with a smile.

The woman, with long dark hair and stunning gray eyes, nodded towards Ladrón. "Almost didn't believe your friend when he said there'd be a man with a raccoon on his shoulder."

Ladrón chittered and waved while Haarlock frowned.

"He's already here?"

"Yep, in the corner over there." The woman pointed. "Been here almost an hour. Keeps flirting with the staff."

Haarlock gave the woman a look. "And you?"

"He tips well and calls me pretty. I ain't one to complain."

She winked and walked off towards another customer. With a shake of his head, Haarlock went to where Roboute sat.

The Illusionist tapped his right hand on the table in time with the music. *Dark Vision* allowed Haarlock to see the red on Roboute's cheeks, and a few dark stains on his otherwise pristine blue tunic. The clothes he wore looked, but definitely weren't, cheap.

Haarlock slipped into the booth as Roboute took a drink, causing him to choke. Amused chitters from Ladrón suddenly stopped when he saw a bowl of peanuts on the table. The animal drug it off the edge and disappeared into the corner of the seat.

"Watch yourself, Roboute. You seem a bit worse for wear."

"Yes." Roboute hacked a few times and wiped his mouth with a sleeve. "This ale is fantastic, and my server is beautiful. Hard not to enjoy a few too many."

Haarlock frowned. "I don't think I've ever seen you drunk."

"The trick is to have a spell handy for every occasion."

"There's a spell to cure drunkenness?"

"Not specifically, no. Alcohol is technically a poison, and that means *Cure Poison* will do the trick."

The Illusionist downed the rest of his drink, then slid his mug to the side and wiped his goateed face with his sleeve. A snap of the fingers sent a small pulse of magic out, and Haarlock watched as the red of Roboute's cheeks faded away and his eyes sharpened.

"And voilà!"

"Your outfit is still...dirty." Haarlock gestured to the stain on his left breast.

A hand wave over top made it vanish, along with the other on his sleeve.

"There we go. Back to being presentable."

"I'm surprised you're not hilariously overdressed for this place."

Haarlock looked around the bar. Thick clothing and hooded cloaks were the staple.

"I'm trying to keep a low profile." Roboute produced a tuning fork from under the table, tapped it once on the edge, then set it in the small vase against the wall. "We may speak freely now."

"First off, why are we at the *Biscuit* and not at your house? Or Marcon's shop?"

"Proximity, my boy. This is the preamble before the theatrics, and where better to have theatrics than the coliseum."

"Theatrics? That means we're playing someone."

Roboute pursed his lips so slightly it was only Haarlock's *Canny Observer* Trait that let him see it.

"Your investigation into Mateo Cabrera has proved enlightening. Unfortunately, that light has shone on someone whose...involvement is less than ideal."

"Anyone I know?"

"You just robbed a bank with her: Justine, second in command of the Ostian Thieves' Guild."

It was all Haarlock could do not to let his jaw hit the table. "What?"

"My sentiments exactly." Roboute used his index finger and thumb to smooth out his goatee. "Mateo's trove led us down many roads, one of which ended at her. And before you ask, the data has been triple-checked by Marcon, myself, and Gerard. Try as we might, we have yet to find a way to invalidate its authenticity."

"*Invalidate its authenticity?*" Haarlock gave the Illusionist a suspicious look. "That's not a very convincing sentence."

"We're not all convinced."

Haarlock crossed his arms and leaned back in his seat. "Please don't play this vague, double-speak bullshit with me right now, Roboute."

"Yes. Of course." Roboute paused for a few seconds as he looked at the remains of his drink. "The data itself is, as expected, not a perfect, one hundred percent guarantee of Justine's guilt. She's a rogue and has been a prolific part of this city's underworld for many years. Illegal things have been done, both through the Thieves' Guild and for it. All of this is well documented, of course. But the devil's in the details, Haarlock."

"Let me guess: her official activities coincide with suspected or confirmed shinobi actions?"

"That's the long and short of it, yes. A few are thin connections at best, but others are irrefutable."

Before Roboute could answer, the dark-haired server appeared.

"Well, darlin', can I bring you another one?"

The woman's bright smile brought an equally expressive one from Roboute.

"Of course!" Roboute gestured to Haarlock and Ladrón. "They're on my tab, so give them whatever they like."

"An ale for me, and..."

*"*Chicken. Fish. Bread. Peaches.*"*

Haarlock shot Ladrón a look of annoyance. *"Pick one, and one only."*

The raccoon squinted his eyes and sniffed his nose several times, then rubbed his paws together.

"**Fish.*"

"And fish for my furry friend."

"Right away."

The server flipped her hair over her left shoulder and gave Roboute a wink. The Illusionist watched her walk away.

"Really? She's literally a quarter your age."

"Just because I'm a hundred and twenty-three years old doesn't mean I can't appreciate a beautiful woman."

"And back to the situation at hand: how convincing is the data?"

Roboute pursed his lips and crossed his arms. "As far as data goes, it's too consistent and self-referential to be a coincidence. I don't know Justine as well as Marcon or Gerard do, so I can't speak to whether it's outside her character."

"She's Gerard's right-hand woman. Is he convinced? What about Marcon?"

"Gerard takes things as they are, feelings be damned. If the data says Justine's guilty, then to Gerard she is. Marcon, though, has known Justine since she was a small child, and even helped her get to the position she's in now. He is finding it difficult to accept."

"Difficult, or impossible?"

"I might be old, but Marcon is twice my age. More than a few friends have betrayed him over the years. It's inevitable, really, when you've been around long enough. Marcon may not like it, but he accepts what is."

Haarlock thought about that. Someone in Marcon's position would be a fool to believe in true loyalty. Then again, people have blind spots for things they care about.

"So why am I here?" Haarlock gestured to the other patrons. "You said there's going to be theatrics, and I'm assuming these people aren't part of it."

"The theatrics are for Justine. She is leaving town to visit family, and you just so happen to be heading the same direction and could use a guide."

"I am?"

"Yes, you are." Roboute gave one of his trademark shark smiles. "Justine is going back to her hometown, Claville. Something she does routinely a couple of times a year. It's a mining town and trade center between the Sathe and Zilgas duchies. Since you're heading to Sathe to hand-deliver a message from Marcon to their Thieves' Guild, you need a guide to take you on a surreptitious path no one will think to find you on."

If the look on Haarlock's face could be put into words, it would be some combination of annoyance and excitement. He liked the outdoors. He liked secret missions. What he didn't like was someone telling him of a secret outdoor mission he's about to be sent on casually over drinks.

Haarlock rubbed his face with both hands, then ran them over his head. "Alright, Roboute. Why am I actually going?"

"To see if Justine contacts anyone, and if she does, what she gives or tells them. The data you found suggests she uses these trips to pass intel between Blue Jira and one of his operatives in Claville. If information is passed, you'll retrieve said info from her contact, and we'll deal with her when she returns."

That's a vague and open-ended statement.

"If she expects me to continue past Claville, how will I contact you? The bird clock isn't exactly subtle."

"With this." Roboute slid a credit card-sized piece of dark, reddish-brown wood to Haarlock. "This is a calling card. It's a piece of hawthorn enchanted with a *Message* spell. When you're ready to report back, take it in your hand and focus on it with your magic. Once activated, you'll have thirty seconds to say up to thirty words before it becomes inert. Those words will come directly to me."

Haarlock took the card and turned it over a few times. Beyond a minute magical aura, it looked and felt like any other piece of wood.

"I can see how these are useful."

"Exceedingly so. They're cheap and easy to make, too."

"Why only one?"

"If Justine has been turned, I wouldn't be surprised if she searched your items on the trip. Honesty, she'll probably search your things either way. And since she'll likely have something similar on her, you having one won't be suspicious."

"Right." Haarlock nodded to himself as he looked over the card. "What about payment?"

Roboute raised an eyebrow. "Payment?"

"Yes." Haarlock met Roboute's eyes. "Since I'm talking to you and not Camilla, it means this quest isn't through Shattersong. That means I'm an independent contractor, and independent contractors get paid. Plus, I'm on vacation."

The flat look Roboute gave Haarlock went away with an amused huff. "I'd offer a stack of coin, but you're a well-to-do lord. Do you have anything in mind?"

"Nothing specific at the moment but know it won't be cheap."

Both men smirked. Something drew Roboute's attention, and his smirk turned into a smile. The server appeared with their order, and the Illusionist tipped enough to make her blush. Ladrón finished his meal before she left.

"Enjoy the ale, Haarlock. Our charade begins in an hour."

14

The bustle of the coliseum surprised Haarlock. Even during the off-days, the massive structure never truly rested, and many of its rooms saw use for various functions. Currently, a large troupe of tumblers practiced in an open area off the main corridor, while the sounds of music came down the side tunnels from the arena. Up to the second floor and halfway around the perimeter lay their destination.

As they approached, one of the many plain wooden doors opened and out stepped Marcon de la Garza, renowned Couturier and spymaster of Lemuria. The dainty elf wore a stiff, tailed tuxedo, with his ultra-thin, platinum hair draping down his back. He gently shut the door and walked forward a few steps.

"Ah, caballeros." Marcon put a hand on his waist and bowed. "Thank you for the opportunity to fit you once again."

It was all Haarlock could do not to react to the comment. Roboute didn't bother to mention the pretense for their meeting.

"Of course!" Roboute smiled wide and offered his hand to the elf. "Only the finest cloth touches this skin."

An almost imperceptible flick of Marcon's eyes across Roboute's outfit caused Haarlock to snort.

"Yes, yes. Ham it up, you two." Roboute looked himself over. "To be fair, I've worn worse."

Marcon nodded several times as he examined the Illusionist. Eventually his gaze fell to Haarlock, and the elf placed a single finger on his lips.

"A set of matching outfits is in order." Marcon tapped his finger twice before he looked up at Ladrón. A nervous chitter brought a smile to the Couturier's face. "Worry not, my furry friend, no frills this time."

*"*Glad.*"*

"You'll have to remind me what this occasion is again." Haarlock eyed Roboute. "I seem to have forgotten."

"Your forgetfulness will be the death of your social life." The Illusionist chuckled and gestured to the door. "Shall we have some refreshments before the fitting?"

"Por supuesto."

Marcon went to the door and opened it, bowing again as the others entered. Inside the long, narrow space sat a hundred bolts of cloth across a dozen tables, with a handful of sewing machines strategically placed throughout. Mannequins lined one wall, each in varying states of colorful dress. At the far end, atop a wooden crate, sat Justine. She waited until the door closed before coming over.

Unlike her usual outfit of tight cloth and leather, she wore a simple gray tunic, black pants and boots, and a green sash around her waist. Her brown hair lay in a ponytail, with a single braid on the left side going behind her pointed ear.

While she looked beautiful before, Haarlock thought the simple outfit complimented her pale skin. Especially without her usual bright lipstick.

"Fancy meeting you two here." Justine smiled as she reached up to Ladrón and gave him a few chin scratches.

Haarlock did his best to seem surprised. "Same goes for you. I didn't know you shopped at *Sew Above, Sew Below.*"

"Marcon and I go back longer than I care to admit." The feigned look of pain brought a huff from her target.

"Poor Marcon." Roboute shook his head at the elf. "Fifty years of friendship and she treats you so?"

Fifty? She doesn't look a day over twenty-five.

"¡Tal falta de respeto!" Marcon started to say something else but stopped and looked at the door. "Ah, the last piece of the puzzle."

A few seconds later, Gerard Parnell walked in. He removed the heavy hooded cloak he wore and sat it on a nearby table, then looked around the shop before coming over to the group.

"Apologies for my tardiness." His expression, as always, betrayed nothing.

"Not a problem." Marcon raised an eyebrow. "Are we ready to begin?"

The bland-looking man nodded once.

"Excellente." Marcon went to the door, locked it, and returned. "Haarlock, this quest is simple but vital. I need an in-person handoff of information to the Thieves' Guild in Sathe. This is something you can do, sí?"

"Yes."

"Good. Justine is going home for a few weeks to Claville, a trading town between here and Sathe. The path you will take will, hopefully, prevent anyone from following you. Or, if they do, allow you to either evade or neutralize them. Haarlock, once you reach Claville, you will continue the rest of the way alone."

Marcon held out a hand, and Gerard removed a wax-sealed envelope and gave it to him. The elf removed a similar one from his jacket. He examined both seals before handing them to Haarlock.

"Give the letter with the rabbit seal to the guildmaster, and the one with the floral seal to the bartender. Repeat back what I just said."

"Rabbit seal goes to the guildmaster, and the floral seal goes to the bartender."

"Leave and come back the next day. One of them will have a reply. Bring their reply straight back to me via whatever means you can secure. You understand that I am the only one the letter is to be brought to?"

"Yes. Bring the letter to you, and only you."

"The only people who know about this quest or these letters are those in this room. Anyone else asking about the letters is a threat. Anyone trying to stop you is a threat. Even those in this room. Both of you reply you understand."

They did, and Marcon let out a sharp breath through his nose. Haarlock could feel the tension coming from the spymaster, and how it hung heavy in the air around him. Even Roboute looked tense.

"I cannot stress the importance of this quest, Haarlock. There is no level of risk or security too great that you can take to bring back the response."

Marcon's eyes burned into Haarlock's, and it was all he could do not to look away.

"What if neither has a letter?"

If the elf's eyes burned before, they seared now. Haarlock reflexively swallowed.

The spymaster clenched his jaw and slowly exhaled. "I am afraid both of my contacts will have been compromised, putting your life in exceedingly grave danger."

"Wonderful."

"I feel wasted on this trip, Marcon." Justine pouted. "It would make sense for me to be Haarlock's backup. My family can wait another week."

"No." Marcon frowned. "A lone noble on foot is odd enough, and you're too well known, my dear."

Justine looked at Haarlock and shrugged. "I've always wanted to go to Sathe."

"Yes, well, when this is all over, we all should take a vacation." Roboute put a hand on Marcon's shoulder, and the elf visibly relaxed. "What say you, Gerard?"

"Perhaps we can all go together." The expressionless man met the Illusionist's eyes and blinked once.

"By the gods, man. Was that a joke?"

It was a smile. Small and barely discernible, but Gerard smiled. The room erupted in laughter.

"Graciosa. Now that we have concluded this business, onto the next." Marcon turned around and gestured broadly to the space. "As you can see, I have set up shop. In four days' time, the performers you saw and heard on your way here will put on a show for the king and his entourage. I am lucky enough to be dressing them."

"You couldn't do that from your shop?" Haarlock looked at the bolts of cloth to his left and right. There had to be thirty just within arm's reach. "Seems like a lot of work to move all this up here."

"Could I have taken their measurements here and then worked at my store? Sí, but I'd be making frequent trips for adjustments or modifications. That, and this is a far less assuming place to have a secret meeting." Marcon winked. "And to keep up appearances, I must craft for each of you an article of clothing. Justine, my dear, what shall I make for you?"

The Couturier went through each person's requests, taking measurements as appropriate. Justine went with a scarf, Roboute a tunic, and Gerard a hat. Haarlock decided on a pair of gloves, and Ladrón a full-body pajama.

"Excellent choices, all. Haarlock, since you and Justine are leaving tomorrow, I will start on your items immediately. I will be at my shop tomorrow morning using some larger equipment, so come by around ten to retrieve yours. Justine, come by at eight."

Haarlock looked at Justine. "We're leaving tomorrow?"

"Better to get on the road as soon as possible. Don't need you carrying around sensitive documentation longer than necessary."

"Fair point. Well, Marcon, I'll see you tomorrow morning. Justine, where are we meeting to leave?"

Marcon nodded his goodbye as Justine put on a hooded cloak and motioned for them to leave. Once they were in the hallway, she wrapped her arm through Haarlock's and leaned against him. Ladrón scurried over to her shoulder and wormed his way into her hood. She gave the critter a few pets.

"Our cover until we get to the street is you're my escort, oh lord of lords." She winked. "As for where to meet, be at pier seven, berth nine at noon tomorrow. We're taking a cargo ship to a village down the canal, then going on foot west through the forest. It's rough terrain and will take us about a week to reach Claville."

"A week? In this weather?" Haarlock groaned. "That's going to be unpleasant."

"It'll be *fine*. We can hunt any monsters we come across, run a dungeon I found years back, and be so far off the trail no one can follow us. The days will *fly* by."

"With you? I doubt that."

The lithe elf smiled.

15

Haarlock walked down the busy street, dodging people so bundled up they could barely see. Granted, he was similarly bundled. The wind blew *hard* today, pulling more cold than normal from the lake in the center of the city. Ladrón huddled in the hood, providing his own bit of insulation for Haarlock.

Through the throngs of people Haarlock went until he finally reached his destination: *Travel Companion*. A week plus of travel in the winter necessitated specific equipment, and the store Justine suggested didn't have all that great a selection. It only took a glance for Haarlock to know why *Travel Companion* was recommended by the Adventurer's Guild.

Even at this time of year, two dozen people browsed the store's tables, bins, and floor-to-ceiling shelves. All looked to be seasoned adventurers; their well-worn equipment having seen blade, claw, and spell alike. They moved through the store with practiced ease, grabbing the usuals one needs for an extended stay outside civilization in the cold.

The front area of the store covered at least 2,000 square feet, with three doorways leading to other areas. Labels hung from the ceiling, denoting different sections: tents, socks, packaged food, cooking supplies, etc.

I need to make sure I don't buy entirely too much stuff.

Haarlock knew it wouldn't be hard to do. He always enjoyed camping as a kid, especially the part where you bought all the little accessories. Did one need a magnesium fire-starting block? Of course not, but it was nice to have just in case.

"Well, buddy, we're going to be eating a lot of rations on this trip. What do you think you can eat every day for a week?"

Ladrón sniffed the air a few times on Haarlock's right shoulder before crossing to the left and sniffing again. Whatever wheels his mind had turned for a moment.

*"*Jerky.*"*

"Are you sure? Because I'm not about to listen to you complain the whole way."

Once again Ladrón sniffed the air, though this time it was with deep breaths.

*"*Jerky.*"*

"Remember, I gave you the option."

The raccoon pointed to a bin in the middle. *"*Jerky.*"*

"Yeah, yeah."

When packing for a winter camping trip, the average adult should have about 3,000 calories, or three pounds of food, per day. The average raccoon, though? Haarlock hoped it wasn't more than a pound a day. That meant four pounds per day, seven days, at least. Not including drinking water. Good thing calorie-dense rations were a thing.

Inside a bin labeled *rations* lay paper packages the size of double-thick drink coasters, each providing one day's calories for 5 silver. When Haarlock knocked two together, they sounded like pieces of wood. The package didn't identify a flavor.

Yeah, no thanks.

The next bin held jerky, but those packages were far larger and quadruple the price. A wax paper envelope contained twenty pieces, and there were only three flavors: peppered, salted, and plain.

*"*Salted.*"*

"Sure you don't want plain? Salt will make you thirstier."

Ladrón's nose twitched. *"*Plain.*"*

"Wise choice."

Haarlock went to the front door for a basket, then returned and put 10 packages of plain jerky inside. Four of the ration squares went in, too, just in case. Better to have dense, terrible food than nothing at all. Two packs of dried fruit for variety, along with four loaves of a dense, oat-filled wheat bread called trencher bread. That should be enough to live off, and if not, they could always source food from the wilderness.

Next, they needed something to carry it all in.

Shelving on the opposite side contained backpacks of all shapes and sizes, from small overnight units to large military-style packs. Each was rated by weight, and Haarlock selected a 50-pound model. While he worked to pull the pack from the shelf, a worker came over to assist.

"Let me get that for you, m'lord." The slender young man easily snatched the pack up and over his shoulder. "I can assist you with whatever you need."

"Ah, thank you..."

"Dominic."

"Hi Dominic. I'm Haarlock and this is Ladrón."

"Greetings, m'lords. I take it this is your first time here?"

"It is. I'm going on at least a week-long wilderness trip and need supplies."

Dominic looked into Haarlock's basket. "If you're wanting to pack for winter, I'd suggest going with a different choice in food or a larger pack."

"Oh?" Haarlock gave the man a confused look.

"Yes, m'lord. Winters in the forest get mighty cold, and this size pack doesn't have much room after your tent, blanket, and so forth."

"Let's hear your suggestion."

"Over here, please." Dominic led Haarlock over to a shelf closer to the register. A sign with the word *Premium* hung from the ceiling in front of it. He gestured to a stack of small, paper-wrapped bars in the middle. "Trail rations, m'lord. A single bite will fill a grown man's stomach for a day."

Haarlock smiled. When he left Milltown, the old Cook there, Bastion, gave him five trail rations as a parting gift. A much smaller Ladrón ate one by himself in a single sitting.

"I'd forgotten these were a thing." Haarlock took one in his hand. "How much?"

"Some ingredients are scarce in the winter, so at the moment they're two gold apiece, I'm afraid."

"Not a problem. Let's go with four of them."

"Jerky. Keep?"*

"Yes, we'll still bring the jerky."

*"*Happy.*"*

Dominic put the bars in Haarlock's basket. "Do you have any cooking tools picked out? Water purification? Sleeping items?"

"Not yet."

"Follow me, please."

Over the next half hour Dominic helped Haarlock select all the assorted things he'd need. While one can boil water to make it safe, that requires a pot, and pots are heavy. An alternative to that is purification tablets, which when added to water cast a *Remove Toxins* spell on up to a gallon at a time. A gallon-sized water skin and three packs of tablets later, along with a small skillet and collapsible metal frame, and a set of wooden utensils, completed the food and water kit.

A canvas tent, bedroll, fur-lined blanket, thick wool sleeping socks and knit cap, plus a firestarter set, finished the sleeping kit. They made a heating box that used an enchanted stone to generate warmth, but those were too large, heavy, and expensive. Besides, Haarlock spent many nights in various cold wilderness areas back in the previous world. He knew techniques to keep oneself warm with minimal extra supplies.

Including 50 feet of rope (everyone needs rope), the price came to 37 gold.

Next was a visit to *Sew Above, Sew Below* to pick up a pair of gloves and a raccoon pajama.

A half-mile west, past a crowded housing area, then south along one of the many canals, Haarlock came to the store. The sign in the window read *closed*, but he knocked anyway. A few moments later the lock clicked and Marcon opened the door.

"Buen día Lord Haarlock and Ladrón. Please come inside." The elf gestured to the bare-bones shelving. "You'll have to forgive the lack of decor; it's all at the coliseum, of course. Por favor, come to the back and we can check the fit. Leave your items."

Through the cloth doorway they went, with Marcon pulling a black felt box from one alcove. He set it on a nearby round table and removed the lid, his eyes lighting up at the contents.

"Seems you're enthralled with yourself." Haarlock shot the Couturier a smirk.

"I rarely make gloves." Lifting out one of the pair with reverie, Marcon brought it to Haarlock. "Your left hand, please."

It slid on Haarlock's hand with a single, smooth motion. Made from thin, supple leather, the material barely impeded finger movement. Haarlock flexed his hand several times, then moved each finger by itself.

"Fits like a...glove."

"Hábil. Now the other."

After a repeat of the first, Haarlock turned his hands over a few times, then made fists.

"These are very comfortable. And warm."

Haarlock examined them.

<u>Dress Gloves</u>

Mastercrafted

Abilities: Second Skin, Thermodynamic

"*Thermodynamic* will keep your hands warm in the winter and cool in the summer. So long as you don't get them wet, that is. And, with *Second Skin*, it'll be like you're not wearing them at all."

"Very nice. Thank you."

"De nada."

"I want to feel them while holding my weapon." Haarlock mentally nudged Ladrón off his shoulder, then pulled his new umbral dirk from the sheath on his lower back.

Marcon watched with interest as Haarlock went through the motions with his blade. Blocks, slashes, stabs, hand changes, reverse grips. Just as Macron said, it was as if he wasn't wearing them at all.

"That is an interesting weapon you have, Haarlock." Marcon frowned and tilted his head. "Very interesting indeed."

"Problem?"

"No problem." The elf held out his hand. "¿Puedo?"

Haarlock handed over the weapon, and Marcon examined it. As he moved the item around, his expression changed from confusion to concern to wonder.

"You have, without a doubt, one of the more truly unique items I've seen."

"I hope that's a good thing."

"Where ever did you get it?" Marcon returned the dirk. "Unique weapons are, by their very name, not something that is acquired with frequency or ease."

"The gnome diplomat I got stabbed in the back for? This was his repayment."

"Ah, yes. I recall that incident. It was quite the talk." Marcon frowned again. "Who is the blessing from?"

"Sjena."

"Interesante." The elf's eyebrows rose. "We shall discuss this more when you return. Now for Ladrón's article."

From another alcove came a similar box, though this one contained a single body onesie. The material matched the animal's general fur color, with four buttons on the chest and drawstrings at the ends of the sleeves and legs.

Ladrón stood on his hind legs and pulled at his armor.

*"*Help. Off.*"*

Once the armor was off and the pajama on, Ladrón darted around the room and climbed up and over everything he could. It didn't appear that the article hindered him in any way. Haarlock examined it.

Animal Pajama

Mastercrafted

Abilities: Durable, Improved Thermodynamics,
Second Skin

"With his fur being so well insulated, I ensured he wouldn't overheat with *Improved Thermodynamics.*" Macon gave the critter scratches behind the ears. "With *Second Skin* he shouldn't notice it under his armor either. And, unlike your gloves, moisture won't affect the material. Except if Ladrón were to swim in it, of course. Lastly, *Durable* will ensure it can survive his scurrying about."

"Thank you, Marcon. These are very generous."

"Mi placer, Lord Haarlock."

When a long silence fell, Haarlock cleared his throat and jabbed his thumb towards the door.

"Anyway. I have to meet Justine in an hour, and it'll take me about that long to get there."

"Before you leave." Marcon's jaw clenched as he flexed his hands. "I wish to ask a favor."

"Name it."

"Please give Justine the benefit of the doubt." Marcon's eyes met Haarlock's, and the elf held them there for several seconds. "The evidence you've found has put her loyalty in question."

"But you're not convinced."

"I don't know." The elf went to the two-person couch against the far wall and sat down. He smoothed out his jacket deliberately before looking up. "The documentation has just the right amount of unknowns to be convincing. If it had unequivocally pointed the finger at her, it would be suspicious. Myself, Roboute, and Gerard have verified the data, and none of it appears fabricated."

"Then what does it appear like?"

"The truth, and that's what worries me."

"Why all the cloak and dagger, Marcon? You've known her for decades, right? Just confront her and be done with it."

Marcon tilted his head. "I groomed Justine to be my informant inside the Thieves' Guild since she was a young woman. There is a soft spot for her, as it were."

"You mean a blind spot."

"Yes."

"So you're testing her with the letters?"

"They're a honeypot, yes. How she reacts to their contents, or what events occur in the coming weeks and months, will confirm her guilt."

"And if she doesn't take the bait?"

"Other methods are in place." Marcon's shoulders slumped, only for a second, before returning to his rigid posture. "Investigate Justine. Thoroughly. I want to know, without a shadow of a doubt, that she has turned. And I would appreciate it if you brought her back alive. I also understand that circumstances may prevent that from happening."

"Done. Anything about her I should be worried about? I know she's classed as a Blade Thief, but I haven't seen her go all out."

"Justine has been my informant longer than you've been alive. Do not underestimate her ability to manipulate you."

Haarlock nodded to himself. "Let's hope I don't."

16

The Ostian Lake shone beautifully in the sun as a dozen boats floated lazily on its surface. Across the other side stood mansions, warehouses, the occasional recreational beach, and docks. Even more vessels were moored there, waiting for cargo to unload or passengers to embark. Ostia, even in winter, was a place of constant motion.

Along the lake's quay wall Haarlock walked, enjoying the sight of so many people at work. Vendors of all sorts hawked their wares, and work animals pulled cargo wagons. Ladrón, ever the connoisseur of meat on a stick, got a treat on the way to meet Justine.

Unlike many of the others designed for dedicated cargo vessels, pier seven's berths held a dozen smaller ships. Three men unloaded baskets of fish, while another counted open-topped boxes of glass jars. A 30-foot single-masted ship lay moored in berth nine. Haarlock's destination.

Several burly humans moved across the ship's deck with purpose. They all carried something, from cloth bundles to wooden crates. More worked on the dock, with one directing a crane operator who loaded large boxes into the hold. When he noticed Haarlock, he stopped him with an outstretched hand.

"You the lord?" The man's wrinkly face belied any emotion. "You look like a lord."

"That's right." Haarlock removed his glove to show the signet ring. "I'm Haarlock. This is Ladrón."

The man eyed the animal. "You're bringing a raccoon along?"

Ladrón chittered in annoyance.

"He's my familiar, and yes." Haarlock frowned. "I assumed Justine would have mentioned this."

"She didn't say it was a raccoon. He going to be a problem?"

"He won't be a problem." Haarlock looked at Ladrón. "Right?"

The animal replied with a nod of its head.

"There you have it. No trouble from Ladrón."

"You can talk to it?" The man's wrinkled face scrunched up.

"I gave him an intelligence enhancing necklace. It makes it so that we can talk, yes."

"That's weird." The man shrugged. "Anyway, I'm Glen, the ship's messer. That means I'm in charge of the cargo. Since you're on the ship, you're cargo. Anything I need to know about, like diseases, curses, dietary restrictions, or the like?"

"Nope. Nothing like that."

"Good. What's in the pack?"

"Basic camping supplies. Nothing fancy."

"I see you got a sword and bow, and I assume you have a hidden blade of some sort. Don't take them out for any reason other than if we're attacked or the captain specifically asks you. Got it?"

Haarlock nodded. "Got it."

Glen grunted and pointed at the gangplank. "Alright, you may board. Welcome to the *Hygeia*."

The wooden ramp up to the ship was wide enough for three people to walk side by side. Once at the top, Haarlock stopped and smiled before he stepped onto the ship itself. It wasn't the first time he'd been on a boat in *The Game*, but he still loved the experience. The scent of wood and pine tar filled his nose, and the way the deck gently swayed, all combined into a feeling of something special.

As he looked around, Haarlock realized he had no idea where he should go. Was he sleeping in the hold on a cot or a suspended hammock? Or did Justine secure him more accommodating quarters? Whatever was fine with him, but he didn't mind a little clout from his noble status, especially on a ship as small as this.

Before he had time to think much more about it, Haarlock heard his name coming from the forecastle. Out of it came Justine, followed by an older, pot-bellied human man in a worn gray greatcoat. The leather tricorn hat on his head looked in far better shape.

"Ah, there's our esteemed lord." Justine gestured to the other man. "Lord Haarlock, allow me to introduce Captain Balthazar. Captain, this is Lord Haarlock."

"Yes, I've heard much about you." Balthazar spoke with a softened, pirate-like accent. The appraising look he gave Haarlock was a cross between amused and annoyed. "Your team did well in the tournament. Lost more than a few gold betting the wrong way."

"Sorry to hear that, captain. I'm sure you'll be glad to know I'm too high level to take part again."

"Guess that'll have to do." Balthazar patted his stomach mindlessly. "Now that you're on board, *Lord* Haarlock, you need to know your title carries no authority here. I'm the captain, and that means I'm in charge. If someone asks you to do something, you do it. No questions."

Balthazar's look gave no room for anything save acceptance.

"Do what I'm told. Understood."

"Now, we here on the *Hygeia* are civilized folk, so you've been afforded our nicest lodgings."

Justine winked at Haarlock. "You and I get to share bunk beds in the hold."

"Who gets top bunk?" Haarlock smirked back.

"Your pet must stay below deck. Too easy for him to fall overboard. If that happens, we aren't stopping."

"**Below. Stay.*"

"Your port of call is Lorth, located where the Clastian River meets the Alligator Canal. That's going to take four days. Until that time, keep yourselves entertained by staying out of the way. Meals are every eight hours, sharp. If you're injured or sick, see the surgeon. If you need supplies, see the quartermaster. Understand?"

"Understood."

"I know you know, Justine, but I still want to hear you say it." Balthazar looked at the woman with a squinted, suspicious gaze.

"Yes, *captain*, I understand." The elf rolled her eyes.

"Excellent. We embark in two hours, and I still have a load of work to do." Balthazar patted himself on the stomach again and smiled. "See you all at dinner."

Justine watched as the captain left, then grabbed Haarlock by the arm and pulled him off to the side. "If anyone asks, I'm a wilderness guide taking you on a week-long hunting trip. Everything else is the same."

"Easy enough to remember."

"Good. It's doubtful anyone could sneak an operative onto this ship in less than a day, but better safe than sorry. So, keep your guard up."

Haarlock looked over his shoulder at Balthazar. "How about the captain? You trust him?"

"We've worked together several times over the last decade, so I trust him about as far as I can throw him."

"Must not trust him at all."

Justine frowned, then smiled. "He is a hefty man, yes. Anyway, we have a long trip ahead of us, so get ready to be bored."

"I was in the military. Boredom is nothing new to me."

***

The four days drug on.

During the endless hours of waiting, Haarlock learned much about the *Hygeia*. The ship itself was a cog, a type of small transport, and could hold 150 tons of cargo and a crew of 24. Balthazar bought the ship with an inheritance two decades prior, but he'd already been the captain for years at that point.

Up and down the Alligator Canal the *Hygeia* went, going as far as the Free Duchy of Trellisborg. It wasn't a glamorous job, but the crew worked it hard all the same. Most of them were humans from Ostia, with the rest a smattering of races from just as many places.

What the ship hauled varied, but it always paid well. Captain Balthazar knew his fair share of traders and ensured his ship's hold stayed full of high-end products. One of his most profitable trips involved hauling half a million bars of soap. They were stored in every imaginable nook and cranny, with even the captain's quarters packed to the brim. No one complained, though. Not only did the ship smell like lavender for weeks afterward, but their bonuses were *sizable*.

Justine spent much of her time between naps and playing card games and dice with the crew. Much to their displeasure, she rarely lost, though an orc rigger named Kordell seemed to never lose. To anyone. When Justine wasn't sleeping or gambling, she rambled on aimlessly to Haarlock about her past exploits. The elf knew little of her own culture, and didn't seem to care to know, either. Her parents abandoned her when she was a year old, so she spent the rest of her childhood in orphanages. She found out in her early 20s that it was Marcon who paid for her to go to school during those years, buying all her clothes, food, and supplies. It wasn't until Justine turned 24 that she cross-classed from civilian into rogue and went to work for the spymaster. Why she wanted to be a baker, she couldn't remember now, but bread still held a special place in her heart.

As Haarlock listened to Justine's backstory, he couldn't help but wonder when she came into Marcon's sights. Ostia had to have thousands of orphans. What combination of personality made him pick her? How did he even learn about her in the first place? Did Marcon have agents searching the city for impressionable children he could manipulate over decades?

No wonder he's the spymaster.

The rest of the *Hygeia's* crew kept to themselves. All were friendly and would chat about whatever random subject when asked, but they didn't start conversations. When Haarlock asked the captain about it over dinner the second night, Balthazar had instructed his crew to leave the guests alone.

Balthazar, though, did anything but. The portly man asked more questions during their first meal together than Haarlock had ever been asked by any single person before. Why did you become a rogue? How many bottles of wine does your vineyard produce each year? Are there any monsters you want to fight again? Does your raccoon like broccoli?

Luckily for them, Justine could divert the captain's curious tendencies towards self-aggrandizement. Especially after a bottle of wine. Balthazar liked to talk about his glory days and how he helped ferry supplies to one warzone or the other, or relief aid to a particularly bad outbreak. It was no doubt the man performed these tasks, even if he made it sound like the *Hygeia* ensured success wherever it went.

Ladrón. Poor, poor Ladrón. Never before this trip had he been fed or paid attention to in any capacity. Whimpers of starvation, both physical and emotional, drew sympathy from numerous crew members. The captain in particular. It took less than 24 hours for Ladrón to con his way onto Balthazar's shoulder, and from there to the top deck. More than once Haarlock had to get him down from the top of the mast with the promise of food.

Though the trip was relaxing, Haarlock couldn't help but wonder about Justine's loyalties. Was she actually going to visit family? Supposedly she took trips like this several times each year, but were they cover to exchange intel with a contact? Marcon assumed she'd search his things, so Haarlock kept the two letters on his person and his pack in the open. Better to let Justine think he wasn't suspicious by not trying to hide more than necessary.

The real question was whether Justine suspected him? Marcon's display of giving Haarlock the two letters, and ensuring everyone in the room knew he had them and who they went to, felt forced.

Hey, Justine, would you mind taking a last-minute courier on a week-long trip through the woods on your way back home? He has super secret documents that are integral to the safety of our kingdom. By the way, here's the route he's taking, when he'll be there, and who they're going to.

Could it be a double bluff? Make it so obvious that it had to be real? Or did they want it to seem fake? Getting Justine to question the validity of the entire operation could force her hand and get her to reveal her intentions. But what would happen if she realized it was a setup? Haarlock was an Assassin, and you don't send someone like that to make a delivery.

Let's hope she doesn't make that assumption.

17

Lorth.

Much like the other small hamlets dotting the coast of the Alligator Canal, Lorth held a smattering of stout wooden houses. It had a quaint, storybook feel with how it sat nestled in a clearing of a dense forest that otherwise came to the river's edge.

The tiny town's single dock looked like a child's toy compared to the *Hygeia*. The cargo vessel was so large, in fact, Justine and Haarlock had to take its tender to get to shore. Balthazar didn't want to risk hitting the dock and breaking either it or his ship.

Several people stood gawking as the pair came ashore in the late morning. Haarlock chuckled to himself about how odd the sight of a raccoon-adorned human and an elf must have looked. Justine tossed a coin to the tender operator, then slung her pack over her shoulder. It took her a moment as she adjusted the straps to notice the onlookers. She watched them for a moment as she wrapped the scarf Marcon made for her around her neck. The newly crafted garment, made of soft-looking wool, stood in stark contrast to the rest of her well-worn equipment. The alternating blue bands down the length of it didn't help, either.

"Every time I come here, these people stop and stare. It's like they've seen no one else in their lives."

Haarlock squinted. "Let me guess, you get off the boat and head straight into the woods without talking to anyone?"

"Yes, and?"

"You know that's like the absolute worst thing you can do, right? These people probably have all kinds of crazy conspiracies about what you're doing and why you chose their home to do it at."

"Hmm." Justine pursed her lips, then nodded once. "You're probably right, but I like to keep it a mystery."

She smiled and winked, then walked off. Haarlock looked at the raccoon on his shoulder.

"Remember, we talked about this. You need to spend as much time on the ground as you can. You're heavy and we have a long way to go."

*"*Shame.*"*

"I'm not fat-shaming you."

A disgruntled chitter preceded the lethargic climb down Haarlock's chest and leg. Once Ladrón touched the ground, he sniffed around until he found Justine's trail, then headed off towards her. Haarlock looked at the now dozen people watching him with blank stares, mouthed *sorry*, and followed his raccoon.

The first few miles into the forest felt like any other hike Haarlock had been on: up and down shallow hills, around jutting cliff faces, and through the occasional clearing. Though they were far from the massive mountains in the north, the land was anything but flat. Few animals made themselves known, leaving the forest a cold, quiet, and stark environment.

It wasn't until the sun left the highest point of the day that Justine had them stop for a break. She picked under a cliff overhang near a stream as their site and asked Haarlock to put together a fire pit while she gathered sticks.

"Whew." The lithe elf dropped a stick bundle at her feet and performed some stretches. "I haven't been this way in nearly six months, and damn if I don't feel it."

"I can relate." Haarlock sat on a rock, poking the smoldering embers. "I thought I did a lot of walking in Ostia, but out here? This terrain is killer."

"Not sure what geology made this part of the forest so rough, but it smooths out a lot another day west."

"Good to know." Haarlock stoked the fire, adding sticks as necessary. "You mentioned dungeon delving."

Justine drank from her waterskin, then took a seat across from Haarlock. She added sticks to enlarge the fire.

"Two days from here is a Level 25 dungeon called *The Fallen Kingdom*. The win condition is to kill the king, Aran. But he's a melee beast. As are his personal guard."

"I imagine we sneak in and take the king out?" Haarlock ran the scenario in his head. "Does the dungeon end right then, or will we have to fight his guards and escape?"

"Oh, no, nothing like that. We're going to rob the place." Justine pulled off her left glove and removed the ring on her pinky, then tossed it to Haarlock. "Snagged that two years ago."

Ring of Projectile Deflection

Uncommon

Abilities - Limited Projectile Deflection

So long as the incoming projectile was classified as light and non-magical, *Limited Projectile Deflection* would deflect up to 5 attacks per day. Haarlock wondered how much better the Rare or Mastercrafted versions of the ring were.

"Very nice, Justine. Did you acquire anything else useful? Or valuable?"

"A few pieces of armor, some gems, and a sword. I don't run it every time I come through. Sometimes I go further south and bypass it or just skip it entirely. As far as I know, I'm the only one that's run it in decades."

"Really?" Haarlock looked around. "Are these woods that secluded?"

Justine gestured widely. “Adventurers come here to hunt, level, and fulfill the occasional quest, but this forest is *big*. I only found the dungeon because I got lost hunting a deer. Damn near ran into one of the guards.”

“Yikes. What are they?”

“Pale skinned elves with red eyes called Dark Elves. Once you get past them, the dungeon entrance is a staircase going underground.” Justine regarded Haarlock. “How acquainted are you with dungeon mechanics?”

“Let’s see, I did one near where I first arrived called The *Hero's Tomb*, then an Event called *The Grand Banquet*. That’s it, really.”

“With how new you are to this place, I was worried you’d never done one before.”

“Fair. *The Grand Banquet* was a mess, but that’s a story for another time. What about you? How many dungeons have you run?”

“I’ve not really done a lot, either. Besides *The Fallen Kingdom*, there’s been *Rats? Rats.*, *Dark Catacomb*, *Brewer’s Despair*, *Elestris’ Puzzle*, and *Final Vacancy*. I spend most of my time in Ostia doing rogue stuff.”

“There’s a dungeon based on rats?” A shiver ran down Haarlock’s spine. “Exciting.”

“It wasn’t.” Justine laughed. “Anyway, let’s get some calories and water in us, then get back on the trail.”

The rest of the day went by with little excitement. That night they made camp in a dried ravine, with alternating guard shifts every two hours.

Day two of the trip came and went much like the first, except for them heading further south to avoid the sound of a battle. What it was, they didn’t know, but they weren’t about to find out. They would reach *Fallen Kingdom* that evening and wanted to stay fresh.

***

"Damn, this place always looks so much different in the winter." Justine stood on a large rock, her hand shielding her eyes from the setting sun as she looked through the trees. "I just need to find the gnarled tree growing out of a rock face."

"Anything else about Dark Elves I should know?" Haarlock took a swig from his waterskin, then let some pour out so Ladrón could drink, too. "The boss specifically."

Justine hopped down from the rock, removed a piece of bread from a pocket, then bit out a huge chunk and ate as she talked.

"Around the dungeon entrance are several types of guards." She washed it down with a drink, then ate more. "You've got rogues in the trees with bows, warriors in medium armor with swords and shields...some have pole weapons. A handful of mages, too. As for the boss." Justine let out a low whistle. "He has special armor that prevents armor-piercing attacks, and a blade that bypasses armor entirely."

"There goes my *sneak up and stab him from behind* idea."

"You don't want to do that. He has an ability called *Perfect Swordsmanship* or something. If you tangle with him, you die."

"Good to know." Haarlock looked at the ground in thought. "Do they have a treasure room, or do we just loot whatever we find?"

"The throne room is where the good stuff is." Justine looked Haarlock over. "Not sure if you'd find much use from any armor or weapons, but hopefully they'll be another magic ring. Maybe something to sell. Money's always good!"

Haarlock laughed at the ridiculous face Justine made.

"Okay, so we get past the outside patrols, then go into the dungeon and make our way to the throne room. Is there anything going on inside? *The Grand Banquet* was an actual banquet with food and guests."

"If we don't get caught up with the storyline, we should be able to get to the throne room before court starts. And so long as we don't cause a fuss, be it by starting a fight or getting caught stealing, there shouldn't be anything to worry about."

"What does the storyline revolve around?"

Justine shrugged. "I don't really listen to what they say, but it's your typical kingdom management stuff. Most of it is in Elvish, so I can't understand it anyway."

"Interesting."

"If you say so." Justine shrugged again, took a drink, then turned around and faced the other direction and pointed. "For whatever reason, that big tree there seems familiar. Let's go that way and see what we can find."

Over the next hour, they found the first signs of civilization. Or what was once civilization. Stone foundations, broken columns, and collapsed towers hid beneath leaf-bare vegetation. The settlement covered nearly a square mile, all centered on a small, long dried-up river. As they progressed, the structures grew denser, though nothing escaped the endless march of time.

Ladrón spotted something in a tree as he scouted ahead. The figure blended well into the bare tree limbs, and if it were summer, he'd be nearly invisible. It wasn't long before the figure moved, climbing higher into the tree, then leaped across to another nearby. Haarlock got a good look at him: elvish features, pale white-blue skin, and red eyes. A few hundred more feet through the ruins of a housing unit and the pair saw the first guard. Like the scout in the trees, this Dark Elf wore a cloak, but wore a metal breastplate and tassets, and wielded a large sword and shield.

Sneaking past the melee guards wouldn't be difficult. They moved in semi-predictable patterns, checking the same few spots in a roughly half-hour cycle. The tree-based rogues would be the only ones to give them trouble. None kept to a noticeable pattern, and each watched with slow, methodical precision. Where the mages were, Justine didn't know, but she wasn't worried. Their hooded cloaks always stayed up, limiting their field of view.

Justine brought Haarlock to a small overlook and pointed out their best path through. A deep but narrow stream bed would let them get close enough to render the rogue's higher vantage point moot; then all they had to do was move between the remains of the courtyard the guards patrolled. The lithe elf knew she could make it with ease, and she wasn't nearly as well equipped to sneak as Haarlock. Plus, as rogues, both possessed *Pass Without Trace*. None would know they had even been there.

With nightfall a few hours away, the pair went further into the forest to make camp and rest.

***

Though it was cold, Haarlock left his cloak behind. Sure, it granted a Skill enhancement to his *Stealth*, but he would be moving with speed. Justine followed suit, though she drank a warming potion. Haarlock's clothing had a liner; hers not so much. This was a night for stealth, so Haarlock left his bow and shortsword behind. Besides, he wasn't that great with either one, anyway.

Luck was on their side. Clouds blocked the light from the moons, casting the entire area in complete darkness. Haarlock and Ladrón's *Dark Vision* let them see with ease, though Haarlock wasn't sure what allowed Justine to do so. Did she have a similar ability, or some kind of magic item? Haarlock saw her drink a potion, so it might be that.

Stop and start. Stop and start. Every few minutes a guard would appear at the edge of the bank and wait. The trio pushed themselves against the stream's walls. Once the armored Dark Elf was satisfied with what it saw, it moved on.

Out of the stream and into the remains of a small building. They waited ten minutes for a nearby rogue to move on, then darted across an open area and into a small ground depression. The three of them made it tight, but it gave them excellent cover and even better sightlines to the dungeon's entrance. Words floated above the broken remains of a massive set of stone double doors.

The Fallen Kingdom

Level 25 Dungeon

They hold the final court of a once great kingdom.

Shall it vanish from our memory like so many stories of old?

Boss: King Aran

Rewards: Heirloom Longsword, 6,000XP, ???

"That rogue there, the one in the slender tree next to the boulder?" Justine waited for Haarlock to notice him. "He's not moving, and if we try to run for it, he'll see us."

"What do we do?"

"Next time, bring your bow."

Haarlock huffed. "Even if I did, I'm not good enough to hit him from here. Can we come from the entrance at a different angle?"

"We'd be more exposed. This is the shortest route from cover."

"So we have to kill him."

"That'll be fun." Justine rolled onto her back and rubbed her face with both hands. "We have nothing ranged."

"We have a Ladrón."

A proud chitter drew Justine's questioning gaze at the animal.

"Him?" She smirked. "I thought he was only good for food disposal."

Ladrón eyed the woman.

"I kid, I kid." The elf ruffled his armored head. "I can see how big and tough you are."

*"*Tough.*"*

"How do you think he can be of use?"

"I don't know if you've ever seen just what kind of damage a regular raccoon can do, Justine, but it's a lot. And Ladrón here is no regular raccoon."

Haarlock looked at Ladrón and jerked his head towards the tree-bound Dark Elf. With speed belying his girth, Ladrón darted out of cover and into a nearby thicket. Even with his enhanced senses, Haarlock had a hard time following where the critter went. Ladrón was a Level 10 rogue, after all.

It took a few minutes for Ladrón to make it to the tree. Once the guard went past, he slowly climbed the trunk, peeking his head out every ten feet to ensure no one was looking. As he approached where the Dark Elf rogue perched, he moved even slower. Five minutes passed before Ladrón's head popped out again above and behind his target.

*"*Ready.*"*

"Get ready to run for it if this doesn't work."

"Ready."

"Get him."

Ladrón leaped onto the rogue's back and bit into his throat. *Sneak Attack* combined with *Vicious Bite* ensured his teeth went deep into Dark Elf flesh. The only noise came from when the dead elf hit the ground. Too bad it was enough to alert the others.

Four guards rushed towards the noise, while a mage appeared from behind a rock formation. Ladrón, though, was already gone. Using the chaos to their advantage, Haarlock and Justine darted across the opening and towards the dungeon.

Arrows landed around them, and one grazed the back of Haarlock's chest armor, causing him to stumble. Without missing a beat, Justine grabbed his hand and pulled him forward into the dungeon.

18

Haarlock landed face-first on a plush red carpet. The sudden change in temperature and light caused his brain to pause for a moment, but he was on his feet, dirk in hand, ready for whatever might come.

"Calm down, *m'lord.*" Justine, leaning against the wall behind Haarlock, chuckled. "This hallway isn't patrolled, and the guards from outside won't follow us in."

The red carpet went forward a hundred feet down a hallway of white stone, stopping at a large set of double doors. Plinths, paintings, tapestries, and foliage lined the walls, only broken by a pair of wooden doors on each side. Large chandeliers hanging from the vaulted ceilings provided light, casting the walls in a dull orange glow.

"Right." Haarlock stood and dusted himself off. "Which way?"

Justine frowned. "We're not waiting on Ladrón?"

"He'll make it when he's able." Haarlock shrugged. "So, where to?"

Justine pointed to the first door on the right, then to the left. "These lead to residential areas with several rooms and a sitting parlor. Sometimes there's a servant or guest, sometimes not. The rooms are locked and about half are trapped. There's a variety of stuff we can steal, but it's different each time I come through. Most we don't want because of size or fragility."

"What kind of traps and goodies?"

"I've only tripped one before, and it was a flame attack of some sort. Only survived because of *Uncanny Dodge* and *Alert*. I'm no mage, so I couldn't tell you what the others are, but they're activated by a rune. As for valuables, there's gold, jewels, paintings, vases, and so on. The occasional outfit, too." Justine pointed to a nearby tapestry. "I'm sure those are worth a fortune."

"This would be a lucrative run if we had a full team." Haarlock looked between the second set of doors, then turned to the elf with a raised eyebrow. "And those?"

"One on the left is another hallway that goes to a kitchen with storage rooms attached to it. I've checked all of them before and found nothing of value. Occasionally there's a guard, but mostly just workers. The right side goes to a soirée, with all sorts of interesting characters to talk to. Again, I don't bother with the storyline, so I'm assuming if I listened to any of them, I'd find out some relevant plot. But they are easy to steal from."

Haarlock huffed. "Good to know."

"I'd suggest taking one of the residential areas. Be a great way to improve your *Pick Locks* if you're needing it."

"Sure. I'll take the left one."

"And I'll check out the party."

The left-side hallway door opened with a smooth, silent motion. Haarlock kept it almost completely closed, peeking his head in at the bottom just far enough to see. The snort behind him made him jump, and when he looked at Justine, she had a hand over her mouth.

"What?"

"The guards and servants only react if they see you acting suspiciously, or if they find someone unconscious or dead."

Haarlock frowned in embarrassment and stood. "So, this is otherwise a passive dungeon?"

"Pretty much. There's a predetermined script they follow, so you're more or less left alone unless you leave something for the guards to find or get caught in the act. Could also be that I'm an elf, so we'll have to see how they react to you."

“Seems a little too easy.” Haarlock looked down the hallway at the double doors. “There’s got to be a catch.”

“I think this is supposed to be a trap, just not for a lone rogue with sticky fingers.” The elf winked and went through her door.

Haarlock went through his and found a large rotunda, complete with light coming through stained-glass panels on the otherwise plain, domed ceiling. The glass depicted various forest scenes, some with buildings, others with water features. More plinths, paintings, and tapestries adorned the walls between arched doors. Directly across from the entrance sat a recessed hearth, its modest fire warming a figure sleeping on a high-backed couch to the side.

Six doors, three to a side, were closed, and Haarlock went to the first on the right. The handle didn’t move, so he examined the lock.

Sturdy Lock

Masterwork

Abilities - Secure

Haarlock removed his tools and went to work. Though he is only *Skilled* at picking locks, his Masterwork platinum pick set ensured there were few places he couldn’t access. *Deft Hands* helped, too, and it only took a few seconds before he heard a quiet *snick*. Opening the door a sliver, then listening, Haarlock waited for any sound. When he was sure the room was empty, he went in and closed the door behind him.

The simple, well-appointed room held a single person bed, a vanity, a wardrobe, and a steaming bathing tub with a shelf of soaps and oils. Other than a six-foot-tall portrait of a Dark Elf woman hanging from the wall, the place was empty. Haarlock made quick work of the space, searching the furniture with practiced ease, finding a handful of coin and a simple pearl necklace.

I bet this will fetch a pretty penny.

Haarlock pocketed the items and exited the room, making his way to the next door. This time the lock made a *clunk* noise when his hand slipped. A yawn filled the rotunda, and Haarlock cursed under his breath. He froze, moving only his eyes to the left to see a pair of arms stretching from the figure on the couch. Next came the white, long-haired head of a Dark Elf woman as she sat up. The lock picks went back into Haarlock's vest as he stood and spoke in perfect Elvish.

"My apologies, my lady, I didn't mean to wake you."

When you're caught, act like you're exactly where you're supposed to be.

The woman's head spun around, and her red eyes went wide as she shot to her feet. She held her gaze for a long time before speaking.

"No apology needed, m'lord." The woman relaxed, then bowed her head slightly. "And I am not a noble such as yourself. Merely my lady's Attendant. She rests after a long day of discussion." She gestured to one of the rooms across from Haarlock. "I didn't know a human would be in attendance." The woman tilted her head. "Lord?"

"Haarlock." He smiled as he thought of how to answer. "I myself was unaware of my attendance until recently. Our monarch has an interest in the final court of your kingdom. May I ask your name?"

"Sofia de Costa." She curtsied, then motioned to the couch. "Please sit with me, m'lord."

Haarlock walked to the couch and looked Sofia over. She wore a floor length pleated black dress trimmed in white floral embroidery. The modest décolletage accentuated a pearl necklace adorned with an emerald brooch. Earrings of hooped gold finished the woman's attire. Up close, her red eyes weren't as creepy as Haarlock thought they'd be.

Sofia de Costa

Level 20 Attendant

Health - 100

Abilities - Dark Vision

"May I ask when court is to be held?" Haarlock sat, followed shortly by Sofia. "The trip here was long, and I would like to rest beforehand if possible."

"And it seems you are in need of different attire." Sofia looked at Haarlock's chest armor and boonie hat, her expression a combination of confusion and intrigue. "You have such strange dress. What kingdom are you from?"

"Lemuria. It's far from here."

"Indeed, it must be, m'lord. As for court, it will be held at the top of the hour." Sofia gestured to the clock next to the hearth. It read 4:18pm. "Do you come alone?"

If he lied, would she freak out if Justine arrived? Better to stick to the truth, or at least a version of it.

"I have an attendant, too. She is taking a self-guided tour of the grounds."

"Yes, the castle is a beautiful place. I wonder what will happen to it when we're all gone."

Haarlock wondered if the ruins outside were of the actual kingdom this dungeon was based. He made a mental note to do some research when he returned to Ostia.

"Only time will tell, Miss De Costa. Perhaps you shall find a new land, or join the ranks of a neighboring kingdom?"

"We shall see, Lord Haarlock. We shall see."

Sofia looked at the clock again, and Haarlock followed her gaze. Though two minutes passed, it remained at 4:18pm. When she looked back at Haarlock, Sofia simply stared at him with a small smile. Haarlock assumed the paused clock meant there was a trigger to advance the story. As for Sofia, was she at the end of her dialogue options, or was she just being polite?

"What is your lady's purpose here?"

"Lady Lucia once held great swaths of land to the north, second only to the king himself. Her voice is equally powerful."

"Ah, yes, the king. What sort of person is he?"

"A proficient statesman and as fine a warrior as has ever lived. Two hundred years he was a soldier before he took the throne."

"Two hundred?" Haarlock's brow raised high. "He must be a prodigious fighter."

"Unmatched, m'lord. While you appear to be as deadly as any, he is beyond you or anyone else here."

That's good to know...kinda.

Haarlock stopped talking again, waiting to see if she continued the conversation. For three minutes Sofia sat there smiling, her delicate hands resting in her lap.

"Well, it seems I will be needing a room. Can you help with that?"

"Of course, m'lord." Sofia removed a key from within her sleeve. "The one between the portrait and the yellow flower vase is open."

Haarlock took the offered key, thanked Sofia for her assistance, and went to the door. Inside he found yet another simple, well-furnished space. A picture of a man using a spear to fight a dire wolf hung from the wall, but otherwise the space was identical to the first room.

*"*Hello?*"*

"Ladrón, hey buddy. Finally get away?"

*"*Sneaky.*"*

"No doubt. I'm through the first door on the left. Hang out where you are, and I'll come get you."

When Haarlock went back into the rotunda, he saw Sofia once again napping. He entered the entrance hallway to find Ladrón sniffing the base of a wooden plinth holding the marble bust of a strong faced elf.

The raccoon looked *terrible,* with most of his fur covered in dark liquid. His armor sported several scratches, rents, and holes. A quick check of Ladrón's stats showed he was down 50 hit points. Nearly a quarter of his total. His armor was even worse off.

NAME: Ladrón	**CLASS**: Fighter/Rogue/Mage
RACE: Raccoon	**LEVEL**: 30 (10/10/10)
AGE: 1	**EXPERIENCE**: 17,276

STATS:

HP - 210	STR - 15	DEX - 23	INT - 6 (17)
WIS - 5	CON - 28	CHA - 20	

SKILLS:

Master	Expert	Skilled	Proficient
		Stealth	Sleight of Hand
		Hunting	Unarmed Combat
			Lockpick

ABILITIES:	**CLASS ABILITIES**:	**FEATS**:	**TALENTS**:
Darkvision	Sneak Attack	Vicious Bite	Nose for Tresure
Familiar	Fighting Style: Brawler	Tough	Nimble Climber
???			Fast Fingers
			Evasion

SPELLS:

Cantrips	1st Level	2nd Level
---	---	---
---	---	

"Damn, dude." Haarlock laughed. *"I thought you said you were sneaky?"*

Ladrón turned his head slowly to look at Haarlock, then chittered once in annoyance.

"Sorry. And, once again, I don't have any health potions for you." Haarlock frowned. *"I really need to start bringing those."*

*"*Fine. Sore.*"*

"Well, you look, and even from here smell, not great."

*"*Bath?*"*

"Yep. Come on."

Ladrón hurried behind Haarlock as they went back to the room. Haarlock helped the raccoon out of his armored harness and pajama, and into the water-filled tub. Ladrón let out a contented sigh as he sunk up to his neck, then dived under as Haarlock poured in a copious amount of soap.

"Lather up while I fix your armor."

With a wave of his hand, Haarlock cast *Mend* and the harness reverted to its undamaged form. Save the blood and dirt, of course. He helped Ladrón finish lathering, mostly because the animal's short arms couldn't reach most of his body. Once he was rinsed, Ladrón made a mess by shaking out his fur. Haarlock threw a towel to him before washing off the armor. Twenty minutes after they started, the animal was clean and smelled like lavender.

"At least now it doesn't look like you climbed through a fresh corpse. Let's find Justine and get this show on the road."

Back in the main hallway, Haarlock approached the doorway to the soirée room. He leaned his ear against the door and listened. Twenty seconds passed without a sound. A turn of the handle showed it to be unlocked, so Haarlock slowly opened the door and had Ladrón peek in at the bottom.

*"*Big. Party.*"*

Haarlock looked inside to find a space far different from the rotunda he had just been in. This room, styled as a courtyard, hosted a party of some three-dozen people. A small reflecting pool, stone columns and benches, pillow-covered rugs, and a variety of small, potted foliage gave the guests plenty of room to socialize. Sections of smooth marble block walls partially encapsulated the area, and another stained-glass dome ceiling covered it. All of it had a pseudo-Roman, even Greek, feel.

The attendees chatted softly as they ate finger food and drank from glass goblets. Three servants in dark clothing moved about with trays of refreshments. Haarlock approached with confidence and a raccoon on his shoulder.

"Be cool, okay? We don't know what's going on, and we don't want to trigger something by accident."

*"*Fine.*"*

One attendee, a well-built male Dark Elf in a bone-white, open chest tunic, turned to face Haarlock. He took a sip of his drink as he looked the newcomer over, then raised an eyebrow. His Elvish sounded different, like a cross between Spanish and Portuguese.

"It appears we have a visitor of some sort." He scoffed, drawing the attention of the woman beside him. "You must see his outfit, Bianca."

Bianca turned around, a small tray of hors d'oeuvres in one hand and a drink in the other. She wore a dark, mid-length silk dress that left little to the imagination. Jet-black hair hung loose, spilling around her shoulders, with several pieces of silver jewelry woven throughout.

"What an outfit indeed, Antonio." Bianca smiled seductively as she took a drink. Her accent sounded like Antonio's, though softer. "Does the visitor speak?"

"The visitor speaks, yes." Haarlock tried not to sound annoyed. "I am Lord Haarlock. This is Ladrón."

"He speaks so well for a human!" Antonio beamed. "And with a northern accent, too. Very traditional."

Bianca nodded. "He's a noble, my dear. They are all about tradition."

"Too true." The male elf shook his head. "Forgive us, lord. We have not made formal introductions. I am Scribe Antonio Rivera Salamanca, and this is Courtier Bianca Molina."

Both bowed in unison.

"A pleasure." Haarlock nodded.

"The pleasure is ours, m'lord." Bianca snapped her fingers, and a servant approached. "Would you like a refreshment? I can see you've recently arrived. You must be famished."

"Yes, thank you." The tray contained several colorful pastries, grapes, and what looked like slices of melon. Haarlock took several grapes. "Traveling in the cold makes me hungry. Him, too."

Ladrón nodded his head as he snatched a pawful of food from the tray.

"The cold?" Antonio frowned as he tilted his head. "Whatever do you mean, m'lord? It's the middle of spring."

Haarlock's eyes widened as he tried to think of something.

Bianca clicked her tongue. "His accent, dear. Lord Haarlock must be from the desert regions to the far north, beyond the mountains. Yes?" She smiled.

"Ah, yes. The desert. Of course." Haarlock laughed nervously. "This weather here is freezing to me."

"What brings you so far south?" Bianca smiled again.

"My king has a vested interest in what will become of this realm."

A look of sorrow crossed Antonio. "As do we all. Do you come merely as an observer, or do you have offers of aid? Perhaps news of immigration? What say your king of the various offers by the faction heads?"

"I am but an observer of these proceedings."

"How unfortunate." Antonio grumbled and looked away.

"Don't be like that, dear. Lord Haarlock does not deserve your ire."

"You are, of course, right, Bianca." Antonio bowed. "Forgive me, m'lord."

Haarlock shook his head. "Nothing to forgive."

"See, all is well!" Bianca beamed. "Now, please excuse us. We have other guests to talk with. There is much to discuss before court. So much politicking and all."

"Of course."

The pair walked off to engage a lone Dark Elf in a toga. Haarlock looked around for Justine, finding her hanging on the arm of a ridiculously thin Dark Elf with sharp features. *Canny Observer* caught Justine removing a piece of jewelry as she caressed the man's ear. She whispered something to him, making his pale cheeks surge with color. It didn't take long for her to see she had an observer and excuse herself.

"Find anything worthwhile in the guest wing?" Justine took a grape from Haarlock's hand and popped it in her mouth.

"Pearl necklace and some coin. Someone was taking a nap in front of the fireplace and caught me before I could get anywhere else."

"Sofia. Sometimes she's in her room, so bad luck for you. Or maybe good?" Justine raised a questioning eyebrow.

"What about you?" Haarlock ignored her and gestured to the elf Justine was just robbing. "Make a new friend? And can they understand Common?"

"It's called *Common* for a reason, Haarlock. And thanks for pointing out that you speak Elvish better than me, by the way." Justine winked. "As for lonely Rolando, he's an easy mark. I make a few dozen gold from him alone each time I come here." Justine patted a belt pouch. "Depending on your *Sleight of Hand* Skill, you might want to try to get friendly with Esmeralda over there. She's got a few hundred gold in her one bracelet. Sadly, she's not into the ladies."

Justine nodded towards a stunningly beautiful woman lounging on a bed of pillows in front of a half-wall. The obscenely sheer, creamy silk dress she wore covered the same amount of skin as her jewelry.

"That seems enticing in all the wrong ways." Haarlock cleared his throat.

"Yes, it does. From what I've overheard, she's a literal man-killer. Likes to seduce and poison." Justine smiled seductively. "Wouldn't be a bad way to go."

Haarlock rolled his eyes. "Anyway. Since the wall clock over there is stuck at 4:18pm, I assume there's some kind of trigger to advance the scenario?"

"Correct. The clock starts once enough people are spoken to. I think you're supposed to gather information about the different factions so you can influence what happens at court."

"You think?"

"I don't stick around long enough to find out. The opening ceremony is *boring*, so I leave before it's over. Usually have enough loot by then, anyway. Want to head into the throne room and see what we can snag?"

"Sure."

Before they could turn around, the door to the space opened, and everyone else in the room went silent and turned to look. The rogues followed their gaze; they saw four heavily armored Dark Elves, two in front and two in back, surrounding another. The center elf, adorned in an ornate breastplate edged in gold overtop a white tunic and pants, wore a simple silver crown upon his head and a longsword on his hip. They stopped ten paces from the gathering.

The center elf spoke in a deep voice, his Elvish accented heavily. “I am Aran, king of these lands. You with the animal. Are you the lord from Lemuria?”

King Aran

Level 35 Master Swordsman

Hit Points - 400

Armor - 250

Abilities - Duelist, Impenetrable Armor,

Perfect Swordsmanship

Haarlock’s brow rose as high as it could go. “Yes.”

“We must speak.”

“What’s going on...” Before Justine could complete her sentence, the guard closest to her stepped forward and put a hand around the hilt of his sword.

“Who are you?” The king regarded Justine with suspicion.

“She’s my attendant, Your Majesty.” Haarlock stood as straight as he could, raising his chin ever so slightly.

“So be it.” The king nodded to the guard on his right. “Bring them both.”

19

The group left the soirée and went down the long hallway to the double doors at the far end, opening them to reveal the expansive throne room.

Its splendor came not from gaudy displays, but from the subtlety of a long history. Statues carved by hands with centuries of experience lined the circular room, each no doubt depicting a hero of old. Tapestries and paintings of nature scenes filled the spaces between the statues, each masterfully crafted. Four stone pillars made of smooth, pale marble supported the vaulted ceiling. The throne, a backless, single-person bench crafted from a solid piece of polished black stone, sat alone on the far side of the room.

King Aran moved with haste, stopping just before his seat of authority as the guards took up station in a wide circle around him.

"They tell me you are called Haarlock."

"Yes, Your Majesty."

Haarlock wasn't sure what to do, so he gave a slight bow. The king looked him over with an appraising eye before doing the same to Ladrón.

"I received no word of your attendance."

"It was a last moment thing. My attendant and I happened to be coming this way, and we were told to travel here just before we left."

Half-truths are better than whole lies, right?

Aran's red eyes tightened for a moment before he nodded once. "Then you are the only ones I can trust. Tonight will be the final court of my once beautiful kingdom." The king sat heavily on his throne. "And still the vultures circle, scheming in hushed tones to carve out whatever they can. Soon they shall come to carve what they can out of me."

"My apologies, Your Majesty, but I know little of your nation's history, nor that it was so soon to cease."

"That is a story too long and sad to tell here." Aran gestured to various paintings and statues. "If you so choose, much can be learned from our art, from our rise to our fall. It is a centuries long tragedy."

Justine cleared her throat and used *Thieves' Cant. "What is he saying?"*

"He's monologuing that people are plotting against him."

As the king gazed longingly around the room, Haarlock thought for a moment about what to ask next. The obvious choice was to find out who these vultures are, but would doing so advance the dungeon's storyline?

Only one way to find out.

"How may we be of service against these vultures, Your Majesty?"

"Tonight's court determines how this kingdom will be divided amongst the remaining nobles. Nobles who vie for every scrap they can get. Any who are alive, that is."

Haarlock frowned. "You worry about assassination?"

"Do you see my guard? There are four now, when once they numbered ten. Accidents and disease do not target so precisely."

"What benefit does your death bring?"

"In truth? Very little. But some find what little I have to be of value." Aran laid a hand on the hilt of his sword. "This weapon is an heirloom from the very founding of our kingdom. Whoever wields it is the rightful ruler of the Dark Elf people. I worry that if another were to claim it, legitimately or not, what little civility exists here tonight would devolve into lethal infighting for decades to come."

"Apologies, Your Majesty, but I don't understand what role myself or my attendant could play in this. I am told none here are a match for you."

"Were it that simple, Lord Haarlock. I have no doubt someone will challenge me for the right to wield this sword." The king tapped his breastplate. "Duels are fought without armor, and without mine I will be vulnerable to assassination."

"You wish for me to guard you?"

"I wish for you to be the first to challenge me."

"What?" Haarlock's eyes went wide.

Aran let out a hearty laugh. "Worry not, lord, it is all a performance. You will challenge me, and I will capitulate. Our laws state that only a noble may challenge another noble. They say nothing of race, creed, or gender. When you claim the sword, you will rightfully be king."

"Ah." A smirk came across Haarlock's face. "I assume no non-Dark Elf has ever held the position of king?"

"Never."

"And you hope the chaos your forfeiture causes will draw out any conspirators."

"Yes. Though your life would be in exceedingly grave danger." Aran gestured to Justine. "As would your attendant."

"Are you talking about me?" Justine signed in short, stiff motions. *"What's going on?"*

"Figuring out the last of it now. Hold on."

Haarlock crossed his arms as he thought for a moment. "What then?"

"Of that I am unsure. There may be no assassin, or there may be several. Perhaps you will be treated with all the respect our ways demand, though I would guess that is unlikely."

"If fighting breaks out?"

"Give me back the sword and try to stay alive."

"I'm going to need a moment to decide."

Haarlock turned to Justine and waved her in close, then gave her a rundown of the plotline.

"So, what do you want to do?" Haarlock gestured with his head towards the king. "Do we stay and risk our lives, or leave with what we took so far?"

Justine put both hands on her head. "Knowing we don't have to fight Aran or his guards, staying seems survivable. Speaking of, I thought he was the dungeon boss? Why is he asking for our help?"

"I may have told several people I'm a lord visiting from another kingdom."

"I should have known. Interactive dungeons like these can have several win conditions."

"Even so, if we're not fighting Aran, then we don't know who or what we will be fighting. I'm willing to risk it, but if you want to go, we will. What's it going to be?"

"When in doubt, ask a raccoon." Justine looked at Haarlock's shoulder accessory. "What say you, Ladrón?"

The animal looked between Aran and the door to the hallway several times, chittering to himself quietly. Eventually he growled and punched the air.

"**Fight. Win.**"

"Attaboy. Let's do this." Justine gave the critter a head tussle.

Haarlock turned back to Aran. "I will help you, Your Majesty."

"Thank you, lord." Aran raised his chin. "Only a fool would risk their life without compensation. What is your price?"

"What do you offer?"

"I have no lands to give, nor titles to bestow. Perhaps gold or jewels?"

"Equipment is acceptable."

Aran smirked. "A wise choice. What would you use?"

"My attendant wears a ring that deflects arrows. I would use something similar."

With a snap of his fingers, the guard to his left approached. The armored elf removed his left gauntlet and took a thin, silver band from his right index finger and handed it over.

"This should suffice, Lord Haarlock."

The king offered the item, and Haarlock took and examined it.

Ring of Spell Deflection

Rare

Abilities - Spell Deflection

Like Justine's ring's ability, *Spell Deflection* would redirect any Level 4 or lower spell away from the wearer up to four times per day. Haarlock could consciously allow a beneficial spell through, though.

"Thank you, Your Majesty, this is acceptable payment."

"Good." The king looked at the doorway into the throne room. "Court begins shortly. Prepare yourself."

***

Haarlock and Justine stood to the left of the king, halfway between the throne and the doorway. The minutiae of Dark Elf culture ensured a rigid process for everything, especially in matters of court. As a visitor and a noble, Haarlock held an elevated position of prominence, but to be any closer to the king would be an insult to attendees of higher status.

Antonio Rivera Salamanca, Scribe, sat on a small stool beside the king. He held a large journal on his lap and a quill poised in one hand. The four armored guards stood in a row behind the throne.

A voice announced the names and titles of the attendees. Each wore a simple wardrobe of white, with men in shirts and pants and women in floor-length dresses. Nobles adorned themselves in gold, and non-nobles in silver. Groups stopped at the appropriate distance, though they all gave odd stares and displeased whispers towards the two rogues. Their lack of proper attire and the faux pas of bringing an animal to court seemed to be quite upsetting to some.

Thirty-one attendees in total arrived. Next came greetings, well wishes, and mild discussions. Haarlock recognized most of those here from the soirée room, but why protocol dictated yet more small talk was anyone's guess. Once the pleasantries finished an hour later, a gong rang out, and the room fell silent. King Aran stood in one smooth motion.

"Welcome, esteemed lords and ladies." Aran gestured to each noble and greeted them by name, waiting to address Haarlock last. "Our guest from Lemuria, Lord Haarlock, has come far to witness these proceedings. Though we must deviate some from established customs this night."

Murmurs filled the space, and the king held up a hand to silence them.

"It has come to my attention that someone in attendance finds my leadership...lacking. There is but one answer to these accusations."

Aran unbuckled his breastplate and let it fall to the floor beside him, the *clang* of metal causing several to jump. He drew his sword and stepped forward.

"By the ancient customs, whomsoever finds my governance lacking, step forward now and meet me in combat."

A heavy silence fell over the crowd. Haarlock waited until Aran met his eyes, then stepped forward and spoke in Elvish.

"I, Lord Haarlock of Lemuria, do hereby challenge your rule. Face me, Aran, or be called a coward."

Ladrón climbed to the floor as Haarlock unbuckled the straps to his armor. The crowd, though, responded with disbelieving gasps. Someone shouted *heresy*, but Aran jabbed his blade in their direction.

"Heresy? Tell me where in our laws it says the challenge must be a Dark Elf. Haarlock is a noble. He speaks our tongue. He said the words. What heresy do you speak save your own cowardice?"

Haarlock handed his armor to Justine, then drew his dirk and walked to within ten paces of King Aran. The king raised an eyebrow as he looked from his longsword to the much smaller blade.

"Your weapon is chosen?"

"It is, Your Majesty. Do you accept my challenge?"

"I do."

Aran brought his sword into a high guard and walked forward. Haarlock, standing casually with his weapon hanging loose at his side, watched as the king stopped two paces from him and kneeled.

"You are the superior warrior, Lord Haarlock. I forfeit and beg for my life." The Dark Elf laid his longsword across his open palms and held it out. "Claim my station and show me mercy."

The crowd erupted. Everyone, from noble to commoner, jabbed their fingers as they hurled curses. Justine, Ladrón on her shoulder, backed away as she drew her dual daggers.

Haarlock sheathed his dirk and took the blade by the hilt and examined it.

Heirloom Longsword

Mastercrafted

Damage (Piercing) - 25

Damage (Slashing) - 125

Abilities - Balanced, Improved Armor Piercing

Alert screamed in Haarlock's head while *Uncanny Dodge* told him to leap to the left. As he did so, an arrow slammed into Aran's chest, knocking him onto his back.

Cries of fear and pain rang out as Haarlock rolled to his feet. Four hooded assassins, all wearing identical black, blank-faced masks, materialized behind the king's guards. In a single motion, they executed the four armored men with glowing daggers. Before the assembled Dark Elf nobles could react, the assassins rushed towards them, slitting throats and stabbing chests with abandon. One woman Haarlock recognized as Esmeralda, the woman Justine described as a *man-killer*, pointed towards Haarlock and Justine.

"Kill the human and his elf bitch!" Venom oozed from Esmeralda's words.

A masked assassin rushed at Haarlock, a curved dagger slashing towards his neck. Haarlock brought the heirloom sword up and knocked the weapon away, but over-corrected and left his chest open. The assassin kicked him onto his back, then leaped onto him, blade once again going for his throat.

With mere inches to spare, Haarlock cast *Magic Armor* on himself just in time to divert the weapon from his skin into the ground next to his head. A headbutt to the assassin's nose and a knee to their groin allowed Haarlock the opening to push them off him. The assassin made an easy target with the longsword once Haarlock got to his feet. The blade went through his chest and into the floor with little resistance.

Looking around, Haarlock found Justine in the chaos. She fought with a short-haired Dark Elf wielding a glowing blade. Justine kept the man on the defensive with her dual daggers while Ladrón nipped at his heels.

Haarlock heard a groan behind him and spun, sword at the ready, to see Aran sitting up. The arrow, actually a bolt from a crossbow, stuck out from just below the ribs on the left side. Blood leaked from the wound, soaking the king's clothing.

"You're alive." Haarlock offered his hand, and the king pulled himself to his feet with a grunt. "Can you fight?"

"A flesh wound. My weapon, please." Aran held out his right hand and grimaced when Haarlock gave him the longsword. "Perhaps it is more serious than that."

With a flash, Aran swung his sword in front of him and cut a crossbow bolt from the air. Haarlock turned to see a fifth blank-faced assassin duck into the shadow of the pillar he hid behind.

That was a mistake.

Haarlock cast *Shadow Tendrils* on the assassin, then gave Ladrón a command to dispatch him. The raccoon darted between feet and bodies, diving headlong into the darkness where writhing shadows held the assassin in place. A few seconds later, Haarlock received an XP notification.

"Very efficient, Lord Haarlock. Thank you."

"My pleasure, Your Majesty."

Taking stock of the room, Haarlock could see two Dark Elves wielding glowing blades guarding Esmeralda as she rushed towards the exit. More than half the attendees were dead, with most of the other half already gone. Ladrón was back with Justine, and the two of them stood at the ready off to the right side.

Aran holstered his sword, pulled the bolt from his chest, then cast a healing spell on himself. The wound sizzled away, and he sighed a breath of relief. He picked up his previously discarded breastplate and slipped it on.

"This strike was intended to decapitate, and it failed. Esmeralda is no fool. She will have reinforcements."

Haarlock waved Justine over. Ladrón stayed on the ground, his eyes darting around, searching for more enemies.

The king switched to Common. "Thank you, Justine. You have done your liege well."

"Liege? Right..." Justine chuckled to herself. "I'm just glad to help."

"This is no longer your fight, Lord Haarlock. Your honor will sustain no blemishes should you choose to leave."

"What will it be, Justine?" Haarlock gave her a raised eyebrow.

The rogue looked around while she bit her lip, then pointed to a six-inch-long burn mark through her shirt. "That glowing knife guy nearly gutted me. I don't think I'll do very well in a stand-up fight. Let's go."

"You heard the lady, Your Majesty. We're leaving."

"So be it." Aran pointed his sword at a painting of an armored figure on a horse. "Behind that image is a secret passage. It will take you into the sitting parlor, and from there you can make your escape."

Just then the room's double doors burst open and a trio of fully armored men wielding broadswords rushed in. It took them only a second to find Aran and charge.

"Go! Now!"

Aran darted forward to meet them, his blade slicing through both the sword and the arm of the first enemy.

Ladrón made it to the painting first, tearing at the canvas and wriggling his way into the passage. Haarlock tore a person-sized rend, then gestured for Justine to enter first.

"Such a gentleman."

The elf went in as Haarlock watched King Aran cut down enemy after enemy. How many there were, Haarlock didn't know, but he was glad they didn't stay. He dipped into the passage to find it dark except for the light from the hole in the canvas.

"You can see in the dark, right?" Justine stood 20 feet further in, looking down a turn in the hallway. "There doesn't seem to be any torches, and I don't have a glow stone."

"Yeah, I can see." Even though Justine was petite, Haarlock still had to squeeze past her in the narrow passage. "Looks like more of the same, ending maybe sixty feet further down."

"See what's down there."

Ladrón chittered his understanding and explored ahead. A few seconds later the passage filled with light as he disappeared.

"Looks like he found the exit." Justine huffed.

The pair followed behind, finding themselves in one of the guest rooms. Exiting, they found the same room Sofia De Costa had been in, though now it was empty.

Justine went to the hallway door, gingerly unlocked it, then opened the door and peeked out. She shut the door and signed in *Thieves' Cant.*

"One guard. Full armor. To the left, back to the door."

Haarlock took Justine's place and drew his dirk. He slowly opened the door, then leaped out and drove his blade through the man's back. *Sneak Attack,*

Chink in Armor, *Silent Kill*, and *Murder* ensured the guard died without making a sound.

With no one else to stop them, they bolted for the exit and out of the dungeon. But outside, in the dark and cold, more enemies waited. Ladrón made an excellent distraction, zigging and zagging between the armored Dark Elves, allowing Justine and Haarlock to rush past. Arrows and spells peppered the ground around them, but none found their mark. Two rogues and a raccoon sprinted into the night at full speed, putting as much ground between them and *The Fallen Kingdom* as they could.

***

Justine collapsed to her knees back at the camp, her chest heaving as she tried to catch her breath in the winter air.

"By the gods!" She laughed as she fell onto her back. "I thought that one guard was going to catch us."

Haarlock, bent over at the waist, hands on his knees, nodded enthusiastically as he, too, took in huge chestfuls of air. He righted himself and put a finger through a hole in his left pant leg.

"An arrow almost got me. That would have sucked." Haarlock waved his hand and cast *Mend*. The hole vanished. "All better."

"Oooo, that's handy." Justine sat up now, her knees to her chest. "I'm going to take the next couple of levels in mage so I can get more spells. Right now, I only have ones useful for thieving. You took a Feat to get magic, right?"

"Yup. *Magic Initiate*. One of the first abilities I got, really." Haarlock frowned. "But I'm not sure what direction to go now."

"What do you mean?"

"I've been working towards a specific sub-specialization. I hit Level 20 from the dungeon, but I don't have the requirements to take it."

Justine huffed in amusement. "Ah, yes, I know exactly what you mean. Do you wait five more levels and hope you get the requirements, or take a different sub-specialization now?"

"That pretty much sums it up." Haarlock sighed. "I need to get *Mastery* with *Stealth*, but I can't seem to reach it. Granted, I don't do all that much sneaking around."

"What are you going for?"

Haarlock pursed his lips. Should he tell her? Would not telling her be suspicious?

"Phantom Blade."

Justine whistled long and low. "That's a doozy. I'd recommend waiting."

"Really?"

"Oh yes. There's like, what, two or three other Phantom Blades operating in this kingdom? You'd be highly sought after once you join their ranks." Justine frowned as she looked at the ground, then looked up at Haarlock with a raised eyebrow. "You're not who I think of when I think of an assassin."

"Thank you?"

"No, nothing like that. Have you even taken an assassination quest yet? Or been to the assassin branch?"

"No to both." Haarlock shrugged. "When I first arrived, I thought this was all some kind of fever dream as I lay dying in the mountains of the previous world. So, I picked my starting levels and abilities based on that premise. Come to find out..."

Haarlock gestured wide and Justine laughed.

"Fair enough, Haarlock. Fair enough. Seems your choices have done you well."

"They really have. Now that I think about it, I should have gone mage so I could really min-max things. Or been like a carpenter or something."

"A carpenter?"

Justine's incredulous look caused Haarlock to laugh.

"I don't see myself as one either."

A shiver ran through Justine. She got to her feet and retrieved her cloak. "It's going to suck when the adrenaline wears off."

"The crash is rough. Ladrón's going to sleep *good* tonight."

"Where is the little guy, anyway?"

"Apparently running for his life was too much fun, and he wanted to stay back to lead away any potential pursuers. He should be back soon."

Justine shook her head. "What a crazy animal."

"You're telling me..."

Both laughed.

"Alright, Haarlock. Put that fire starter of yours to work and get us warm." Justine pulled her cloak tighter.

Five minutes later their fire burned at a steady pace. Haarlock, sitting on a log and wrapped in his hooded cloak, reviewed his notifications as he idly poked the flames with a stick.

Congratulations! You have completed the dungeon: The Fallen Kingdom. *You have been awarded 6,000 experience.*

You have leveled up! Would you like to apply one (1) levels to Rogue?

Your one (1) levels have been applied to your Rogue class. Your stats have been adjusted accordingly.

You have received the following rogue Class Ability: Improved Sneak Attack.

You receive one (1) Talent every two (2) levels. You currently have one (1) Talents to choose.

You receive one (1) Feat every five (5) levels. You currently have one (1) Feats to choose.

You may pick a new class sub-specialization at Level 20. If you do not choose a sub-specialization at this time, you will have

THE CHANCE EVERY FIVE (5) LEVELS. WOULD YOU LIKE TO CHANGE YOUR SUB-SPECIALIZATION NOW?

First, *Improved Sneak Attack*. It increased *Sneak Attack's* damage multiplier from 2x to 3x. Combined with *Murder*, it now did 6x damage. Add in the increased damage from *Sjena's Gift* and the bonus from Haarlock's *Mastery* with *Daggers*; few enemies would survive such an attack.

Haarlock already knew which Talent to pick. Not too long ago, a Trainer told him he lacked the necessary movement abilities to allow his class to really shine. Hence *Agile*. That ability came in handy when he scaled the side of a building, looking for Mateo Cabrera's apartment. But he still had trouble doing it. That's why *Climber* was Haarlock's next Talent.

What Feat to pick was a difficult choice. They allowed otherwise physically impossible abilities, and there were oh so many to pick from. Haarlock looked through the choices, weighing if he should pick one to increase his offense or survivability. Increased magical capabilities would be nice, but until he reached *Magic Theory: Skilled*, he was stuck on that front. After what felt like an eternity of waffling, Haarlock picked *Increased Reflexes*.

As the name suggested, Haarlock's overall subconscious reflex action increased roughly 20%. This would open other fun avenues, like being able to deflect, or even catch, incoming arrows. Overall, though, this further improved his already considerable skill with daggers. Being able to block and riposte faster than the average opponent would be invaluable.

NAME: Haarlock		**CLASS**: Shadowdancer	
RACE: Human		**LEVEL**: 19	
AGE: 30		**EXPERIENCE**: 72,627	
RENOWN/INFAMY: 670/288		**TITLE**: Lord	
STATS:		**GUILD RANK**: Copper	

HP - 130	STR - 25	DEX - 70	INT - 30
WIS - 25	CON - 53	CHA - 40	

SKILLS:

Master	Expert	Skilled	Proficient
Dagger	Stealth	Tracking	Sleight of Hand
	Survival	Athletics	Simple Weapons
	Unarmed Combat	Spycraft	Skinning
	Lock Pick	Bow	Vintner
		Bartering	Estate Management
			Magic Theory

CLASS ABILITIES:	**FEATS**:	**TALENTS**:
Thieves' Cant	Alert	Canny Observer
Sneak Attack	Magic Novice	Resilient
Uncanny Dodge	Pass Without Trace	Hidden Blade
Deft Hands	Wrapped in Shadow	Improved Animal Bond
Darkvision		Shadow Dance
Chink in Armor		Nondescript
Murder		Silent Kill
		Agile

SPELLS:

Cantrips	1st Level	2nd Level
Mage Hand	Umbral Step	Shadow Tendrils
Mend	Magic Armor	
Shadowstep		

A few minutes later Justine added another armful of wood to their stockpile, then sat down next to him.

"It feels like it'll get colder by morning." The elf stretched her hands out to the flames.

"Yes, it does." Haarlock looked up at the walls of the dry riverbed they were in. "At least we're out of the wind."

Justine scooted a little closer. "We could share cloaks and keep the heat in even better."

"Could we now?" Haarlock's eyebrows rose as he continued to poke at the fire.

"I don't know about you, but I'm still wired. Be a nice way to wind down after such an exciting dungeon delve."

She had a point. Haarlock's adrenaline may have worn off, but he was still wide awake, and would be for a few more hours, at least. Plus, it didn't hurt that Justine was a beautiful woman.

Could he? Obviously. Should he? Now there was the problem.

Bringing physicality into the mix would complicate things. Sex, no matter how casual, still altered two people's relationship, even if minutely. Even before this whole spy game started, Justine flirted with him. Was this a natural progression of that, or a ploy on her part to gain some kind of emotional advantage over him? Would it be suspicious if he said *no*?

Haarlock thought about the whys and the why nots, but it only took him a minute to decide: he would take what was given.

20

Just after noon, eight and a half days after they disembarked from the *Hygeia*, Haarlock heard the sounds of civilization. A dull drone permeated the otherwise quiet forest, along with the distant, regular *ding* of a blacksmith's forge.

Justine stopped a few hundred feet from the forest's edge. "Alright, Haarlock, Claville is just over the ridge. It's grown a lot in the last twenty years, so it's a mess of winding streets and dead ends. Try not to get lost."

"What's the growth for?" Haarlock kneeled and pulled Ladrón off his shoulder. The animal growled in displeasure.

"The town's always been an overland midpoint between Sathe and Zilgas, so that and the otherwise mediocre iron and copper mining prospects in the area kept it alive. Then, two decades ago, someone found a rich silver vein. Before Claville's population held steady around a thousand people. Now? Easily five thousand permanent residents along with another few thousand or so transients."

"Went from a stopping-off point to a trade hub."

"Exactly." Justine shrugged. "But where there's money, there's crime. The Thieves' Guild here sees its fair share of action. Speaking of which, that's our first stop."

"It is?" Haarlock raised an eyebrow. "I'd like to hit up someplace where I can take a bath. A *hot* one."

"Plenty of time for that." The elf laughed. "Marcon wants me to make a delivery first thing. Plus, we need to find you a ride to Sathe, and Simon will know the schedule better than anyone."

Haarlock frowned and then sighed. "Of course Marcon gave you a delivery."

"He's a sneaky one, that's for sure." Justine smirked. "Makes me wonder what he asked you to do."

"Oh, a little of this and a little of that." Haarlock did his best to shrug nonchalantly, putting faith in his ring of obfuscation to make himself convincing.

"No doubt." Justine looked over Haarlock. "No one is going to bat an eye at the two of us coming out of the woods. Lots of would-be prospectors and hunters in the area. Just keep to yourself and don't flash your signet ring around."

Haarlock held up a gloved hand. "Got it, literally, covered."

Justine nodded once and walked towards the tree line. Haarlock looked down at Ladrón.

"Remember, keep her in sight no matter what."

Ladrón chittered once and fixed his gaze on the woman.

It took another ten minutes for the town to come into view. A small river cut through the center, leading from distant mountains in the southwest and heading north into the woods. The main road, easily wide enough for three carts to pass side by side, wove from east to west. This split the town roughly into four equal sectors.

Buildings along the main road were the most developed, all reaching at least three stories tall. Those further back looked to be residential or storage, with most of the manufacturing clustered on the north side by the river, its current providing power to the massive water wheels dotting its banks.

Like Justine said, this place was a trading hub. The road held a steady stream of covered wagons, stretching into the distance. Mustering areas on each side of the road held even more.

They reached the town's edge in twenty minutes, blending in with a trio of well-guarded caravans and their escorts. Justine struck up a conversation right away, asking about the goings-on in the area. Apparently, bandits were a problem to the east, hence the extra muscle.

As they approached, Haarlock caught sight of some kind of official speaking to each caravan. When their group arrived, the man, a rail-thin human in a red cloak, took the driver's origin, destination, and copied his manifest. He didn't bother to ask either Haarlock or Justine anything, nor make eye contact.

Once inside the town proper, things became *far* more cramped. Two carts could pass with ease down the main thoroughfare...if there weren't any people. Or stalls. With those things, it made for a winding, shouting, unruly mess.

Justine grabbed Haarlock's hand and pulled him through the crowds with ease, crossing the street to avoid a busy stall or dodging a stopped cart. Once they were three blocks in, she took him through a winding path north through several alleys, then west across the river and back south again to a small manufacturing hub. Two blacksmiths, a glassblower, and a silversmith huddled around a simple stone well, and the constant *ting* of metal on metal filled the space.

"We're two blocks north of the main road on the west side of the river. As you saw, the roads are a nightmare to navigate, so if you're trying to get to the Thieves' Guild, get to this spot then go down that alley." Justine pointed to a narrow space behind the glass blower, tucked between a pair of two-story wooden housing blocks. "You'll see the cant sigils soon enough."

"Getting here will be the real trick." Haarlock huffed as he looked around. "This place really could have used a city planner."

"It's what happens when you triple in size in as many years."

Justine gestured for Haarlock to follow before walking into the alley. They went a hundred feet before they saw *Thieves' Cant* sign for *guildhall* above a sturdy-looking door. Inside and down into an empty basement, then through a brick tunnel for another hundred feet. At the end stood a muscled orc with a face a mother probably couldn't love.

"Hey there, Pierre." Justine shared a handshake with the orc. "This is Haarlock. He's new."

"Right." Pierre gave Haarlock the once-over. "Nice pet."

"Thanks." Haarlock reflexively patted Ladrón's side.

"Back to visit family?"

"Yup. My idiot brother keeps bothering me about making the trip more often. He needs to come up to Ostia sometime." Justine huffed.

"I feel ya." Pierre nodded.

"Anyway, see you around."

Pierre opened the door, and Haarlock followed Justine inside the guildhall. Much like the others he'd been to, this place looked similar. A large job board hung on the far wall, and a bar filled the opposite corner. Tables with hooded figures lay in between, and a single room next to the job board was likely the guildmaster's office.

"Someone will let Simon know I'm here, if he doesn't already. Let's get a drink."

Justine nudged Haarlock with her elbow and headed to the bar. He joined her, and they each ordered an ale, with Ladrón receiving a bowl of water and pretzels.

"Simon sounds like an important person."

"He's the guildmaster, so a little, yeah. I've known him for a *long* time. Too long."

"What's that supposed to mean?"

"We became rogues at the same time. Spent a few years together in Ostia before he moved back home. He became the guildmaster about ten years ago."

Haarlock looked around the space. "This place couldn't have been very busy before the mining boom."

"It wasn't. The last guildmaster led a very comfortable life before things got crazy. They've had to move the guildhall twice."

"That sounds...fun." Haarlock downed half his ale, then regarded his drink. "This is good."

"Sathe makes excellent ale, and a good deal of it comes through here." Justine clinked her glass to Haarlock's. "I've had many late nights and rough mornings on this stuff."

"Somehow that doesn't surprise me." Haarlock laughed as he finished his drink. "But one is enough for me."

A voice came from behind them. "Your advice is almost as good as Justine's scarf."

Justine spun in her seat and stood, then rushed to the diminutive figure standing there. The older human man huffed as the elf crushed him in a hug.

His lime green tunic stood in stark contrast to the mostly gray, fire-red hair draped over his shoulders. Especially compared to Justine's brown hair and muted earth-tone clothing.

"And it's mighty good to see you, too." Simon patted Justine's back, then took a deep breath when she let go. "Your brother's been bothering me to strong-arm you into coming back more often."

"Meh." Justine waved dismissively. "He'll see me when he sees me."

"Of that I have no doubt. Who's your friend?"

Haarlock stood and offered his hand. "Haarlock. That's Ladrón."

"Simon, guildmaster of this branch." Simon shook the hand and gave Haarlock a once-over. "What brings you to our guildhall? Jobs, what little there are, won't be posted till midnight. Doubt any will be of use to someone of your level."

"Oh, nothing like that. Just a stopping point on my way to Sathe. Justine offered to keep me company from Ostia to here."

"Couldn't have you getting lost in the woods." Justine looked at Simon and gestured with her head towards Haarlock. "We cleared out *The Fallen Kingdom* on the way. That's a story you're going to need to hear."

Simon grimaced. "Come on, Justine. You have to stop doing that. It'll get you killed one of these times."

Something in the man's voice triggered *Canny Observer*. Haarlock didn't know what it was, but the words he said didn't seem to match how he said them.

"Is anything wrong, Haarlock?" Simon tilted his head.

"What? Oh, no." Haarlock laughed to himself. "That dungeon was a little rough, is all."

Justine gave him a momentary look of confusion before returning to the conversation.

"Anyway. We literally came straight here, and I haven't had a decent meal in a week. Want to meet for dinner in an hour or two? I'm going to get a hot soak right after this."

"Excellent idea. A new stew place opened on the main road, and I haven't been there yet."

"Sure." Justine looked at Haarlock and raised an eyebrow. "Join us?"

"No. I'm going to get on the road again as soon as possible."

Justine pouted sarcastically. "Aw, that's too bad. We could take in a few sights before you go. Maybe do some shopping?"

"Sorry. I want to get there sooner rather than later."

Simon jabbed his thumb over his shoulder. "Two blocks west of the river and one block south of the horse stable is a popular mustering yard. I'm sure you can find a caravan to ride along with."

"Thanks for the recommendation." Haarlock mentally nudged Ladrón. "And with that, I'll take my leave."

"Make sure to come find me when you're back in Ostia, okay?" Justine winked seductively.

Haarlock smirked, said goodbye to Simon, and he and Ladrón made their way out into the cold air. He went back to the main road, then into the cheapest-looking inn he could find and bought a room. And a hot bath for both him and Ladrón.

As the heat suffused his body, Haarlock thought back to what Simon said and *how* he said it. Why did his comment about Justine getting killed trigger *Canny Observer*? Was it the man's worry for his friend, or could it be that he knew something more? Something sinister?

Whatever the case, Haarlock needed to see what Justine would do now that they were here. The question was: when would she do it?

Not only did Haarlock have no idea *if* she would do something, but he also had no idea *what* she would do, let alone when. Would it be as simple and neigh undetectable as a dead drop, or a hand off in passing? Unless Haarlock was there, watching every move she made, he wouldn't see it happen. And, while he soaked in a tub of hot water, Justine could be passing on information to Simon.

No, that wasn't it.

Haarlock felt Justine was here for something more than a simple hand off. He couldn't place why, though. Maybe it was the fact that she had come all this way. That much effort meant she was going to meet someone face to face.

But when and where?

It wouldn't be tonight. There was no way for her to know when they'd arrive, let alone be able to get word to...the calling cards. Roboute mentioned she might have one.

Haarlock shook his head. There were too many variables, too many what ifs to think yourself into a corner of indecision. Something told him Justine wouldn't act until at least tomorrow. Like him, she'd want to decompress and relax. Mistakes were made when you were in a rush, and Justine didn't seem the type to rush a job.

And this all hinged on the idea that Justine was a subversive agent on a secret mission, not someone coming home to visit family.

Ugh, I really dislike all this spy crap.

Haarlock dipped his head underwater. When he came back up, he looked over at Ladrón and laughed. The animal floated on his back in his own tub, suds almost entirely covering him. Taking his cue, Haarlock poured in more soap, lathered himself up, then sank in as far as he could.

21

Following Justine proved more difficult than Haarlock expected. The woman kept an active, if benign, schedule, going from shop to restaurant to her family's home on the eastern side of town in seemingly no pattern. The frigid weather didn't slow her down, and Haarlock lost her more than once in the dense, winding streets. Especially when she left the busier areas of town to head home. Huddled masses, hooded cloaks, and incomprehensible city planning didn't help any either.

Her family lived in a modest two-story house with a blue tile roof and a small garden plot in front. Like the surrounding structures, the wooden building needed some TLC. More than a few lights shone through the walls at night, and the chimney's mortar crumbled in several places. Luckily, there were plenty of windows for Haarlock to spy through, even if it made him feel uncomfortable. Especially crouched on someone else's roof. In the dark.

Four people lived there. Haarlock assumed the skinnier, dark-haired elf was a cousin or nephew, as Justine treated him with far more care than the bulkier one with blonde hair. That had to be the brother. The female elf, who could be Justine's sister by her looks, carried herself like a mother, providing drinks, snacks, and the occasional soft touch. Justine's father rarely made an appearance. The few times Haarlock caught a glimpse of him showed he was in poor health, with an obvious limp and, even for an elf, pallid skin.

Justine and the two younger men made regular trips out. Most were to the market for ingredients, though on the third day they went to another residence for a few hours. Likely friends, as much exclaiming and hugging were directed at and given to Justine. What they did was anyone's guess, but the trio spent most of the day inside before returning home at dusk.

By the fifth day, Haarlock wondered if Justine would actually do anything suspicious. At least, anything suspicious he could witness. Once, back in his first year of Delta Force, Haarlock was assigned to follow a Brazilian businessman. The powers that be didn't want him, but his contact in the cartels. So, for 10 *long* days he followed the businessman, sitting outside his office, coffee shops, and even his mistress' apartment, all in the sweltering heat of a South American summer. In the end, another of his team caught the mistress with a manila folder hidden in an oversized handbag. She was the go-between, leaving the businessman clear of any direct connection.

Did Justine employ such a measure? Were her friends, relatives, or Simon her go-between? It took another two days for time to tell.

An insistent raccoon shook Haarlock out of his nap. He'd been curled up in his cloak, huddled between a chimney and a shed to keep out of the wind.

"Seriously, what?"

*"*Person. Strange. Visit.*"*

Haarlock shot to his feet, adrenaline turning his mind from asleep to awake in an instant. A quick look around in the dim morning light showed no one in sight.

"Where?"

Ladrón scurried across the ground, hugging the wall, and went down a short connector between two alleys. He stopped and pointed at a gap between houses.

Three roads met behind Justine's family home to form a small courtyard, and in it stood a figure in a brown hooded cloak. Whoever it was had their back to Haarlock, though they were either young or on the short side. After a few seconds they threw something at the house, and a very soft *tink* filled the area. If it wasn't for *Canny Observer*, Haarlock doubted he would hear it over the sounds of city life.

Tink.

Tink.

Finally, a door opened, and the figure straightened. Ladrón, who'd climbed higher to get a better vantage point, commentated from his point of view.

"**Justine. Approach.*"

The elf rogue was bundled up, the ends of her blue-banded scarf hanging out from under her hood. Justine walked over to the figure, and the pair spoke in hushed tones. The streets made enough of a funnel that Haarlock could just hear them.

"Seriously? You're throwing stones now? And it wasn't even at the right window."

"Sorry." The figure shrugged. "I know what address you're staying at, not which room."

"What's so important that we must talk before I'm done with breakfast? *And* meet me in person, at my house, no less? We're rogues. Subtlety is what we do. This isn't subtle."

The figure looked over their shoulder, and for the briefest moment Haarlock could see their face. Simon's face. Ladrón confirmed with a psychic message.

"Your friend made contact not twenty minutes ago."

Justine perked up. "It's about damn time."

"I know the guildhall is supposed to host your meeting, but something spooked him. Now he wants a one-on-one, alone, at the ruins."

"For the love of the gods." Justine rubbed her face. "That's at least a two-hour hike into the woods. And in *this* weather?"

"Listen, I don't know what his deal is, okay? He showed up during the morning rush while I was getting my coffee. I barely got a dozen words in before he ran off."

"Did you follow him?"

"I tried to, but it was the morning rush." Simon shrugged again.

"Fair enough. He must have uncovered something important."

"Agreed. He said to meet at four o'clock tonight and to come alone. If anyone else is there with you, he'll vanish."

Justine crossed her arms. "Did he say anything else?"

"Nothing."

"Damn. Alright, thank you for the update."

"You want me for backup? Could be a set up."

"Oh, please. You think everything is a set up."

"Hey, I offered."

"Yes and thank you. But if he's as spooked as you say, I'd rather not take the chance." Justine paused for several seconds. "I'm going to get there early. If you don't hear from me by tomorrow morning, assume something happened and come search for me."

Simon dropped his shoulders. "That's a *long* walk."

"What are friends for?" Justine laughed, then turned serious again. "I'll be back when I can. If you're not there, I'll leave a message."

"Good luck."

The two exchanged handshakes. Justine went back to her house, and Simon went the opposite way, coming around the corner to Haarlock's left. Haarlock watched Simon stop, turn to look behind him for a long moment, exhale slowly, then turn around and keep going out of sight.

What was that look for?

It didn't trigger *Canny Observer*, but the small man was far away and mostly hidden by clothing. Whatever it meant, Haarlock didn't have time to contemplate it for very long. He needed to find out what and where *the ruins* were.

It was 8am or so now. A two-hour hike, plus her getting there early, meant he only had a handful of hours to find out where she was going. Sure, he could simply follow her, but she was a rogue with *Pass Without Trace.* All it would take was for him to lose sight of her in the forest and she'd be gone...without a trace. Plus, he didn't want to risk keeping too close and triggering her abilities. If she didn't suspect him already, that'd be a dead giveaway.

Haarlock waited until Ladrón signaled the all clear, then rushed to the main road. As usual, hundreds of people went about their business, all of them a mess of bodies and horse-drawn carts. Haarlock needed somewhere that sold maps, and there just so happened to be a business called *Treasure Hunter's Dream* near the river.

Twenty years ago, a silver mine was discovered, bringing untold wealth to the town. It also brought thousands of people looking to get rich off their own vein of precious metal. *Treasure Hunter's Dream* provided every tool and resource imaginable to help do that.

Inside the store, an expansive space smelling of oil, two people browsed a shelf of metal digging tools. They gave Haarlock, and Ladrón in particular, a weird look when he rushed in through the door. Behind the counter, the shop owner, an old, weathered-looking human, put down his paper and stared wide-eyed at the pair.

"Can I help ya?"

Haarlock walked to the counter and sat ten silver coins on top. "Yes. I need a map of the local ruins. Specifically, an old map that would have locations of little value to people."

"What?" The man's weathered face scrunched up.

"It's important." Ten more silver joined the first stack.

The man exhaled as he looked at the money, then kneeled behind the counter. He rummaged around for almost a minute before grunting in satisfaction. When he came back up, he held a large wooden crate of rolled-up papers. Most of the documents' edges were frayed and cracked, and all were yellowed to various degrees.

"Got anything more specific than that? This area is lousy with ruins, both large and small, above ground and below."

"They're inside a wooded area approximately a two-hour hike away, but I don't know which direction. I'm going to assume they're in a secluded location, though."

"Got to be on the north side, then." The man slid the coins to the side and sat six of the scrolls down, then put the box on the floor. He spoke as he unfurled the first, placing round, flat stones on each corner to keep it flat. "The real trick will be narrowing it down more than that."

Haarlock looked at the dozens and dozens of symbols marked on the map: caves, ravines, old riverbeds, ruins, and more.

"How accurate is this?"

"This one was made, oh, a hundred years back. Granted, this won't have all the ruins marked on it, but it's probably the best one I have."

"Why not all of them?"

"Those woods are big, and this is one map."

"Fair enough." Haarlock couldn't find a distance marker, so he pointed to a symbol marking an old homestead just inside the forest's edge. "How far away is this one here?"

"Two miles or so. Probably an hour's walk this time of year."

With that as his scale, Haarlock used a nearby ruler to find where a two-hour walk would get him. Sixty-three markers fell within that area, 19 of which were ruins. But a large ravine cut across the northern section of the area.

"Is this ravine traversable?"

"It's a hundred feet deep in most spots and about thirty across. I'd say not."

That puts a barrier in one direction.

"Do you have newer maps of the area, ones with established prospecting sites?"

"Listen, what are you doing?" The old man raised a bushy eyebrow in annoyance. "I don't actually care, but are you trying to go lay claim based on a rumor?"

"What?"

"Just by your gloves, I can tell you're rich. And rich boys like yourself come here all the time throwing around money based on a so-called *sure thing*."

Haarlock frowned for a moment before things clicked. With a subtle look over each shoulder, he made sure the shop's other patrons were minding their own business, then leaned in towards the old man and whispered.

"I'm not a prospector, I'm an adventurer." Haarlock took off his glove to show his signet ring. "And a noble."

The man's wrinkly forehead rose in surprise.

"You see, the ruins I'm looking for are part of the Elven kingdom that spanned this whole area centuries ago. I hired a guide, a good one, to take me out to the ruins to search for documents. Right now, everyone else is out there rummaging around in the dirt, looking for any sign of wealth. But what if you knew exactly where to look for old gold and silver mines? Or better yet, where they kept their treasury?"

It was all Haarlock could do not to laugh at the shop owner. He hung on every word, his eyes as wide as saucers.

"Those documents I'm looking for? My companions betrayed me, leaving me sleeping in my bed to go off and find their secrets without me. If they get there before I do..." Haarlock gave a knowing look as he placed a single gold coin on the map. "I'm sure you understand my rush."

The old man gulped. "You spin a good yarn, friend."

"It'll remain one unless I catch up to, or better yet, beat my so-called friends to the prize. What can you do to help me with that?"

"Toss another gold on the pile to show me you mean business."

Haarlock smirked as he complied. The man slid them all off the edge and into his hand and put them in his pocket. He went through a small doorway behind him, then came back with a set of cartography tools.

"We'll need something to scale so we can narrow down the search area with some semblance of accuracy. Won't do you no good to be wandering around miles off course."

Over the next twenty minutes, the man consulted a dozen different maps, laying out the distances between markers with calipers and a ruler. He took a fresh, to-scale map of just the forest and copied over the ones only from the older map. When he finished, 28 sites were marked and six were circled.

"Those six there are your best bets, all within approximately a two-hour walk. Unexplored in the last fifty years, at least."

Haarlock looked over the map for a moment. "How far apart are the two furthest sites?"

"A straight-line walk would take you an hour. But that doesn't include elevation changes or natural features blocking your path. Please realize that this map is as good as I can get. It's not going to be perfect."

"Right." Haarlock nodded as he chewed his lower lip. "At least I only have six places to search. Do you have a compass?"

"Least I can do." The man walked over to a shelf and came back with a compass, stopping next to Haarlock. He laid it on the counter but didn't remove his hand. "If there be any documents in those ruins you don't want, I'd appreciate first dibs."

"I think that's more than reasonable." Haarlock looked down at the man's hand. He laid another gold coin next to it. "I hope you can wait a couple of days before any rumors make their way to the wider world."

"For you?" The man moved his hand from the compass to the coin and smiled. "I'll wait a week."

***

By the time Haarlock acquired the map and made it back to Justine's house, she was gone. In fact, the entire house was empty.

Fuck.

Haarlock stood in the street, motionless as he thought about what to do. Ladrón crossed the street back and forth as he sniffed around the ground.

*"*Justine. Scent. Follow.*"*

"Really? You think you can?"

Ladrón didn't reply, instead focusing on the ground where Justine stood as she talked to Simon. Several deep breaths later, the raccoon took off to the north. Haarlock smirked as he rushed after him.

Through winding alleys and streets, they went. How anyone could traverse this place, Haarlock didn't know. They crossed west over the river, went north a few hundred feet, then back east across the river again. Was Justine being paranoid and trying to throw any would-be followers off her trail? Whatever the case, it took Ladrón half an hour to reach the edge of town.

It was a half-mile to the forest, and all that lay between them was open ground. Nothing disturbed the light layer of snow save for a few animal tracks.

"You sure she went this way?"

*"*Yes.*"*

Haarlock took out his map and compass. He faced north by northeast, and of the six sites, the southernmost two were closest. They lay roughly a mile apart inside a dale between the hills. Since he had nothing else to go on, Haarlock set out.

22

Try as he might, Ladrón couldn't follow Justine's trail through the blowing wind of the open countryside. Haarlock wasn't sure how he could follow her in the first place, considering she obviously possessed *Pass Without Trace*. He looked up the relevant entry in his menu as they walked.

Pass Without Trace only affected things like leaving footprints, disturbing dust or tree leaves, and other such small, incongruous things. An upgraded version, *Improved Pass Without Trace*, able to be taken as a Feat at Level 30, would negate more subtle things like scent and residual magic. Even with the ability, it only worked if the user was attempting to move surreptitiously. If one were to run through a snow-covered field, or a dense forest, for instance, the ability's efficacy suffered.

I hope Justine didn't take the improved version.

Then there was Ladrón. With his pajama and armor on, his stomach hung only an inch below the snow. That meant he left a *very* obvious trail behind him.

When they reached the forest, Haarlock stopped and kneeled.

"Come here, Ladrón."

The animal scurried over and sat back on his haunches. *"*Yes?*"*

"You might be sneaky, but I want you to have an edge if you're going to be my scout. Let's make sure this ring's Talent blocking ability doesn't overcome Improved Animal Bond. *Won't do me any good if I can't talk to you."* Haarlock removed his glove, then the ring of obfuscation. He looped it onto the intelligence enhancing bangle around Ladrón's neck. *"Can you hear me?"*

*"*Yes.*"*

"Good. Stay ahead of me, but don't go so far that we can't talk, okay?"

*"*Close. Stay.*"*

"Exactly. Be sure to keep hidden and don't do anything until I tell you."

*"*Understand.*"*

Haarlock ruffled the animal's head. The ring wouldn't do much, especially since it couldn't block Class Abilities like *Uncanny Dodge* or *Alert*, but it was better than nothing. And sometimes, that was enough.

With a mental nudge, Haarlock sent Ladrón forward. Hopefully, he'd be able to see Justine in the distance, but probably not. Raccoons are nocturnal animals with notoriously poor eyesight. But, just like the ring around his neck, every little bit counted.

An hour and a half later, Haarlock peered between two rocks overlooking the remains of a small stone building in a large clearing. Moss covered the slab it once sat on, and several shrubs grew between the weathered cracks. Only the bottom row of bricks remained of the walls. While this would be a great place for kids to play, it was far too exposed for a secret meeting place.

The second location lay half-a-mile northeast, but it required going over a partially frozen stream. By the time Haarlock found a place to cross, it took him almost an hour to get there. Unlike the first place, these ruins looked to be the remnants of a large basement or cellar. Collapsed stairs on the south end dropped twenty feet into a pool of dark, frozen water. Thick walls of vines and roots hung from the edges, and the dense canopy of trees kept the whole place in shadow, even in winter. A search around the perimeter found no trace of activity, human or otherwise, for some time. The feeling of this place having been forgotten sent Haarlock on his way.

Next was a crumbling watchtower on top of a rocky cliff. Lost to time was the structure's former height, as only a dozen feet of it remained. Hundreds of stone bricks lay haphazardly at the base, with many having fallen to the ground far below. The height provided great sightlines in all directions, and it took Ladrón several long minutes to find a path up to the top of the cliff. Anyone, familiar with the place or not, would be hard pressed to make it up safely or undetected. Haarlock marked it as a possibility.

But he wasn't sure if he should wait here or go to the next site. He didn't even know if any of the six locations marked on his map were the right ones. Another dozen lay within range, and Justine's contact could very well have picked any of them. Time ticked ever onward. He had, at most, two hours before the meeting started. Justine could be there already.

No. He couldn't second-guess himself. Even if he didn't find their meeting place, he still learned that Justine used this trip to contact someone, and that Simon was helping her. Or planning to, at least. That information would be more than valuable on its own.

Catching Justine in the act would be icing on the cake.

The fourth site lay the furthest from town, nestled against a small lake. Several streams snaked out from there, one of which passed within a few hundred feet of the watchtower. Haarlock followed the stream, breaking off once Ladrón was within sight of the lake. He had the raccoon keep to the forest's edge while he snuck in from the south.

And what a beautiful sight it was.

Nestled low in the terrain, the lake was protected from much of the wind, leaving its partially frozen surface a crisp reflection of the sky. What was once an estate sat on the western bank, though time left only a handful of pillars and walls standing. A small dock, or perhaps a walkway, jutted out into the water twenty feet. From his vantage point, Haarlock could see the overgrown paved walkways leading to and from the forest and along the lakeside. The cold, quiet winter left a somber note on what would otherwise be a breathtaking location in the green of the summer.

*"*Someone. Coming.*"*

Haarlock's reverie broke, and it felt like hours went by before he saw a figure moving between the trees in the distance. They went behind one of the partial walls but didn't come out the other side.

"Where did they go? I can't see them."

*"*Sitting.*"*

"Who?"

*"*Justine.*"*

Haarlock let out a breath he didn't know he held. Should he confront her now, or watch things play out? Maybe snag her contact as he leaves and interrogate him later, letting Justine think everything went smoothly? Then again, rogues were a sneaky lot by nature, and perhaps this all seemed nefarious and was anything but. How many times had Haarlock taken too many precautions while home on leave because of simple habit?

No, he should act before, not after.

"Move back as far as you can without losing sight. Keep an eye out for her contact and do nothing until I say. Okay? You're my ace if this is an ambush."

Ladrón acknowledged.

Haarlock crawled forward, keeping the partial wall between him and Justine. Once he reached it, he slowed his breathing and listened.

From the other side came a faint, soft humming. It carried on for over several minutes before Justine stopped, let out a noise from stretching, then cracked several joints. She yawned and walked forward, from Haarlock's left to his right. She must have picked up a rock, because she let out a light grunt before something splashed into the lake.

With Justine's attention focused elsewhere, Haarlock moved further left and from behind the wall to between two stone benches next to what was once a manicured green space. Brambles and lumpy earth filled it now. He stood 50 feet from her.

"Hello, Justine."

In a flash of motion, Justine spun in place, ending in a crouch with daggers drawn and at the ready. Haarlock's hands were visible and open, and his hood was down.

Justine's jaw clenched and her eyes bored into Haarlock. "I wasn't sure if they'd gotten to you or not. You had me convinced when you didn't make a move on our way here."

"What?" Haarlock shook his head.

"Don't!" The elf snarled as she stood and jabbed a blade towards him. "Are the letters even real? Or did you pass them off before we left?"

A thousand things ran through Haarlock's mind as he took in the situation. Justine's eyes were hard, but wide, and her hands trembled ever so slightly. This wasn't surprise; this was terror.

"Look, Justine..."

"Where's Krtek? Where?!"

"Justine!" Haarlock drew his blade and put a hand up. "Something's not right. I was sent to see if *you* were the mole."

Justine's head jerked to the left and right as she brought her daggers into a defensive stance. "How long have you been here?"

"Ten minutes before you arrived."

Haarlock turned around to face the woods and focused every ability he had on them. Only the rustling of leaves and the chirping of birds sounded in the distance. When he turned to face Justine, she slowly walked backward toward him.

"Anything?" The elf stopped 20 feet away.

"No. The woods are empty."

"Then why are you here?"

Something caught Haarlock's attention: the sun. With the short winter days, even in the mid afternoon the glowing orb hung low in the sky, directly behind Justine, casting long shadows across the ground. But her shadow faced the sun.

Towards the source of light.

Haarlock's eyes widened as he went to speak, but the shadow moved before he could utter a sound. It hinged at Justine's feet, standing in a single smooth motion. A black tendril wrapped across her chest, pinning her arms against her sides. Another formed into a thin, bladed edge, cutting her flesh as it moved through her scarf and across her throat. Blood sprayed onto the ground at Justine's feet.

The shadow held Justine there until she stopped convulsing, then let her drop in a heap. It took form as it stepped over her body, coalescing into a hard-featured human man in a jet-black hooded cloak.

"Greetings, Lord Haarlock." The man dipped his head and smiled. "It is a pleasure to make your acquaintance."

23

Haarlock's eyes flicked from the man to the motionless form of Justine and the pool of blood soaking into the mossy stone beneath her.

"Fear not, Lord Haarlock. You shall die as quickly as she."

The man's neutral tone contrasted heavily with the blood dripping from the dagger in his right hand.

"You're here for me, too?" Haarlock relaxed his shoulders and straightened his back.

"Unfortunately, yes."

"Unfortunately?" An eyebrow raise.

The man shrugged. "Though I cannot speak for the others, I, for one, would have liked to see another Phantom Blade join our ranks."

Haarlock watched the man for a moment before speaking. He couldn't be younger than his mid-fifties, and stood almost casually, weapon hand hanging relaxed at his side. In fact, his entire body was relaxed. This man was a professional killer, and Haarlock was nothing more than his next target.

His appearance didn't match what Haarlock thought a Phantom Blade would look like. The man before him wore a pristine white tunic and pants and a pair of simple rabbit fur boots. Beyond the black leather kidney belt around his waist, it didn't look as though he wore any armor. Though his jet-black cloak shimmered ever so oddly in the setting light.

"So why am I not dead?" Haarlock gestured to Justine. "I'm sure your abilities would make just as quick work of me."

"You are what, Level 18?"

"Twenty."

The man smirked. "I am nearly thrice that, Lord Haarlock. You would be dead before you could blink."

"Again: why am I not dead?"

"It is few and far between that I get the chance to test my skills against another with *Mastery* in *Daggers*."

Haarlock scoffed. "You want to duel? That's cliché."

"True, but I hope you will indulge me."

"No abilities?" Haarlock tightened his grip on his weapon. "Just blades?"

"Just blades. No pets either." The man looked to each side, then past Haarlock and into the woods. "Speaking of which, where is your companion?"

"I wasn't sure which ruins Justine was meeting her contact at, so we split up to cover more ground."

"Hmm, I hoped to meet Ladrón. I am told he is a fierce beast."

More than you know.

The man unclasped his hooded cloak and tossed it to the side, revealing his bald, shapely head. "I tire of talk. Make your decision."

Haarlock weighed his options. Or the lack thereof. He looked over his shoulder and into the woods, and the long, dark shadows filling it. If he tried to escape through them, the Phantom Blade could, at the least, *Umbral Step* right next to him. What about the lake? Even if he reached it, the ice-cold water would freeze his muscles before he made it more than a few dozen feet from shore.

No. The only way out was through.

Unclasping his own hooded cloak, Haarlock let it drop behind him, then brought his dirk up and entered a combat stance. With a smirk, the man crouched low with his blade held to the side, far from his body.

The man surged forward, his blade flashing up towards the inside of Haarlock's knife arm. Haarlock's left hand batted the weapon away, turning into an elbow strike to the face. A forearm blocked, then both blades stabbed forward, the metals ringing oddly as they deflected each other.

Knee, elbow, fist, blade. Strike, block, riposte, deflect. Back and forth they moved, trading attack and defense as they felt out one another's fighting style.

Every move of Haarlock's weapon was meant to disable. To kill. By the time he turned 24, no one in the seven squadrons of Delta Force could match him. His skill with a blade honed by youthful talent and the best teachers the previous world could offer.

But this man fought from decades of experience.

His opening attack, a deliberate, all-or-nothing move, left Haarlock with little to reply. A truly masterful feat of martial skill. And now he fought with methodical simplicity, wasting no energy to defend against obvious feints, nor trying for sloppy, last-second strikes. He exploited every opening and defended every angle of attack.

Across the stone-inlaid ground they moved, as each took turns between attack and defense. But each exchange brought Haarlock closer to failure. The man's strikes hit *hard*, and it was all Haarlock could do to put leather armor between blade and flesh. Without his recently acquired *Increased Reflexes*, he knew the fight would have ended long ago.

In the previous world, Haarlock watched a lot of television. One show, the name long since forgotten by *The Game's* memory-altering effects, had a character perform a ridiculous hand switch with her dagger. A trick Haarlock spent the better part of a year practicing for no other reason that it looked cool. The one time he used it during a sparring match, it earned him great recognition from his peers and greater admonishment from his superiors. They were right to say it was a foolish thing that would only get you killed in the real world.

Haarlock switched weapon hands mid-block, using the change in rhythm for a backhanded cut towards the man's face. Though he jerked his head back with speed, the man didn't fully escape the dirk's extra length. The two rogues separated, and the Phantom Blade touched the wound on his right cheekbone.

"Clever move." The man frowned as he looked at the blood covering his two fingers. "Few risk a hand change like that."

"If you weren't so fast, that would have taken your eye." Haarlock lifted his right arm to show a deep gouge in the leather bracer. "And not for my armor, this would have disabled my hand."

The man smirked. "Were I using my abilities, my blade would have passed through your armor and severed the limb entirely."

Haarlock's eyebrows raised high on his forehead as he looked at the rend. When the blade hit him, it felt like a kick, not a blade slash. This man was *strong*. And when Haarlock looked at him, he noticed his lack of exertion. Even now, in the frigid air, beads of sweat ran down Haarlock's face as he breathed heavily. It looked as if the man had done little more than go for a long walk.

Now that Haarlock thought about it, when his blade touched the man's skin, it felt...odd. Almost as if he struck hardly anything at all. In fact, the man's wound seemed *less* than it should have been. It bled, but nowhere near as much as a cut to the face should. What did Roboute say when they first met? *The more powerful sub-specializations confer abilities that are no longer physical in nature*. Roboute said he became the illusion, so did that mean this man became a phantom?

Haarlock looked down at his blade and how it shimmered in the light. Was its *Dual Natured* ability the reason the man frowned at the blood on his fingers? Was that the only reason he could injure him at all?

"That wound is too shallow for as hard as I struck you."

A smirk. "Honestly, I am surprised your weapon could wound me at all."

Haarlock scoffed. "And here I thought this was supposed to be a fair fight."

"Oh, no." The man shook his head. "As you can see, you tire as I do not. And though I thought you possessed nothing capable of injuring me, that weapon of yours will not suffice. You lack the necessary Talents and Feats for it to be a threat to me."

"So, you're toying with me?" Haarlock raised an eyebrow in mock disbelief.

"I am merely seeing if the rumors of your prodigious talent with a blade are true. To your credit, you have met expectations."

"Thanks, I think."

The man dipped his head in respect. "It was a compliment, and you are welcome."

"The outcome of this fight is already determined, then?"

"I have yet to fail a contract in the twenty years since becoming a Phantom Blade. You will die today, Lord Haarlock."

Lucky me...

"Shall we continue?" The man tilted his bald head. "Perhaps luck is on your side, and you will deal me a fatal wound."

Haarlock took a moment to look out across the picturesque lake, and the mirror-like reflection of the setting sun on its surface. The wind dislodged a handful of leaves from the corner of a crumpled wall section, blowing them towards the wood line and across Justine's prone form. She lay 20 feet to Haarlock's left, her own blood freezing on the ground around her.

"Yeah. Sure. Why not?"

The man walked forward with purpose, blade in his left hand this time. Haarlock matched grips and juked to the right before crouching and going for a sweeping kick. He wasn't fast enough. The Phantom Blade planted his left foot, stopping Haarlock's leg dead, then stabbed forward and down, his blade tip aimed at Haarlock's right eye.

Using the man's momentum, Haarlock grabbed his wrist and rolled backwards, twisting the blade from his hand and knocking it to the side as they rolled over. In a moment they were on the ground and Haarlock was on top, the grip of his weapon reversed and stabbing down with all his might.

With blinding speed, the man reached out and grabbed Haarlock's wrist, stopping his weapon mid-thrust. At the same time, he grabbed Haarlock around the back of the neck with his other hand. Though Haarlock resisted, he felt himself moving against his will. The man pulled down on Haarlock's neck and twisted his wrist, so the dirk's blade turned towards his chest. Haarlock pushed back with his legs, but the man's strength was too great.

The umbral dagger, gifted to Haarlock by Basterlit Cratery, pierced through the armor on his chest and into his right lung. Haarlock froze, pain searing through his body. He coughed and blood filled his mouth, then his body went slack.

The man pushed Haarlock to the side and stood, then dusted off his clothes before straightening them. He watched for a moment as a coughing fit overtook Haarlock's prone form before kneeling.

"Well fought, Lord Haarlock." The man picked up his dropped blade, then dipped his head in respect. "I am not too proud to admit you almost had me a few times."

Haarlock looked up, but the pain kept him from meeting the Phantom Blade's eyes for more than a second. He knew blood filled his lungs with every beat of his heart. He'd watched it happen to others more times than he cared to remember.

Another coughing fit. Pain wracked through him, again and again...then stopped. He blinked his eyes open and found himself standing off to the side, looking at his own dying body. A body froze in place. Frozen like the leaves blowing across the ground. Like the birds in the sky. Like the man who Haarlock just lost to.

Motion on the right caught Haarlock's eye, and he turned to see someone standing near the edge of the forest. He was young, no older than 20, with smooth, pale skin and jet-black hair kept in a tight ponytail reaching to the middle of his back. Though he had rounded ears, the man's facial structure resembled an elf's, with prominent cheekbones and a shapely chin. His tailored, form-fitting clothing, a pair of black slacks and a white shirt under a black overcoat, glimmered ever so slightly as he moved. Four shadows, one pointing in each cardinal direction, stretched out far from the man's shoeless feet. They stayed fixed in their positions even as the man approached to stand next to Haarlock's frozen form.

Haarlock blinked several times as he realized the pain was gone. He touched where the blade entered his chest and found no blood there. None in or on his mouth, either.

"What's happening?" Haarlock regarded the newcomer with caution. "Who are you?"

"You don't know?" The newcomer looked at Haarlock's dying body and tilted his head.

Something drew Haarlock's gaze to the weapon impaled in his chest. His other body's chest. He knew who this was.

"Sjena."

The newcomer smiled, his too-white teeth turning the expression into something sinister.

"It is a pleasure to make your acquaintance."

24

Haarlock stared at his own frozen form. To see himself there, dying, and the man who dealt the fatal blow standing over him. And the god next to him.

"That man's name is Kilec." Sjena looked the Phantom Blade over with disappointment. "For fifteen years he's tried to gain my attention. Too boring, really. But not you, my dear Haarlock. Not you at all. You should consider yourself lucky."

"I don't know what I should be right now." Haarlock swallowed hard, his stomach churning.

"Since you'll be dead in, oh, thirty seconds, I'd say you should be grateful." Sjena tilted his head as he looked at Haarlock's other self. He pursed his lips in thought, then shrugged. "Kilec will cut your throat to end your suffering. He's a professional like that."

"How do you know that?"

"I know many things."

"Because you're a god?"

Sjena shrugged. "Something like that."

"That's not an answer."

"It's the best one I can give. Sorry."

Haarlock gestured sharply at the scene before him. "Then what's happening here?"

"As I said: you're dying. But I come with an alternative to that. Well...the opportunity for an alternative."

"Which is?"

"My, my. You are *not* one to beat around the bush, are you?"

Letting out a heavy breath, Haarlock relaxed. "Sorry. It's not every day you're a disembodied ghost looking at your own dying body. And the person who put you there."

Sjena crossed his arms and looked at the scene for a moment before walking around it once. He stopped next to Haarlock and nodded.

"Valid point. As to your question, you have two choices: live or die." Sjena gave a sinister smile once again. "The choice is simple, of course, but the consequences are not. If you choose to live, you join my flock and incur the responsibilities that entails. If you choose to die, Kilec here cuts your throat, you bleed out, and no one ever knows what happened to you." He huffed. "Guess the second option isn't nearly as complicated."

"That's a Hobson's choice."

"But it's still a choice."

The part of Haarlock's brain that made him human weighed the options. He knew, deep inside, that there was only one answer. The other part, the animal brain, decided in an instant.

"Why? Why offer me the choice? Why have me become one of your followers?"

"Darkness encroaches. You will help me cleanse it."

Haarlock frowned again. "Aren't you the god of darkness?"

"I'm the god of *shadows*. A shadow cannot exist without the light that creates it."

"I need a better explanation than that."

"War is coming, Haarlock. At the head of that war is one who seeks to spread the darkness."

The connection clicked. "You're talking about the shogun. He's infected with the corruption."

Sjena nodded. "You will stop him. Or die trying."

"You're a god. Why not snap your fingers and solve the problem?"

"There are certain...protocols that must be followed."

"Then are you really a god?"

"In this world, yes."

"That's not an answer."

A shrug. "We're running out of time. Make your choice."

"I choose to live."

"Then you shall live."

Haarlock shook his head. "The whole *bleeding to death* thing I have going on might put a damper on that."

"No weapon with my blessing can hurt you. Remove it and you will be without injury." Sjena turned to leave but stopped and looked over his shoulder at Kilec. "You still need to defeat him, though. Good luck."

Sjena took another step and faded away.

"You're supposed to say *good hunting*." Haarlock pursed his lips as he looked at his frozen self.

Pain started in Haarlock's chest. Where the blade would be. Where it is. It grew in intensity as his vision doubled, overlaid with what he saw standing and while lying on the ground, bleeding. But what to do about Kilec, the Phantom Blade?

The man was monstrously fast and strong, and until now, hadn't used his abilities. Haarlock needed something, anything, to give him an edge. Would his newfound lack of injury be enough? Maybe. But there was one trick left up Haarlock's sleeve. If anything saved him, it would be that.

Haarlock blinked, and he was there, the wind blowing across his face, the blade burning in his chest.

"Tell me, Lord Haarlock, do you have any last words?"

Another cough, and though there was pain, it was far less than before. Haarlock pushed himself up to sit on his knees, facing Kilec.

"Wait." Haarlock half-raised a hand towards the man in front of him. "Please."

Kilec scowled. "I would not expect this from one such as you. Begging for a few more seconds of life will not stop the inevitable."

"I'm not begging for a few more seconds of life."

It hurt to breathe, but with each breath the pain faded. Haarlock swallowed hard and looked up at Kilec. Their eyes met.

"I'm buying time for my raccoon."

25

Kilec spun in place, the tip of his weapon perfectly timed to intercept the raccoon soaring through the air at his head. Too bad *Mage Hand* wrapped around his wrist and pulled him off balance.

The area flooded with magic as Kilec cast several spells at once. Haarlock anticipated this and activated the nullstone necklace, and Kilec's hesitation at his failed spells was the opening needed. Withdrawing the dirk from his chest felt odd, but Haarlock didn't have time to think about it as he leaped forward.

The moment Ladrón slammed into Kilec's face, putting *Vicious Bite* and *Sneak Attack* to work, Haarlock stabbed the dirk into the man's back. *Improved Sneak Attack*, *Chink in Armor*, and *Murder* ensured the wound bit as deep as Ladrón's teeth.

To his credit, Kilec didn't panic. Though his body tensed with the twin attacks, it took him only a moment to recover. He ripped Ladrón from his face and slung the animal to the side, then jerked his elbow back into Haarlock's stomach. Haarlock stumbled back, his breath gone.

Ladrón wasted no time returning to the fight, darting in and tearing into the flesh of Kilec's right calf. As the assassin screamed and collapsed mid-step, the raccoon climbed up his back and tore the man's ear off. Ladrón received a backhand for his troubles, hard enough to break four teeth and knock him unconscious.

Haarlock slammed into Kilec, tackling him to the ground, dirk sinking into the man's chest just below the heart. Haarlock's left arm blocked a counter stab, but the blade sank deep into his forearm, cutting through armor, tendons, ligaments, and muscles, disabling the hand. So, he slammed his forehead into Kilec's nose, shattering it. With his opponent dazed, Haarlock withdrew his blade and reared back for the killing blow.

Kilec's eyes focused, and his blade darted towards Haarlock's left lung. Armor, flesh, and bone would have collapsed under the Phantom Blade's attack, but it lacked any power. Haarlock's dirk was already sunk to the hilt in his neck, just below the jawline. Kilec took one last ragged breath before he went limp.

With his own ragged breath, Haarlock fell to the side. Notifications pinged in his mind, but he pushed them all to the side as he looked for Ladrón. The animal lay in a patch of dry grass, breathing slowly. Haarlock let out a sigh of relief. That's when the pain came.

The worst part wasn't that the fingers on his left hand wouldn't move; it was all the bleeding. And by the volume, it was likely Kilec severed the radial artery. He'd never make it back to town before he bled out.

I really need to carry healing potions.

Removing his belt, Haarlock clumsily tied it above his left elbow and pulled it so tight he almost passed out from the pain. Once the makeshift tourniquet was in place, he went to the dead man to look for a potion.

Nothing. Whatever other gear Kilec had, if he had any, must be stored elsewhere. Haarlock cursed under his breath as he looked around. That's when he saw Justine. She lay on her side, facing away. If she weren't in a pool of frozen blood, it would look like she was simply sleeping.

Haarlock limped over to her and put a hand on her shoulder. "Sorry."

Luckily, the woman carried a belt pouch of six potions, two of which were healing. Relief flooded Haarlock once he drank the first one. It stopped the bleeding but didn't fully heal the wound, leaving his left hand only partially functional. With his belt returned to his pants, Haarlock went to Ladrón.

The animal wasn't in as terrible a shape as Haarlock expected, just steadily breathing as if asleep. Granted, if Kilec had connected with the first attack, it would have killed Ladrón outright. The Phantom Blade only hit Haarlock's forearm, and it nearly killed him.

A check of Ladrón's status showed he was down to a third of his hit points. His Feat, *Tough*, provided excellent damage reduction and was the only reason he was alive. Haarlock checked his own sheet and saw that, even after taking the potion, he was at less than half of his total health.

Sorry, little guy, I need this more than you.

Haarlock took the second potion. Though he regained the use of his left hand, it didn't feel right. Much of the strength was gone, along with a good deal of coordination. This would take a proper healer to fix.

A gentle shake didn't wake Ladrón, so Haarlock retrieved his cloak and wrapped the animal in it, then laid him out of the wind behind a partial stone wall. He didn't know if magical healing could fix Ladrón's broken teeth, but he hoped so. The top left canine was completely knocked out, and the one on the bottom was broken in half. Ladrón would never let him hear end of it if they couldn't be fixed.

Haarlock surveyed the scene. Justine's contact, Krtek, was assuredly dead, which meant that if anyone else was going to come, they would have by now. That meant, thankfully, no backup for Kilec. All Haarlock wanted to do was sit down and rest, but he needed answers.

Too bad it involved something Haarlock never liked: searching the dead. It wasn't so bad searching a nameless enemy but rummaging through the pockets of someone you knew seemed...inappropriate. And now, standing over Justine's prone form, it felt even worse.

Haarlock undid the clasp of her cloak, then removed the garment and set it aside. Justine's belt pouch, the contents of her pockets, jewelry, weapons, and her boots were laid out on the cloak. A thorough search of her items revealed no hidden pockets, spaces, or liners. Nothing stood out. Beyond the potions, she had nothing to stay in this weather overnight. She even wore Marcon's scarf and her sapphire brooch necklace. Would Justine wear those if she came for a fight?

When Simon told Justine about this meeting, it appeared her contact had information to pass along. It would be odd for her not to have something to give to them as well.

Depending on how sensitive the data is, she might very well not have written it down.

Whatever she came here for, it wasn't a fight. Kilec, though, didn't come. He was *sent*. The question was why and by whom. And did he come here for one or both of them?

Haarlock stood over the man's body, thinking back to his words: *I have yet to fail a contract in the twenty years since becoming a Phantom Blade. You will die today, Lord Haarlock.* That sure made it seem as if he was the target. And if so, why bother with Justine? Kilec could have attacked at any point in the woods, dispatching him without worrying about a possible ally.

Unless she was a target, too.

And if so, it would have been easier to assassinate them deep in the woods on the way here, not risk a change of plans and for them to separate. Besides, Justine's whole reason for coming here, the meeting with her contact, Krtek, was a last-minute occurrence. What if he hadn't overheard the conver...a chill ran down Haarlock's spine.

Was this a setup from the start?

The chill went to Haarlock's knees, and he had to sit down. He swallowed hard as he stared at the dead Phantom Blade before him. Who could arrange something like this? How did they even know about the meeting? The mission itself? A thousand things burned through Haarlock's mind before he shut them out.

Focus on the moment. Work the problem backward to the source.

Haarlock was here because he followed Justine to a secret meeting. How did he learn about the meeting? By overhearing her and Simon's conversation. Why did Simon tell Justine about the meeting? Krtek, Justine's contact, told Simon about it.

No. There's no proof Krtek told Simon, only that Simon said he did. Loose end #1.

How did Haarlock come to overhear their conversation? Because he was tasked with following Justine to see if she would meet with anyone. Who tasked him? Marcon, with additional information from Roboute. Why task him with following Justine? They believed her to be a potential defector. Why? Because of the cache Haarlock found while chasing Mateo Cabrera. Why was he chasing Mateo Cabrera? His guild, Shattersong, tasked him with it. Who at Shattersong gave him the mission? Their guild leader, Camilla Albertine. Who gave her the quest, or where did she get the information about Mateo? Unknown.

Loose end #2.

It all started with Mateo, but how could that lead to here and now? Too many steps with too many unknowns...unless that was the point. What did Mateo say right before he blew himself up? *I know what you're here for. You've ruined everything.* Haarlock blinked in realization.

Mateo was in on it. He knew I'd find the cache, only I found it too soon, and he panicked.

And if Haarlock was supposed to find the cache, then Justine was supposed to be discovered as a defector. Did that mean she was set up? It explained why she said *I wasn't sure if they'd gotten to you or not*. But if this was all put in motion to eliminate her, why eliminate both of them? What did Haarlock know, or they think he knew, that made him such a threat?

I have no idea what I know that would warrant an assassination. Loose end #3.

What did Justine know to warrant an assassination? Loose end #4.

Again, why would the assassin strike out here and not in town, or any time before? Why kill Justine first? Why have a knock-out-drag-out knife fight to the death? Was Kilec really that arrogant, or did he have a reason?

Haarlock moved to the assassin's body and searched it, finding only two things: his dagger and a packet of letters tied together with a piece of twine. Opening and laying them out, each of the four letters were written in a flowing script and obviously encrypted. It looked as though it could be the cipher used by the shinobi, but Haarlock wasn't sure.

Makes me wonder if these were to be planted on Justine's body, and if the handwriting is hers, too.

If that were the case, then her body would eventually be found. And likely Haarlock's, too. But what was the story supposed to be, that they killed each other? Maybe Justine's contact, Krtek, would come out here and find them? Was he already dead, waiting to be found, or in on it?

Who and where is Krtek? Loose end #5.

Haarlock stared at the letters for a long time as he ran through the situation, only breaking his concentration when Ladrón finally came around.

*"*Hurt. Head. Ouch.*"*

The animal climbed out of the cloak and limped over to Haarlock.

"Hey there, little guy. You okay?"

*"*Good. Gone.*"* Ladrón growled at the dead Kilec before him.

Haarlock snorted and gently petted his familiar. *"I agree completely."*

Ladrón looked up and whimpered. *"*Justine. Gone. Sad.*"*

"I know. I'm sad, too." Haarlock looked at Justine's prone form, then up at the sky. *"It's maybe an hour until dark. We need to get back but first let's put her to rest."*

That presented a problem. Frozen ground and no tools made it impossible to dig a grave. Haarlock put away the letters, then stood and looked around, stopping as he gazed across the lake. A water burial was better than leaving her to the scavengers.

As Ladrón went to find vines, Haarlock collected stones. Once they had gathered enough, he brought Justine out onto the small dock, filled her cloak with stones, then tied it around her with the vines.

"Sorry you got caught up in whatever all this is, Justine." Haarlock pushed her into the water, watching as she slowly slid under the surface. "Let's hope I can find who's responsible and give you some kind of closure."

Once he was sure she'd stay submerged, Haarlock turned his attention to Kilec.

What to do with you?

The desire to let him rot was strong, but, like Haarlock, acceptance of a job brought him here. How many times did Justine take a job that resulted in someone's injury or death? How many times has Haarlock? No, Kilec would receive a burial if for no other reason than to hide his body.

But I'm not about to waste his cloak.

Haarlock went to Kilec's cloak and examined it.

Veil of Shifting Shadows

Unique Cloak

Durability - 10/100

Armor - 20/200

Abilities: Enhanced Stats (Night), Self-Mending (Night), Shadow Form

When the cloak's hood was put over the wearer's head, *Shadow Form* encased the user in total darkness. Be there mundane light shining on them or not, they would be a walking shadow. Without the use of magical attacks or magical sources of light, this rendered the user effectively invulnerable. While powerful, the ability would only last 20 minutes, three times per day. The cloak's armor and durability stats altered based on the time of day, increasing tenfold in value at night. And at night, the garment automatically repaired itself over the course of a few hours.

Haarlock let out a low whistle. This would be a *powerful* addition to his equipment.

The rest of Kilec's possessions were high quality, though nothing special. He didn't have food, potions, or even lock picks on him. Assuming he had a pack stashed somewhere, Haarlock sent Ladrón to find it.

Like with Justine, Haarlock used his old cloak, stones, and vines to weigh down Kilec and bury him in the lake. As the Phantom Blade disappeared into the water, Haarlock wondered why someone like him was sent. It couldn't have been cheap, but then again, if this entire thing was a setup from the start...

Who put this in motion?

If the cache pointed the finger at Justine, then whoever created it had to know Justine and her actions intimately. Marcon said both he and Gerard confirmed the data, and who better to verify than the one who created it? Or say they verified it.

The kingdom spymaster and/or the head of the Ostian Thieves' Guild? That's just great.

But who approved the quest for Shattersong? The guild worked for the Crown, so any number of people would have the authority to send the Mateo quest to them. But whomever sent it needed to ensure Haarlock found the cache.

Or did they? Camilla could very well have fabricated the quest's origin and picked me because I'm new. It wouldn't be suspicious to send the new guy on a simple fetch quest.

It was convenient, sure, and made Haarlock's investment in the situation stronger, but he didn't need to be the one to find it. Anyone in the guild could have. But Camilla did send him on the quest. She also pointed him towards Acorn and her bank robbery gig. Did she know Justine would be involved in it? The two worked for some time on the problem before Haarlock joined their team.

And Gerard is the one who picked Acorn for the job in the first place.

Haarlock shook his head. There were entirely too many variables. Anyone could have put this in motion, even Roboute.

Roboute. He has entirely too many fingers in too many pies. He makes, what, loose end number nine? Twelve?

No, this line of thinking wouldn't do. Haarlock needed to focus. To start where he could and pull on every loose end until he found the answer. And the closest loose end was in Claville.

26

Before they left the ruins, Ladrón found Kilec's stash. The assassin packed light, with enough supplies for an overnight stay. Ten potions, two health restores, and the rest for keeping warm, were the only other equipment Kilec carried.

Minimalist much?

One restore went to Ladrón, bringing him up to nearly full health, and the other to Haarlock, topping him off. It didn't fix the raccoon's teeth or completely restore functionality to Haarlock's hand, though. It seemed a trip to a proper healer was in order.

What the Phantom Blade provided in droves was experience. Enough for seven more levels. Renown and Infamy wise, Haarlock received the same amount: 570. The fact that killing Kilec was as helpful to the world at large as it was a terrifying feat to perform, the quantity made sense. Overall, this gave him two more Talents and another Feat, along with a unique opportunity.

There was time enough for picking abilities later. Haarlock needed to have a talk with a guildmaster.

Dozens and dozens of people came and went along the road to Claville. Even now, standing among the throng of carts, Haarlock wasn't given a second glance. It felt hollow.

They were oblivious to what had happened to Justine. To Haarlock. The life of a soldier is fraught with danger, and more than once Haarlock's life was put in jeopardy. Sure, people came to kill him, but *he* wasn't the one they were after.

They were there to kill whoever was trying to kill them. To kill an unnamed, faceless soldier. It wasn't personal. It wasn't an assassination. But dwelling on the past, even the very recent past, wouldn't solve the mystery. Intel and action would.

Past the customs agent and into the city proper, Haarlock found himself in a throng of bodies. The dinner rush ensured shouting vendors, drunk patrons, and the scent of fresh food filled the densely packed street.

The street layout made zero sense, with dead end after dead end. After nearly an hour of backtracking, Haarlock found the small manufacturing hub he was looking for. The blacksmiths, glassblower, and silversmith were closed for the evening, their shops dark and cold. Down the attached alley would be the door leading to the guildhall. All Haarlock needed to do was wait for Simon to leave. But when would he?

During Simon's final conversation with Justine, he mentioned getting coffee during the morning rush. People like routine, and morning coffee is a nearly universal one to have. With luck, the diminutive man would need another fix to keep him awake through the night.

One of the dead Phantom Blade's warming potions kept the cold off. It didn't quite make Haarlock comfortable in the blowing wind of the rooftop, but it prevented his muscles from locking up. Ladrón stayed back in the hub area, finding the perfect place for an interrogation.

An hour passed. Then two.

Several people came and went in that time, none nearly as small as the guildmaster. A group of four went inside but left a handful of minutes later. Odd, but not suspicious.

Three hours.

Simon exited at what Haarlock guessed to be 10pm. The graying, red-haired man put up his hood and gathered his cloak together around him, sighed heavily enough his breath extended out several feet, then slowly walked off. The last time Haarlock saw him, Simon moved with purpose, head high and shoulders back. Now, though, he hunched over and moved at what could be described as a plodding stroll.

Is that guilt?

Haarlock *Shadowstepped* from the roof to the ground far behind Simon, then followed him as he walked towards the manufacturing hub. When the guildmaster reached the stone well, Haarlock *Shadowstepped* again directly behind him and placed a blade against his throat.

"Good evening, Simon. We're going to have a little talk."

The guildmaster nodded only once.

"Go to the structure to your left. The one with the green door."

The door opened as they approached, and Ladrón appeared in the threshold, broken teeth bared. Simon went without resistance into the dark interior. The otherwise empty storeroom held only a single chair.

"Don't worry, Haarlock. I'm not going anywhere."

Simon went to the chair and sat, then removed his hood and folded his hands on his lap. Ladrón stayed near the door, eyes locked on the man.

Haarlock removed his hood, too. "I assume you already know my first question."

"I've asked myself that over and over again since this morning." Simon shook his head. "The answer is simple: family. Obviously, that's why they picked me."

"Who is *they*?"

"Wish I knew. About a year ago, someone came to me and told me to inform on Justine, or the local baron learns of my family's illegal activities. They had very detailed records, of course."

Haarlock frowned. "Illegal activities?"

"My father and two brothers smuggle any number of illicit items, and I use my position as guildmaster of the Thieves' Guild to ensure they remain safe while doing so."

"What did they ask you to do?"

Simon flashed a look of sorrow for just a moment. "Who Justine meets and what they meet about, who she visits and what she does while here, and to get copies of any documents she may give or receive."

"And this morning? Did her friend, Krtek, ask her to meet at the ruins, or did you send him there, too?"

"They knew within a day when the two of you would arrive. Same with Krtek. He went to the ruins the night before you did."

Haarlock threw Justine's bloody, torn scarf at Simon's feet.

"Yeah, I know." Simon squeezed his eyes shut. "We were friends for a long time. Since my teens."

"And you sent her to her death. Sent us."

"You think they wouldn't kill me and my whole family if I said no?" Simon met Haarlock's eyes. "The guy brought me my mother's necklace. The one my father keeps in our family safe."

It was hard for Haarlock not to feel sympathy for the man. Hard, but not impossible.

"I want everything. Times, requests, documents."

"I don't know much, but I'll answer what I can." Simon straightened his back.

"Krtek. Who was he and why did Justine meet with him?"

"He was some kind of economist Justine knew from way back. About three years ago she asked me to make arrangements to pass documents. Justine would come to town and give me letters, then a few weeks later Krtek would come and take them. Sometimes he had letters to give to her, sometimes not. This was the first time they were going to speak face-to-face since that first meeting."

"And this went on for two years before someone blackmailed you to spy on Justine?"

"Like clockwork."

"You said you copied the letters. What did they say?"

"Just a bunch of economic data."

"Like what?"

"Business names, tax records, market prices. Stuff like that."

Haarlock shook his head. "Both of them sent that?"

Simon shrugged. "I assume it to be code of some kind, but I couldn't break it."

"Did you keep copies?"

"No. Being shown my mother's necklace kind of freaked me out. I didn't want to push what little luck I might have."

"Damn." Haarlock reflexively squeezed his blade handle. "Why were they meeting? Did the letters change in some way?"

"Like I said, I think they were coded. The last time Justine came, she asked to set up the in-person meeting for around this time of year. A few weeks later, the anonymous man came and threatened me."

Obviously Justine found something out, but what about me? Why was I targeted?

"When did they contact you about our arrival?"

"Eight weeks ago."

"How?" Haarlock's mind raced. That was during the kingdom tournament. Before he joined Shattersong.

"I don't know how they knew about you, but Justine advertises her trips well in advance. She has responsibilities as second-in-command of the largest Thieves' Guild in Lemuria."

Her boss, Gerard Parnell. She would have at least told him. Probably Marcon, too. How many other friends, acquaintances, or coworkers would she tell in passing?

"My affairs are in order, Haarlock. I knew my life was forfeit the moment I sent my friend to her death."

Haarlock looked at the guildmaster with confusion. "I'm not going to kill you, Simon. But you are going to help me uncover who's behind all of this."

"No, I'm not." Simon's shoulders slumped and suddenly looked tired. "I've told you all I can. It's time for me to pay for my betrayal."

Simon gave a small smile before he clenched his jaw. White foam filled his mouth as a seizure racked his body. Haarlock rushed to the man and pulled open his mouth, but he was already dead.

"Fuck!"

Haarlock pushed Simon back in the chair, then stepped back and put his hands on his head. When the Phantom Blade didn't report back, whoever was behind the assassination would come searching for the guildmaster. If they found him dead, would they think Haarlock and/or Justine were still alive?

No. They might suspect but couldn't prove.

Justine and Kilec's bodies were on the bottom of a lake. If someone came looking, and if they found the site, the only evidence remaining was blood. They wouldn't know who it belonged to, which meant they couldn't figure out what happened.

There was no way Haarlock could move Simon's body without being seen. But that wasn't necessarily a problem. The man obviously poisoned himself, and without defensive wounds, there was no reason to think otherwise. Sure, it might be odd for him to be dead in a random storeroom, but suicidal people sometimes killed themselves in places and ways comprehensible to them only.

It might be messy, but it worked. And sometimes, that was enough.

27

Haarlock moved the drape to the side and looked out the carriage window. He and Ladrón were in a forest now, still two days from the small port town of Bent. The plan, such as it was, would see him take a surreptitious route back home via carriage, boat, and his own feet. All told it would take close to 10 days for Haarlock to return, giving him plenty of time to think.

He wondered how fast the word of a raccoon toting lord receiving specialized magical healing before contracting a private carriage would spread back to whomever sent the Phantom Blade. With magic, it could be as little as minutes. If not, it could take days or weeks. Whatever the case, things were the way there were, and Haarlock would deal with things as they came. No sense in worrying about what one couldn't control.

The most pressing matter was what to do when he returned. Did he go straight to Marcon and reveal everything that happened? The king? Or did he go to Gerard, or Camilla, or the city guard? What would he tell any of them?

Someone set Justine and I up for assassination. I have no proof; save her bloody scarf and the unique cloak of a Phantom Blade I shouldn't have been able to kill. Oh, and her decades-long friend, who's been spying on her for a secretive third party, told me a bunch of stuff before he poisoned himself. But since I'm conveniently the only person left alive, you believe me? Right?

Haarlock wouldn't believe himself, either. What he needed was a list of whom he could trust. That required more data.

It seemed Justine and her contact were working on something. But what? How would he even find out what it was? Did she have a safe spot, and if so, where?

The frustrated grunt Haarlock let out startled Ladrón awake. Displeased raccoon grumbles filled the carriage, and it was all Haarlock could do not to laugh. Since their departure for Claville, the animal slept far more often than usual. Ladrón's top left canine remained missing, even after a bout of professional healing, and Haarlock attributed his lethargy to whatever the raccoon equivalent of depression was.

Can raccoons even get depression?

Ladrón's intelligence, according to his character sheet at least, hovered around that of a preteen. Did that mean he had the same emotional range? Obviously, he knew jealousy, anger, joy, and sadness, so it made sense he'd feel depression, too.

Haarlock looked over Ladrón's sheet, noticing he still sat at 10 levels each in rogue, mage, and fighter. In fact, Ladrón had enough stored experience for dozens of levels more.

What was it he said? He was waiting for me to get stronger.

Pulling up his own notifications, Haarlock saw his seven outstanding levels to apply. The Phantom Blade provided an incredible amount of experience, and after Simon's interrogation, he hadn't been keen on much of anything, let alone leveling. That whole thing was a revealing, if somewhat horrifying, experience.

Another thing Haarlock's level up notifications showed was a new sub-specialization opportunity.

Your patron, Sjena, has provided you with an alternate sub-specialization: Anointed Umbral Blade.

This particular sub-specialization wasn't in the menu, so Haarlock had no way to know what benefits it might incur. Whatever they were, he assumed them to be substantial. Add in the abilities, specialization, and sub-specialization Ladrón would eventually take, and Haarlock wondered just how powerful he'd become.

Now would be the perfect time to level, especially for Ladrón. There would be little privacy once they boarded a ship. Unless they had a private cabin. No, the carriage left too much of a footprint as is.

With the acceptance of the Anointed Umbral Blade sub-specialization, you have lost the following Class Abilities: Chink in Armor. You have lost the following Talents: Shadow Dance, Hidden Blade. You have lost the following Feats: Wrapped in Shadow.

With the acceptance of the Anointed Umbral Blade sub-specialization, the following spell has become a cantrip: Umbral Step. You currently have one (1) 1st Level spell slots available.

You have received the following Anointed Umbral Blade Class Abilities: Sjena's Kiss, Dual Natured - Umbral.

You receive one (1) Talent every two (2) levels. With the loss of your previous Talents, you currently have four (5) Talents to choose.

You receive one (1) Feat every five (5) levels. With the loss of your previous Feats, you currently have three (2) Feats to choose.

NAME: Haarlock	**CLASS**: Anointed Umbral Blade
RACE: Human	**LEVEL**: 27
AGE: 30	**EXPERIENCE**: 95,863
RENOWN/INFAMY: 1,220/808	**TITLE**: Lord
STATS:	**GUILD RANK**: Silver

HP - 210	STR - 42	DEX - 85	INT - 30
WIS - 25	CON - 60	CHA - 40	

SKILLS:

Master	Expert	Skilled	Proficient
Dagger	Stealth	Tracking	Sleight of Hand
	Survival	Athletics	Simple Weapons
	Unarmed Combat	Spycraft	Skinning
		Bow	Vintner
		Bartering	Estate Management
		Lock Pick	Magic Theory

CLASS ABILITIES:	**FEATS**:	**TALENTS**:
Thieves' Cant	Alert	Canny Observer
Improved Sneak Attack	Magic Novice	Resilient
Uncanny Dodge	Pass Without Trace	Improved Animal Bond
Deft Hands	Wrapped in Shadow	Nondescript
Darkvision	Increased Reflexes	Silent Kill
Murder	Increased Endurance	Agile
Sjena's Kiss	Increased Strength	Climber
Dual Natured - Umbral		Blade Twist
		Reflexive Spell
		Pain Tolerance
		Increaed Swiftness
		Intercept Projectile

SPELLS:

Cantrips	1st Level	2nd Level
Mage Hand	Magic Armor	Shadow Tendrils
Mend	---	
Shadowstep		
Umbral Step		

The wave of change that flowed over Haarlock left him chilled to core. It felt as though all warmth was sucked from his body, like he was cast into a dark, wet pit. But that feeling left as quickly as it came, the heat returning like a summer day's warm breeze.

Haarlock shivered as a visceral reaction when he looked down at his hand. The one hidden in the shadowy interior of the carriage. He willed it to fade from view, for his whole body to fade, until he could see himself as almost an outline against the dark.

Both creepy and cool.

Though Haarlock lost abilities, his new ones replaced them and synergized far better. *Sjena's Kiss*, combined with his new Unique weapon, *Sjena's Gift*, allowed his blade to bypass armor entirely. The wound dealt by this attack would require a specialist to heal as it was no longer fully physical in nature. Nor would it leave evidence as having passed through any intervening material, armor or not. Additionally, with both he and the weapon possessing *Dual Natured*, Haarlock could summon his weapon from, and hide it in, any shadow, even one cast by his own body.

Dual Natured - Umbral gave Haarlock an interesting, if somewhat unnerving, ability. It turned him into a being of both light and darkness, allowing him to meld into static shadows and vanish from sight entirely, replacing his previous Feat of *Wrapped in Shadow*. This also gave him a substantial damage reduction from purely physical attacks while active. Now with *Shadowstep* and *Umbral Step* as cantrips, he could hide in and move through shadows like a wraith.

And with Haarlock now a member of Sjena's flock, the *Blessed* ability on the dirk revealed its function. Guided by Sjena's hand, the blade would strike true no matter the difficulty. Once used, the ability needed to recharge while remaining in total darkness for three consecutive days, the number most pleasing to Sjena.

Two Feats and five Talents. While the Talents would provide useful, their enhancements were overall not *that* powerful. On the other hand, the Feats were almost too good to be true. They were truly powerful, giving abilities that bordered on superhuman.

With Haarlock having seen just how absurdly powerful the Phantom Blade was, he knew he needed to make better selections. Before he went for the class' minimum requirements, not bothering to fill out his weakness beforehand. This time would be different.

Feat wise, Haarlock chose *Increased Endurance* and *Increased Strength*. While he could take the less powerful Talent versions, the Feat forms would boost his physical abilities immensely.

Blade Twist, Reflexive Spell, Pain Tolerance, Increased Swiftness, and *Intercept Projectile* rounded out Haarlock's Talents. *Blade Twist* increased the damage multiplier from his *Daggers: Mastery* by one, giving him even greater lethality. With *Reflexive Spell*, Haarlock designated his 1st Level spell *Magic Armor* to be cast instantly, providing an excellent increase in survivability. *Pain Tolerance*, like it says on the label, reduces the negative effects of pain, allowing Haarlock to fight through grievous injury. Finally, *Increased Swiftness* and *Intercept Projectile* would allow him to move more quickly, and, well, intercept incoming projectiles, be it by catching or deflecting. Combined with *Increased Reflexes* and *Alert*, he could theoretically catch an arrow, though this wasn't a guaranteed thing. It sure would be cool if it worked, though.

Then there was Ladrón.

For several months now, the animal's class progression had halted at 10 levels each in mage, fighter, and rogue. By now he should have specialized, and even sub-specialized, with as much experience as he'd received. From what Haarlock understood, animals advanced based on instinct. A sneaky wolf would naturally take levels in rogue as it leveled, eventually specializing into a shadow wolf. Alternatively, a more aggressive one would take levels in fighter and become a dire wolf. Haarlock's teammate in the yearly tournament, Win, mentioned encountering a stealthy deer and a lightning squirrel.

But with Ladrón's intelligence enhancer, and him being a familiar, altered his natural development. Instead of leveling on pure instinct, he paused his development while waiting for Haarlock to get stronger. It seemed with his progression to an Anointed Umbral Blade, Haarlock achieved whatever threshold Ladrón set as *stronger*.

"Alright, little fella. You were waiting on me, now I'm waiting on you."

Ladrón perked up, then gave a grunt of affirmation before looking into the distance. Much like Haarlock, a shiver coursed through the animal's body. Ladrón's fur, normally a mix of brown, black, and gray, shimmered in the soft light of the carriage as it changed to a dark mix of purple and blue. Eventually the colors evened out, leaving his coat darker overall, though with a hint of purple at the edges of the black.

The animal faded into a translucent outline, though Haarlock could still see him in the shadowed seat, before returning to normal opacity. In a blink Ladrón vanished, only to appear next to Haarlock. He disappeared again, this time fading out of existence as he crawled sideways into Haarlock's shadow.

*"*Fun. Hidden.*"*

Haarlock looked around, though he couldn't find his familiar.

"Are you hiding in my shadow?"

*"*Yes.*"*

A few seconds later Ladrón faded into existence on the floor between Haarlock's feet. He chittered excitedly before darting back into the darkness and vanishing. Haarlock looked at his feet, blinked once, then looked back up at the carriage wall and frowned.

That's not going to be a problem. At all.

He reviewed Ladrón's updated character sheet.

NAME: Ladrón **CLASS**: Umbral Brawler
RACE: Raccoon **LEVEL**: 52
AGE: 1 **EXPERIENCE**: 38,251
STATS:

HP - 307	STR - 22	DEX - 27	INT - 6 (17)
WIS - 5	CON - 31	CHA - 20	

SKILLS:

Master	Expert	Skilled	Proficient
	Stealth	Unarmed Combat	Sleight of Hand
		Hunting	Lockpick

ABILITIES:	CLASS ABILITIES:	FEATS:	TALENTS:
Darkvision	Fighting Style: Brawler	Savage Bite	Nose for Treasure
Familiar	Improved Sneak Attack	Survivor	Nimble Climber
Stalk	Dual Natured - Umbral		Fast Fingers
			Charming
			Relentless
			Evasion

SPELLS:

Cantrips	1st Level	2nd Level	3rd Level
---	---	---	---
---	---	---	

Ladrón, no longer a mere raccoon, became a fearsome Umbral Brawler. By virtue of Haarlock's own recently acquired Dual Nature Class Ability, Ladrón's status as a familiar, along with his penchant for getting into scraps, it made sense.

The first thing Haarlock noticed was that the critter's hit points went up by nearly a hundred. That would increase his survivability a *lot*. Boosts to his strength, dexterity, and constitution would help in that regard, too.

Skill wise, Ladrón increased his *Unarmed Combat* from *Proficient* to *Skilled* by way of a Talent. Other Talents included *Relentless*, which gave him increased endurance to run down his targets, and *Charming*, to help against targets of an altogether different variety.

A significant boost to Ladrón's efficacy came in the form of upgraded Feats. *Viscous Bite* turned into *Savage Bite*, and *Tough* became *Survivor*. Not only would he be far, far more durable, he'd deal a significantly increased amount of damage, too.

Couple *Savage Bite* with the Class Ability *Improved Sneak Attack*, and Ladrón would be nearly as deadly as Haarlock in the shadows. Proportionally, at least. The Class Ability *Dual Natured - Umbral* matched Haarlock's ability of the same name, making the animal substantially sneakier and, it seemed, allowed him to hide in Haarlock's shadow.

Ladrón's levels in mage provided him spell slots, and now that he spent the rest of his experience to add even more, he gained an additional second level and a new third level slot. Haarlock would still need to figure out how to teach Ladrón spells, but that was a problem for another time.

Last, but not least, was the revelation of Ladrón's *???* ability. Since the day Haarlock found the gluttonous beast, Ladrón's ability was a mystery. Sophia Blanc the Coach said it wouldn't be overly powerful, instead meshing with another ability in some capacity. She wasn't wrong, but she wasn't exactly right either. *???* turned into *Stalk*, synergizing with Ladrón's other abilities, allowing the critter to effortlessly track down his prey without them realizing he was there. With *Relentless* and *Dual Natured - Umbral*, there would be few who could escape him.

Haarlock dismissed the screen and let out a long breath. With both his and Ladrón's new abilities, they were a *powerful* combination. He hoped they would be powerful enough to figure out and stop whoever sent them to meet their end at the hands of a Phantom Blade.

28

Once Haarlock disembarked at a service port just south of Ostia, he made the day-long trip on foot to Huerto de Vid Azul.

A heavy snow fell the days before, and carts left deep ruts with their passing. Haarlock followed along, taking the winding route back to his estate. The endless blanket of stark white lent beauty to the rolling hills, and each smoking chimney the image of a storybook picture.

The first structure to come into view was Father Jessup's steeple, by far the tallest structure in the area. Once Haarlock crested the next hill, he saw the bodega. Its single chimney bellowed with smoke, evidence of guests enjoying Dubois' cooking.

Well, Aripine, I'm really screwed if they got to you.

***

Mayordomo Aripine's mechanical chair stopped in the foyer. The elderly gnome took a deep breath as she reviewed the bodega's status. Guests ate in the dining area while Chef Dubois and his team worked in the kitchen, and Janice swept the floor.

Everything just as it should be.

With a smile, Aripine proceeded up the stairs to the second floor where, decades ago, she had converted one of the children's rooms into an office. A key opened the lock, and she entered to find...not everything was just as it should be. In the center of the room sat a single bottle of Vid Azul brandywine, a piece of paper folded underneath it.

Aripine's jaw clenched as she closed the door behind her and approached the misplaced bottle. Her chair angled down and forward, and she gingerly slid the paper out in a smooth motion. She looked around the room once before reading the note.

We need to talk.

She knew by the handwriting who it was, and it did nothing to ease her worry.

Bundled in her thickest coat, Aripine exited the warmth of the bodega. She went around the back of the structure to where an iron gate sat nestled at the base of the hill. A large key opened it, and into the cave she went.

Click. Click. Click.

The sounds of Aripine's mechanized chair filled the cavern as she entered the aging room. She went through a small path between the four dozen barrels to an exposed section of the wall. There she removed a signet ring from her vest pocket and pressed it into a particular brick. As the illusory wall shimmered out of existence, Aripine found the secret room devoid of anything but bottles.

"Alright, m'lord. You can come out now." Aripine turned around and surveyed the barrels. "I never much cared to play hide-and-seek."

***

Haarlock deactivated the *Shadow Form* ability of the *Veil of Shadows* and stood up from Aripine's shadow.

"How unfortunate."

The gnome slowly turned to face Haarlock. They stood five feet apart.

"Neat trick. Even neater cloak." Aripine squinted and tilted her head. "You've changed."

"Things have happened."

"Enough with the cloak and dagger. Come out with it." Aripine folded her hands together in her lap and gave her lord a flat look.

"Someone sent me to die." Haarlock sat on a barrel and watched the gnome for a moment. "Someone with far-reaching connections who knew my schedule down to the day I would arrive."

Aripine's left eyebrow rose on her forehead. "Are you insinuating I had something to do with it?"

Haarlock laughed. "I figured you wouldn't bother to have me killed, considering you could effortlessly crush me like a bug and all."

"That *is* true." Aripine nodded to herself. "But I've been out of the game for far too long. I don't even get regular updates as to the goings-on in the adventuring world."

"Has anyone asked about me or my travel plans? Anything?"

"Not out of the ordinary." Aripine regarded Haarlock. "You think they'd come here for information?"

Haarlock looked up at the ceiling. "I take it we have guests?"

"A well-off silversmith and her family from Lady Fantom's land. She's passing through on the way to Ostia to sell her wares."

"How much longer until she leaves?"

"I would imagine another hour. Dubois is probably serving dessert right now."

"Send everyone home for the day once they're gone. We need to talk, and I'd rather not do it in a cave."

"How long have you been here?" Aripine shivered. "And how are you not frozen?"

Haarlock pulled out one of the warming potions and gave it a shake. "These things work wonders."

"They'll also make you go blind."

Haarlock's eyes went wide, and Aripine laughed.

"You really are wound tight, aren't you, m'lord?"

***

Two hours later Haarlock sat by the fire, a cup of warm tea in his hands. Ladrón lay in Aripine's lap, half asleep, his belly full of leftovers.

Haarlock laid out the situation for Aripine, from how it started with Mateo until the conversation with Simon. He left out sensitive details, like who the kingdom spymaster was, but otherwise didn't hold back. Better to have a well-informed ally than one with only half the picture.

The room was quiet for a long time before Aripine spoke.

"This is most disturbing."

"You're telling me." Haarlock huffed and drank his tea.

"How do you think I can help?" Aripine gestured around the room. "I've been here for twice as long as you've been alive. That's a long time to be out of the game."

"I need information on Camilla, Gerard, and Roboute."

"The spymaster, too, but I understand why you won't tell me his name. Though I fear that may hinder your investigation."

"Perhaps, but I have a plan for him."

Aripine absently petted the sleeping raccoon in her lap as her face scrunched up in thought. She stayed that way for nearly a minute.

"I may know someone."

Haarlock perked up. "Really?"

"Believe it or not, there's a gnome even older than I still working for the crown. She's a Clerk for Lemuria's Department of State. They'll have records of Camilla's official diplomatic activities through the Crown."

"Do you think someone could access and alter those records?"

The gnome shook her head. "Something somewhere always gets missed, and there's no better way to miss something than in the gears of bureaucracy."

"What about the others?"

"Any rogues I knew have long since died, so that leaves out Gerard. Roboute is in a similar position. He's worked with my old adventuring guild, the Unbound Legionaries, but there's no one left from my time."

"You can't use your previous tenure to pull some strings?"

"The roster's changed, oh, I'd say three times since I left. Anyone still alive would long since have retired."

Haarlock nodded to himself as he stared at his drink. When he looked up, he saw a smirk on Aripine's face.

"What?"

"You're forgetting something, m'lord."

"Which is?"

"You should start at the beginning: Mateo."

"He's dead, and I have no other leads."

"Sure you do. This all started when he was caught in that illegal tobacco snuff raid. If sending you after Mateo was always part of the plan, so was his arrest."

Haarlock snapped his fingers. "Damn it, you're right. I just need to find records of the arrest but that was months ago."

"Good thing you know a captain of the Ostian guard."

***

Lord Micca Barecna spent his weeks in the city and weekends on his lands, meaning he would return in two days. Haarlock finished his letter, a request for a security audit of his own estate, and had Aripine give it to Bailiff Jan for rush delivery. The urgency of the request might be suspicious, but Haarlock didn't want to wait another week or two for Barecna to pay a visit.

During this time, Aripine drafted a letter to her friend at the State Department. Though she wrote in her native tongue, Gnomish wasn't so rare as to be useful as a cipher. Considering the sensitive nature of the request, she needed to ensure not too much was revealed while still asking for the needed information. It took the Mayordomo several days to carefully blend a narrative of allegory and riddles from Gnomish culture and personal knowledge between the two women. When she finished, Aripine sealed the envelope with wax and handed it to Haarlock with a smile.

"Having fun?"

"Oh, yes." Aripine looked off as she reminisced. "When you get to my age, it's hard for anything to truly excite you. This cloak and dagger stuff was never my forte, but I could see myself slinking around in the dark."

"I couldn't imagine you as a rogue." Haarlock huffed in amusement. "Not after that story of you attacking the front gate of a castle. By yourself."

"I *was* a force to be reckoned with." Aripine punched her palm.

"Remind me never to piss you off. Anyway, what do I do with this letter?"

"If whoever they are thinks you're alive, it's reasonable they'll be watching the comings and goings of the estate. Better to hand-deliver it, even if it means waiting a few extra days for the records."

Haarlock nodded. "Right. But when do I go? The last time I was at the castle was when we broke out of the *Dolphin* during the tournament. I have no idea of the layout, let alone where the State Department is."

"I can draw you a map, but as for when to go, that's tricky." Aripine let out a *hmm*. "Court is held on the last Friday of every month. That's in, what, nine days? You would be far safer with so many other nobles in attendance."

"Good point." Haarlock frowned. "I'm going to assume an actual medieval court is nothing like how the previous world portrayed it."

"I couldn't attest to that, m'lord, but I can tell you it's quite the event. Anyone who's someone attends, all trying their best to advance their place in society. Lots of complaining, too."

"Actually, that sounds pretty similar. And it would be a good place to meet Roboute. He's never one to shy away from social advancement."

"Excellent plan. Do you have one for Gerard yet?"

Haarlock shook his head. "Still working through what to say to Roboute. But one problem at a time. When did Barecna say he'd arrive?"

"Tomorrow morning. Unless he's changed, that means he'll be here at first light. The man wakes early." Aripine shook her head. "Too early."

"Sounds like I'd better get to sleep then."

***

The morning sun showered the land in orange light, giving the snow-covered landscape a beautiful glow. Haarlock watched from his third-floor room as a single carriage approached in the distance, the only sign of something awake at this hour. Besides himself, of course. Hot cup of coffee in hand, Haarlock went downstairs, leaving Ladrón bundled in his bed, snoring quietly.

Though people traveled at night, the bodega wouldn't see a customer, if they did at all, until closer to lunch. It was too easy in the dark to accidentally leave the road because of a snowdrift or miss a sign and head in the wrong direction. With large distances between civilization, getting stuck in the freezing cold far from help was less than ideal.

Haarlock finished his cup and prepared another pot. It was hard to turn down a warm drink on a wintry morning, even for a stoic like Barecna.

Twenty minutes later the carriage stopped at the bodega, and a large, heavily cloaked figure stepped out and hurried inside. Lord Micca Barecna tossed the garment to the floor, and Haarlock could see him visibly shaking. The imposing man eyed the steaming cups in Haarlock's hands.

"Please tell me those are for me."

"Oh yes." Haarlock held both forward, and Barecna took them, pressing the cups to his cheeks. "What happened to you?"

"The damn heating crystal in my carriage broke halfway here. Spent the last hour slowly freezing to death."

Barecna drank one entire cup in a single go, eliciting a look of horrific fascination from Haarlock.

"Isn't that really hot?"

"Scaldingly so, but the benefits of my Feat, *Improved Resilience*, keeps it from actually hurting me, painful though it is." The man drank the second cup just as quickly. "I'd like another, please. One I will actually enjoy the flavor of."

"Of course."

Haarlock led his guest to the fireplace, then went to retrieve the pot of coffee. When he returned, Barecna's boots and overshirt were off, and he sat on the floor in front of the fire. He looked over as the coffee entered.

"Ah, yes. Thank you." Barecna nodded enthusiastically as Haarlock handed him a fresh cup.

"You know, you didn't have to come all the way here, Micca. You could have gone back and gotten a replacement carriage."

"The urgency of your message precluded that." Barecna looked over his coffee with a raised eyebrow.

"Right." Haarlock sighed as he sat on the nearby couch. "Long story short, someone tried to have me killed."

Barecna's other eyebrow joined the first, then he blinked once.

"My thoughts exactly."

"I noticed you seemed...different when I first arrived. Whoever made the attempt must have been powerful."

"A Phantom Blade."

"That's concerning." Barecna's jaw clenched. "What have you done or learned to warrant an assassination by someone of that caliber?"

"I've spent considerable time reviewing things, and as far as I can tell, I know nothing."

"Unlikely."

"I arrived in this world less than a year ago. Granted, in that time I've made powerful friends, but anything I've learned is known by others. Others with more power and reach than I will ever achieve."

Barecna frowned. "So, someone came to kill you out of the blue?"

"No. I was sent to investigate a Courier named Mateo Cabrera."

Haarlock explained his first quest through Shattersong, how he tracked Mateo to his cache of evidence, and finally, the assassination attempt. To keep both him and Barecna safe, Haarlock kept the details to a minimum, only mentioning necessary names and places.

"That's quite the tale." Sufficiently warmed, the guard captain moved to the couch. He leaned forward, staring into the fire. "And a disturbing one."

"Tell me about it."

"What do you need from me?"

"Just like that, you're willing to help?

Barecna turned to Haarlock. "Despite what you may think, you've learned something that makes you a liability. They sent a Phantom Blade after you, which means whatever it is involves powerful people. And when powerful people are involved, it usually means corruption. Any help I provide will help root out that corruption, leading to a safer nation, if not just my city."

"You'd be putting a target on your back."

"I'm a captain in the Ostian guard. I've been putting away petty criminals, corrupt businessmen, and traitorous nobles for years. Adding one more target won't make much of a difference."

Try as he might, Haarlock couldn't hold back a laugh when he saw the sly smile Barecna shot him.

"Fair enough." Haarlock shook his head. "But I don't need you to do anything overtly dangerous. Just find me the records of Mateo Cabrera's arrest."

"That's not a problem. Are you wanting anything specific?"

“I don’t really know what I’m looking for, so the more information the better: arresting officer names, incident location, others involved, everything I can get.”

“As a captain, I can access the archives, but I’m no scribe. It’ll take some time to copy the documents.”

“How long?”

“There are a few things I must attend to when I return to the city. I’d say no more than a week.”

Haarlock let out a *hmm.* “I’m attending court in nine days. Meet me there?”

“No, too conspicuous.” Barecna shook his head, then smirked again. “I can meet you somewhere the day after and pass the documents then.”

“What, like we’re spies?” Haarlock gave the man a sideways look.

“Something like that. I’ve always wanted to do covert work.”

“Hearing the call of the rogue lifestyle, I take it?”

Barecna gave a dismissive wave. “No, just a fantasy of mine. Once they promoted me to captain, my days turned into paperwork, inspections, and interviews. Your stunt at *Raven Rock Holdings* was the most excitement I’ve had since your stunt at the *Dolphin.*”

“Sorry about that.” Haarlock grimaced. “But it’s kind of interesting how you’re the second person to tell me they thought about being a rogue.”

“Really? Who else?”

“Aripine.”

“I can’t imagine her as a rogue.” Barecna laughed, then stopped and frowned. “Actually, I can. My great-grandfather knew her, and his journal tells some *wild* stories. No doubt they’d be far wilder if she were a rogue.”

“I’d like to read those sometime. Learning about her firsthand would be an experience.”

“Of course.” The guard captain finished his drink. “But first, if there truly are sinister forces at work, we need to fabricate a reason for my visit.”

"I've thought about that already. You've provided me with an excellent list of security upgrades, which include the purchase of weapons."

"It sounds like something I'd do."

Barecna smiled. On their first meeting, he gifted Haarlock a Masterwork short sword, one crafted by the artisans of his own lands. It only made sense to purchase more of the same.

"But you'll have to tell me what I need and how much it'll cost."

Haarlock handed Barecna a sheet of paper with the demographics of his land's hamlet, Farncombe. The man looked it over for a second before doing some mental math.

"Swords are terrible weapons for defense, especially for the untrained. I'd suggest two dozen spears, a dozen shields, along with a half dozen leather chestpieces with matching bracers and greaves. That would give your populace more than enough umph to take on any monsters or bandits that might wander in."

Haarlock curled his lip. "I can't imagine that will be cheap."

"Spears are cheap, as are shields. The armor will be the largest expense. I'll get figures for the cost, but I wouldn't expect it to be more than five hundred gold for Common quality equipment."

"Not as bad as I thought."

"You're getting the family discount."

29

Janice arrived in short order and prepared a quick breakfast. Her cooking roused Ladrón, and she sang a soft song to him as she worked. The attention she paid the critter, physically, emotionally, and culinarily, ensured he kept out of Haarlock and Barecna's hair.

Barecna waited until Aripine arrived before he said his goodbyes. Come to find out, as a child his father would send him to work on the vineyard during the harvest. Aripine would regale him and the other youths with her exploits as an adventurer in the evening, and they would pick grapes by hand during the day. For nearly a decade Barecna did this, and the two stayed friends ever since.

With the guard captain gone, Haarlock prepared to head into the city. Marcon would expect him around this time, as would Roboute and Gerard. Camilla Albertine, and by proxy Shattersong, theoretically didn't know what Haarlock was up to. What would they do when he failed to show up? Send people out to find him? Though Ostia's population hovered around a million people, magic would allow someone to find Haarlock with both speed and ease. Better they knew he was here, sooner rather than later, and better to do it on his terms.

But how soon? An extra week's delay wouldn't be suspicious. Then again, Roboute wanted him to use the wooden calling card to send word if Justine contacted anyone. That was long enough ago now that Roboute might get worried and start looking for him.

Haarlock went to the enchanted bird clock in his room. The wooden dove perched gracefully on the timepiece, waiting to accept its next communication. He stared at it, wondering what to send to Roboute. He needed something to pique the Illusionist's curiosity but also keep him from prying into Haarlock's affairs for the time being.

Keeping it simple and to the point, with a bit of aggression and suspicion, would do nicely. Haarlock removed a sheet of paper from the nearby writing desk, dipped the quill in ink, then wrote in the nicest script he could.

There's been an incident.

I am attending the next scheduled court. If you are not in attendance, I will assume you are complicit.

If you, or anyone else, attempt to contact me before this time, I will consider it a hostile act and respond accordingly.

With his letter complete, Haarlock rolled it up and placed it into the feet of the bird, then called for Aripine. When she arrived, he taught her the words to activate the clock's enchantment and asked her to wait three days to send it.

Once he had gathered his equipment, loaded his backpack with extra clothes and supplies, and with Ladrón hiding in his shadow, Haarlock headed out on foot. He wasn't sure how easily recognizable his own carriage would be, and besides, the carriage moved roughly as fast as someone walking, anyway. *Increased Endurance* and *Increased Swiftness* would keep Haarlock moving with speed, allowing him to make it to the capital in record time. Hopefully, he had enough warming potions left to make the distance.

***

Even with the frigid cold, hundreds of thousands of people went about their business, all moving with purpose. Be it day or night, summer or winter, Ostia never slept and never stopped.

But where to go? Haarlock thought back to his time in the tournament and what someone had said. *If you ever need to lie low, go to any larger inn and ask the purveyor for a room on a floor they don't have.* That was code that you were on the lam, and for a premium, the inn would give you a key to the back door and a room as close to it as possible. Anyone who came asking about you would get the runaround and you'd get a heads-up.

Most transients found themselves on the eastern and southern sides of the city, so it took Haarlock a while to find a two-story tavern/inn elsewhere. Even in the daytime the interior was dimly lit, the windows boarded up to keep the heat in. Of which there was ample. Fireplaces on either side of the room crackled with burning logs. Servers brought steaming cups to the smattering of patrons, all of whom wore furs and thick clothing. None looked to be adventurers, but then again, cloaks covered their bodies. A handful of people came and went from the open doorway in the back labeled with a hanging sign that read *accommodations*.

Haarlock walked to the bar and sat down, dropping his pack next to him, then placed three silver coins on the counter. The bartender, a human man with well-styled dark hair, came over and set a cup of warm cider in front of him.

"Evening, m'lord. What brings you in?"

"I didn't know it, but this." Haarlock put his hands around the cup, sighing as the heat soaked into his flesh.

"It's a popular drink this time of year, true." The man chuckled. "Anything else? We have salted pork, vegetable stew, and, if I remember, some ginger cakes left."

*"*Cakes. Want.*"*

"Yeah, yeah." Haarlock mentally sighed. "You allow animals in here?"

"So long as it isn't dangerous."

"He's only dangerous to food."

Haarlock opened his cloak and Ladrón hopped out, then climbed up on his own stool. The animal sat back on his haunches and met eyes with the bartender.

"Not sure if you're psychic, but he wants some ginger cakes."

"Don't need to read minds to know what he wants." The man chuckled again. "Yourself, m'lord?"

"A bowl of stew sounds great."

The man nodded and went into the back, returning with the order a few minutes later. Ladrón's cakes, of which there were five, vanished before Haarlock made it to his second spoonful. Ten minutes went by before the bartender checked in.

"Need a refill?" The man pointed to Haarlock's empty cup.

"Not, but I could use a room."

"We got plenty available, but nothing fancy."

"I don't need fancy, but I could use a room on the third floor." Haarlock didn't look up from the bowl.

The man nodded once. "We can accommodate that request. How many days?"

"As long as this will get me." Haarlock laid three gold coins on the counter.

"Three weeks sound good?"

"Perfect."

"Excellent, m'lord. We'll get your room ready right away." The bartender snapped his fingers to get a server's attention, then gave a head jerk towards the rooms. Ten minutes later the bartender laid a key in front of Haarlock. "Go to the left, second to last on the right."

"Much appreciated."

Haarlock downed the last of his third drink, took the key, and went towards the room, waiting in the hallway for a few minutes to ensure no one followed him. Though on the smaller side, the room held more than enough amenities: a bathtub, a dresser, a bed, and a sturdy chest. He laid his sword, quiver, bow, and backpack in the corner, then removed his adventuring attire and changed into pajamas. The long walk in the cold and the warm meal called him to sleep.

Ladrón popped out of the cloak before Haarlock neatly folded it and laid it on top of the dresser. He explored the room, sniffing around every piece of furniture before he stripped out of his armor and buried himself under the covers. Considering the bed wasn't big enough for both of them, Haarlock resigned himself to a furry bedmate.

Slowly Haarlock drifted to sleep, the comfort and warmth of the bed seeping through him. Dreams eluded him, and morning came in what felt like an instant.

As his mind returned to the waking world, something buzzed in the back of it. Something in his room. Magic. It wasn't powerful, just different. He recognized it as being with him since he first arrived in Ostia. With all the background noise, both mundane and magical, he paid it no attention.

Is that a tracking spell?

Haarlock's eyes shot open as he sat up in bed. He went to his backpack, where the effect originated, and removed everything from it. It wasn't in his clothes or his supplies. It came from Justine's items. Haarlock took the bundle and unwrapped it on his dresser, laying out each item and focusing his magical senses on them.

Her pendant. Made of silver, the circular design held a trio of small sapphires in the center. Whatever magic suffused it wasn't there at the bodega, nor at Claville. Haarlock searched everything he left with to ensure it wasn't tracked before he returned to his estate. It had to self-activate when he arrived in Ostia. But why?

The magic wasn't strong. Just enough for him to sense it now. Haarlock searched back through his limited magical theory, recalling a section on enchantments, and specifically about items enchanted as pairs. Like a lock and key.

What did it go to? And if this was the key, how close would the lock need to be for the enchantments to react to one another? He had to be close enough now for it to be active, but with how weak the magic was, the distance could be quite far.

Haarlock sat on the end of his bed, staring at the pendant. Did Justine wear this the first time they met, when she brought him into the Thieves' Guild guildhall? He knew she wore it when he helped plan the heist with Acorn. And Gerard.

Gerard. The guildmaster. Haarlock grumbled to himself as he tried to fit it all together. Was this pendant something important, or just another loose end? It felt important. Jewelry this valuable wouldn't be from her family. They lived too modest a lifestyle. But why bring it on a cross-country trek where it could easily get lost or damaged?

No, this was important.

Rousing Ladrón, Haarlock helped the animal suit up, then did likewise. He needed answers as to what this enchantment went to, and he had an idea of how to find them.

An hour north he went until the coliseum came into view. The massive stone edifice loomed over the other buildings, by far the largest in the area. Banners hung from the top, each depicting common creatures like rabbits and horses to monstrous ones such as dire wolves, dragons, and merpeople. What event, if any, they signified was lost on Haarlock.

Through alleys and down main avenues Haarlock went, doing his best to randomize his path to evade any potential followers. Even using the occasional *Shadowstep* to jump across busy intersections.

Once Haarlock reached the coliseum he found it to be busier than he would expect in the winter. Granted, he had no frame of reference for how busy it should be at this, or any other, time of the year. Groups of people went to and from the structure, some loading crates, both large and small, onto flatbed wagons. When they finished one, another would replace it, and the process repeated. Once Haarlock moved close enough, he could see steady bursts of steam coming through the barred opening at the top of one massive crate.

Is this a menagerie?

On cue, a roar came from inside, and the enormous man moving it yelled something and hit the side with his fist. He entered the line of people going inside.

Haarlock watched for a while, then joined a large group as they approached the building. They chatted amongst themselves about pedestrian topics, doing their best to avoid the crates. Once in the outer corridors, Haarlock broke from the group and moved to the side where he could see into the inner courtyard. Dozens of crates, organized into neat rows, filled the space.

Guards, both private and from the city, patrolled the area. Each held an electric prod Haarlock recognized from his time in the *Dolphin*. Some carried nets made of thick rope on their hips, too.

Around the coliseum Haarlock walked, making nearly a full circle before he found someone who looked official. The obese man wore layers of subdued colors, though his fur hat stood out by how tall it was. He and a group of much smaller men stood obnoxiously in the middle of the corridor, blocking the paths of others as they discussed the events of the coming days.

"Kint, you'll ensure sector four's vendors are in the correct spot. We don't need another incident like last year. Bret, keep the guards out of the damn whiskey." The obese man flipped through several pages on a clipboard. "Jerell, Amon, and Theo, you're on runner duty. If you need help, grab Serek."

The three men looked at one another and nodded.

"I'll be set up on the second floor, southern side. Things should go as smoothly as they've done in the last few years, but don't get complacent. We'll have one last meeting tomorrow morning at my office. See you then."

Haarlock approached once the others left, coming up on the large man's side. He needed the man to help him while forgetting him after he left. A little unrequited crush would do just the trick.

"Hello, excuse me." Haarlock had his gloves off and waved with his left hand. The one with his signet ring. "Apologies for the interruption."

"Ah, good morning, m'lord." The man tipped his sizable hat, but otherwise kept his expression neutral. "How may I assist you?"

"I'm looking for someone I met a few months ago. During the Academy tournament."

The man's eyes hardened as he gave an *oh great* smile. Haarlock smiled back with as much enthusiasm as he could muster and put on his best pleading voice.

"I realize it's a long shot, but it would mean everything if I could see her again."

"Who is it you seek?"

"A Seer named Zeline." Haarlock slumped his shoulders. "Her fortune came true, as I knew it would, and I've been stricken ever since to know more of what my future holds."

An eye-roll and a shake of the head. Haarlock had the man just where he wanted him.

"She has that effect on people." The man gestured for Haarlock to follow. "We should have her business address on file in the records office."

"Most excellent. I didn't catch your name."

"Portreeve Haverstrand, m'lord. What may I call you?"

"Love struck, I'm afraid."

"Of course."

Haarlock could hear the subtle groan Haverstrand let out and stifled a laugh.

It took them several minutes to make it to the records office on the second floor. Once inside, the Portreeve found the correct box on the second try and pulled out a single sheet of paper.

"Here we are. Zeline Aetos." Haverstrand found a scrap piece of paper and wrote on it. Once done, he returned the file, then handed the scrap to Haarlock. "Your muse is at this address. It's about a thirty-minute walk due east, nestled between two narrow canals next to a marketplace."

"Many thanks, Haverstrand. You've ensured my success no matter the endeavor." Haarlock gave a formal bow.

"Of course, m'lord. It's been my pleasure."

His smile showed it was anything but. Even so, Haarlock gave him a head nod and walked off without another word.

The winding path Haarlock took added another half-hour to the trip, and just as the large man said, Zeline's shop stood alone on a small sliver of land between two canals. It looked as though the builders had chopped off the edges of the two-story building to fit in the cramped space, with symmetry a foregone conclusion. The door sat offset to the left, with one large and two small windows on the ground floor, and three small windows on the second. A high-arched, single-person bridge connected the small island to the mainland, leading visitors into what would be a verdant herb garden in the summer. A wooden sign over the door identified the building as *Zeline's Oasis*.

The front door opened as Haarlock approached, and a young orc woman in a pleated green dress greeted him.

"Good morning, Lord Haarlock. Zeline has been expecting you."

30

The interior of *Zeline's Oasis* looked exactly as Haarlock predicted.

Every manner of esoterica filled shelves and tables, from animal skeletons to crystals, dried plants, books, and jars of preserved animal parts. Incense floated heavily in the air, diffusing the incoming light into a milky, spiced scented haze. Plants of all sizes occupied windowsills and corners, giving the space a primordial vibe. A set of stairs in the back right corner led to the second floor, but otherwise this was the only room on the first.

"Would you like a refreshment, m'lord?" The orc smiled, revealing gold bands on her tusks.

"No, thank you." Haarlock looked around. "This is quite the place."

"Thank you." The woman dipped her head. "Zeline offers only the best."

"Of that I have no doubt."

The orc watched Haarlock with a curious expression, and when Haarlock met eyes with her, she smiled again.

"Yes?"

"It is rare Zeline is flustered, with her being a Seer and all."

Haarlock frowned. "My presence flusters her?"

"Yes, it does." Another voice called out from the haze, echoing everywhere at once.

"Neat trick, Zeline." Haarlock looked into the air. "I could use your help with another."

"So the river of fate has shown me. Among other things."

"Good things?"

"Not necessarily."

That's not foreboding at all.

Wood creaked behind Haarlock, and when he turned around, there was now an open door in the back corner. Zeline, wearing a simple white linen dress and no shoes, stepped out of the doorway, a dark expression on her face.

"Close up the shop, Lilou, and leave for the day. If anyone approaches you, about anything, don't answer the questions and go immediately to a guard post. I will come to get you if you do."

Lilou nodded. "I understand."

"Haarlock, come with me. Leave the animal in your shadow."

Mouthing *sorry* to Lilou, Haarlock followed Zeline into the other room. Sporadically placed tea lights revealed a recessed sitting area in the center filled with thin, square pillows. Images of alchemical formulae hung in frames on one wall, with another covered in shamanistic ritual items. The far wall remained bare, as did the wall with the doorway.

"Wear this."

Zeline held out a braided hemp necklace adorned with long, thin pieces of dark wood, colored stones, and small animal bones. Her piercing green eyes left no room for refusal.

When Haarlock draped the necklace around his neck, he could feel the subtle workings of magic wash over him.

"What is..."

A finger pressed against Zeline's lips. She went to the door and locked it, then to each of the room's corners and lit incense. Once in the recessed sitting area she put a similar necklace around her neck before waving Haarlock over and gesturing for them both to sit.

"No one will be able to scry our conversation, nor will any attempt at locating you now, or where you've been for the last few hours, succeed." Zeline eyed

Haarlock and took a slow, calming breath. "What exactly have you roped me into?"

"That's what I'm trying to figure out." Haarlock removed the triple sapphire pendant and offered it to Zeline. "The person I was sent on a quest with carried this, but they died."

"Died how?"

"An assassin came for us both."

"And you lived." Zeline took the item, holding it in her hand as if it might break. "Do you believe this will help you discover why they died?"

"I do."

"At least now I know why a sense of foreboding overtook me early this morning."

Haarlock huffed in amusement. "I wondered if you could sense I was coming."

"Typically, my abilities only work close to when the person will arrive, but with how much possibility revolves around you at the moment?" Zeline shuttered.

"I'm going to assume that's not a good thing."

"Your future is tumultuous, to say the least."

"Wonderful." Haarlock gestured to the pendant. "If you can help me figure out what that goes to, perhaps my future will be a little quieter."

The Seer fixed her green eyes on the pendant, and her gaze went far away. She blinked once and looked up at Haarlock.

"I will help you, but I demand a steep payment."

"Name your price."

"You will never seek my services again."

Haarlock shook his head in disbelief. "Things are that bad?"

"They have the possibility to be. The further I am from you, the less those possibilities involve me."

"As I have no one else to go to, I must agree to your terms."

Zeline's shoulders relaxed. Without knowing how tense he was, Haarlock's own shoulders followed suit.

The woman reached under the pillow she sat on and removed a leather pouch, then took three bundles of herbs from inside. She removed the pillow between them to reveal a metal brazier inset into the floor, then placed the pendant inside and sprinkled one bundle over the top. Magic coursed through the air, slow and steady. The woman took up a soft, rhythmic chanting, changing tempo as she added each of the two other herb bundles to the metal bowl. Over the brazier she moved her arms, first in wide, flowing patterns, building speed as the shapes grew closer and more intricate.

In a flash, almost too fast for Haarlock to see, Zeline clapped her hands together and a shockwave of force burst from them. Smoke rose from the brazier as the herbs caught fire. It took only seconds for the flames to consume them, leaving the sapphire pendant covered in fragrant soot. Zeline removed the pendant with her left hand, using her right to mark her face, once above and below each eye, with the fine black powder.

The woman closed her eyes and tilted her head to the right. "This is a key...to a door. But not a door. It's secret, hidden in plain sight." She frowned and tilted her head to the left. "A counter-scrying spell works its will against me."

Reaching out to Haarlock with her free hand, Zeline removed one of the wooden sticks from his necklace, then a matching one from her own. She placed them both in her mouth before performing intricate hand gestures over the pendant. Once done, Zeline sat the sticks to the side and closed her eyes again.

"West. South. Near still water." Another head tilt. An eyebrow raise. "It's large, empty, with a blue feather." When Zeline's eyes opened again, they changed from a milky haze back to their normal green. "Whatever magical defenses this place has, they're potent. I can provide no more."

"Then that will have to suffice."

"Good luck to you, m'lord." Zeline held the pendant out to Haarlock. "Keep the necklace you now wear and break one of the wooden sticks when you wish to obfuscate your movements. Each will last a single day."

By her expression, Zeline had nothing further to say. Haarlock took the pendant and left.

***

West and south.

Haarlock walked for two hours, taking a random, winding path. Though he had no reason to think someone was following him, he still took precautions: sudden turnarounds, nonsensical shortcuts, and so on. *Nondescript* would help anyone visually trying to identify him, as would the tightly pulled hooded cloak. Ladrón's new abilities kept him hidden and not riding on Haarlock's shoulder. That would *significantly* lower Haarlock's silhouette. Plus, the ring of obfuscation and one of Zeline's enchanted wooden sticks.

With luck, these precautions would throw off anyone following him. Who, though, was still the question. Haarlock doubted Roboute would risk sending someone, but then again, he was a powerful mage. He had already traced Mateo's movements with only a scrap of paper. Camilla, as the leader of a guild and a high-ranking official, could send any number of people to find Haarlock. But the only way past is through, and Haarlock needed to find a secret door.

But how to find which door the sapphire pendant unlocked? *Still water* could mean anything from a swimming pool to a filled bucket. *Large* and *empty* could mean a fresh worksite or a warehouse. And a *blue feather*. Is that a sigil? Perhaps for a menagerie like what's happening at the coliseum? Or any of the likely thousands of businesses that filled Ostia. It could even be graffiti.

Haarlock sighed. He could easily ask someone for directions, but that left a trail, even a minute one. On he walked, up and down the streets, for several more hours.

Lunch came and went, then dinner. As the sun dipped low in the sky Haarlock found himself at the western docks, not too far from where he first arrived in Ostia. Even with the fading light, people hurried about their business, pulling carts and unloading ships. Food vendors shouted discounts before they closed, and buskers ended their runs.

It was easily an hour's walk back to the hotel, and Haarlock's feet started hurting long before now. He looked around for any sort of housing, be it reputable or not. Walking all the way back just to turn around and do it again in the morning would *suck*. The moisture from the lake gave an edge to the cold, and for whatever reason Haarlock just wasn't feeling it. Another twenty minutes of searching and he broke down and asked for directions.

"Excuse me." Haarlock approached a man standing next to a stack of boxes by a dock entrance. He looked cold and miserable, bundled up as best he could in clothing not nearly thick enough. "I need directions."

The man eyed Haarlock with suspicion. "Ask a city guard. I'm busy."

"Will a silver free you up?" Haarlock held out his gloved hand, a single coin resting in it.

"Whatever." He snatched the silver and shoved it in a pocket, looking around with a frown. "Where do you need to go? I know a few good places to warm you up on a chilly night like this."

"No, nothing like that. I just need directions to a cheap place to sleep. One that doesn't ask questions."

Once again, the man looked at Haarlock with unease. "And you're paying me a silver?"

"You're going to forget about this conversation, right?"

"Mister, I don't even know what you're talking about."

"Exactly. So where am I going?"

The man jerked his head to the left. "Two blocks down, head west another block, then you'll see a signboard. The inn is the building the board is on, but you've got to go around through the alley to the left to get to it."

Haarlock nodded once and headed off. Ten minutes later he found the sign board and noticed one symbol on it. A stylized feather. What color it had been he didn't know; the wood was weathered with divots and splinters.

You've got to be kidding me.

No directions pointed the way, but Haarlock knew it had to be close. He looked around, but even with his *Dark Vision* he couldn't see a corresponding feather sign.

"Alright, time to get to work." A raccoon head poked out of the shadow on the ground between his legs. *"See this feather symbol? Find a building with the same one on it."*

Ladrón looked at the symbol, chittered once, then bolted out onto the ground and into the darkness. Haarlock headed in the opposite direction.

South two blocks, then west one, and back up north four. Haarlock did this three times before the mental callings of a raccoon filled his head.

*"*Sign. Found. Come. Now. Where?*"*

"Calm down, little guy. I'm west of where we started."

*"*West?*"*

"You don't know directions? The way the sun sets."

*"*Come. Now.*"*

"Yeah, yeah."

As Haarlock made his way east, he finally caught sight of Ladrón in the middle of the street. If he wasn't expecting to see the animal, he would have found the sight of an armored raccoon all alone in the dark entirely unnerving. Good thing they were in a narrow back alley, far from any nightly foot traffic.

"Come on then. Where are we going?"

Ladrón led Haarlock north through two alleys, then west one block. A hanging sign with the same stylized feather, this one a vibrant blue, adorned a two-story corner warehouse. Haarlock told Ladrón to return to the shadows and keep an eye out for anyone following, then continued towards the building.

He walked past, not paying it any attention, turned left down an alley, and activated the *Shadowform* ability of his cloak.

This wasn't the first time Haarlock used the *Veil of Shifting Shadow's* ability. On his way to Ostia, he activated it while inside a carriage. It would do him no good to use it for the first time in a rush, or when it was life or death. And boy, was Haarlock glad he experimented with it.

When the effect activated, a rush of unnatural cold coursed over his skin. It wasn't painful or uncomfortable, but it was just odd enough to cause a moment's hesitation if you didn't know it would happen. And the perspective change was disorienting, too. The world desaturated into black and white, while the contrast ramped up, giving Haarlock's *Dark Vision* a massive boost. Before he could see in the dark well enough, like night vision from the previous world, but now it was like daytime. Haarlock could even see Ladrón as he moved within the darkness like a black blur.

Haarlock turned his attention back to the building. No light source came from inside. Ladrón slinked into the alley on the left, coming back out onto the street to the right. Nothing there either.

"Can you get inside?"

*"*No. Windows. Door. Locked.*"*

In an instant Haarlock *Shadowstepped* across the street before *Umbral Stepping* through the wall and into the building. He found himself in an office long since abandoned by anything but scavengers. Scraps of decayed paper lay strewn about, and the furniture, a shoddy desk and broken chair, were the only other things inside.

Out into the hallway Haarlock crept, his dirk at the ready. Two more offices, a meeting room, and the reception area looked as well-kept as the first room. A doorway across from the entrance led into a warehouse. The space was maybe 10,000 square feet, with regularly spaced columns holding the roof aloft. Rectangular windows near the ceiling let in what little moonlight shone through the clouds, and a pair of large barn doors occupied the street side corner in the back. Beyond a smattering of crates, barrels, and discarded *stuff*, the space was empty.

Haarlock deactivated the cloak's ability when he returned to the office. When Ladrón called the all-clear, he opened the front door and let the animal in. Ladrón immediately went into search mode, his nose to the ground, following every scent. Haarlock now stood with hands on his hips in the reception area.

A door that's not a door, hidden in plain sight. What does that even mean?

If there were a secret door to be found, Ladrón's *Nose for Treasure* would literally sniff it out. In the meantime, Haarlock went back into the warehouse to search the crates and barrels.

The first box, empty save for broken glass, smelled like lemon. Same with the next one, also empty. The third, though, held a dozen bars of lemon-scented soap, each wrapped in wax-lined paper and tied with a string and stamped with a stylized blue feather. Two more crates contained the remains of broken glass, though they smelled of lavender. Residue of some kind lined the bottom of the box, having soaked into the wood. A search of one barrel found it partially full of vinegar, while another, empty, smelled like olive oil.

On the far side of the space, Ladrón sniffed through a pile of packing material, filling the deathly quiet place with soft rustling.

Haarlock looked at the crate of broken glass. This place was obviously a cleaning supply company of some sort, which allowed large quantities of people and cargo to come and go without suspicion. He had to admit; it was a good place for a secret hideout. Or a drug lab. The glass triggered a thought.

Jars have lids, and a lid is a type of door. And there are, or were, a lot of jars here. Is there a specific jar I need to find?

No, that wasn't it. The lid of a crate could be seen as a door. So could a window, or even a drawer. Those were the only things Haarlock had yet to look through.

Back in the office, Haarlock went through each piece of furniture, emptying the contents of the filing cabinets and desks onto the reception room floor. Once he had collected everything, he sat down in front of it and examined each piece, putting *Estate Management* into use.

Bills of lading, supply orders, news articles, and one financial ledger showed *Blue Feather Cleaning* as a profitable business. It seemed after a decade of steady business, supplying dozens of apothecaries, general stores, and larger estates, the owner suddenly died. Less than a year later, his sons ran the place into foreclosure after a series of poor investments. Actually, as Haarlock compared dates on receipts to the purchase of supplies, it appeared those investments were illicit in nature. While he didn't know the finer points of medieval soap making, he could see the trend of ingredients changing once the father died. Overly large quantities of tallow, more than triple the amount, started coming from a new supplier.

Your basic money laundering scheme cropped up in the financials, too. A new set of office furniture, far too much for the small space, was ordered two months in a row. Next came new windows, triple what was needed, and finally a hilariously exorbitant remodel of the sewer intake in the alley.

Haarlock sat the ledger down as he laughed out loud. Was this entire thing really a front, from the abandoned warehouse to the failed business, all made to obfuscate the fact Justine did something to the sewer?

Calling for Ladrón, Haarlock sent the critter outside to look for a sewer grate, and sure enough, he found one in the alley. An *Umbral Step* outside, and Haarlock looked at the recessed metal cover. Haarlock took a deep breath through his nose. It didn't smell great, but it didn't smell anywhere near as bad as a sewer. He kneeled and pried the lid open with his dirk to find a metal ladder going down ten feet.

Everyone expects to see a sewer, but no one pays them any attention. Justine, you clever girl.

A small, single-person hallway at the bottom went under the warehouse some thirty feet, ending at a brick wall. In the top left corner, nearly indiscernible to his bare fingers, Haarlock felt a small recess. It took him a moment to orient the sapphire pendant correctly before it clicked into place and a weak magical effect went off. Haarlock waited, motionless, for something to happen. A trap? A trap door? A few seconds passed before the air pressure changed and the wall itself hinged open.

The space inside looked as if it had once been the warehouse's basement. Two wooden supports from the first floor extended down through the ceiling, and the floor and walls were made from large pieces of rectangular stone. A living space occupied one corner, and along one wall hung dozens of pieces of paper above a long wooden table. More pages covered the table and filled boxes sitting in front of it. An empty equipment rack hung to the left of the door. Altogether, it couldn't have been more than fifteen hundred square feet in size.

What kept the space comfortably warm, Haarlock didn't know. It wasn't far enough underground for the temperature to stay regulated, and the mattress in the corner only had a single blanket on it. He assumed whatever enchantments warded the space from scrying included provisions for comfort. A small globe on each of the two pillars provided soft light throughout the room.

"Damn, this is an awesome secret base."

Ladrón chittered his agreement as he sniffed the air.

Haarlock moved to the bench. The papers, hundreds of them, included maps, hand-written notes, sketches of people, receipts, and what looked to be neatly penned government records. Books lay hidden under piles, as did sketches of people from varying races and economical means. Some pages held a single date, others just names, while still more contained coded messages in what looked like a modified form of *Thieves' Cant*. He assumed there was some kind of organizational scheme here, but it would take hours to decipher it.

Good thing he had little else to do until court. With the secret wall-door sealed behind him, Haarlock stripped out of his warmer layers and set to the task of working through the intel.

Focused determination set it as Haarlock sorted the documents, at first trying to understand the general flow of Justine's system. Receipts for a cobbler business were bundled with the family trees of three noble houses, none of which still existed, while the quest activities of an adventuring team sat between the dinner order of a merchant from another country. Either Justine possessed a photographic memory, or she kept a synopsis off-premises, because none of it made sense. Three hours passed before Haarlock gave up and started his own methodology.

Haarlock used the blank pages for his own notes, and within the first hour he filled three of them. Hours more went by as Haarlock followed each plot thread, consolidating page after page into a handful of bullet points. By the time Ladrón woke up, Haarlock was in the center of the floor surrounded by stacks of his own papers.

*"*Food?*"*

"What?" Haarlock blinked as he looked around.

Ladrón climbed out of the corner bed and yawned. He shook out his dark fur, long since removed from the armored harness, then stretched.

*"*Morning. Breakfast.*"*

Haarlock suddenly felt the soreness in his muscles and the exhaustion behind his eyes. Then he noticed how much work he had completed.

"Did I work through the night?"

*"*Yes. Breakfast?*"*

Standing and stretching out his muscles, Haarlock felt his stomach grumble with hunger pangs.

"Good idea."

Though he tested *Shadowstep* and *Umbral Step*, Haarlock couldn't leave the confines of the base. A magical effect blocked him, but he felt as if he could attune to it. *Magical Theory: Proficient* told him it could be done, just not how. So, he left the mundane way, ensuring the sapphire pendant stayed clutched tightly in his hand as he sealed the secret door behind him. He also broke one of the thin wooden sticks Zeline gave him.

A quick breakfast, fresh air, and some light stretching brought life back into Haarlock's body. *Increased Endurance* kept him going, but he knew it wouldn't last forever. Eventually he'd need sleep, and the longer he put it off, the worse his analysis would become. He could even miss some critical detail. With discretion being the better part of valor, Haarlock returned to the secret base and slept.

31

A rested mind is a productive mind, and Haarlock made great headway into Justine's research over the next few days. Fresh eyes helped bring perspective, too.

Overall, Justine's investigation focused on seven nobles, four adventurers, and a dozen merchants, all based in Ostia. She linked them together, tracking investments, purchase orders, Thieves' and Adventurer's guilds activities, and even their dinner arrangements.

Haarlock remembered back to the secret meeting during the Academy tournament, and how evidence of market manipulations, all with disastrous results, were found. A new merchant would come into town, drive down the price of material goods to the point of crashing the market, and then leave. Prices would skyrocket, and another merchant would arrive to take advantage. Not only did this throw the entire supply chain into chaos, but the new merchants would also send their profits outside Lemuria, slowly draining the nation of liquidity.

Were these merchants part of that conspiracy? Justine had traced the involvement of two of them and four of the nobles to the same company, an import/exporter called *Far Waters Trading*. She had little other information on the business, though one thing caught Haarlock's attention. Gerard Parnell, guildmaster of the Ostian Thieves' Guild, once met for coffee with one of *Far Waters Trading's* board members, who also happened to be a noble on Justine's list.

It was only a single line, and as far as Haarlock could tell, Gerard wasn't mentioned anywhere else. That in and of itself wasn't suspicious, as dozens of others were mentioned once in passing. Besides, people in important positions often cross paths for any number of reasons. Gerard might know the man personally or was asked to consult on a security matter, like he did with *Raven Rock Holdings*.

The others not linked directly to *Far Waters Trading* seemed to all be working towards the same general goal. The nobles smoothed the paperwork for merchants, allowing them access to markets they otherwise couldn't. Targeted efforts, usually illegal, by the adventurers ensured no one remained in the way. In an odd twist, it didn't seem the nobles reaped much in the way of monetary rewards, just favors and people placed in positions beneficial to them in the future.

But who knew who those people were and what they planned to do? If and when the war with Sanyo started, those people could assassinate or sabotage or even drag their feet to slow Lemuria's defensive efforts.

Justine's dossiers didn't follow her targets outside their interconnected relationships. Trying to trace the business maneuverings of a merchant was like trying to hold a flopping fish. Same for a noble's social escapades. Even the adventurers seemed content to limit their efforts to the quests provided by the others, then spending their generous payments on a life of relative luxury.

Though Justine's targets based themselves in Ostia, their reach far exceeded the capital. Krtek, her accountant friend with whom she exchanged information in Claville, worked the problem from the Sathe duchy. He followed every coin, person, and crate *Far Waters Trading* moved between Ostia and Sathe, and from Sathe to elsewhere.

The lack of concrete evidence wore on Justine. Haarlock, during a break as he thoroughly searched the secret base, found a journal behind a loose stone. While coded in *Thieves' Cant*, a language meant for quick, discrete communication, Haarlock parsed enough of the woman's meaning. Justine knew her suspicions of *Far Waters Trading* needed to be backed with hard evidence. They had too much reach and too many powerful benefactors for her to accuse without it. She regularly commented with a saying Marcon taught her during her first years as a rogue.

Cutting off the head allows the body to grow another. Find the heart and lungs, then rip those out.

Haarlock understood the metaphor. An organization's success rarely relied on the visible leader, but on those key people who kept that leader in power. Remove them and the whole thing will fail.

And that's what Justine was doing. Each person, each event, was traced back to *Far Waters Trading*, then out again to other events. Unfortunately, her target was no fool. Beyond the occasional shady dealing or heavy-handed negotiation, *Far Waters Trading* stayed above board. Which made sense: a secret cabal working towards the downfall of a nation wouldn't want to get caught by a sloppy paper trail. Sure, she could turn in what she had to the authorities and maybe get a handful of people arrested, fined, or otherwise run out of town, but what would that accomplish? How many of those in power, ones not working towards the downfall of Lemuria, pulled strings or made bribes to further their own interests? Justine wanted, *needed*, the smoking gun. She also knew she had to be discreet, too. With as much money and as many powerful people *Far Waters Trading* dealt with, she could find herself shut out if she played her hand too soon.

Justine remained suspicious of whom to trust. Decades in the Thieves' Guild gave Justine an extensive network, from cut purses on the street to senior advisors to the Crown, but too many of them traced back to *Far Waters Trading*. Even Marcon, her mentor and spymaster of Lemuria, occasionally purchased bolts of exotic cloth from them.

But what was the reason for all of this? Something three years ago caught her attention, and the investigation ramped up steadily from there. Nothing

Haarlock found in Justine's journal or notes said what it was, though. Whatever the reason, it was enough for her to invest significant time and resources into it.

Haarlock lay on the corner mattress, staring at the ceiling, the journal on his chest. He needed to talk to someone else about this. Someone he could trust with the resources to corroborate Justine's findings. Who did he trust enough to bring down here? Who did he trust enough to even tell?

With a heavy sigh, Haarlock sat up and laid the journal on the stack of papers next to him. By the stiffness of his muscles and the beggings of a raccoon, he figured yet another day had passed. That meant court took place tomorrow evening. Haarlock stood and looked down at his clothing. His disheveled, much in need of washing, clothing. Even freshly laundered, he was in no way presentable at court.

Guess I should get a new outfit.

Haarlock needed to put his trust in someone, and who better than the kingdom spymaster? Besides, if Marcon de la Garza was a shinobi, everyone in Lemuria was well and truly fucked. Better to find out sooner rather than later.

***

Later that night, Haarlock watched as the front door of *Sew Above Sew Below* creaked open, and as a warmly bundled Marcon entered. His long, platinum blonde hair flowed from under a rounded fur cap, draping down past his shoulders. The jacket he wore, crafted from the same animal as the hat, made him look three times his normal size.

The Couturier removed the coat and hat and placed them on the rack next to the door, revealing a stiff, tailed tuxedo underneath. He rubbed his hands together as he blew on them, then let out a shiver.

"Maldito el frío."

Into the fitting room Marcon went, stopping halfway between the entrance and a buffet holding a tea service. He turned his head to the left to see a scarf of blue bands wrapped around the shoulders of the otherwise empty mannequin standing against the wall. A torn scarf stained with blood.

The elf's jaw tightened as he looked around the room. Moonlight filtered in through the small windows near the ceiling, casting the space in long, deep shadows.

"Buenas noches, Lord Haarlock. Courtesy dictates that you schedule a fitting, not arrive unannounced."

Haarlock pulled back the *Veil of Shifting Shadow's* hood, fading into existence as he stepped out from a shadow on the far side of the room.

"You'll have to forgive my lack of decorum. I've been distracted."

Marcon's eyes moved to the dirk in Haarlock's right hand, then to the raccoon peering from the shadow at his feet. He kept his hands visible and at his sides.

"Understandable. How may I assist you this evening?"

"By providing some much-needed clarity."

"May I ask a question first?"

Haarlock nodded once.

"Is that Justine's blood on the scarf?"

"It is."

Marcon's jaw clenched as he exhaled a slow breath. He gestured to the sitting area in front of the mannequin.

"Please join me."

The elf moved with deliberate slowness, once again keeping his hands visible as he sat in one of the overstuffed chairs. Haarlock sat across from him, dirk still in hand, resting on his knee. Ladrón moved between Marcon and the fitting room's exit, his eyes never leaving the spymaster.

"As I'm sure you've already guessed, there's been an incident."

"And this has put my loyalty into question?"

"Something like that." Every one of Haarlock's abilities focused on the elf. "Did you know what would happen before we left?"

Nothing. Marcon didn't react. At all.

"Someone tried to kill you?"

"*Have* me killed."

Marcon looked at the scarf. "And Justine?"

"The assassin."

"Your survival means justice for her death has been served. Who did it?"

"A Phantom Blade named Kilec."

"I have crossed paths with him before." The elf's left eye twitched. "A most unpleasant man. How did you survive him?"

"He underestimated me. And Ladrón..."

As Haarlock's mouth opened to speak, he felt the cold, sharp edge of a blade press into the left side of his neck just above the collarbone. When he tried to move his arms, bands of writhing darkness held them to his legs. None of his spells would activate either. Out of the corner of his eye, he saw Marcon's ultra-fine, platinum blonde hair drape down as the elf leaned over to whisper in his ear.

"And you have underestimated me, Lord Haarlock. If I wanted you dead, you would be dead."

Haarlock sent commands for Ladrón to escape, but the animal didn't respond. His eyes darted to the left to see his familiar, from tail to muzzle, bound in the same bands of darkness. When he looked across at Marcon, Haarlock couldn't believe the elf still sat there. But like a mirage, his image faded from existence, leaving an empty chair.

"I hope after I release you, we can continue this discussion peacefully, sí?"

The blade's pressure against Haarlock's skin released enough for him to safely nod *yes*.

"Bueno."

Marcon's weapon left Haarlock's skin, and the bands of darkness faded from existence. The ones on Ladrón remained. Haarlock rubbed his neck, feeling the faint mark the blade left on his skin.

The elf walked around Haarlock and went to a shelf, removed a bolt of cloth, then reached into the back and retrieved a small tin. When Marcon opened it, the scent of fish filled the air. He kneeled in front of the bound Ladrón.

"I trust this payment will allow you to forgive me." Marcon laid the food in front of Ladrón.

The raccoon's hatred filled eyes softened as he sniffed at the fish. His eyes darted back and forth between Marcon and his apology.

*"*Forgive.*"*

"He says he forgives you."

"Bueno."

Ladrón leaped to his feet when the bands of darkness left him, and he snatched the food tin and dragged it into a dark corner.

*"*Forgive. Yes. Happy. No.*"*

Haarlock snorted. "He forgives you, but he isn't happy about it."

"Such is life." Marcon took his previous seat. "Now, please tell me what happened."

Was this a ploy for Marcon to get information? No, with the amount of groundwork laid to get Haarlock and Justine into position, whoever sent them didn't need information. They needed them out of the city and dead with no trace. Marcon wasn't an enemy.

"Once we made it to Claville, I followed Justine to a meeting between her and a contact, an accountant from Sathe named Krtek, at some ancient ruins deep in the woods. The Phantom Blade knew we'd both be there. Down to the day."

"This is...distressing news." Marcon thought to himself for a moment, eyes focused in the distance. "Do you have proof?"

"A confession from the Thieves' Guild guildmaster, Simon."

"I know of him. Where is he now?"

"Dead." Haarlock held up a hand. "And no, I'm smart enough not to kill potential leads. He used a poisoned tooth. Whoever is behind this used knowledge of his family's illegal dealings as leverage."

"How could they have known what day you'd arrive? Justine's trip was well known in advance, but not your joining her. Or that you would follow her." Marcon tapped a finger on his knee.

"I've been asking myself that." Haarlock ran a hand across his short beard. "From what I can gather, I stumbled onto *something*. I have no clue what it could be, but it's big enough for them to go through significant, directed effort to have me removed from the board."

The spymaster squinted at Haarlock. "Sounds like you've researched this on your own."

"I have." Haarlock removed a sheet of paper from his armor and tossed it to Marcon. "That's a timeline of events as I understand them."

Marcon scanned the document, his face hardening when he reached the end.

"You believe your involvement started when you attended the secret meeting at the tournament."

"They had Simon informing on Justine for close to a year. Then they changed their tactics right in the middle of the tournament. What else could it be?"

"Let's say you did discover something at that time. Why both of you? What did Justine know to warrant her death?"

Haarlock thought about how to answer. Did he reveal her secret base and everything she learned about those involved with *Far Waters Trading*? It would be smart to have someone else in the know in case he was injured or killed. Then again, the best-kept secret is one only a single person knows.

"I assume she stumbled onto something, too."

Marcon watched Haarlock for a moment, his head tilting ever so slightly to the side. "You have more than an assumption."

"I'm working on it."

"I would very much like to assist with that."

"It's not that I don't trust you Marcon...but I don't trust you. Or anyone at the moment, for that matter."

"A prudent choice." Marcon watched Haarlock for a moment. "Back to your assassination attempt. I still don't believe they could have planned for you to arrive in Claville on a specific day that far in advance."

"Why not? They ensure I'm recruited into a certain guild, then have that guild assign me a quest to follow someone. It just so happens that it leads to enough information that suspicion falls on Justine just before she goes on her regularly scheduled trip back home. Someone needs to follow her to see what she does, and lo-and-behold, here I am again, both with a working relationship with Justine and ties to several important people involved in the invasion conspiracy. Roboute's my pseudo-mentor. He works for you, and you're Justine's mentor. Granted, that's a lot of *ifs*, but not so many that it wouldn't work."

"How could it be assured you would choose to join Shattersong? Or for Shattersong to offer membership, for that matter?" Marcon raised an eyebrow. "Roboute would naturally press you to join a guild that puts you in a better place for him to use you. Then they would need someone in Shattersong to offer an attractive membership package and ensure you were assigned the task once recruited. As for who assigned Shattersong the quest to track Mateo, that was handled by an intermediary at my request."

Haarlock watched the wheels turning in the spymaster's head.

"Camilla."

"Or Jean-Baptiste. Or any of the others." Haarlock shrugged. "I don't know the guild's internal politics well enough to say for sure who pushed for me to join. Maybe it's none of them, or several. Hell, it could even be our Steward, Aldo."

"Who else do you suspect?"

"Gerard."

"Parnell?" Marcon's posture straightened. "Your proof?

"Beyond him being in a position to arrange things and knowing I was leaving with Justine? Nothing."

Marcon frowned. "Then why mention it?"

"Like I said, Marcon, I'm working on it. You can work on it from your side, too."

Even though the elf sank back into his chair, his posture remained exquisite. He stayed that way as he tapped on his leg once again.

"While you think of that, perhaps you can help me in another matter. I'm meeting with Roboute tomorrow at court." Haarlock gestured to himself. "I am less than presentable and could use a new outfit. Know any reputable tailors?"

"I would suggest myself, but considering the recent discussion, I will be far too distracted to craft a worthy ensemble. Let me get you a list of the names and addresses of where you can find adequate attire."

The elf went to a small table in the back and wrote out the information of four businesses. Haarlock stood as Marcon handed him the list.

"You've discussed this with Roboute?" Marcon's face betrayed nothing.

"I sent him a vague, mildly threatening message about needing to meet me at court. Other than that, no. Why, don't you trust him?"

"He's been an ally for over forty years."

"That's not an answer, Marcon."

"Roboute's loyalty is, without a doubt, to Lemuria. No one else."

"Would he betray you if he thought it necessary?"

"There are few things Roboute wouldn't do if he thought it necessary." Marcon gestured to the door. "I hope you'll keep me informed of your progress?"

"I will, and when I have actionable intel, you'll be the first to know. But until then, anyone following me will be treated as a threat."

Marcon nodded once. "Good evening, Lord Haarlock."

32

Haarlock looked into the mirror, admiring the simple, yet elegant tunic he wore. Though not specifically tailored to him, it still fit like it was. Solid black, with highlights in soft purple, the garment gave an air of subtle nobility. It also went well with Ladrón's new fur color.

"Ah, quite fitting, m'lord."

Fine, Fancy, and Fashionable's owner, a bland looking human man named Frederick, stood next to Haarlock, examining him with a keen eye. Frederick's outfit, a simple frock of white linen, gave him the air of a priest.

"That's a good one, Frederick." Haarlock smirked.

"Yes, indeed. I slip the puns in when I can."

Ladrón sat next to Haarlock, his head turning side to side.

"**Like. Want. Mine.**"

"I'll see what he can scrounge up."

Haarlock smoothed the material over his chest. "This will do nicely for my debut at court."

"Wouldn't you like a piece with more statement? Ostentatious displays are an important part of the social ladder."

"No, Frederick, I'm wanting to keep a low profile."

Frederick raised an eyebrow. "As you wish, m'lord. Will you be needing anything else?"

"Do you have anything that fits him?" Haarlock pointed to Ladrón.

"I'm sure I can whip something together."

An hour later Haarlock and Ladrón left *Fine, Fancy, and Fashionable* dressed in their new attire. The *Veil of Shifting Shadows* covered most of Haarlock's, but still. They boarded the waiting carriage and rode towards the glistening white castle perched several hundred feet up the side of the snow-capped mountains. Its heraldry, a horse beneath two crossed lances, blew in the wind, each banner massive enough to be seen from any point in the city.

How many people it would take to siege the castle, Haarlock didn't know, but it had to be tens of thousands. Jagged rocks and steep cliffs flanked a snaking road four carts wide, the only way to the front gates, each a massive slab of metal anchored to equally massive blocks of marble. There was no doubt that the gate and walls both harbored extensive enchantments to ward off any foe. When Haarlock passed through the gates after he and his team escaped *The Dolphin*, he could feel the magic leaking off them in his teeth.

The walk to the castle would be exhausting, and that's why Haarlock found a transportation service and booked a carriage. Not only would it save his legs, but no self-respecting noble *walked* to court. It took an hour to wind through the city, then another waiting in the long line of carriages leading to the castle. Haarlock wasn't the only one with the notion to arrive early.

When Haarlock exited the carriage, his jaw almost fell open at the sight before him. Walls forty feet high enclosed an enormous courtyard, with shiny armored guards manning the battlements. More guards flanked each doorway, and more still patrolled in squads of ten. Manicured hedgerows, beautiful in the starkness of winter, lined the bottom of the walls. It took a voice from behind to knock Haarlock out of his revelry.

"Pardon us."

Haarlock turned around to see a foppishly dressed elf and his orc attendant, having just exited their own carriage, staring blankly at him.

"Yes, of course." Haarlock moved to the side, watching the pair go by with, literally, their noses in the air.

Let's hope their level of pompous jackassery is on the high end, because damn.

Considering he knew not where to go, Haarlock fell into step behind them. He followed them up the stone stairs and through the large oak arch doors. A bright red carpet ran the length of the hallway they entered, stretching hundreds of feet in both directions. Suits of armor, tapestries, paintings, and plinths adorned with busts, vases, and relics decorated the space, giving it the feel of a museum.

They went left, then right, then up a wide stone staircase. The second floor contained more of the same, though the imposing forms of King Raoned Shein's honor guard stood in the distance. Purple tabards covered their gold-accented black full plate, and each of the six stood at attention with longswords and tower shields. On Haarlock went, following the pair between the honor guard and through six sets of double doors into the throne room.

Eight columns of carved stone held up the vaulted ceiling, with a chandelier of sparkling crystal hanging from the archways between them. The throne, a monstrous, high-backed thing of ornate marble and black metal, sat on a dais at the far end. Two smaller chairs, each of simple design, flanked it. Stained glass lined the sides of the ceiling, each panel depicting the likeness of a great warrior. Even with a hundred people already in attendance, the enormous space felt empty.

Haarlock received looks of amusement, confusion, and disgust as he took his place near the middle right. Not only was he *far* less dressed, but he had a raccoon on his shoulder. A big, heavy raccoon. Luckily, his Feat *Increased Strength* kept Ladrón's girth from being more than a nuisance. If, by some small chance, Haarlock's return to Ostia wasn't well known before, it would be now.

Three hundred more people filtered in over the next hour, each as overdressed as the last in animal furs, bright colors, and swirling patterns. Few arrived alone, though none came in groups of more than three. Humans comprised the vast majority, with elves being the second most represented. Dwarves and orcs, perhaps two dozen each, and a smattering of dragon-kin and lizard folk, filled out the rest. All congregated in small groups, speaking in hushed whispers.

A bell sounded, and the room fell silent. Heavy, metal-clad footsteps echoed throughout as six honor guard marched from the back left and lined up on the stairs in front of the throne. A hunched man in a brown robe with a large tome under one arm, and a tall, thin elf in a sky-blue gaberdine came next. They stood beside the chairs to the left and right, respectively.

When the second bell chimed, the elf spoke, and the acoustics of the space brought his voice, clear and strong, to every corner.

"His Majesty, King Raoned Shein."

Save the honor guard; everyone in the room bowed. Haarlock followed suit, as did Ladrón.

King Shein, his blonde hair draped loosely around his shoulders, wore a black tunic and matching trousers. Embroidered into them were intricate designs of flora and fauna. The cut of the fabric accentuated his shoulders and chest, and the high, stiff collar framed his square jaw.

Once the king sat on the throne, those to either side of him took their chairs, too. The elderly man opened his thick, leather-bound book and readied a quill. He nodded once, and the elf spoke again.

"On this day, the twenty-sixth of December, court is hereby called to order."

The elf spent the next hour going through an established procedure, with unresolved items from the previous months addressed first. A deed transfer between two senior nobles was finally resolved after six months of legal battles; the Namedian Commonwealth, Lemuria's eastern neighbor, won a contract for shipbuilding; and the source of a persistent plague was finally identified in the Nolon duchy. Various attendees asked clarifying questions on the subjects.

Finished with the old, new business moved forward. King Shein, as required by law, revealed his intention to make a winding, months-long trip south, visiting as many hamlets and towns as he could before spring. Any who wished to join him needed to be ready to leave by mid-February. A refresh of the Ostian Guard armory was coming up, and any who wished to bid on the first wave of equipment could submit their application to the Regent of Arms by the end February.

Lastly, the king's sister, Elizabeth, would marry on the summer solstice, and planned to have a party to rival all others. This caused a great deal of joyful murmurs in the assembled nobility...until the clarification that only those of count and higher could attend. Haarlock chuckled at the ruffled feathers of those around him and their quick change in opinion of the bride-to-be's generosity.

With the docket cleared, the elf opened the floor to any who wished for an audience with the king. Shein, who until this point had remained quiet, called forward each supplicant. They bowed, announced their name, status, and where they hailed from, then made their request. Most brought minor issues to the king's attention or announced to the group a party or new business venture. Some were minor nobles, like Haarlock, and other commoners who pleaded for their entire communities.

As the tenth person addressed the king, Haarlock felt a presence behind him. Before he could look, Ladrón chittered and jumped from his shoulder, eliciting a grunt and laugh from the newcomer.

*"*Friend.*"*

"Yes, hello there." Roboute's accent was unmistakable, quiet though his voice may be. "You've gotten bigger."

Haarlock turned around, and to absolutely no surprise, was greeted by Roboute's ostentatious attire. The man's well-manicured goatee, waxed to a gloss, matched his coiffed pompadour in both poise and form. His jacket, a solid purple as deep as night, lay over a shirt of dazzling forest green. Loose, pleated trousers came down to mid-calf to give focus to his extra tall, suede boots. Each with a large, shiny buckle, of course. Last but not least, a raccoon lay in his arms.

"And you've looked less ridiculous." Haarlock gave the Illusionist a once-over.

"This *is* court. I can't let my reputation falter." Roboute looked at those around him, giving the occasional smile or nod as appropriate. "When I bother to attend, that is."

"I'm glad you heeded my request."

"Yes. It was strongly worded."

"It got you here, didn't it?" Haarlock smirked.

"So it did. I assume you chose this location for safety?" Roboute gave Haarlock his own examination, frowning as he did so. "It appears you might not be so unsafe yourself. Dare I ask what brought on such a potent change?"

"All part of the tale, Roboute."

One of the nearby nobles, a human woman with golden hair in an elegant dress of soft pinks and blues, eyed Haarlock suspiciously. She turned to her partner, a man wearing the masculine version of her own attire and whispered something to him.

"Which we probably shouldn't talk about here." Haarlock stared at the couple with an uncomfortably blank expression until they moved away. "Do you have one of your special tuning forks?"

"It wouldn't work here, nor anywhere else on the premises. Various counter-enchantments negate such devices."

Haarlock looked up at the ceiling. "I thought I felt something when I first arrived."

"Yes, the entire castle is coursing with magic. It's quite impressive once you learn what all they've done."

"Of that I have no doubt." Haarlock nodded towards the king. "Want to stay?"

"Not unless you do. The afterparty is always a sordid affair of the most entertaining kind."

Haarlock huffed. "With this many powerful people in one place? I can only imagine."

"Then where to?"

"I have a letter to deliver." Haarlock patted his left pocket. "Do you know where the Department of State is in this place?"

Roboute pursed his lips. "Of course."

"Something wrong?"

"Of course not. Follow me."

Once the pair pushed their way through the crowd, Roboute took Haarlock back down to the first floor and deeper into the castle. They passed through hallways, foyers, and rotundas, eventually crossing an open-air garden towards a separate building perched atop a rocky outcropping. Well-manicured hedges, now brown and without leaves, lined the stone staircase up to the metal door.

Roboute narrated during the walk, pointing out some innocuous feature or commenting on an interesting piece of art. He stopped before they reached the secondary building's stairs and transferred Ladrón back to Haarlock.

"Before we go in, I am curious as to the nature of your letter."

Haarlock looked around. "How safe is it to talk here?"

"Physically? The safest place in all of Lemuria. Socially it is by far the riskiest."

"Fair enough. The long and short of it is Justine was killed by a Phantom Blade. He almost got me, too, were it not for a certain raccoon familiar."

Roboute's mouth dropped open, then shut just as quickly. "That is troubling."

"No shit." Haarlock grunted. "Someone sent us there to die, Roboute."

"You have proof?"

"I have suspects."

"Who are?"

"You and Marcon, for starters, but I ruled the two of you out with a fair amount of certainty."

"Marcon?" Roboute gave Haarlock a suspicious look. "What cleared his name?"

"I was shown just how easily he could kill me if he wanted. That is one scary elf."

"And myself?" Roboute grumbled as if wounded by Haarlock's suggestion. "I can't imagine why you'd suspect me."

"You might be Machiavellian, but there's no way your plans to have me killed would be *that* convoluted."

"I don't know that word, but I assume you use it with affection." Roboute crossed his arms as he thought to himself. "You said *someone sent us there to die*, and if you ruled out Marcon and myself, it's only natural for you to suspect others directly involved with what led you to join Justine on her trip home. That means Mateo, which means Shattersong. Considering we're standing in front of the Department of State, I believe you suspect Camilla Albertine."

Haarlock scoffed in disbelief. "Impressive, Roboute."

"I do try." The Illusionist nodded in self-appreciation. "But she's not the only one involved. Gerard Parnell, of course, attended the meeting where Marcon paired you and Justine. He was part of the team who verified the authenticity of Mateo's stash, so it is possible he had some hand in your attempted assassination, too."

"Speaking of. Who all was on that team?"

"Myself, Marcon, Gerard, and a handful of trusted others."

"How trusted?" Haarlock squinted.

"As well as any can be trusted." Roboute shrugged. "As well as Camilla. Or you."

"About Camilla." Haarlock stared at the building's door. "How secure is that place?"

"Worried that someone snuck in and made changes?"

"Essentially."

"Nigh impossible, I'd think. Lemuria's most sensitive records reside there. After your stunt at the *Dolphin*, they've over-corrected any ability for teleportation, and, like the outer fortifications, the walls of that building are so absurdly reinforced you'd destroy the rest of the castle trying to breach them. If you're not attuned to pass through the wards in the non-public areas, you'll be hit with numerous disabling spells, and the vault itself is located deep underground. I'm not sure of the defenses there, but I can only imagine they're just as potent."

"And the employees?"

"Decades long veterans if they have access to the sensitive areas, but anyone else will have been vetted extensively."

"Guess that'll have to do. I can only be so paranoid."

Haarlock waved for Roboute to follow him, and the pair walked up the stairs and into the Department of State building. Much like the rest of the castle, paintings of impressive figures covered the bare stone walls. Strategically placed greenery kept it from feeling cold and uninviting. Across the waiting area, a wide, four-station desk crafted from dark wood dominated the space. Two female gnomes, one young and one middle-aged, each dressed like a stereotypical librarian with spectacles perched on their noses and their hair in buns, worked on stacks of papers with machine-like rhythm. The wall behind them held a single door in the center, flanked on either side by two bushy ferns.

"Hello..." Haarlock walked up to the younger woman on the right and looked at her name placard. It read *Elaria - Clerk.* "Elaria. My name is Lord Haarlock. This is Ladrón."

Elaria looked up and over her glasses, first at Haarlock, then Ladrón, then back to Haarlock. When Ladrón waved at her, she raised an eyebrow and slowly laid down her quill.

"Good afternoon, m'lord. What may the Department of State do for you this day?"

Her Irish accent, unlike most of the younger female gnomes Haarlock met, didn't have the squeaky, high-pitched quality. Elaria's voice was as even and methodical as her demeanor.

"I have a letter for Callista Sooztorn. Is she here today?"

"Miss Sooztorn is here, yes. Would you like to leave it for her, or give it in person?"

"In person, if possible."

Elaria simply nodded before turning around on her stool, hopping to the ground, and going through the door in the back. Haarlock looked at Roboute, who only shrugged, then looked over at the other gnome. The middle-aged woman, who could have been Elaria's mother with how similarly they looked and dressed, continued her writing. A few minutes later Elaria and another gnome, one *far* older, returned.

Though she walked with a cane, the older gnome moved with speed. She went to the left and through a small doorway in the desk and stopped a few feet from Haarlock and looked up. Unlike the others, this gnome wore her hair in Dutch braids, each so long that even with two loops, they hung down the middle of her back.

"You have a letter for me?" Her voice, equally scratchy and wobbly, sounded confused. "I haven't received a letter in some years. Quite unusual."

"Yes, Miss Sooztorn, I do. It's from a mutual friend of ours."

Haarlock took Aripine's letter from inside his shirt and handed it over. Sooztorn draped the cane's handle over her arm as she took the letter, smiling as she ran a finger over the wax seal of Huerto de Vid Azul. She opened the letter and read it as she hobbled her way to a chair between two plants on the left. With a nimbleness that surprised Haarlock, the ancient woman climbed into the seat and continued to read. After a few minutes, she looked up and adjusted her spectacles.

"I see." Sooztorn eyed Roboute.

"Um, he's with me."

Haarlock looked back at Roboute. The Illusionist did his best to seem interested in the dirt under his nails.

"I can see that, young man. The letter doesn't mention him."

"I actually don't know what the letter mentions."

"It mentions a raccoon." Sooztorn patted her lap. "Come here, little fella."

With little in the way of grace, Ladrón clambered down Haarlock and up onto the woman's lap. She groaned as he smashed her into the seat, and she could barely put her arms around the animal's body.

"My word, he isn't so little." Sooztorn grunted and squealed as Ladrón adjusted himself on her lap. "But he is cute, especially with the outfit he's wearing.

*"*Like. Friend.*"*

Haarlock had to admit, a raccoon in a ruffled orange onesie was a sight to behold. He approached, laughing as he scratched Ladrón under the chin.

"He's a big boy, yes."

Sooztorn considered Haarlock for a moment while she absently stroked the massive animal in her lap. Her eyes flicked to Roboute for a moment, then back to Haarlock.

"It can be done, yes. Is the offer valid?"

"Offer?"

"Yes or no, lad."

"Um, sure. Whatever you were promised I will provide."

Sooztorn chuckled to herself. "You must need those documents quite badly."

"A great deal rides on access to the information they, hopefully, contain."

"Then it's done. Give me, what, four days?"

Haarlock grimaced. "What did Aripine have me agree to?"

"A month long, all-expense paid trip to the vineyard."

"Oh. That's not so bad."

The look of pure, unadulterated mischief that crossed Sooztorn's face sent a wave of dread through Haarlock.

"I don't think you appreciate how much wine I can drink, my dear boy."

***

Haarlock sat across from Roboute in the *Crimson Biscuit,* the Illusionist's magic tuning fork enclosing them in a bubble of obfuscation. Each nursed an ale, while Ladrón gorged himself on chicken scraps. Roboute listened intently to the story of Justine's death, the fight with Kilec, Sjena's offer, and Simon's confession. Haarlock included the existence of the secret hideout and Justine's research, but not its location. When he finished, Roboute downed the last of his mug.

"That's one hell of a story, Haarlock."

"You're telling me."

"I'm still surprised you're telling me this without actually verifying my loyalty."

Haarlock nodded as he stared into his drink. "I wasn't convinced of it at first. Too many unknowns with too many powerful people. But once Marcon showed me he could have killed me anytime he wanted, I asked myself, *does it make sense for Roboute to set me up*? And no, it doesn't. If I'm right and this entire plot started after I attended the secret meeting, you wanting me there means it wasn't you. Or Marcon."

"But you think it could be Camilla." Roboute scoffed quietly. "Or even Gerard."

"Camilla might not be the mastermind behind it all, but she, or someone else in Shattersong, is complicit. And beyond that one entry in Justine's research, I have nothing to tie Gerard to it. Nothing to rule him out, either. His position as the Thieves' Guild guildmaster gives him a great deal of access to add, remove, or manipulate data."

Roboute shook his head. "These people are well vetted, Haarlock. We would know if they were turned."

"Would you?" Haarlock leaned in. "I worked black ops for long enough to know greed is a hell of a motivator. Back in the previous world, my country had an entire organization dedicated to turning people into double agents. And let me tell you, they did it with no abilities and no magic."

"Let's say it is Gerard. A single meeting between him and a businessman isn't proof. He meets with clients across every social and economic line, for personal and professional reasons."

Haarlock let out a sigh. "I don't know. I've delved deep into Justine's research, and as far as I can tell, she didn't suspect him."

"Alright then, Camilla. Or someone else in Shattersong. How did your visit to the Department of State help on that front?"

"It's a long shot, but maybe Camilla's activities as a diplomat can be cross-referenced with Justine's research. If enough things line up, we have somewhere to start. And if it's not her, then we investigate the next likely suspect: Jean-Baptiste."

Roboute smirked. "I still can't believe that old gnome is working."

"You know her or something?" Haarlock shot the Illusionist a sideways glance.

"We've crossed paths. Like Callista said, she is quite fond of wine."

Something about Roboute's tone left more to be said.

"Tell me, Roboute, did the two of you have a tryst?"

Haarlock's smile caused Roboute to blush. He cleared his throat and drank the last few drops of his ale.

"Anyway. What do we do while we wait for the records to arrive?"

"I'm meeting with a contact tomorrow who will, hopefully, have intel on Mateo and how he was brought into all of this."

"You've put quite a few things into motion since your return. Impressive."

"What can I say? I don't like it when people try to have me killed."

"Perfectly reasonable." Roboute leaned back and thought to himself. "If there's a mole in Shattersong, I have an idea how to force their hand."

"Oh?"

"First, how many people know you're alive? Beyond the entire royal court, that is."

"Aripine and the Maids, Micca Barecna, Marcon, the owner of *Fine, Fancy, and Fashionable*, some administrator and his cronies at the coliseum, a Seer who, funny enough, never wants to see me again, and about a dozen other random shop owners and bartenders."

"Then I think I should arrange a meeting with Camilla to discuss your return. Seeing what she, or anyone else in Shattersong does afterwards, will be telling."

Haarlock nodded and smiled. "Better make it urgent. And vague. Really amp up the curiosity."

"Perfect."

33

The city's public library, a stout, square building near the College of Magic, held the third largest collection of books on the continent. The private collection of Baron Droff Fulix counted as second, and the *National Reserve of Knowledge* in Nippon took first place. Even with the *Ostian Public Library* being third, the sheer number of volumes took Haarlock's breath away.

Shelves 30 feet high and a hundred long stretched into the distance. The second floor, a balcony surrounding the outer perimeter, was a single shelf that wrapped around the entire circumference of the building.

Captain Barecna waited impatiently in the reading area, trying his best to look interested in whatever book he barely paid attention to. He wore plain clothes, though it was obvious his oversized tunic covered a breastplate. Haarlock stood on the second-floor mezzanine with his own book, using it to obscure his face. With how high up he was, combined with *Nondescript*, it was doubtful Barecna would recognize him.

Ten minutes. Twenty. Haarlock couldn't see anyone acting suspiciously, but then again, a hundred people sat quietly reading all around Barecna. They could be his backup. Or not.

Fortune favors the bold.

Haarlock returned the book and made his way down the stairs and towards Barecna. The captain might be good at his job, but he was a far better guard than he was a rogue. A simple hat would do wonders to hide his *very* identifiable red hair.

"Hey there." Haarlock stepped up next to Barecna without making a sound.

Barecna jolted, his chair squeaking loudly as he pushed it backwards. A dozen people all stopped and looked at him, most with scowls on their faces. The captain cleared his throat and hunched over.

"Not funny, Haarlock."

"Sorry." Haarlock sat down next to Barecna and pulled his book over and read the cover. "*Marsupial Migration Patterns*. Really?"

"I honestly just grabbed the closest thing."

"Nervous?"

A low grunt answered. "I feel as though everyone's watching me. Even at work when I was copying the files, every time someone came into my office, I was sure they were there to catch me. I have no idea how you rogues do it."

"I'm no fan, either. I only picked rogue when I came to this world because I thought I was hallucinating a video game. If I'd have known the truth, I probably would have picked mage."

"Really?" Barecna gave Haarlock a once-over. "Never picked you as a spell-slinger."

"Anyway, I take it you have the records?"

"I do."

Barecna looked around suspiciously as he reached into the neck of his shirt and removed a leather-wrapped bundle. With deliberate slowness he set the package on the table and slid it to Haarlock.

"You know trying not to look suspicious makes you look way more suspicious, right?"

"What?" Barecna's eyes went wide as he froze.

"Acting normal is your best disguise. No one really cares what anyone else is doing."

Haarlock took the pouch and opened it. Like Barecna said it would, it contained copies of arrest records, incident reports, witness and suspect statements, and the names and addresses of everyone involved.

"This is good. Very good."

When Haarlock looked up, the guard captain stared at him intently.

"Yes?"

"Can you do me a favor, Haarlock?"

"Of course."

"If anyone in those pages is involved in this, turn them over to me. Don't kill them. That's not justice."

Haarlock nodded. "My goal is to question these people, not hurt them."

"Good." Barecna exhaled and slumped in his chair.

"If there are accomplices, I'll need you to keep them safe."

"I've already put measures in place to secure them in the *Dolphin*."

"Seems fitting. And safe."

"I thought so, too." Barecna smirked, then stood and offered his hand. "Good luck, Lord Haarlock."

***

Barecna's documents, laid out on the floor in the secret base, showed a timeline of events around Mateo's arrest.

On May 14th Ostian Guard Lieutenant Marcus Eplin raided the tobacco shop *Puff of Smoke*, resulting in the arrest of three individuals, one of whom was Mateo Cabrera. Mateo was detained for two hours, then released with a fine of 12 silver. The others were released the next day, also with fines.

Four months later, during a routine cataloging of evidence, Clerk Patricia Lee discovered an encrypted message in a tin of untaxed snuff recovered during the raid. As this was not recorded by the arresting officer, she reported it to her superior. Cue a chain of reports up to the district watch commander, Major Gale Berrial. Eventually Berrial forwarded the encrypted letter to the kingdom spymaster just before Haarlock joined Shattersong.

With no reason to look further, the whole thing came together in one tidy package. But Barecna looked further.

Major Berrial died at home in his bed two days after he submitted his report to the spymaster. An attached medical report showed the otherwise healthy 45-year-old man's cause of death to be a heart attack.

For his actions in performing the raid, Lieutenant Eplin received a citation and transfer to a larger guard post in a better area of town. Clerk Lee likewise received a transfer, though to a small administrative building close to where she lives.

Conveniently, the names of the other guardsmen who took part in the raid were omitted from the report. Barecna noted this wasn't unheard of, though uncommon. What was uncommon and suspicious was the absence of the names of those arrested. Additionally, *Puff of Smoke* seemed to exist only as a name in the incident report, with no public filing in the city's business records. Lieutenant Eplin didn't even list the store's address.

Haarlock couldn't help but appreciate Barecna's thoroughness. The guard captain knew the inner workings of the bureaucracy, and without him, Haarlock wouldn't have uncovered even half of this information.

But what to do with it? Turn it all over to Marcon? The elf had the resources to investigate it further, but would he share his finding with Haarlock? Would he make any meaningful headway without Justine's research? Would Haarlock?

Growling in frustration, Haarlock stood and walked to the center of the secret base and began a quick stretching routine. He just exercised his brain, and now he needed to do the same with his body. Pushups, body squats, and lunges would burn off the stress, freeing his mind to get back to the problem at hand. Specifically, how to approach those named in Barecna's documents.

Major Berrial's death tidied up one loose end. Considering Barecna included the addresses of both Eplin and Lee, Haarlock would need to tidy up the two of them.

***

Patricia Lee, a human woman of some girth with dark hair and dark skin, lived a mile north of the secret base. The apartment complex she called home was nothing special, with well-priced, two-bedroom units for middle-class workers. Luckily for Haarlock, she was a homebody.

Shelves of books filled Patricia's home, with more stacked neatly on tables and in corners. The first two nights Haarlock observed her, she came home from work, drank wine, and read. On the third, Patricia met with friends for dinner, though she left early. One volume, the title of which Haarlock couldn't see from the adjacent rooftop, Patricia burned through in a single night. She also finished a bottle of wine while doing it.

Haarlock waited until Patricia was two glasses in before he made his move, using the *Veil of Shifting Shadows* to make a memorable entrance. He melted from the woman's own shadow as she took a drink of wine, scaring her so badly she poured the whole thing down her front. The scream Patricia let out only lasted a moment before a coughing fit overtook her. With how badly she coughed, it was lucky she was already sitting down.

"Please, take your time, Miss Lee." Haarlock removed his hood, changing back from a shadow to his normal form.

Patricia composed herself, though her eyes remained wide and fixed on him. "I've honored our arrangement. No one has asked, and I haven't told."

"We have no arrangement." Haarlock crouched down to pick up her dropped book before the trickle of wine reached it. He set it on top of the others on a nearby table. "But I am going to ask, and you *are* going to tell."

"You're not with him?" The woman took a sudden, deep breath. "Oh, gods, someone else found out."

"I know what you've done. And I know you were compensated for your efforts." Haarlock removed five gold from his vest and sat them on the stack of books next to him. "You will be compensated again."

"Money won't get me to talk." Patricia shook her head. "I know what happens if I talk."

"Which is?"

"They told me, in no uncertain terms, I'd be sent to the *Dolphin* for the rest of my life for falsifying records."

"Who said this? The person you thought I was with?"

"You'll not get another word from me." Patricia crossed her arms and hunched down in her chair.

Haarlock huffed in amusement. He wasn't sure what he would do if she wouldn't talk, but now that he was here, he knew he needed to apply a little theatrics to the problem.

The room's only light source, a small oil lamp next to where Patricia sat, cast dark shadows throughout the room. Haarlock used *Mage Hand* to extinguish it, then *Shadow Tendrils* to bind the woman to her chair. She went to scream, but Haarlock was already clamping his hand across her mouth. He knew she was blind in the near-total darkness, and it was all he could do not to laugh as her absurdly wide eyes darted back and forth.

"We're going to play a little game. I will ask you a question, and you will answer. Each time you don't, I cut off a finger."

If Patricia's eyes were big before, they were enormous now.

"Nod if you understand."

Several seconds passed before she nodded in short, rapid motions.

"Good. First question: will you scream if I remove my hand?"

Patricia shook her head *no* and Haarlock removed his hand. The woman took a deep breath and swallowed hard.

"Listen, I can only assume that whatever it is I did hurt you or someone you know. I'm sorry. I really am."

Haarlock watched as her eyes continued to dart around the room, desperate to see where he was. He let her stew for a minute, and when he spoke, she jolted so hard it almost broke her chair.

"What are the names of the person or people who paid you to falsify records?"

"I don't know their names."

"There was more than one?

"Yes. Two men. One was like you, a rogue, and the other some kind of administrator."

"Describe them."

"The admin guy, he was fat, with big jowls and a bigger stomach. Dressed in too-bright clothing. He had a strong smell, like bad incense layered with cigar smoke and perfume. It almost made me gag."

"And the one like me?"

"I don't know. Some faceless rogue in a hooded cloak. I couldn't tell you what they looked like. They never spoke, just handed me documents to sign."

"What were the documents?"

"Pre-filled forms, all in my own handwriting. Things like chain-of-custody receipts and transfer logs. The fat man told me what to do with them and what to say if anyone asked."

"When did this happen?"

"October...maybe the second week?"

Haarlock watched the woman again. The answers poured from her like a faucet, and with the panic in her voice, he could only assume she was telling the truth. He figured he should make sure, though.

Materializing his dirk, Haarlock drug the tip of the blade down Patricia's left arm. The woman tried to jerk her arm back, but the tendrils kept it in place.

"I'm telling the truth!"

"Oh, I know." Haarlock smiled. He was enjoying himself in a perverse way. "I'm making sure you understand what happens if you don't. Now tell me about the encoded letter found in the snuff tin. The one you passed up the chain to your superiors."

"The fat man provided both the tin and the document, but I never actually told my superiors about either. Major Berrial, the district watch commander, came to me two days later and retrieved it himself."

"That sounds unusual."

"It was. He seemed haunted."

"Haunted how?"

"Like how I felt. Like I feel. Used by others against my will."

The look on Patricia's face sent a wave of sympathy through Haarlock.

"What do they have on you?"

"About a year ago, I lost evidence. Important evidence that would have sent a murderer to the gallows. A week later he killed again, and the look on the face of the victim's husband is the reason I drink."

"And now they have something else."

Patricia nodded her head as she fought back tears. "If I hadn't helped, they would have revealed how I covered up my mistake, and I'd be in prison, or worse. If I did, they'd make sure no one else ever found out, plus transfer me out of the evidence locker. It wasn't really a choice."

"I know, Patricia." Haarlock used *Mage Hand* to turn the lamp back on. Its light burned away the shadow tendrils, and Patricia immediately rubbed where they had held her to the chair. "That's why I'm going to help you."

She scowled. "You are?

"It's likely your blackmailers will find out about our conversation. And soon. If you want to live, you'll confess everything you know to Captain Micca Barecna. Do you know who that is?"

"I've heard of him, yes."

"Good. He will ensure your safety."

"How do you know that?" Patricia's scowl softened. "Why are you helping me?"

"You're as much a victim as you are an accomplice." Haarlock pulled his hood back up, turning once more into a shadow. "I leave the choice to you, Patricia."

34

Four days after his visit to the Department of State, Haarlock once again found himself walking up the staircase to it.

Callista Sooztorn sat at the front desk, the quill in her hand moving with fluid grace across the open book in front of her. The middle-aged gnome was absent, though the younger one, Elaria, tended to an elf woman in basic but quality attire, to the right. When Haarlock entered, both Elaria and the elf looked at him, and the raccoon next to him, with mild interest before returning to their conversation.

Haarlock walked up to Callista and rested his hands on the counter. The gnome didn't look up or even slow her writing as she spoke.

"Back right on time, m'lord."

"I figured you wanted to see Ladrón sooner rather than later."

"You know the way to an old gnome's heart." Callista put her quill down, and when she looked at Haarlock, her face turned from mild boredom to surprise. "My, my, young man. You look like quite the dashing hero."

Unlike last time, Haarlock wore his full adventuring kit. He adjusted his boonie hat with both hands and smiled.

"I try."

"Now where's my friend?"

Ladrón chittered with excitement as he climbed up Haarlock to get onto the desk. Callista already had part of a sandwich ready for him, giving him bites of it as she scratched under his chin.

"Ladrón is quite the adventurer himself with all that armor."

"Oh yes. He is a fierce warrior. And mage and rogue."

"Really now?" Callista gave the animal a once-over. "He took a specialization?"

"And a sub-specialization. Ladrón's an Umbral Brawler. It's a long story."

"I'll have to hear all about it during my vacation." Callista tilted her head as she looked at Ladrón, then pulled out the gold band tucked under his armored harness. "This is an intelligence enhancer."

"That's right."

The old gnome shook her head. "I can't imagine why you'd do such a thing."

"Trust me, I regret it every day."

*"*Rude.*"*

"I can only imagine." Callista laughed as she used the rest of the sandwich to coax Ladrón off to the side. "To business."

"You have the documents?"

"They are far too sensitive to give to any random lord that comes asking, even one vouched for by someone like Aripine."

"Oh." Haarlock frowned. "Do you have *anything* for me?"

"Dates and locations."

"Going back how far?"

"Three years. I could get more, but it would take me far longer to retrieve the records from storage. Aripine's letter spoke of urgency, so I figured you'd want something now."

Callista removed a folded sheet of paper from her vest and handed it to Haarlock. He opened it to find almost the entire page filled with dense print, with each line a separate entry.

"She's been a busy woman."

"Indeed, she has, lad. I hope whatever it is you're looking for was worth my having to go to the healer for my wrist."

"Arthritis?"

The woman's entire hand showed heavy signs of the disease.

"Yes. Getting old ain't for the faint of heart."

"I believe it." Haarlock patted his left leg. "I already feel my years in this knee, but I can't imagine what it'd be like in...how old are you?"

"Four-hundred-and-sixty-six in January."

Haarlock let out a low whistle. "Impressive."

"That's one way to put it." Callista chuckled to herself. "You have what you need, yes?"

"Yes, ma'am, I do." Haarlock slid the paper into his vest and gave it a few taps.

"Good. I'll write to Aripine to schedule my trip. Do you have any of the blue vine brandywine in stock?"

"Callista." Haarlock leaned forward on the counter and gave the gnome a look of mock disbelief. "Those are two thousand gold a bottle."

"Better put back two then."

The old gnome winked, sending a hearty laugh through Haarlock. The other two in the room gave scowls, eliciting a small chuckle from Callista.

"I'm sure we can make the necessary arrangements." Haarlock mentally nudged Ladrón to return to his shoulder. "Thanks again."

Callista and Ladrón waved goodbye to one another before the gnome returned to her work.

***

Roboute's meeting with Camilla wasn't scheduled for another week. The marquise was out of town on business, and most of the other members of Shattersong were off on their own quests, too. Haarlock put himself to work investigating Ostian Guard Lieutenant Marcus Eplin.

The lieutenant's citation provided him with upward movement in the guard force. Marcus went from dealing with street level cut purses, thugs, and corner drug dealers to investigating crime rings and suppliers. Now that he no longer worked in the part of town where muggings were par for the course, he took lunch at a marketplace one block east.

Marcus' lunch routine comprised either a sandwich or soup from the same vendor, then a seat in a small courtyard shielded from the wind by the plethora of stalls. The cold weather kept most people indoors, but Marcus seemed energized by it.

Haarlock waited for four days, when a particularly cold day appeared, to make his move. Like clockwork, Marcus left the guard post at 11am, purchased an extra-large bowl of soup, then nestled himself at a small table between two stalls. The location had the added benefit of keeping the table's occupants from being easily seen.

With his own bowl of soup, Haarlock hurried over to the table and plopped himself down with a grunt. His hood stayed up, and he gave an authentic shiver.

"Talk about a cold one, eh?" Haarlock put his hands around the bowl and let out an *ahh*. "You found yourself a good place, friend."

"We don't know one another, so it's presumptuous of you to call us friends."

Marcus didn't look up from his bowl of soup as he scooped a spoonful into his mouth.

"Fair enough. Didn't catch your name."

"I didn't offer it."

"You're one of the guardsmen, right? Work at the building the next block over?"

"I'm on my lunch break. Where I prefer to eat quietly and alone."

Haarlock smirked. "Man of few words. I knew someone like that once. An elf named Mateo."

Marcus' spoon stopped mid-air. He paused for only a second before putting it in the bowl and looking up. Haarlock didn't give him a chance to speak.

"Your address is 8 Westing Place, where you live with your wife, Sarah, and three children: Robert, Bryce, and Jason. She is a stay-at-home mother as your children aren't old enough to attend school."

"Threatening my family? How cliché."

"Perhaps, but I want you to understand what's at stake here."

"If you're going to extort me, name your price. I only have twenty minutes left on my lunch break."

Haarlock huffed in amusement. "You're not one to mince words."

"I believe that discretion is the better part of valor. You want something I have, and it's important enough that you're willing to threaten the well-being of children to get it. That makes you either desperate, stupid, or in a rush. Either makes you dangerous, and I'd rather not see my family injured because of my ego and pride. What do you want?"

"Mateo Cabrera. Tell me who came to you and what they asked you to do."

The sigh Marcus let out was quiet, almost imperceptibly so over the wind.

"Two men came to me one night when I was working late by myself. They wanted me to falsify documents, and in return I'd be given a citation and transferred out of my watch post."

"You don't seem the kind of man to take someone's word at face value."

"Absolutely not. They had both the signed transfer order and the citation with them. Along with a sizable bonus."

"How could you tell they were real?"

"Citations come with a foil embossment of the district watch commander. I received one two years ago, so I know what they look like."

"And the transfer form?"

"Their coin helped ease my doubt about its authenticity."

"How much?"

"A year's salary to the coin."

Haarlock watched Marcus for a moment. Other than the fact that he hadn't let go of his spoon, he seemed entirely at ease with the situation.

"I understand the transfer, but why a citation?"

"It's for exceptional excellence in the performance of one's duties. With it, I'll make captain by the end of next year."

"The two men. Tell me about them."

"One was fat, with jowls and a stomach, and smelled of the Central Administration building."

"How do you know that?"

"It's the incense they burn there. It has a very distinctive odor."

Haarlock nodded. "Continue."

"The first man did all the talking while the second, some faceless rogue, handled the forms and the bribe."

Some faceless rogue. The exact same description Patricia Lee gave.

"Describe the rogue."

"What?" Marcus blinked rapidly.

"The rogue. What did they look like? Were they a man or woman? An elf? An orc?"

The lieutenant looked into his soup and frowned. "I, uh, don't know. I can't see their face."

"As in you never got the chance to see what they looked like?"

"No, the rogue stared at me the entire time. I remember looking...and noticing..." Marcus clenched his jaw and looked up at Haarlock. "There's nothing."

Haarlock could see the confusion on Marcus' face. He wasn't faking it.

"What forms did the first man, the one with the jowls, give you?"

"Incident reports filled out in my own handwriting, prisoner meal request forms, an injury report, and overtime approvals, too. Almost fifty documents in total. Everything you'd need to falsify a raid and subsequent arrests."

"When did all of this happen?"

"The sixteenth of October, if I remember correctly."

Right around the time they visited Patricia.

"I believe you, Marcus." Haarlock ladled out a spoonful of his soup and blew on it before slurping it down noisily. "Now, what are we going to do about it?"

"We? There is no *we*. I gave you what you asked, now go away and never bother me again."

"That's not how this works."

"Yes, it is." Marcus shook his head in disappointment. "Major Berrial is dead, and I can only assume it's because he asked questions. If they can get to him, they can get to me. Which means they can get to you, whoever you are. I told you what happened so you wouldn't go after my family. Now kindly *piss off* before I have you arrested for harassment."

Haarlock's brow rose in surprise. "Fair enough."

With bowl in hand, Haarlock left the lieutenant to his thoughts.

***

All I need is red string.

Slips of paper, sketches, reports, and handwritten notes covered a significant portion of one wall, detailing the timeline of Marquise Camilla Albertine's activities.

As a Consular General, Camilla greased palms and plied egos for Lemuria. She attended galas, greeted new arrivals, and presented gifts. With the woman's penchant for the finer things in life, it's a perfect career.

Though Camilla kept to Ostia much of the time, she made frequent trips to the kingdom's different duchies, and more than a few excursions to the Namedian Commonwealth. Namedia, a maritime nation of islands and a single small peninsula attached to Lemuria's eastern coast, was a poor country, relying on the bounty of the Goswell Gulf to feed its people. It's also where *Far Waters Trading* operated its primary import facility.

From what Justine gathered, *Far Waters Trading* used their Namedian facility as a tax loophole. Because of Namedia's wealth inequality, Lemuria provided a significant discount on all imports from them. This allowed *Far Waters Trading* to keep a high profit margin on exotic goods.

Justine tracked everything *Far Waters Trading* brought in and sent out, and who bought from and sold to them. And when. Her records went back two-and-a-half years, and in that time, Camilla made four trips to Namedia. Within a handful of weeks of Camilla's visits, the market position of *Far Waters Trading* received a significant boon: competitors disappeared, vocal dissenters suddenly went quiet, and new opportunities opened. Justine's notes mused on the reason for this, and she assumed, as the evidence showed, that someone in the government was providing *Far Waters Trading* with insider knowledge.

But all of this was circumstantial. Not every boon coincided with a visit from Camilla. Of the other events Justine attributed to *Far Waters Trading*, or those associated with it, only a small percentage came close to aligning with Camilla's official travel records. None of this proved guilt.

Haarlock ran his hands across his face, exhaling with exaggerated gusto. The raccoon playing with, literally, a stick next to him stopped and looked up.

*"*Problem?*"*

Haarlock spoke aloud, more to the wall than to Ladrón. "You could say that."

He looked at the clock on the desk to his left. The meeting with Roboute was in two hours. Hopefully, it would provide them with answers, or at least something to do besides gathering and reviewing data.

With nothing else to do until then, and his mind thoroughly fried from all the thinking, Haarlock laid down for a nap.

35

The walk to the *Crimson Biscuit* refreshed Haarlock in a way he didn't realize he needed. Spending so much time in the secret base, comfortable though it may be, left him feeling cooped up and on edge. Several deep breaths of the frigid air sent a wave of energy through him.

Ladrón felt much the same way. With his newfound abilities, he stayed within the shadow of Haarlock's cloak, reaching out from time to time to grab handfuls of snow. What he did with them, or how snow could exist within a shadow, was something Haarlock figured better to be left alone. Raccoons need their secrets after all.

Inside the *Biscuit* Haarlock found Roboute at a table near the fireplace listening to a musician play a jaunty tune. The song, a lay describing a duel between a hero and a sea monster, finished before Haarlock sat down, and as he did so, Roboute clapped enthusiastically.

"I take it you like this song?"

"Very much so!" Roboute tossed a coin onto the floor at the musician's feet. "I haven't heard it in ages, and this man here did a fine rendition."

The musician, a muscular human in an orange outfit, bowed and thanked the crowd. He gathered the few coins before him, nodded once to Roboute as he picked up a gold, and left.

"Make me wonder if any songs from the previous world made it here."

"Yes, actually. Though I'm told many of the instruments of *The Game* are insufficient." Roboute waved his hand dismissively. "But onto more important business."

The Illusionist removed his tuning fork, gave it a whack on the edge of his seat, then propped it up against the napkin holder. Haarlock felt the wave of magic wash over him as the ringing of the fork faded away.

"I hope you took precautions when coming here." Roboute looked around the room.

Haarlock pursed his lips. "I can teleport through shadows, and my cloak lets me literally turn into one. So yes, I took precautions."

"Good. Because I have a plan."

"A plan for what?" Haarlock shook his head. "Are we going to talk about your meeting with Camilla?"

Roboute flashed his signature shark-like grin. "That's why I have a plan."

"I'm hoping that's a good thing."

"It is. While Shattersong and I have worked together in the past, it's rare I reach out personally. That's usually handled by others. Naturally, Camilla was quite eager to know why I needed to speak to her alone, especially regarding you. We met at the Shattersong guildhall and I explained how Marcon sent you on an ultra-top-secret mission, one related to the cache you found, but that it was a setup and Justine's dead. Now you're back and don't know who to trust. I explained how we met at court and that you told me Justine revealed something before she died. What she told you, I have no idea, but it made you suspicious of everyone involved. Even to the point you no longer trust Marcon."

"Nice touch. Did she buy it?"

"Hard to say. Camilla put all her diplomatic abilities to work to stay unreadable."

"Then what's the plan?"

"Wait and see what she does. I told her you and I have been conversing about the situation and are working to uncover who is behind it. Hopefully Camilla's actions, or lack thereof, reveal her level of involvement. Any luck with her travel records?"

"Eh? There's some overlap with Justine's research, but it's not enough to look like anything more than circumstance."

Roboute let out a *hmm*. "An operation this well-hidden wouldn't leave a pattern. They might only use her for specific kinds of messages, or just when her schedule lines up with their needs."

"Which has me thinking. Why hasn't anyone come after me?"

"What do you mean?"

"They sent one of the most dangerous killers in the kingdom after Justine and I. We weren't supposed to survive, but now here I am, announcing to the world I'm still around and no one has tried to finish the job. No one's even really bothered me beyond a few beggars. As I walk around, I've been putting myself in places where it would be easy to assassinate me again, but so far nothing."

Roboute squinted in disbelief. "Are you upset that they haven't tried again?"

"Kinda." Haarlock shrugged.

"Beyond the fact that you might need to see a professional, it makes a sort of sense."

"Really?"

"Think about it. Whoever *they* are, put a lot of things in motion to get you and Justine to a specific place at a specific time. That meant anywhere else wouldn't suffice."

"Right, right." Haarlock shook his head, mostly at himself. "Because if they wanted me dead for the sake of it, they could have done it with a lot less effort."

"Precisely. It's smart of them to keep quiet and let things play out as they will. They might reveal more than intended by trying to cover their tracks, as well covered as they obviously are."

"Maybe not. I'm working on a lead with some promise, but I'm going to need help getting in somewhere."

Roboute frowned. "Which somewhere?"

"Central Administration."

"I assume your entry will be of the illegal variety?" Roboute chuckled. "Who am I kidding? Of course it will."

"Worried I'll do something stupid?"

"As the name suggests that building is the central hub for the successful operation of Ostia. It never sleeps and is almost as well guarded as the castle. Whatever you want to do there will be done under the gaze of surly old men."

Haarlock smirked. "Good. Surly old men are anything if predictable."

"That is a well-known fact, yes."

"But we still need to know what, if anything, Camilla will do. Thoughts?"

Roboute leaned back and crossed his arms. "She likes data. It would be reasonable for her to either investigate your return herself or send someone to do it."

"That's right, she has, what, fifteen levels in rogue?"

"Indeed, she does, but Camilla's skills focus on the social aspects of espionage. It's likely she'll send someone to find and follow you. How well have you been covering your tracks?"

"Pretty well. I've been using movement spells to hop between alleyways, and I try to come to and from Justine's hideout from different directions. *Pass Without Trace* and the ring of obfuscation you gave me should be helping a lot. Plus, I've been keeping Ladrón hidden as often as I can. He enjoys staying in my shadow."

"Yes, how does that work?" Roboute leaned forward and stared into the dark recesses of the cloak. "Does it have some kind of pocket dimension?"

"No. Ladrón received the *Dual Natured - Umbral* ability when he took Umbral Brawler."

Roboute huffed. "Seems as though giving him that intelligence enhancer was a wise choice."

"You don't have a psychic raccoon living in your shadow, Roboute."

"That is very true. But I believe we can use Ladrón to our advantage."

"How?"

"There are few people who have a raccoon as an animal companion. If you let him out more often, perhaps it will draw the attention of those looking for you. Someone sent by Camilla, perhaps?"

"Ah, right. See who follows, then capture and interrogate them in Justine's secret base?"

"It's *your* secret base now, Haarlock."

Haarlock sighed and hung his head. "You just want to see it, don't you?"

"Duh, it's a secret base."

***

Over the next few days Haarlock incrementally exposed his movements.

At first, it was his lordly status. Nothing big, just a careless glove removal here to show off his signet ring and only having a gold to pay for small things there. Then came Ladrón. It just so happened the animal's armor needed an adjustment, then he rode on Haarlock's shoulder while on their way back to the base. Haarlock also used his movement spells less, opting to walk through busy marketplaces with his hood down rather than *Shadowstep* between alleyways the next block over.

Canny Observer triggered two days after Haarlock began the relaxed security procedures. It was a quick thing, a movement in an alleyway out of the corner of his eye, but it was there. Haarlock had to will his reflexes not to look towards it. Whoever it was couldn't know he noticed them.

Another two days passed before Haarlock relaxed his security around the secret base. Though he couldn't yet teleport directly inside, he would do so into and out of the underground tunnel. And he would always use movement spells to get at least three blocks away before walking on the street. Now, though, Haarlock walked on foot the entire time.

A day later, they sprung the trap.

***

The shadowed figure watched from rooftops as Haarlock and Ladrón surreptitiously wandered their way down alleys and side streets. Finally, they came to the same place: an old warehouse. Six times they came here, and six times vanished in the vicinity. But not last night. And not tonight.

Into the alley they went, but they didn't come out onto the other side. The figure waited. One hour. Then two. It had to be the sewer cover. There was nothing else in the alley it could be. No doors, no low windows. Nothing.

A third hour passed. Then a fourth. By the positions of the moons, it was soon to be midnight.

Finally, pressed down behind the parapet wall, the figure watched via a mirror as Haarlock and his pet exited the sewer. The rogue gingerly reseated the cover, making barely a sound even in the dead of night. He mumbled something about food to the animal and walked around the corner, then headed north.

The figure waited half an hour to make sure Haarlock didn't circle back.

Over the wall and down the side of the building the figure moved. They approached the metal cover, examining it with keen eyes and deft hands. No traps, no alarms, no wards. A heavy thing, it took the figure considerable effort to silently move it to the side.

A peek into the recess showed a hallway. Odd. Once again, nothing to alert or subdue attached to the ladder. Once in the hallway, the figure moved with methodical slowness, checking every surface, crack, or puddle of water. Then the smooth stone wall.

Ungloved fingers moved across the surface, feeling the subtle variations in the material. Tool marks, erosion, and...something else. A recess, round with flourishes on the outside edge. Something like a locket, coin, or brooch fit here.

The figure removed their tools and set to work on the mechanism. It was magical, but all locks, magic or not, still have moving parts. Latches need to open, and that means...*snick.* A subtle rush of heated air pushed through the wall before it hinged open. The figure slipped through the small gap before the door opened all the way, closing it behind them.

Documents, dozens of them, hundreds, plastered the walls and lay in piles on the floor. The figure rushed to a nearby stack and looked over them, memorizing at a glance. Each page contained...gibberish? It wasn't coded, it couldn't be. Nothing made sense. Same with the next document. And the next.

A wave of unease slammed into the figure. They turned to leave, only the door wasn't there. It had been *right there*, next to the board. Someone cleared their throat from behind.

"Fancy meeting you here, Acorn."

***

Haarlock threw up his arms as the tiny rogue spun and drew a curved dagger.

"Whoa, now! No need for violence."

Acorn's eyes darted around the room. "You expected me."

"We weren't sure who it'd be." Haarlock showed his empty hands to the gnome. "Put the weapon down, please. We just want to talk."

"We?"

"Roboute, come out, please."

The Illusionist faded into existence next to Haarlock. "Good evening, Acorn."

"Nice trick making me see them leave, Roboute." Acorn huffed in annoyance.

"I do like my tricks. Now, as Haarlock said, we just want to talk."

"No talk."

Haarlock's *Alert* triggered, but the gnome was too fast for him to stop her. Acorn yanked a pouch from her belt and threw it at her feet, engulfing the room in a searing flash of white light and a deafening clap of thunder.

How long it took for the ringing to subside, Haarlock didn't know, but he found himself staring up at the ceiling, the world spinning. Roboute stood over him, looking down with a smile. Whatever he said came out muffled.

"What?!"

Haarlock shook his head, but nothing helped. The Illusionist laughed silently before snapping his fingers. In a rush, the world stopped spinning, and Roboute's laughter came into focus. Haarlock sat up and rubbed his eyes.

"Did I just get flash-banged?"

"Actually, yes. I'm surprised you know what those are."

"We use them in the previous world." Haarlock took Roboute's hand and pulled himself onto his feet. "Never got hit with one, though."

"They're quite dangerous in an enclosed space like this."

Roboute frowned as he looked over Haarlock's shoulder. When Haarlock turned to see, he found a gnome suspended in the air by ethereal chains. They wrapped her arms to her sides and her legs together, and one even went across her mouth.

"What's with the gag?" Haarlock blinked and turned to Roboute. "Actually, how did that not affect you?"

"Auto-activating enchantment." Roboute tapped a plain gold ring on his left pinky. "As for the gag, our friend might be small, but she has quite the colorful vocabulary."

Acorn struggled against the chains to no avail, screaming incoherently as she did so.

"I think I understood that." Haarlock smirked at Roboute, then turned back to Acorn. "Listen, you're caught. Even if you break out of those chains and take us out, this room is sealed shut. Plus, you'd have to get through Ladrón."

The gnome's eyes went wide as they filled with tears. She looked around the room before she saw the critter's head poking out of the shadow of Haarlock's cloak. Haarlock reached down and picked up Ladrón, sitting him on his shoulder.

"You don't want to hurt Ladrón, do you?"

With crackerjack timing, Ladrón let out a sad chitter, bringing a look of utter pain across Acorn's face. She shook her head emphatically.

"Good. We're going to let you go now. No funny business, alright?"

Acorn nodded, and Roboute dissolved the magical chains with a wave of his hand. The tiny rogue dropped nimbly onto her feet, then stood and smoothed out her clothing.

"You two are a nasty combination."

Roboute bowed.

"Alright, then, Haarlock, what's going on? Since when did you get a secret base, and why the hell didn't you come back to the guildhall?"

Haarlock let out a weak laugh. "You're going to need to sit down."

Over the next half-hour Haarlock laid out the plot, starting from when they found Mateo's cache, through Justine's death and finding her hideout. Acorn sat and listened, softly stroking the sleeping Ladrón in her lap.

"That's one wild story." Acorn took a deep breath and let it out in a sharp exhale. "And if I wasn't sitting in a secret base, I probably wouldn't believe you."

"I find it difficult to believe, too, Acorn." Haarlock nodded solemnly. "Someone set me up, and there can only be a handful of people capable of pulling it off."

"You suspect someone in Shattersong, don't you?"

"You're here, aren't you?"

Acorn frowned. "Me?"

"No." Roboute shook his head. "You're too new a member. Someone with seniority."

"Like Jean-Baptiste. Or Camilla."

Haarlock tilted his head. "Why those two? Seline, Zachary, and Samantha are also senior members."

"Seline's been away on a special quest since long before you arrived. Samantha is harmless, and Zachary would have tried to bring me into any scheme he was part of."

"He would?" Roboute raised an eyebrow. "Why do you say that?"

"Zachary is one of the best Grifters in the city. He's told me stories, *crazy* stories of the stuff he's done. Even convinced me to join him a few times. These are things that would put him and everyone involved in prison for longer than we gnomes typically live. If he planned your assassination, Haarlock, there'd be no tracing it back to him."

The two men shared a look, then Haarlock stared at Acorn until she met his eyes.

"If you had to pick, who would be in the best position to set me up? Jean-Baptiste or Camilla?"

Acorn didn't hesitate. "Camilla."

"Why?"

"She's a diplomat with access to sensitive people, data, places, and, frankly, her sending me to look for you was suspicious to begin with."

Roboute. "Suspicious how?"

"Shattersong is upfront with its members about what everyone is doing and why. Even for the more hush-hush sort of stuff, the guild is very transparent. Camilla tried to keep the fact that you and she met, Roboute, and she didn't even do a very good job at it either. Then the next day she pulled me aside and asked me to find you, Haarlock. Said something went south on a non-Shattersong quest and you'd gone on the lam and was worried you would do something, and I quote, *stupid, reckless, or both*. Since she didn't know what happened, Camilla wanted me to keep it quiet until more information was gathered."

"Sounds reasonable." Haarlock looked at Roboute.

"Camilla is a reasonable woman."

Haarlock thought to himself for a moment. "That can't be all, Acorn. I don't think Camilla's current behavior is suspicious enough to believe she's acting with ill intent."

The gnome reflexively chewed her lip as she pulled Ladrón closer to her.

"Acorn?" Roboute leaned forward. "This is important."

"She has a daughter."

Roboute straightened in his chair as his face went slack. "How do you know about that?"

"What's wrong?" Haarlock looked at Roboute.

"The existence of Camilla's daughter is a secret kept well enough that someone shouldn't be able to find out about it."

"Yeah, well, Zachary found out." Acorn shrugged as she ran a hand across Ladrón's back. "It was during research for one of his schemes. He needed access to a certain location, which just so happened to be owned by Count Justinian..."

Roboute shot forward and jabbed his finger at the gnome. "Do *not* speak another word."

Acorn's eyes went wide as she nodded profusely.

"Hey now, Roboute." Haarlock put a hand on the Illusionist's shoulder. "We're all friends here, right?"

"Sorry." Roboute took a deep, calming breath and relaxed. "Zachary shouldn't have been able to learn about Camilla's child."

"Well, he did." Acorn swallowed hard. "Whatever steps were taken to hide the child weren't enough."

Haarlock watched Roboute for a moment before speaking to Acorn. "How did he put the pieces together?"

"Easy enough, actually. Zachary's plan was to impersonate a relative of...the father. Zachary did some searching through his family tree and who he may be able to recognize in person. That digging led to a few too many paths crossed with Camilla, then add some more digging into her backstory and it wasn't hard to put two and two together."

Roboute shook his head. "The devils in the details."

"Why is it so important to keep the child's parentage secret?" Haarlock thought about it for a second, working it out as he spoke. "Does it have to do with inheritance?"

"Exactly so." Roboute gestured to Haarlock's signet ring. "You are a noble, Haarlock. If you ever have an heir, they will inherit both parent's belongings, be they land, money, or titles. In Camilla's case, the father impregnated her and his wife within days of one another. Camilla's daughter was born first."

Haarlock jaw dropped.

"Yes. Quite. The inheritance laws of this kingdom are those of absolute primogeniture, where the eldest legitimate child, regardless of gender, inherits all lands and titles.

"But Camilla's daughter was born out of wedlock, so what's the problem?"

"Bastards do not inherit unless they are the only direct relative remaining. The father's only other child died a few years ago, leaving Camilla's daughter the legitimate heir."

"So?" Haarlock looked between Acorn and Roboute. "What's it matter that she inherits the father's estate?"

"She is a secret, and the father is sickly. If he dies before siring another heir, all his considerable inheritance is hers by legal right. All it would take is for someone to reveal her existence, and then suddenly a very normal young woman receives a great deal of power. Camilla would be asked some hard questions regarding the situation, and that is an excellent pathway to subversive coercion. She is in too important a position to have such leverage held against her."

Haarlock laughed. "And whatever distant relative that would have inherited the father's estate would be left high and dry. I assume they wouldn't find that very funny."

"The financial stalemate, legal battles, and high-society chaos would be something for the history books." Roboute looked at Acorn with sadness. "I'm going to need to have a long talk with your Grifter friend."

The gnome nodded.

"But a secret, illegitimate child isn't proof of anything." Haarlock shook his head. "I'm not convicting someone without actual evidence."

Roboute eyed Haarlock. "You mentioned needing access to Central Administration before. Does the proof reside there?"

"The devil's in the details." Haarlock smirked. "It seems in their rush to set up the backstory for Mateo, they didn't bother to hide one of the conspirator's scent. He reeked of the incense Central Administration uses."

Acorn and Roboute both reflexively scrunched up their noses.

"Is it that bad?"

Roboute grimaced. "The incense isn't the worst, but after decades of use it has permeated the very stone itself. Combine moisture and stale air, and you have a potent odor. Every one and thing from that place smells of it."

Acorn looked at Haarlock with confusion. "Why would proof of Camilla's guilt be in there?"

Haarlock gestured to the pile of documents against the far wall. "Justine's investigation led her to an import/export company called *Far Waters Trading*, along with several nobles, merchants, and adventurers involved with it. A business with that much pull needs someone on the inside of the city's bureaucracy to help them along. What better way to coordinate a massive undertaking like that than with a veteran administrator at the center? And what better position could someone like Blue Jira have? Plus, no one is talented enough not to have reference documents, which means they can be found. And if we can get the guy working there, we can get his accomplice."

"Accomplice?" Roboute tilted his head.

"Yeah, some kind of rogue. The admin did the talking while the rogue provided the materials. It was weird, too. Both people they approached described them the *exact* same way: some faceless rogue. One of them, even though he stared right at the rogue, couldn't remember what their face looked like, let alone tell me their gender or race. He blanked completely. Do either of you know what kind of ability that is?"

The color visibly drained from Roboute's face. Haarlock looked at Acorn, and even her nut-colored skin went pale.

"What? What is it?"

Roboute swallowed before he spoke. "I know several Blank Faced rogues operating in Ostia, but only one who is the guildmaster of the city's Thieves' Guild."

***

With a whip-crack of thunder, Roboute and Haarlock teleported into *Sew Above, Sew Below's* fitting room. Seconds later Marcon de la Garza burst into the room, dual blades at the ready. Once he recognized who the intruders were, he let out a huff and threw up one hand.

"¿¡Que coño, Roboute?!"

"Apologies for the hour of our calling, Marcon, but we seem to have a problem."

"I would assume so." The elf took a centering breath before straightening his posture, then, with daggers still in hand, smoothed out his silk, baby-blue pajamas. "Take a seat, you two. I'll ensure we are not overheard."

"No need." Roboute pulled a crystal from his pocket and crushed it in one hand. A pulse of energy rushed out, leaving behind a thick magical haze in every direction.

Marcon tried to hide it, but Haarlock could see the concern in his eyes. The elf gestured to the nearby chairs as he sat on the room's only bench.

"What is the issue at hand?"

Haarlock gave Marcon the breakdown of what he, Roboute, and Acorn had discussed earlier. It was all Haarlock could do to not talk so fast his words blended into an incoherent mumble. For his part, the elf listened quietly as he took everything in. When Haarlock finished, Marcon shook his head.

"There are nine Blank Face rogues in Ostia. I need more before I can act."

"Damn it, Marcon!" Roboute's voice oozed venom. "Don't you remember who brought this whole shinobi problem to your attention in the first place?"

Marcon's eyes narrowed. "Circumstantial."

"Wait, Gerard started this whole thing?" Haarlock looked between the two men. "You're kidding, right?"

"No." Marcon let out a slow breath. "Gerard brought me the first encoded message. He said it was found during a quest to steal documents from a merchant."

"And you don't suspect him?"

"I vetted Gerard Parnell, *thoroughly*, before he took the position of guildmaster."

"You said *before*, Marcon." Haarlock shook his head. "People change. Press hard enough on their weak points and they change however you want."

"Gerard has no weak points. I ensured that."

Roboute scoffed. "Don't be a fool. Someone discovered Camilla's daughter by pure happenstance. If mistakes were made then, who's to say they weren't made with Gerard?"

Marcon rubbed his thumbs against his index fingers nervously. Haarlock leaned forward and stared at the elf.

"Do you, in your heart of hearts, trust Gerard?"

"A fool trusts, Haarlock." Marcon grunted as he shook his head. "Gerard's maternal grandfather is from Sanyo. He still lives in the south, two days' travel from the border. Gerard went to visit him once, three years after he became guildmaster. Fifteen weeks later he brought me the first encoded message."

"We need to act, Marcon. Decisively." Roboute stood and ran both hands down his face as he looked at the wall clock. It read 4am. "It'll take me an hour to assemble a team to raid Central Administration. We'll lock it down magically, then detain everyone inside. It's the weekend, so there'll be reduced staff. Those not at work will have to be apprehended at their homes."

Haarlock stood and looked between the two men. "What about Gerard? Raiding a government building will spook him."

Marcon remained seated. "We have protocols in place to meet when circumstances demand it. The raid can happen then."

"How long?" Roboute looked back at the clock.

"Two hours after I alert him. He picks the location, though."

Haarlock shook his head. "Wherever it is, it'll be a trap."

"That's why you're coming with me."

"What?"

"Gerard is a strategist and killer, through and through. I am a tailor first and a rogue second. On my best day, I'm not confident I could take him, and we'll be the ones flat-footed."

"Won't my presence be a problem?"

"You have shadow abilities. Use them."

Haarlock looked at Roboute. "Should we tell Shattersong?"

"They'll be part of the raid, too. Camilla might not be the only mole, so I want them where I can see them."

"We go in blind. Fantastic."

Roboute stroked his goatee. "Do you still have my calling card?"

"Yes."

"Activate it either way. If the message I receive is empty, I'll know something went wrong and backtrace the spell. I don't know what help I'll be able to provide, but it's better than nothing."

Marcon finally stood. "Let's get to it, sí?"

36

Haarlock and Ladrón followed Marcon, both using their newfound abilities to remain hidden in shadow. The elf made his way on foot, weaving through alleys and streets to Gerard's meeting place.

The guildmaster chose the warehouse of a large bakery owned by a retired adventurer. Marcon knew the place well, as more than once he had used it for clandestine meetings with others. Located on the northern side of the city, *Dough Re Mi* sat on a well-traveled street near a busy market. It was as safe a location to meet as any could hope.

The dainty elf, well disguised in an oversized wool cloak, stopped across the street from the bakery. Haarlock stayed behind him, though within sight of the store's entrance. People came and went from the quaint, cottage-like structure, each with a bundle under their arm. In the side alley, a team of men loaded a carriage with trays of steaming loaves from the attached warehouse in back. Though his sense of smell was essentially muted while phased into the shadows, Haarlock could just smell the yeast in the air. No doubt the three stout, smoke-spewing chimneys spread the scent far across the city.

Several minutes passed before Marcon flashed the *Thieves' Cant* sign for *begin*. Haarlock nudged Ladrón to go left as he went right. A *Shadowstep* later and Haarlock was under the carriage.

An *Umbral Step* brought Haarlock through the wall and into the warehouse itself. Rows of ten-foot shelves lined three of the walls and filled much of the floor space, with golden-brown loaves of bread in every shape and size filling them. Six large stone hearths covered the fourth wall, and ten men kneaded dough on long, sturdy tables in front. They loaded metal sheets with a dozen boules before glazing and scoring them. Once the sheet was loaded, they placed it onto a rack and started again.

The morning sun, still low in the sky, barely filtered through the skylights. Fire from the hearths gave the men in front of them light to work; otherwise, deep shadows filled the warehouse. A perfect place for a clandestine meeting.

Eleven people moved through the warehouse, none of them Gerard. All were bakers moving with the confidence of someone who'd done this a thousand times. A door creaked open in the back, and a woman pushed a large cart of dough to the kneading tables. Haarlock moved to see inside the additional space to find two other women mixing flour and water in large bowls.

When Haarlock returned to the warehouse, positioning himself between two shelves across from the hearths, he saw someone come from the storefront. The man, an older human with a long, jagged scar running down his right arm, whistled to those in front of the hearth. He flashed them a sign before saying it's time for a break. They all nodded. One woman hurried into the back, and a few seconds later all three women joined the men by the hearth to clean up. It took several minutes for the current round of bread to finish baking, and once the fresh loaves were stored, the entire group headed to the front.

Marcon entered from the alleyway and went straight to the kneading tables. He looked around for a moment before removing his cloak and folding it neatly on a corner. As usual, the elf wore his stiff-looking tailed tuxedo. A minute went by before Marcon absently scratched his neck and coughed.

"Good morning, Marcon."

Haarlock and Marcon both turned to the new figure standing between two shelves. The figure, obscured by the all-too-common hooded cloaks, stepped forward. Haarlock couldn't see their face from his angle, but Marcon tensed.

"Buenos días a ti también, Gerard."

Gerard stepped forward and lowered his hood. The man's plain face betrayed nothing.

Blank face indeed.

"It's been some time since you've used this protocol. You have me worried."

"I am worried."

"About?"

Haarlock desperately wanted to move closer, but he wasn't sure what abilities Gerard might have to detect someone. Better to stay put. He sent a command to Ladrón to ensure the animal stayed where he was, too.

"Information regarding our ongoing problem has come to light. The diplomat is compromised."

"The delivery succeeded, then?"

Neither used *Thieves' Cant*, nor did they use hand signs to alter the meaning of their words. Both stood with their arms at their sides and hands relaxed.

"No. That is the problem."

"The second hand?"

"Assassinated."

"Her shadow?"

Marcon coughed. "Brings ill tidings. Much has been revealed."

"Where is he?"

This drew a split-second look of suspicion from Marcon. The elf shrugged as he once again scratched his neck. He went to a nearby shelf and removed a fresh loaf, then pulled a hunk off and ate it.

"The reason for the shadow was a source of false light. One that was extinguished. I hope you can provide information on who lit it."

Gerard tilted his head. "I know nothing of false light."

"Lies."

The spymaster continued to nonchalantly eat pieces of bread as he watched Gerard. For many long seconds the two rogues stared at one another until Gerard broke the silence with a sigh.

"We hoped to delay this moment." The guildmaster shook his head. "I voted to end their lives with less complication, and it seems that was the right choice."

Marcon straightened and dropped what remained of the loaf. "You're on the side of the enemy."

"They're not the enemy."

"What happened to you, Gerard?" Marcon coughed again, this time more forcefully. "Do you really believe that?"

"Lemuria is rotten, from the center out. I have seen it. As have others. Sanyo will cleanse this nation with fire."

Haarlock moved forward, right to the edge of the shelving's shadow.

"Is there anyone hidden in this room?"

*"*No.*"*

This didn't make sense. Gerard couldn't be foolish enough to come alone, and he had to assume Haarlock, or even Roboute, waited nearby. The scenario ran through Haarlock's mind as he...Marcon coughed again.

That must be it.

But what was *it*? Marcon would protect himself against poison, right? If anyone managed to poison him, they would have poisoned Haarlock too. No, it had to be something here, and recent. As Haarlock inhaled, the scent of fresh bread filled his nostrils.

The yeast.

Was it magically infused somehow? Is that why he could smell its overwhelming scent even while melded into the shadows?

Marcon coughed so hard this time that he grimaced.

"Don't make this harder than it needs to be, Marcon." Gerard slowly raised his hands to show them to be empty.

"You know me, Gerard. I'm not one to make anything easy."

With a flash, Marcon's left hand flicked forward, sending a blur of metal surging towards Gerard. The guildmaster stepped back and caught the slim blade by the handle, its tip an inch from his face.

Haarlock rushed forward, dirk materializing in his hand as he exited the shadows. His first breath burned heavily in his chest as a wave of nausea overtook him. Gerard looked at Haarlock, his face expressionless as ever, then crouched and leaped up onto the prep table. A shortsword appeared in the guildmaster's hand.

Another breath and Haarlock stumbled, his knees losing their strength. His vision swam as drums pounded in his ears.

*"*Help?*"*

"No! Stay back. I don't know what's doing this. Get out and find Roboute. Anyone."

Haarlock grabbed a nearby cart to hold himself upright. The room spun as he looked to see Marcon on his knees, clutching at his throat as he gasped for air. Gerard, on the other hand, stood calmly on top of the table, sword held loosely at his side.

"Lord Haarlock. I wondered when you'd make yourself known. I'm glad to see my trap worked on you, too." Gerard's eyes flicked to either side. "Where is your pet? If he hasn't attacked by now, I imagine you sent him for help."

"Yeah." Haarlock coughed so hard he thought he'd break a rib. "Just hang around for a few more minutes and see."

"I think not."

Haarlock's knees gave out, and he tipped the cart over as he fell. The overpowering scent of yeast burned his sinuses and mouth, and his eyes watered so much that he couldn't see. With his last conscious action, he slammed his fist against his vest, breaking the thin piece of wood inside.

***

*"*Wake.*"*

*"*Location?*"*

*"*Where?*"*

*"*Wake.*"*

An upward lurching motion and burning arm muscles brought Haarlock back to consciousness. When his eyes opened, all he could see was white. It took an agonizingly long time before his vision resolved, showing him a brightly lit brick room. Where the light came from, Haarlock didn't know. It seemed to come from everywhere at once.

Haarlock's muscles ached because he hung by his wrists from chains, with the balls of his bare feet just able to touch the floor. Though he wore his insulated leggings, the cold dampness of the room seeped into his bare chest and arms. He shivered.

*"*Frustrated. Location? Where? Wake. Where?*"*

"Yeah, yeah, I hear you."

Haarlock followed the chains over ten feet to the eyelets on the domed ceiling, then down again to two grim-looking men in black outfits. They attached the links to floor hooks on either side and left the circular room through a thick steel door, shutting it behind them. Haarlock groaned as he pulled at his bindings, but in his position, even his enhanced strength couldn't help.

"You are an interesting individual, Lord Haarlock."

Gerard's even-toned voice came from behind, out of Haarlock's sight.

"Thanks, I guess."

"How ever did you defeat Kilec? He was one of the most prodigious killers alive."

*"*Where?*"*

"I don't know. Give me a damn minute."

"Kilec?" Haarlock strained to see over his shoulder but couldn't. "A dash of arrogance on his part. A bit of luck on mine."

"That's not the whole truth."

"Is that what's in the air?" Haarlock smacked his lips. "I thought I could taste an active spell."

"Yes, you are under a *Detect Truth* spell. You were saying about how you defeated Kilec."

"Right." Haarlock groaned as he tried to adjust himself into a more comfortable position. It didn't work. "He wanted to see if my skills were a match for his."

"It appears they were."

"Actually, no. I lost." Haarlock smirked. "Am I telling the truth?"

"Yes. You are." Gerard stepped into view. He still wore the hooded cloak from before, and the bright, flat light cast a sinister tone over his utterly expressionless face. "Your new sub-specialization interests us. It wasn't what we expected you to have. Neither is the Unique cloak."

Haarlock smirked again.

"You will answer, or there will be pain."

"You didn't ask a question, Gerard." Haarlock adjusted himself again. "If you could just lower me down a little, I'd be more comfortable to talk."

Gerard gestured to the side. "You will find your shadow and umbral related abilities neutralized by the light. The position you're in is to negate your enhanced physical attributes. And your rather lackadaisical attitude won't help you overcome the discomfort of this interrogation."

"How unfortunate for me."

"Answer, or there will be pain."

Haarlock scoffed. "Just kill me now. I'm not going to talk."

"As I'm sure you well know, Lord Haarlock, everyone talks in time. One benefit of this world is the existence of magic. We can break your body in many interesting ways, then put you together again as if it never happened."

Gerard's coy smile sent a shiver down Haarlock's spine.

"Seems it's in my best interest to cooperate, huh?"

"Indeed, it does."

Remember your SERE training, Haarlock. Focus, observe, plan, and envision. Just got to keep him talking.

"How about this: I answer a question, then you answer a question." Haarlock looked at the ceiling, walls, and floor, noticing the aged state of the bricks. "Come on, Gerard, I'm not going anywhere. You've got me, what, in the tunnels under the city? A dozen guards between me and the exit? What's there to lose?"

"You are four stories underground. Every tunnel for three hundred feet is, just like this room, magically enchanted with light, and, no matter what tricks you might have, there are more than enough guards to ensure you don't escape. This only ends one way."

"All the more incentive for me to make it easier for you." Haarlock tried to shrug. "Answering a few of my questions can't hurt, can it?"

"Where is your pet?"

"I don't actually know."

Gerard's jaw clenched. "That is a half-truth."

"I don't think *Detect Truth* works that way. It's your turn."

"Ask your question."

"Is Marcon dead?"

"Yes."

Haarlock's heart sank.

"Who else is aware of my defection?"

"Roboute and Acorn at least. Hard to say who else they've told by now. You did something to the bread, didn't you? Was it magic yeast?"

"Excellent guess. A few years ago, a Poisoner developed a prolific strain of magic-eating yeast that can survive the baking process. You consume the bread or breathe in the yeast spores, and the more magic you have around you, the faster the yeast multiplies and the faster its waste products build in your system. Confusion, rash, nausea, and organ failure occur within minutes to hours."

Haarlock thought back to how the yeast smell slammed into him when he left the shadow.

"Oh, I get it. You spiked their dough, and as they baked it into bread, it filled the warehouse's interior with your trap. Marcon didn't need to eat anything.

He just needed to be present. Then, when I came out of the shadow, it hit me all at once. That's some last-minute planning you came up with, Gerard."

"Marcon is known to employ extensive protective enchantments, and eventually he would activate the meeting protocol. That scenario was but one of thirteen methods of neutralizing him. As for you, Haarlock, now that you are an Anointed Umbral Blade, you are partially magical, so the yeast attacked your very essence. Unlike Marcon, you only survived because you weren't able to cast any spells before passing out."

"That's actually..."

Gerard held up a hand. "My turn. The assumption is Justine told you of her investigation before her death, then you put the pieces together and discovered something to lead you to me. What did she find to lay suspicion on me, specifically?"

"Funny enough, if she did suspect you, nothing in her notes or research alluded to it. The only entry about you was a meeting you had with an investor at *Far Winds Trading*. That's it. Nothing else."

"Then how did you come to suspect me?"

Haarlock extended a single finger. "That's two in a row, Gerard. But don't worry, I'll answer. I did a little work of my own and found the two people you bribed to plant evidence of Mateo's arrest. That ability you used to mask your appearance? They both described you in exactly the same way. When I mentioned it to Roboute, he immediately thought of you."

The low, slow breath Gerard let out filled the quiet room.

"You may ask your questions, Lord Haarlock."

"First question: why me? I've been asking myself this whole time what I could possibly know to warrant my assassination. Second question: why such a complicated plan? Wouldn't it have been easier to just, I don't know, kill us both in our sleep or something?"

Gerard walked backward towards the metal door, his eyes never leaving Haarlock. When he reached it, he leaned against it, then crossed his arms and tilted his head.

"You posed an interesting conundrum. In a short amount of time, you became one of Roboute and Marcon's pawns, then showed up at a meeting between the most powerful people in this nation. When Roboute pushed to have you join Shattersong, it became a concern you were there to investigate its members."

"Ah, so you do have a mole in their ranks."

No reaction.

"As for why such a complicated plan? We couldn't be sure who Justine shared her investigation with, nor what, if anything, she shared with them. Nor did we know if failsafes were in place to release her findings should she die. Thus, killing her far away from Ostia, in a method that would cover any suspicion of her disappearance and prevent her body from ever being discovered, was necessary. We weren't entirely sure how to accomplish that until you showed up at the secret meeting. Then it was only a matter of how to get the two of you together and going to the same place. It seems in our haste we left a few strings for you to unravel."

*"*Friends. Soon.*"*

Haarlock looked up at the manacles on his wrists again, then followed the chains to the eyelets in the ceiling. "Devil's in the details, so they say."

"I tire of this game."

Gerard removed a shock stick from under his cloak and tapped it to Haarlock's bare stomach. The jolt of electricity seized Haarlock's muscles, causing him to flex so hard his feet lifted off the ground. Haarlock's jaw clenched tight enough to make his ears ring.

"Every time you answer a question in anything other than a direct, concise manner, that will happen."

A ragged coughing fit overtook Haarlock, and he hacked up phlegm.

"Seems I hit a chord, Gerard."

The process repeated itself. Haarlock cursed when his muscles finally relaxed.

"I am amending the rules. If you speak other than to answer a question in a direct, concise manner, that will happen. Do you understand?"

"Yes!" Haarlock's body jerked involuntarily as sweat beaded on his skin. "Fuck!"

"Where is your pet?"

"I don't know." Haarlock jerked as far back as he could when Gerard moved the shock stick towards him again. "I'm telling the truth!"

Gerard held the shock stick out menacingly. "Where is Roboute?"

"Last we spoke, he was going to raid Central Administration in the early morning and arrest any employees who weren't at work."

"Why?" Gerard lowered the stick.

"Your friend, the one with the jowls? Blue Jira, right? He really should have covered up that incense Central Administration uses. Very recognizable."

The guildmaster looked into Haarlock's eyes, holding his gaze as he adjusted the shock stick in his hand. He spun in place and rapped twice on the metal door. It opened to reveal one of the grim, black-outfitted men who strung Haarlock up earlier. Another five men, each armed with shock sticks, waited down the long tube of a hallway. Like the spherical room, bright light filled every part of it.

Gerard looked back over his shoulder at Haarlock for a moment. "If anything happens, kill Lord Haarlock immediately."

The two men left, and the metal door shut and locked behind them.

Dramatic much?

Haarlock gently swung in the now empty room. He tried to cast his least exerting spell, the cantrip *Mage Hand*, but his mind was too fried from the shock stick. Even if he could manage a spell, the all-consuming light left no shadows for him to use his more versatile magic.

How long he hung there, Haarlock didn't know, but he passed out at least once. The psychic voice of a raccoon woke him up.

*"*Coming. Fight.*"*

"Oh yeah? You better be sneaky about it, because I'm the first person they're killing when things kick off."

*"*Loud. Fun.*"*

"For you, maybe."

*"*Where?*"*

"I told you, I don't know where I am."

*"*Tunnels. Where?*"*

"Four stories down, at the end of a hallway. I think. Not sure if that helps."

*"*Yes. Coming.*"*

Haarlock looked up again at the eyelets holding his chains to the ceiling. If this place was anything like Mateo's secret stash, these bricks were old. And with the dampness in the air, the foundation probably wasn't the most structurally sound. It also appeared each of the eyelets were secured to the ceiling by four bolts. That meant shallow threading.

Let's see how good an idea this is.

Though his abs burned from the shock stick, he pulled his knees up to his chest. With a kick out, Haarlock brought his legs down and back in a swinging motion, then back up again, giving him just enough momentum to lift his entire body.

But it wasn't enough.

His weight slammed down on his manacled wrists. A second time. A third. Each time he came down, the metal bands cut further into his wrists, finally breaking the skin. Blood trickled down his arms.

Focus. Pain is subjective. You've got literally magically enhanced endurance and strength. This is nothing.

Once. Twice.

More blood and pain.

Three times. A fourth.

Purchase.

The index and middle finger of Haarlock's left hand wrapped around the chain. It wasn't much, but it gave him slack on his right hand. He started swaying to get the right angle and...his right hand went completely around the chain. Once both hands were secure on the metal rungs, Haarlock pulled himself up.

His shoulders burned as his tendons and ligaments strained to their limit. Something tore, but he pulled himself off the ground and up the chains. Once he reached the top, he took a deep breath.

"Ladrón, I'm about to do something really stupid. I hope you guys get here soon."

Haarlock released his grip and let gravity take over.

37

The fall isn't what gets you; it's the sudden stop at the end. And Haarlock stopped suddenly when he hit the brick floor. Which was good because that meant he could unhook the chains and escape. Considering his right arm wouldn't move very well, it meant he had probably broken it. That wasn't so good.

Haarlock's mind swam with pain as he lay on the cold floor. The sound of the door's mechanism opening brought him back to the present. Even with the broken arm, Haarlock was on his feet and against the wall in a moment, metal chain at the ready.

Two guards rushed in, each with a dagger in their hand. The second it took them to realize Haarlock wasn't strung up was all the time he needed.

The closest guard ate a mouthful of chain, and as he grabbed his now ruined face and screamed, Haarlock kicked him into the man behind him. Both went down in a heap, and both received a bare foot to the face to keep them down.

Sjena's Gift needed darkness for Haarlock to summon it, and with the endless white light coming from every surface there was nowhere for a shadow to form. Haarlock even shoved his hand between the two men to find darkness, but his weapon wouldn't appear. He thought about taking one of the guard's daggers, though with the chains attached to his wrists he wouldn't be able to use it effectively. But he had chains attached to his wrists.

Haarlock darted into the hallway to meet the other armed men coming towards him. The five-foot wide tunnel made an excellent barrier against more than one person attacking him at a time.

Even with one arm disabled, Haarlock matched the next guard in skill. That, and the pain re-energized him, allowing him to cast *Magic Armor*. It wasn't much, but it kept his enemy's blade from wounding him further.

Down the third guard went, then the fourth. The next two got smart and didn't come at Haarlock one at a time. One changed grips so their blades were in opposite hands.

"Alright, fellas. Who thinks they have what it takes to knock me down?"

Before anyone moved, an explosion rocked the entire area, and all three lurched to the side. Haarlock's broken right arm slammed into the wall, sending mind-numbing pain through him. As he lay panting on the ground, the two guards stood, looked at one another, and took a step forward.

That's when a wave of counter magic pulsed down the tunnel and cast everything in darkness. Before Haarlock could react to his good fortune, he saw a dark shape dart through the shadows towards the guards.

The shape slammed into the man on the right, moving across him like a snake. He screamed as he tried to beat the thing attacking him with his fists, but it was too fast. The second man ran towards Haarlock and tripped on one of the previously dispatched guards, hitting the ground so hard that he knocked himself out. It didn't take long for the shape to find something vital, and the screaming of the last guard ended as quickly as it began.

"Hey there, Ladrón."

*"*Fight. Happy.*"*

"Yes, you did. Good job."

The shape approached Haarlock and snuggled up to his side.

*"*Help. Coming.*"*

"Can you get these off me?"

The dark shape that was Ladrón moved across Haarlock's left wrist, and within seconds the manacle fell off. Luckily Ladrón did the right manacle with far more grace, eliciting only the most minor grunt of pain from Haarlock.

As Haarlock got to his feet, a bright golden light appeared in a side tunnel, approaching slowly. *Sjena's Gift* materialized in Haarlock's hand while Ladrón took a defensive stance in front of him.

Into the main hallway the light moved, shining from the feathers of an enormous black raven. The bird hopped along the ground for a few feet, and once it saw Haarlock, it cawed a single time before it blinked out of existence and its master took its place.

"Ah, there you are, Haarlock. I wondered where you'd gotten off to."

Roboute may have shone with the same golden hue as the bird, but he looked like he'd just been through a fight with an especially angry badger. His hair, normally coiffed to perfection, lay haphazardly on his head, one whole side singed almost to the scalp. His clothing, a set of light leather armor, had fared much the same.

"Oh, you know me. Always sticking my nose where it doesn't belong." Haarlock pointed to his busted arm. "Little help?"

"Yes, of course." Roboute put two fingers in his mouth and blew out an ear-piercing whistle. "I brought the cavalry."

A rustling jingle of metal, glass, and cloth slowly approached, and a pixie-cut, gray-haired woman in her fifties popped out from the side hallway. Samantha the Enchanter. She held a glass bottle in each hand. Her red fox, Jaakuna, followed closely behind.

Both looked as good a Roboute did.

"Hey there, Haarlock!" Samantha's bright smile melted away when she saw his condition. "Good thing I brought plenty of these."

The Enchanter handed the bottles to Haarlock. He drank them, and within moments the healing potions worked their magic. Wounds closed, bones knit together, and pain vanished.

Jaakuna approached slowly, eyeing Ladrón with suspicion. The raccoon sniffed the air and grumbled.

Haarlock let out a sigh of relief. "That is *much* better. Thank you."

"It's literally what I'm here for. That and violence." Samantha winked. "I'm dual purpose."

Roboute laughed. "That you are, my dear."

"So, what's going on?" Haarlock gestured to the unconscious men on the ground. "I assume there's more of them."

"Many more." Roboute ran a hand through his disheveled hair. "We fought through a dozen just to get here, and there's at least twenty more the others were fighting."

"Others?"

Samantha nodded enthusiastically. "Manuel, Quinn, and Acorn."

"Zachary, Jean-Baptiste, and several platoons of city guard are mopping up any who escape topside." Roboute looked over Haarlock's shoulder, then back the way Samantha had come. "Any idea where Gerard is?"

"No." Haarlock shook his head. "I passed out for a little while, so I'm not sure how much of a head start he has."

"Couldn't be much. We teleported in maybe twenty minutes after Ladrón first started communicating with you."

"Really? It felt like hours, at least."

"With as bad as you look, I bet it did." Samantha shrugged.

"Fair enough." Haarlock knocked on a wall. "How big is this place? Gerard said we're four stories underground."

"It's a maze." Roboute looked down. "There's at least three more levels below us."

Alert screamed in Haarlock's head as a figure leaped from a shadow behind Roboute. Before Haarlock could do more than take a defensive stance, the Illusionist held up a hand, and the would-be assassin froze in place. Samantha and Jaakuna both chirped in surprise and jumped back.

"And what do we have here?" Roboute turned around to look at his attacker. "Goodbye."

Roboute flicked his wrist, and the man vanished with the whip-crack of a teleport spell.

Haarlock frowned. "Where'd he go?"

"Twenty or so feet to the left."

"What's twenty feet to the left?"

"I have absolutely no idea."

Samantha and Haarlock shared a look and shrugged.

"Now that those damn lights are out, I can use my spells to move with speed." Haarlock readjusted his dirk. "I'll find Gerard."

Roboute looked at Samantha with a smile. "My dear, I'm sure we can find some more goons to vent our frustrations on."

"Yes, I believe we can." The Enchanted clicked her tongue at the fox. "Jaakuna, lead the way."

The red fox, who'd been sitting patiently to the rear, perked up. It let out a chirp before sniffing the air, then headed back the way it came.

"Good luck, Haarlock."

"You never say *good luck*. You say *good hunting*."

***

The underground tunnels stretched on for what seemed like an eternity. Sometimes only a wall separated them from a basement, or even a canal. How they kept it a secret from the rest of the city would be a mystery for someone else to solve.

Both Haarlock and Ladrón moved like wraiths through the shadows. Down they went into the furthest recesses of the tunnels, first two levels, then three. Here they found a handful of others, all scrambling to assemble piles of documents, or to destroy them with chemicals and fire. Each died without ever seeing what killed them.

Four levels further down, their target appeared. Gerard, unflustered by the chaos surrounding him, directed a score of men in evidence destruction. Some fed a barrel of steaming liquid a steady diet of parchment, while others brought single pages to a leather satchel on the ground next to the guildmaster. Glow globes floating beside them illuminated what they did, the light casting shadows across every surface. Gerard, though, stood in a ring of globes, completely safe from the darkness.

Their room, a massive, square space with tool-worn stone walls and floors, looked to have once been the final stopping point of a mining crew. Since then, it has become a work area, with desks in the center, beds lining one wall, and a kitchen against another. An elevator hid in a shadowed recess in the back, its shaft going so far up Haarlock couldn't see the end.

Haarlock circled the room as he watched Gerard, dipping between the dark recesses of the furniture. Even Marcon, a centuries-old elf, wasn't confident he could defeat the guildmaster on his best day, and Haarlock only had a blade. Though none of the others present looked to be threatening, twenty unarmed people could overwhelm even the most prodigious fighter.

Should he leave to warn Roboute, then wait for the cavalry? If he did, Gerard might use the elevator, or some kind of teleportation spell, to make his escape. Something told Haarlock that whatever was in the satchel was important. Important enough for the guildmaster to wait for what the others put into it.

Fortune favors the bold.

Haarlock stepped out of the shadows inside the elevator. If the higher levels were cold, it was absolutely frigid down here. The damp, stale air sucked every iota of heat from Haarlock's bare arms and chest.

"Sorry to interrupt, Gerard. Looks like you guys are busy."

The guildmaster turned to face the newcomer. "I didn't realize you were fishing for information on our location until the attack started. Very skillful of you, Lord Haarlock."

"Thank you." Haarlock tipped his head. He looked around the room at the people still going about their business as if he wasn't there. "You know the jig is up, right? Why bother trying to salvage anything here? Give up while you can."

"*The jig is up*? I'm not familiar with that phrase." Gerard shrugged. "Either way, our belief is unwavering, even in the face of certain defeat. We will accomplish what we can in the time allowed."

"It's hard for me to believe you'd betray your nation like this."

"There's nothing difficult about it. I fought for Lemuria, then I was shown the truth and now I fight for Sanyo." Gerard's posture straightened ever so slightly.

Haarlock frowned. *Shown the truth*?

"What truth?"

"One this entire nation will learn soon enough. Your actions today will force the shogun's hand, Lord Haarlock."

"Oh, please, Gerard." Haarlock mockingly laughed. "Like he wasn't going to invade, anyway."

"True enough, I suppose." Gerard spoke to the others without taking his eyes off Haarlock. "We're done here. Leave what's left and escape if you can."

The others gave murmurs of acknowledgement before leaving through the room's only hallway. Gerard kneeled and closed the satchel, then twisted a medallion on the flap. The satchel blinked out of existence in a whip-crack of noise.

As the guildmaster stood, he noticed something to his left. Ladrón. The raccoon stepped out from underneath a bookcase, teeth bared. Haarlock used his dirk to cut the elevator's ropes, then walked forward.

"You're not leaving this place, Gerard."

"Of that, Lord Haarlock, I have no doubt." The guildmaster drew his sword and plunged it into the nearest floating orb.

***

Haarlock and Ladrón collapsed out of the shadows and into a tunnel three levels higher, a coughing fit overtaking them both. The hair on Haarlock's face and head was singed to the skin, and a sizable portion of Ladrón's fur not covered by his harness was gone, too. A reflexively cast *Magic Armor* saved Haarlock from the worst of it.

Destruction reigned around them. Light and water poured in from a rend in the ceiling to their left, flowing underneath them and into the crater to their right. Steam bellowed from the massive hole in the floor, and what little of the air wasn't filled with smoke was thick with water vapor.

"Ladrón! You alright?"

The raccoon coughed a few times before shaking the water from his head. He looked up at Haarlock and chittered once.

"Yeah, I'm fine."

Haarlock realized he was yelling. And speaking out loud. Probably because of the ringing in his ears.

"Can you hear? Because I can't."

*"*Loud. Ouch.*"*

"No shit."

Haarlock used the wall to get to his feet and stumble away from the hole. Something further down the tunnel emitted light, and that meant people. Ladrón darted ahead, his nose to the waterlogged ground.

*"*Friend. Hurt.*"*

"Who?"

*"*Quinn.*"*

The Sky Druid lay in a pool of water in a side room a hundred feet further down. Her head bobbed in the dark liquid, face under the surface. Haarlock grabbed the petite woman and drug her out of the water and onto her back. He began chest compressions with a steady rhythm.

"Damn it, Quinn, come on."

Ten pumps on her chest and she still wasn't breathing. Haarlock sat her up and went behind her to do the Heimlich. It took five dangerously forceful thrusts before she coughed up the water in her lungs.

"There we go." Haarlock laid the woman gently on her side and rubbed her back as she took in lungfuls of air. "You're fine."

Quinn finally caught her breath and sat up. She saw Ladrón sitting in front of her with a worried look on his singed face.

"Oh, hey there, Ladrón." Quinn wobbled as she shook her head, then looked over at Haarlock. She wiped the dark brown, water-soaked hair from her face and smiled. "Fancy seeing you here. Were we supposed to go on a date?"

"No, Quinn, we weren't." Haarlock leaned in to see her pupils were two different sizes. "It looks like you got knocked around a little."

"There was this really loud noise and then something hit me in the head, I think." The Sky Druid touched the back of her scalp, and she pulled her hand away to see blood coating it. "Yep. Hit it pretty good it looks like."

"We're all a little banged up."

Haarlock looked the woman over. A leather pouch on the small of her back contained only shards, which meant no healing potions. With a groan from both, Haarlock got Quinn to her feet.

"There was an explosion, and I'm pretty sure by the giant hole in the floor it destabilized the entire area. We need to leave."

"I came with others. We can't leave them behind."

"We won't. But we need to get to safety first, okay?"

Haarlock smiled at the woman. She smiled back and nodded her head a single time, then bent over and puked. When she regained her composure, Quinn slicked her hair back and took a deep breath.

"Feel better?"

"Much. I'm still not sure where I am."

"If it makes you feel any better, I'm not entirely sure where we are either."

Two humans and a raccoon made their way through the ruined tunnels, over collapsed ceilings, and up flooded stairs. The explosion wasn't big enough to kill Haarlock, but it was big enough to destroy the centuries-old foundations under the city. It took them an hour to find their way up the four stories to the surface.

The surrounding buildings lay on their side, with many more gone into an enormous sinkhole a hundred feet across. How many went in with them was anyone's guess. Hundreds of people cried out for loved ones, while dozens more searched the rubble. First responders healed who they could with potions and spells, while other mages used their magic to erect barricades and stabilize the ground. The city guard did its best to contain the chaos.

Where they were, Haarlock wasn't sure. It had to be on the western side of the city based on their position to the castle. Dust and smoke floated thickly in the air, mostly pouring from the sinkhole.

"Quinn, did anyone make it out before the explosion?"

"Is that what caused the big hole in the ground?"

The Sky Druid's face drained of color right before Haarlock's eyes as her skin turned clammy to the touch.

"Okay, let's get you on the ground."

Once Quinn was propped up against a piece of rubble, Haarlock flagged down a medic. The skinny orc who jogged over wore a vest covered in so many potions it was any wonder he could stand. With practiced ease the medic examined Quinn, diagnosing a severe concussion, and fed her two different potions. The red one healed the wound on her head, while the green one put her to sleep.

"Don't worry, she'll be fine when she wakes up. What I gave her will take time to work, and I'll make sure she's looked after till then."

"Got anything for me? I look worse than I feel, but I don't feel too good, either." Haarlock jabbed a thumb at Ladrón. "Same with my friend."

The orc looked between the two with confusion but shrugged and handed each a small phial of red liquid.

"I've got to save the stronger stuff for those not upright. But these should keep you going."

Both downed their potions at the same time, then Haarlock patted the orc on the shoulder.

"If you ever see me again, I owe you a very expensive drink."

Haarlock jogged off towards a squad of guards trying to herd a group of panicked civilians away from the sinkhole. One guard turned towards him and raised a hand.

"Sir, you need to move away. This area is dangerous."

"I know. Listen, I need to find..."

"Like I said, move away. We'll help you find whatever it is you lost once the area is safe."

"Hey! Listen to me." Haarlock pointed at the sinkhole. "The team that raided the tunnels? I'm the one they were looking for. Do you know where any of them are?"

The guard stopped, looked Haarlock up and down, then made a face like he had just heard the most grandiose lie ever.

Haarlock couldn't help but laugh at what this guy must be thinking about the shirtless man covered in dirt, soot, and grime, and his severely disheveled, mostly hairless raccoon companion.

"Um, sir, I think you might need to see a medic."

"I already did. Was there some kind of cordoned-off area before the explosion? Real hush-hush?"

The guard frowned. "Actually, yes. About three blocks east."

Without waiting for more information, Haarlock ran east. Luckily for the city, the destruction stopped after a few hundred feet, though crowds of gawkers blocked every roadway to and from the scene. It took Haarlock four tries before someone knew of a police cordon before the explosion. A whole company of city guard blockaded the area an hour before, and, as far as they knew, it remained so.

When Haarlock came around the corner, he was met with a line of armored sentries. They stood, weapons drawn, on the street, in the alleys, and in the doorways of every building in the area. More than a few eyed Haarlock with a combination of suspicion and amusement.

"Hey there, fellas. This is going to be a weird question, but is there a gnome, an orc, and a couple of humans running the show?"

One guard, an officer by his cloak, spoke up.

"This area is under guard. Because of the nature of the incident, we cannot give you further information. Please move along."

"Whatever you say." Haarlock sent Ladrón a mental ping.

The raccoon sat on his haunches and waved his arms excitedly at one guard. When the burly man looked down and tilted his head in confusion, Ladrón darted forward and slipped between his legs.

"Sir, you're responsible for the actions of your pet. Once we capture him, you will have to pay a fine."

"Good luck with that." Haarlock looked past the man's armored shoulder. "But I don't think that will be necessary."

Captain Micca Barecna approached, spoke to the officer for a minute, then waved Haarlock through. Barecna took Haarlock down an alleyway to a large, black tent attached to a warehouse.

Inside was a bustling command center. Guards came and went, sometimes depositing a prisoner in a makeshift cell in the corner or bringing intel to those at the tables. Mages off to the left coordinated via *Message* spells, relaying information to and from with calm professionalism.

The wall of warmth that hit Haarlock caused him to shake.

"I wondered when you'd finally realize you were cold." The captain let out a deep laugh, then grabbed a blanket on a nearby chair and handed it to Haarlock.

"Adrenaline is a hell of a drug." Haarlock wrapped the blanket tightly around himself. "Got anything warm to drink?"

With a snap of his fingers, Barecna summoned someone with a mug of steaming liquid. Haarlock held it in both hands for a moment before holding it under the blanket. Ladrón found his own pile of linen and disappeared into it.

"Not going to drink it?"

"My skin feels like it's on fire. I need to warm up my outsides before I worry about the insides."

"I don't think that's how it works."

It took no time for a squeaky Irish voice to fill the tent.

"Haarlock!" Acorn bounded over. She looked about as good as Roboute did when Haarlock last saw him. Burns, cuts, and tears covered much of her armor, while dirt and soot smeared her face. "Glad to see you're alive, but where's my raccoon?"

"Under there." Haarlock gestured with his chin. A dirty, shivering, partially furless paw popped out of the blankets, gave an enthusiastic wave, then disappeared back inside. "He says he'll greet you properly once he's done thawing out."

Acorn pouted. "Guess that'll have to do. Again, glad you're alive."

"Same. Gerard tried really hard to kill me, though."

"Is that what the explosion was?" Barecna turned to look towards the door.

"He detonated a glow globe, which caused a chain reaction with the others in the room. Damn near took me with him. I didn't know those things were so volatile."

Acorn closed her agape mouth. "A single globe has a lot of magic in it, sure, but it's ridiculously stable. What did he do to rupture it?"

"Stabbed it with a sword."

Barecna huffed. "That'll do it."

"Say, where are the others?" Haarlock looked around the tent. "Quinn made it out with me, but she's banged up pretty bad. A medic near the sinkhole is taking care of her."

Acorn sighed in relief as she patted her chest. "Thank the gods, we were worried about her. As for the others, Roboute and Samantha are interrogating prisoners in a makeshift holding area in a stable to the south. Zachary and Jean-Baptiste are helping to rein in the chaos, but Manuel got caught when the ground collapsed and is on the way to the hospital. He's in a bad way now but should be fine, eventually."

"Glad to hear we didn't lose anyone."

"Same."

Barecna cleared his throat. "Now that everyone is caught up, where are your clothes, Haarlock?"

"Somewhere underground."

Acorn grimaced. "You had some nice stuff, too."

"I'm aware." Haarlock grumbled into the mug as he sipped from it.

"My men will search every inch of those tunnels. If it's not under a city block's worth of rubble, we'll find it."

"Tell them whoever does gets fifty cases of wine."

Barecna and Acorn looked at one another, then back to Haarlock.

"What? I want my stuff back."

***

How many slipped through Captain Barecna's cordon, no one would ever know. The sheer chaos of the situation overwhelmed every aspect of the city's response, and besides, there were too many exits for the guards to cover.

The documents on those who were caught, and those recovered from the rubble, painted a grim picture of how deep the shinobi's tendrils stretched. Nearly three hundred nobles, merchants, and adventurers were implicated. Barecna's relentless charge stopped at nothing to arrest every person accountable.

It didn't matter what title a noble possessed, nor what position in society they held; all went away in chains. Many attempted to blackmail their way to safety, but King Raoned Shein himself decreed that any involved with the shinobi plot would pay dearly. The die-hard believers, or just the petty ones, released their secrets anyway, bringing hundreds more down with them.

The merchants inflicted their own petty revenge before their capture: mass selloffs of stocks, shuttering of vital storefronts, and the disappearance of vast quantities of liquidity. Market fluctuations threw everything from necessities to bulk goods into financial uncertainty. Every aspect of Lemurian society would feel the effects for months, if not years.

Surprisingly, none of the adventurers tried to fight their way to freedom. While many escaped before Barecna's men came calling, those who didn't went without so much as a fight. Senior members of the Adventurer's Guild stripped them of their memberships and banned them from all guildhalls across the continent, and when possible, the world. Those who outlived their sentences would find their adventuring careers effectively ended.

The scouring didn't stop at just those involved with Gerard directly. With the chaos caused by the nobles and merchants, and the looming war with Sanyo, King Shein wanted his city cleansed of any liability. Roboute, appointed interim spymaster, descended upon Ostia's Thieves' Guild with a vengeance. Every quest that passed through the guildhall and its branches, and every coin it paid out, was scrutinized. Hundreds of rogues, from petty thieves to violent assassins, were identified and prosecuted. Those who posted the quests received similar fates. Shuttering the Thieves' Guild wouldn't stop crime in the city, but it put an end to the more prolific criminals, be they people or institutions, for a time. But power abhors a vacuum, and eventually those voids would fill.

It took fifty mages more than a week to stabilize the sinkhole and the surrounding area. Even with all their efforts, the city engineers would need to redirect one of the nearby canals to stop the underground flooding. Thousands would need to be relocated while the sinkhole was filled in, and dozens of businesses would likely close their doors forever. A conservative estimate suggested a cost of 850,000 gold, with the project lasting into the summer. How far the tunnels stretched was anyone's guess, but a concerted effort to map and then seal them was put on the docket.

38

Haarlock returned to Ostia in the last week of February. Things calmed down by then, and Roboute requested a meeting at the castle.

A vermin of a man met Haarlock in the courtyard and brought him to Roboute's new office. The path led them through several halls, down two flights of stairs, and through a small passageway Haarlock had to duck to fit through. Wherever in the castle they were, it looked much like any other, sans windows and natural light.

The nameless guide stopped in front of a simple wooden door, bowed, and pushed it open. He gestured for Haarlock to enter, then closed the door behind him.

Roboute worked in the center of the room, the round table in front of him covered in stacks of papers. The Illusionist held one document in each hand as he looked at them with confusion and annoyance.

"Troubles?"

"Yes, very much so." Roboute huffed and laid the pages down. He picked up two more and repeated his expression. "Cleaning up the last bit of Gerard's mess is proving to be more difficult than imagined."

"No doubt." Haarlock sat down across from Roboute. "What is the *last bit* you're working on?"

"You were right about Blue Jira working out of Central Administration. After the debacle in the tunnels, we rounded up every person associated with Central and gave them a *robust* interrogation. An older gentleman, far too worried about spending the rest of his life in the *Dolphin*, ratted out his compatriots for a lighter sentence. Come to find out, Blue Jira isn't just a person, but a small group with their fingers in oh so many pies." Roboute sat down the pages and gestured to the stacks before him. "This is about a tenth of the documents we pulled from Central. Luckily for us, they liked to keep blackmail material."

"Damn." Haarlock guessed there to be at least two hundred sheets.

"Yes. *Damn*."

Both men laughed.

"Anyway, glad to see your equipment was recovered."

Haarlock looked down at himself. His armor, fatigues, cloak, boots, and boonie hat all looked clean and new.

"All except the gloves Marcon made for me."

A flash of sorrow crossed Roboute's face before he frowned. "Yes, that is unfortunate."

"I never asked: what were his last wishes, if any?"

"In lieu of him having no family, his will requested a handful of heirlooms be returned to his homeland and donated to a museum. I arranged for the items to be sent via ship a few weeks ago. As for Marcon himself, he was buried at sea. Seems he liked the idea of being eaten by fish rather than by worms."

Haarlock nodded more to himself than to anyone else. "His shop?"

"*Sew Above, Sew Below* leased that space, and by now someone else will have moved in. The stock was sold and any unfinished items were refunded."

"It's as if he never existed."

"Given enough time, Haarlock, all of us will be forgotten."

"That's weirdly comforting, actually."

Roboute cocked an eyebrow. "It is, isn't it? Speaking of being forgotten, where's my favorite raccoon?"

From within the shadows of Haarlock's cloak came an excited chitter, immediately followed by a purple tinted black-gray ball tumbling out onto the floor. The animal's fur was mostly grown back, though it would be several more weeks before it reached full length again.

"Ah, there you are!" Roboute waved his hand, and a plate of neatly stacked berries appeared in front of Ladrón. "I see he's healed nicely."

"The healing was the easy part. Growing back all the fur wasn't." Haarlock squinted at Ladrón as he shoved handfuls of fruit into his mouth. "The first week was torture for both of us."

"Both?"

"He did nothing but complain about how badly it itched, and how he's still missing a tooth, to anyone who would listen. I am unfortunate enough to be psychically connected to him."

"That sounds quite unpleasant. Anyway, to business."

"I was wondering why you asked me here." Haarlock leaned in with a smirk. "Does the Thieves' Guild need a new guildmaster or something?"

"Hardly." Roboute rolled his eyes. "The Thieves' Guild will be rebuilt, in time, but long before that happens there are more pressing matters to attend to. As I said, Gerard's network ran far and wide. The vast majority comprised low-level informants, with only a few dozen having any real reach or sway."

Haarlock gave the Illusionist a sideways look. "Am I going to be *cleaning up* some of the loose ends?"

Roboute's brow rose. "Looking for a little payback, are we?"

"Not particularly, but it's been a boring few weeks."

"Sorry about sending you away like that. No one wanted you around, itching for a fight."

"Oh, I get it. Decompressing with copious amounts of wine and food did wonders to help with the whole betrayal thing."

"That I understand." Roboute leaned back and regarded Haarlock for a moment. "Not going to ask about Camilla?"

Haarlock mirrored the pose. "Sounds like you want to talk about her more than I do."

"It seems I do."

"What about her? No one at the guild has written about her, or anything else for that matter."

Roboute pouted. "You seem wounded."

"Please." It was Haarlock's turn to roll his eyes. "While I feel...somewhat betrayed by Camilla's actions, I never counted her as much more than a coworker. Granted, she kept herself apart from everyone to maintain an air of detached leadership, so that could have something to do with it. Besides Acorn, I never worked that closely with the others. They're far more coworkers than friends. Not hearing from them hasn't hurt my feelings."

"If it makes you feel any better, Shattersong has been, how do you say, put under an appraising eye."

"No news in or out while you vet their stories?"

"Officially they're still contracted through the Crown, so they've been hired to do nothing but twiddle their thumbs."

"Any concern of another mole in their ranks?"

"All have passed every stringent investigation anyone can think of doing."

"I take it you've used spells to elicit honest responses?"

"Of course. Every member volunteered for an extensive, and invasive, memory audit."

"You can do that?" Haarlock blinked several times.

"There are few things magic cannot do. Granted, fewer still can perform such an audit, and it takes a mostly willing subject."

"Good to know."

"Indeed." Roboute sighed. "As for Camilla, we are unsure what to do with her."

"I assume she followed everyone else involved into the *Dolphin*."

"There are mitigating circumstances." Roboute leaned forward and rested his arms on the table, taking a less relaxed pose. "Despite the *official* proclamation from the king, not all went into the mountain. Those who were coerced, like Camilla, received lighter sentences."

"How light?"

"Her diplomatic position and noble titles will be revoked." Haarlock sat up and went to speak, but Roboute held up a hand. "The memory audit showed her involvement truly was minimal. With the threat of revealing her daughter's inheritance and the dangers that posed, combined with the fact she only delivered letters with no knowledge of their purpose, the punishment fits the crime."

"You said you weren't sure what to do with her."

"A partially formed timeline shows her letters corresponded with significant shinobi activity. Though her actions may have been minimal, the consequences most assuredly were not."

Haarlock nodded. "Someone needs blamed."

"There are those who want more than a proverbial slap on the wrist."

"I don't think stripping away everything that made someone who they were is what I'd call a *slap on the wrist.* Will she get banned from the Adventurer's Guild, too?"

"She will."

"Looks like her prospects will be few and far between."

Roboute nodded. "Indeed, it does."

"So, what's the problem?"

"Camilla's guilt is absolute, but her expertise and contacts are invaluable. Simply removing her from the board would be a detriment to Lemuria."

Haarlock huffed. "You're wondering if she should be used in a less official capacity. Send her to be an unofficial voice of the nation or some such."

"That's the gist of it, yes." Roboute shrugged. "The decision is ultimately not up to me, though the outcome will weigh heavily on my opinion. And my opinion weighs heavily on yours."

Something in Roboute's head tilt triggered *Canny Observer*. Haarlock squinted at the Illusionist as the wily mage waited for a response. A long moment passed in silence.

"This is another one of your tests, isn't it?"

Roboute's face lit up with his signature shark-smile and waved his right hand towards the wall. The otherwise featureless stones shimmered to form a doorway, and out through it came a hulking figure in gold-accented black full-plate armor. Behind the honor guard walked the king of Lemuria.

Haarlock shot to his feet, awkwardly standing at attention. It took him a second to regain composure, then he looked at Roboute, then at the king, then back to Roboute.

With a laugh, Roboute stood and bowed slightly to the king. "Your Majesty, welcome."

"Thank you, Roboute." The honor guard stood next to the newly revealed door as King Shein walked to the table. "Please sit with me, Lord Haarlock."

Roboute moved to the side, standing with his hands clasped behind his back as the king took his seat.

It was difficult for Haarlock not to be impressed by the air of regal power radiating from the monarch. He assumed it was some kind of ability at work, but even still it took concentrated effort to shake the feeling. Shein's long, blonde hair and defined, masculine features gave him the look of someone from a romance book cover. The white, gold-trimmed tunic he wore, though plain, was sure to be anything but.

"How may I be of service?" Haarlock sat with his best posture.

"Tell me about your opinion on the measures I took in the wake of Gerard's betrayal."

Haarlock cleared his throat as his eyes flicked to Roboute. The Illusionist gave a minuscule nod.

"I'd say they were extreme, but then again, it was and is an extreme situation." Haarlock waited for a response, but the king only looked at him. "Taking that into account, it was better to rip the bandage off, otherwise you'd likely never have caught as many as you did. Would I have done that? Probably not, but I'm not a king."

"And the punishments?"

"I doubt it will happen again anytime soon."

The king raised his chin slightly. "What of Camilla Albertine?"

"I'm told there were mitigating circumstances."

"Her situation doesn't seem to be a measure of hypocrisy?"

"I can't imagine everyone connected to this debacle, no matter how small, would receive the same punishment as the most die-hard believer."

"No, they haven't." The king leaned back in his chair. "Far too many people are connected, some guilty by simple association. Throwing every single one of them in prison would cripple the economy even further."

"Justice and practicality can be a difficult balance."

"Indeed, they can, Lord Haarlock. Indeed, they can." The king tapped a finger on his thigh as he looked down at the raccoon still devouring fruit on the floor nearby.

Haarlock glanced back and forth between the king and Roboute, confusion on his face.

"This feels like an interview, Your Majesty."

"It is."

"For what, exactly?"

Roboute spoke. "Your report stated Gerard activated a teleportation spell on a leather satchel. That satchel arrived at a messenger service with a standing contract to immediately dispatch a priority rider to Turbenton. From there the satchel was placed on a small cutter that traveled south to the Goswell Gulf, eventually docking in Nippon. Four days later, our spies reported the mobilization of Sanyo forces."

"That was weeks ago." Haarlock bolted forward in his chair. "Are we mobilizing our own forces?"

The king laughed softly as he held up a hand. "There is no need for panic, lord. War in this world does not occur in winter. Besides, it will take months for them to organize, and another month or more to make the trek north."

Haarlock sat back and exhaled a heavy breath. "Sorry. Where I'm from, we could deploy within days to anywhere on the planet, anytime of the year."

"We seem to be given the luxury of time." The king huffed. "However good that will do."

"What do you mean?"

"You were at the tournament meeting. Armies cost money, and after recent events, Lemuria's treasury is in dire straits."

"Are you telling me Lemuria has lost before the war even begins?"

"Of course not." The king gestured to Haarlock. "As a former soldier, tell me, what ensures a military's success?"

"Logistics."

"Correct. We can only assume Sanyo will conscript every able-bodied citizen to lay siege to our nation. Thus, we must do the same to defend it."

"And pulling them all to fight a war will further strain the economy."

"It will destroy it." Shein's expression turned to sorrow. "And that will be the end of the supply line."

"Then what's to be done?"

"Grecklewood Pass is the only land route from the southern duchies to the north. If Sanyo takes control of the castle defending it, they will have unfettered control of nearly a quarter of this kingdom. There is no doubt they will attempt to capture it, and that is where we will break them."

"A siege?" Haarlock blinked. "Can the castle withstand Sanyo's army?"

"The shogun could throw fifty thousand men at those walls and fifty thousand would be cast back." Shein's voice oozed pride and arrogance.

"His Majesty would be correct..." Roboute tilted his head to the side as though he wasn't sure of how to phrase his next words. "If it weren't for what we believe to be the workings of a Relic."

Haarlock's jaw dropped ever so slightly. Relics were the highest classification of quality in *The Game,* each with incredible abilities. King Shein himself possessed a Relic, as did the shogun. The effect of such a Relic, or any other for that matter, on the battlefield would be extreme.

"What makes you think that?"

"Those we caught escaping the tunnels, along with others in higher positions, all acted in a certain way."

"Like true believers, right?"

Shein looked at Roboute, and both turned to Haarlock at the same time.

"Before Gerard blew himself up, he said something like he was *shown the truth*. It stood out because of the way he said it, like it was a programmed response."

Roboute nodded. "That's the same language the conspirators used when asked about the reason for their involvement. The *exact* same. Several killed themselves before we realized what was happening. Once we did, we learned that each was shown an image, after which they were utterly convinced of Sanyo's inevitability."

"Relics are powerful enough to just take you over like that?"

"Not exactly. Based on its description and effect, we identified the Relic to be a military standard known as *The Eternal Vigil*. So long as it is within your sight, your resolve is nigh unbreakable."

"Assuming the Relic didn't leave Sanyo, how did they convert Gerard and the others, and how did they remain under its power? And assuming they were loyal to begin with, how did it turn them away from Lemuria?"

"The victims all traveled near Sanyo in the last three to five years, and it's assumed they were taken to where the Relic was housed." Roboute swallowed hard, as if the words didn't want to leave his mouth. "They are still under its sway because we believe the Relic is corrupted."

A shiver ran down Haarlock's spine as his ears rang. It took him a moment to regain his composure.

"You believe the Relic's ability to be permanent?"

"We do. It appears to override one's beliefs with whatever message the owner wishes. In this case, the inevitability of Lemuria's defeat."

"Are you saying we'll be fighting an army of actual true believers, not just conscripts?"

"That is the current working theory, yes." Roboute's forlorn tone matched his expression. "It is our belief that the shogun will attack in two prongs. First, he will land troops along the length and breadth of our northern coastlines to raid and pillage. Their purpose will be to divert as many resources as possible, both in soldiers and material, from defending against the primary force attacking from the south. Second, their primary force will march en masse and head straight towards Grecklewood Castle. If this force is under the influence of a corrupted Relic, it is almost assured they will fight without regard to their own survival."

"What of the Relic? If it's brought to bear on the castle's defenders, won't they be overtaken?"

"*Any* who see it will be overtaken."

"Then what can we do?"

"Actions are being taken as we speak to provide a counter to the Relic's effect. The means to do this are relatively simple, though the materials necessary are difficult to come by in any quantity. Hence the reason for this meeting, Haarlock."

Roboute looked at Shein, and the king took over the conversation.

"You will be part of the forward mobilization team. At each muster point, you will assist them in organizing troops and supplies to be absorbed into the primary force as it moves south. Under this guise, you'll gather the needed components for the anti-Relic charms. With luck, the other requisitions will obfuscate your efforts. Any who hinders you, or the mobilization in general, is to be dealt with quickly and severely. Once the forward team arrives at the duchy of Jerell, you will break off and make haste to Grecklewood Castle with the charms."

Haarlock gave the king an uncertain look. "What do you mean by *severely*?"

"I leave that to your discretion." Shen held out his hand, and Roboute placed a wax-sealed scroll in it. He placed it on the table between him and Haarlock. "This document will ensure your word carries sufficient weight."

"What does it say?" Haarlock frowned at the rolled parchment. "Because unless you, Roboute, or a higher-ranked noble are coming with me, I don't think a piece of paper will count for much."

"Roboute will accompany me on a scheduled trip south, which will conveniently take us to the southern duchies and Grecklewood Castle before hostilities are likely to ensue. But it's funny you should mention a higher-ranked noble."

Haarlock looked up at Roboute to see his shark-like smile.

39

The carriage rolled smoothly to a stop in front of an estate in the north of Ostia. Though well into winter, the heavy layer of vines coating the rough-hewn, dark stone fence still retained much of its color. A well-bundled guard stood by the metal gate, and he opened it to allow Haarlock through.

Much like Roboute's holdings, this estate didn't cover a large, expansive area. The grounds themselves were perhaps half an acre, and the two-story house, the only structure, was built from the same stones as the fence. A light color wooden door, embellished with finely wrought metal accents, opened as Haarlock approached. The thin figure gestured for Haarlock to enter.

"Good evening, Lord Haarlock." The elven Footman, Gabriel, bowed. "Miss Albertine welcomes you to her home. May I take your cloak?"

It didn't take an ability to hear the twinge of pain and anger in Gabriel's voice about addressing the former marquise as *miss*.

"And a good evening to you, too, Gabriel. Thank you."

Ladrón hopped out of the cloak's shadow before Haarlock handed it to the Footman as he went inside.

"Ah, it appears Master Ladrón possesses a new ability."

"Indeed, he is. I can assure you my back appreciates it."

"I have no doubt." Gabriel hung the cloak in a nearby closet. "Miss Albertine waits for you in the study. Please follow me."

The elf led Haarlock to the left and down a short hallway adorned with floral artwork and live plants of all types and sizes. At the end Gabriel opened a pair of doors between two masterfully sculpted ferns.

"Miss Albertine, may I welcome Lord Haarlock and Ladrón." Gabriel bowed slightly. "Refreshments will arrive shortly, and if you are staying, m'lord, dinner is served at 7pm sharp."

Haarlock nodded once to the Footman and turned back to Camilla. She sat in one of the many high-backed chairs, hands folded neatly in her lap. Her hair, as colorful as ever, lay in a simple ponytail. The dress she wore, a plain red garment, matched the simplicity of her hair.

"I'm surprised you came to see me."

"To be honest, I'm surprised to be here."

"You were sent." Camilla's questioning expression went as quickly as it came.

Haarlock didn't answer, only moving to the left towards the bookcase covering the entire wall. Busts of various people and animals dotted the shelves, separating the larger sets from individual volumes.

"House arrest treating you well?" Haarlock ran a finger across the supple leather spines of several books. "It'd take me a *long* time to get through these."

"It may be a well-stocked prison cell, but it's still a prison cell."

"Want out?"

Camilla frowned when Haarlock flashed her a smile over his shoulder.

"And what *favor* does Roboute want for that to happen?"

"The king, too."

A scoff filled the otherwise quiet room. Ladrón perked up at the noise, then went back to sniffing the furniture.

"I can only imagine the caveats attached to that offer."

"They're not that bad, Camilla." Haarlock turned to face the woman, then leaned back against the shelving and crossed his arms. "You're to help convince the more obtuse nobles of this land to donate their stocks when the time comes."

Camilla stood in one smooth motion. "Sanyo is mobilizing?"

"Nothing extensive, mostly weapons and supplies. I'm told troops won't be mustered until mid-spring."

"Wars aren't fought in the wintertime."

"I'm told that, too."

The former noble thought to herself, hands folded behind her back. "And what concessions is the Crown willing to make for my assistance?"

"You get to leave your prison." Haarlock gestured broadly to the room. "And stay out of any others."

"I may be good with words, but I doubt many will listen to a disgraced former noble and diplomat. What are my options?"

Haarlock reached under his vest and removed a sealed envelope. "Either you accept the offer I have here, as presented, or you're charged with aiding and abetting a criminal conspiracy. I'm not sure if you've paid attention to what's happened to the others involved, but it isn't pretty."

"Take the carrot or get the stick. Roboute's typical strong-armed, underhanded negotiation technique."

Haarlock remained quiet as Camilla stared at the letter in his hand, chewing her lower lip. The woman finally held out her hand.

"Let's have it, shall we?"

Camilla took the offered letter and cracked the wax seal, pacing the room as she read, her face in a scowl.

"The gist of the letter is you'll be transferred to the War Department as special liaison. So long as you act with Lemuria's best intentions in mind during that time, you'll keep your titles and lands and receive a full pardon for all crimes once hostilities cease. Beyond the few who already know, no one else will learn of your involvement with Gerard."

Camilla stopped and looked up at Haarlock. "They're placing me under your direct command?"

"They need someone to look after you during all this."

"No doubt my executioner if I fail to live up to my end."

Haarlock shrugged.

"No offense, but lords are a silver-a-dozen. Your title won't exactly carry weight in the wider kingdom."

"Lucky for me, I got a letter, too." Haarlock removed another envelope. He opened it and read aloud. "Lord Haarlock, for your selfless actions in service to the Kingdom of Lemuria, I, Raoned Shein, do hereby..."

"Oh, by the gods, of course they promoted you."

Haarlock looked up from the letter with a smirk.

"You said it yourself, Camilla: lords are a silver-a-dozen. You may address me as *Baron* Haarlock from now on."

Haarlock's Destiny continues in Book 4

Invasion

Character Sheets

NAME: Haarlock
CLASS: Anointed Umbral Blade
RACE: Human
LEVEL: 27
AGE: 30
EXPERIENCE: 101,687
RENOWN/INFAMY: 1,220/808
TITLE: Lord
STATS:
GUILD RANK: Silver

HP - 210 STR - 42 DEX - 85 INT - 30
WIS - 25 CON - 60 CHA - 40

SKILLS:

Master	Expert	Skilled	Proficient
Dagger	Stealth	Tracking	Sleight of Hand
	Survival	Athletics	Simple Weapons
	Unarmed Combat	Spycraft	Skinning
		Bow	Vintner
		Bartering	Estate Management
		Lock Pick	Magic Theory

CLASS ABILITIES:	**FEATS**:	**TALENTS**:
Thieves' Cant	Alert	Canny Observer
Improved Sneak Attack	Magic Novice	Resilient
Uncanny Dodge	Pass Without Trace	Improved Animal Bond
Deft Hands	Wrapped in Shadow	Nondescript
Darkvision	Increased Reflexes	Silent Kill
Murder	Increased Endurance	Agile
Sjena's Kiss	Increased Strength	Climber
Dual Natured - Umbral		Blade Twist
		Reflexive Spell
		Pain Tolerance
		Increaed Swiftness
		Intercept Projectile

SPELLS:

Cantrips	1st Level	2nd Level
Magc Hand	Magic Armor	Shadow Tendrils
Mend	---	
Shadowstep		
Umbral Step		

NAME: Ladrón
CLASS: Umbral Brawler
RACE: Raccoon
LEVEL: 52
AGE: 1
EXPERIENCE: 40,157

STATS:

HP - 307 STR - 22 DEX - 27 INT - 6 (17)
WIS - 5 CON - 31 CHA - 20

SKILLS:

Master	Expert	Skilled	Proficient
	Stealth	Unarmed Combat	Sleight of Hand
		Hunting	Lockpick

ABILITIES:	**CLASS ABILITIES**:	**FEATS**:	**TALENTS**:
Darkvision	Fighting Style: Brawler	Savage Bite	Nose for Treasure
Fámiliar	Improved Sneak Attack	Survivor	Nimble Climber
Stalk	Dual Natured - Umbral		Fast Fingers
			Charming
			Relentless
			Evasion

SPELLS:

Cantrips	1st Level	2nd Level	3rd Level
---	---	---	---
---	---	---	

ABOUT THE AUTHOR

After spending more than thirty years in Springfield, OH (twice rated "most depressing city in the country"), J Tyler Pennington moved to Dayton and threw himself into acting, film making, photography, and, of course, writing.

Blog: https://www.jtylerpennington.com
Royal Road: https://www.royalroad.com/profile/367185
Facebook: https://www.facebook.com/JTylerPennington
Instagram: jtylerpennington

Support the author directly through their Patreon:
https://www.patreon.com/JTylerPennington

Further Reading

If you would like to know more about the LitRPG genre, please visit these Facebook groups:

- **LitRPG & GameLit Readers**
  - https://www.facebook.com/groups/940262549853662
- **GameLitRPG Society**
  - https://www.facebook.com/groups/LitRPGsociety
- **LitRPG**
  - https://www.facebook.com/groups/LitRPGGroup

www.ingramcontent.com/pod-product-compliance
Lightning Source LLC
LaVergne TN
LVHW041102080826
845145LV00007B/1666